THE ROMANCE OF THE FOREST

ANN RADCLIFFE (neé Ward) was born in London in 1764. Her father was in trade, but she passed much of her childhood in the households of more prosperous and socially elevated relations. In 1772 her family moved to Bath, where she may have attended a school run by Sophia and Harriet Lee, early innovators in the writing of Gothic fiction and drama. She married in 1787 William Radcliffe, who later became proprietor and editor of the *English Chronicle*. It was apparently with his encouragement that she took up writing as a pastime. Her first attempts in the genre of romance, *The Castles of Athlin and Dunbayne* (1789) and *A Sicilian Romance* (1790), were published anonymously. They received some favourable attention from the reviewers, but it was *The Romance of the Forest* (1791) which established her as the supreme practitioner of the Gothic mode, then variously dubbed 'the Terrorist System of Novel Writing', 'the hobgoblin-romance', or eventually, as a tribute to her influence, 'the Radcliffe romance'. Two further novels published in her lifetime, *The Mysteries of Udolpho* (1794) and *The Italian* (1797), served to consolidate her reputation as 'the Great Enchantress'. Her works were translated into many languages. Radcliffe also was an enthusiastic traveller. She authored a work based on her sole excursion to the Continent, *A Journey Made in the Summer of 1794, through Holland and the Western Frontier of Germany . . . To Which Are Added Observations of a Tour to the Lakes* (1795). But the tours of southern Europe undertaken in the novels were more exotic, based on travel books, fashionable landscape paintings, and a vivid imagination; the scene-painting sometimes heightened by verse. Walter Scott was to describe Radcliffe as 'the first poetess of romantic fiction'. In spite of her celebrity, Radcliffe clung to privacy, and retired from publishing in 1797. In later life she suffered from asthma, and died of an attack in 1823. A final novel, *Gaston de Blondeville* was published in 1826, together with a narrative poem, *St Alban's Abbey*, extracts from her travel diaries, and a memoir of the author by Thomas Noon Talfourd.

CHLOE CHARD is a lecturer in English Literature at the University of Osijek, in Yugoslavia, and has previously taught at the University of Sheffield. Her academic research has mainly been concerned with seventeenth-century and eighteenth-century travel literature.

KT-571-336

OXFORD WORLD'S CLASSICS

*For over 100 years Oxford World's Classics have brought
readers closer to the world's great literature. Now with over 700
titles—from the 4,000-year-old myths of Mesopotamia to the
twentieth century's greatest novels—the series makes available
lesser-known as well as celebrated writing.*

*The pocket-sized hardbacks of the early years contained
introductions by Virginia Woolf, T. S. Eliot, Graham Greene,
and other literary figures which enriched the experience of reading.
Today the series is recognized for its fine scholarship and
reliability in texts that span world literature, drama and poetry,
religion, philosophy and politics. Each edition includes perceptive
commentary and essential background information to meet the
changing needs of readers.*

OXFORD WORLD'S CLASSICS

ANN RADCLIFFE

The Romance of the Forest

Edited with an Introduction and Notes by
CHLOE CHARD

Ere the bat hath flown
His cloister'd flight; ere to black Hecate's summons,
The shard-born beetle, with his drowsy hums,
Hath rung night's yawning peal, there shall be done
A deed of dreadful note.
                                        MACBETH

OXFORD
UNIVERSITY PRESS

OXFORD
UNIVERSITY PRESS

Great Clarendon Street, Oxford OX2 6DP

Oxford University Press is a department of the University of Oxford.
It furthers the University's objective of excellence in research, scholarship,
and education by publishing worldwide in

Oxford New York

Athens Auckland Bangkok Bogotá Buenos Aires Calcutta
Cape Town Chennai Dar es Salaam Delhi Florence Hong Kong Istanbul
Karachi Kuala Lumpur Madrid Melbourne Mexico City Mumbai
Nairobi Paris São Paulo Singapore Taipei Tokyo Toronto Warsaw

with associated companies in Berlin Ibadan

Oxford is a registered trade mark of Oxford University Press
in the UK and in certain other countries

Published in the United States
by Oxford University Press Inc., New York

Introduction, Note on the Text, Select Bibliography,
and Explanatory Notes © Chloe Chard 1986
Chronology © Terry Castle 1998
Updated Select Bibliography © E. J. Clery 1998

The moral rights of the author have been asserted

Database right Oxford University Press (maker)

First issued as a World's Classics paperback 1986
Reissued as an Oxford World's Classics paperback 1999

All rights reserved. No part of this publication may be reproduced,
stored in a retrieval system, or transmitted, in any form or by any means,
without the prior permission in writing of Oxford University Press,
or as expressly permitted by law, or under terms agreed with the appropriate
reprographics rights organizations. Enquiries concerning reproduction
outside the scope of the above should be sent to the Rights Department,
Oxford University Press, at the address above

You must not circulate this book in any other binding or cover
and you must impose this same condition on any acquirer

British Library Cataloguing in Publication Data

Data available

Library of Congress Cataloging in Publication Data
Radcliffe, Ann Ward, 1764–1823.
The romance of the forest.
(Oxford world's classics)
Bibliography: p.
I. Chard, Chloe. II. Title.
PR5202.R7 1986 823'.6 95–28545

ISBN–13: 978–0–19–283713–4
ISBN–10: 0–19–283713–3

9

Printed in Great Britain by
Clays Ltd, St Ives plc

CONTENTS

ACKNOWLEDGEMENTS

I wish to thank Roger Lonsdale for identifying the author of the poem 'Virgil's Tomb', quoted in an epigraph on p. 271, and referring me to one of the editions of Dodsley's *Collection of Poems* in which 'Virgil's Tomb' is included. I should also like to thank Brian Jenkins, of Cambridge University Library, for his help and advice when I was arranging to use one of the Library's copies of *The Romance of the Forest* as the basis of the text.

I am indebted, too, to the Research Fund and Press Committee of Sheffield University, for providing me with a grant towards the research expenses which my work on this edition entailed.

INTRODUCTION

Adeline, the heroine of *The Romance of the Forest*, is portrayed, towards the middle of the novel, reading an old and partially illegible manuscript which she has found in a concealed room in a ruined abbey, and which tells a story of imprisonment and suffering within the confines of this same building. As she comes to the words 'Last night! last night! O scene of horror!', her reactions are recounted as follows:

Adeline shuddered. She feared to read the coming sentence, yet curiosity prompted her to proceed. Still she paused: an unaccountable dread came over her. 'Some horrid deed has been done here,' said she; 'the reports of the peasants are true. Murder has been committed.' The idea thrilled her with horror.

In describing the process by which Adeline reads the manuscript, *The Romance of the Forest* underlines the promise of horror and terror on which its own narrative structure is based. Like all works of Gothic fiction, the novel constantly raises the expectation of future horrors, suggesting that dreadful secrets are soon to be revealed, and threatening the eruption of extreme—though often unspecified—forms of violence. The passage just quoted affirms very strongly the power of a narrative of mystery and impending violence to produce such moments of horror and terror: in anticipating imminent confirmation of her suspicion that 'murder has been committed', Adeline is so overcome with horror that she is prevented—for a while—from reading further.

The narrative pattern which the Gothic novel actually follows, however, differs in one very important respect from that which it promises—and which is dramatized in the account of Adeline's reaction to the manuscript. The reader of a work of Gothic fiction, far from being thrown into fits of such overwhelming horror that he or she casts the novel aside unfinished, is constantly urged onwards by that very emotion of 'curiosity' which, in Adeline's case, fails to conquer her fear of what she may discover if she reads further. In order to stimulate this response of curiosity, the moments of climactic horror and terror which the reader is led to anticipate are, in fact, regularly deferred: the dangers which threaten the heroine are continually averted, or displaced by new developments in the narrative. An article by Michel Foucault, 'Language to Infinity', provides an analysis of this process of deferral, as it operates in French eighteenth-century novels of terror, which is highly relevant to the English Gothic genre as well. In these novels, Foucault argues:

it is necessary to approach always closer to the moment when language will reveal its absolute power, by giving birth, through each of its feeble words, to terror; but this is the moment in which language inevitably becomes impotent, when its breath is cut short, when it should still itself without even saying that it stops speaking. Language must push back to infinity this limit it bears with itself, and which indicates, at once, its kingdom and its limit.[1]

It might be noted, in considering this analysis of the Gothic narrative, that all Gothic novels, whilst they prevent any full realization of impending threats and dangers, do, on the other hand, eventually reveal the dreadful secrets which, like these threats and dangers, are presented to the reader as potential sources of terror. Instead of producing this promised effect of terror, however, the revelation of such secrets actually dispels the reader's emotions of anticipatory dread. The secrets themselves, moreover, may prove rather less horrific than the novel has originally suggested: as the contemporary periodical the *Critical Review* remarks, in its assessment of another of Radcliffe's novels, 'curiosity', in the Gothic novel, 'is raised oftener than it is gratified; or rather, it is raised so high that no adequate gratification can be given it'.[2]

The Romance of the Forest, published in 1791, was one of the earlier novels to construct a narrative of mystery, suspense, and ever-impending horror and terror. It was preceded by several other works which are usually regarded as 'Gothic':

---

[1] In Michel Foucault, *Language, Counter-Memory, Practice: Selected Essays and Interviews*, edited by Donald F. Bouchard, translated by Donald F. Bouchard and Sherry Simon (Oxford, 1977), 53–67 (p. 65).

[2] *Critical Review*, 9 (1794), 361–72 (p. 362). (This review is attributed to Coleridge in Garland Greever, *A Wiltshire Parson and his Friends*, London, 1926.)

Horace Walpole's *The Castle of Otranto* (1764), Clara Reeve's *The Old English Baron* (1777), and Ann Radcliffe's own earlier works, *The Castles of Athlin and Dunbayne* (1789) and *A Sicilian Romance* (1790). Many more novels which promised the reader moments of extreme horror and terror, however, were to follow: the Gothic novels which succeeded *The Romance of the Forest* include, for example, Radcliffe's *The Mysteries of Udolpho* (1794) and *The Italian* (1797), Charlotte Smith's *Montalbert* (1795), Matthew Lewis's *The Monk* (1796), Eliza Parsons's *The Mysterious Warning* (1796), Mary Robinson's *Hubert de Sevrac* (1796), Regina Maria Roche's *Clermont* (1798), and Eleanor Sleath's *The Orphan of the Rhine* (1798).

The Romance of the Forest is now less well known than the two novels by Ann Radcliffe which followed it, but it was received by contemporary reviewers with an enthusiasm rather greater than that which greeted either of these later works. The account of *The Mysteries of Udolpho* in the *Critical Review*, for example, includes the comment that 'while we acknowledge the extraordinary powers of Mrs. Radcliffe, some readers will be inclined to doubt whether they have been exerted in the present work with equal effect as in The Romance of the Forest'. The review of *The Italian* in this same periodical suggests that *The Romance of the Forest* is superior to both of Radcliffe's later novels. A review of *The Romance of the Forest* itself—also in the *Critical Review*—praises very highly the way in which, as the reader progresses through the narrative, 'the attention is uninterruptedly fixed, till the veil is designedly withdrawn'.[3]

This ability to 'fix the attention'—or, in other words, to maintain the reader's curiosity—is not, however, the only pleasure which the Gothic novel offers. Gothic fiction also provides an extravagant dramatization of various forms of excess and transgression, which are defined as sources of intense fascination precisely by virtue of the expressions of

[3] *Critical Review*, 9 (1794); 361–72 (p. 362); 23 (1798); 166–9 (p. 166); 4 (1792), 458–60 (p. 458): (The first two of these reviews are attributed to Coleridge in Garland Greever, *A Wiltshire Parson and his Friends*, London, 1926.)

horror and censure which are directed towards them. Instances of the unrestrained indulgence of the passions, and of varieties of transgressive behaviour which are portrayed as the products of this unrestraint, assume a central role both in *The Romance of the Forest* and in every other work of Gothic fiction (including *The Monk*, which, by its different handling of these same themes, provoked contemporary reactions of moral outrage).[4]

Lack of control over the promptings of violent passion is presented, in the Gothic novel, as a failing which is found in all except the most virtuous. Such lack of control assumes a particularly dramatic form in the case of Ambrosio, in *The Monk*, who finds that 'no sooner did opportunity present itself, no sooner did He catch a glimpse of joys to which He was still a Stranger, than Religion's barriers were too feeble to resist the over-whelming torrent of his desires.'[5] Radcliffe's novels, too, however, frequently dwell on the theme of unrestraint. In *The Mysteries of Udolpho*, Signora Laurentini warns the heroine: 'Sister! beware of the first indulgence of the passions; beware of the first! Their course, if not checked then, is rapid—their force is uncontroulable—they lead us we know not whither.'[6] In *The Romance of the Forest*, the ability of 'strong passion' to confuse 'the powers of reason' is emphasized in the account of Madame La Motte's jealousy of the heroine, and a more extreme example of the dangers of indulgence is provided by the description of her husband's similar lack of self-control: La Motte, the reader is told, 'had been led on by passion to dissipation—and from dissipation to vice; but having once touched the borders of infamy, the progressive steps followed each other fast . . .'

In their representation of unrestraint, Gothic novels—like the novels of Sade, which appeared over roughly the same historical period—focus above all on those characters who

---

[4] The *Monthly Review*, for example, commented: 'A vein of obscenity . . . pervades and deforms the whole organization of this novel' (23 (1797), p. 451).

[5] Edited by James Kinsley and Howard Anderson, World's Classics (Oxford, 1980), p. 238.

[6] Edited by Bonamy Dobrée, World's Classics (Oxford, 1980), p. 646.

indulge their passions with particular ruthlessness: the feudal
and monastic oppressors, who exercise an almost unlimited
power within the confines of the castles, country houses,
monasteries, or convents which constitute their primary area
of operation (and who enjoy a certain authority even beyond
the boundaries of these isolated domains). The characteristic
passions of the Gothic oppressor are those of lust and cruelty,
and the utter rejection of any form of moderation by the
oppressor, in seeking the gratification of these passions, is
always emphasized very strongly indeed. *A Sicilian Romance*,
for example, describes the two central agents of oppression, a
Marquis and his wife, as characters whose lives 'exhibited a
boundless indulgence of violent and luxurious passions'.
Montoni, the villain of *The Mysteries of Udolpho*, whose castle
is perceived by the heroine as a haven for 'vice and violence',
is represented as a man 'in whom passions . . . entirely
supplied the place of principles', whilst Schedoni, in *The
Italian*, is reported by his confessor as declaring that 'I have
been through life . . . the slave of my passions, and they have
led me into horrible excesses'.[7]

In *The Romance of the Forest*, the most extreme instances
both of unrestraint and of oppression are provided by the
figure of the Marquis de Montalt, who is consistently
characterized by 'the violence and criminality of his passions',
and is described, in a fit of anger, 'giving himself up, as usual,
to the transports of his passion'. Lesser practitioners of
unrestraint are entirely outshone by this more powerful and
energetically unprincipled 'votary of vice': La Motte, for
example, is depicted in a state of extreme dismay when
urged by the Marquis 'to the commission of a deed, from
the enormity of which, depraved as he was, he shrunk in
horror'.

The Marquis, in his extremity of unrestraint, indulges in
the two forms of transgression which Gothic novels—again,
like the works of Sade—regularly present as the usual
manifestations of lust and cruelty within the feudal family: the

[7] *A Sicilian Romance*, 2 vols (London, 1790), II, 205; *The Mysteries of
Udolpho*, ed. Bonamy Dobrée, World's Classics (Oxford, 1980), pp. 329 and
435; *The Italian*, ed. Frederick Garber, World's Classics (Oxford, 1981), p. 339.

crimes of murder and incest. These two crimes are accorded a closely analogous role within the Gothic genre: both are presented as forms of forbidden physical contact, both are portrayed as acts of violence (incest, in Gothic novels, almost always assumes the form of incestuous rape), and both are defined as particularly extreme forms of transgression by the family relationship which exists between the oppressor and the victim (a very large proportion of the murders in Gothic fiction take place within the family).

The close analogy between the two crimes is emphasized particularly strongly in Lewis's *The Monk*, in which one follows the other in swift succession. Ambrosio feels his first presentiment that the heroine, Antonia, is his sister just after he has raped her ('There was something in her look which penetrated him with horror; and though his understanding was still ignorant of it, Conscience pointed out to him the whole extent of his crime').[8] Very soon afterwards, he kills her. In Radcliffe's novels, the incestuous intentions of the oppressors are never in fact carried out (except between non-blood relations, as when Schedoni, in *The Italian*, rapes his brother's wife, having killed his brother). Both *The Italian* and *The Romance of the Forest*, however, in portraying the threat of incest, construct a very close relation indeed between incest and murder. Schedoni's attempt on the life of the heroine, in *The Italian*, thwarted by his apparent recognition of her as his daughter, is presented as an act which at the same time constitutes a form of incestuous assault: the moment of recognition is situated just as he has gone to Ellena's bedroom and is pulling back her garments: 'Vengeance nerved his arm, and drawing aside the lawn from her bosom, he once more raised it to strike: when, after gazing for an instant, some new cause of horror seemed to seize all his frame.'[9] In *The Romance of the Forest*, the Marquis's unwittingly incestuous designs on the heroine are, when he discovers their close family relationship, swiftly replaced by a plan to murder her.

---

[8] Edited by James Kinsley and Howard Anderson, World's Classics (Oxford, 1980), p. 387.
[9] Edited by Frederick Garber, World's Classics (Oxford, 1981), p. 234.

In its portrayal of murder, incest, and other manifestations of 'vice and violence', the Gothic novel, adopting an imaginative geography of a semi-feudal, Roman Catholic Europe, appropriates from contemporary travel writing an equation between the foreign and the forbidden. (Almost all English Gothic novels have foreign or partially foreign settings; *The Old English Baron*, an early example of the genre, constitutes a rare exception.) The assumption that, in a foreign, Roman Catholic country, all kinds of excessive and transgressive behaviour are to be expected, is found not only in overtly censorious eighteenth-century travel writings such as Samuel Sharp's *Letters from Italy* (1766), but even in works such as Hester Piozzi's *Observations and Reflections Made in the Course of a Journey through France, Italy, and Germany* (1789), in which the traveller proclaims some sympathy with the foreign. Gothic fiction, incorporating this same assumption, implicitly promises the reader the pleasures of a glimpse of the forbidden as soon as it names a foreign setting (as recognized in the ironic allusion, in Jane Austen's *Northanger Abbey* (1818), to the role played in the Gothic genre by 'the Alps and Pyrenees, with their pine forests and their vices').[10]

In its use of the foreign as a setting for the forbidden, *The Romance of the Forest* differs from most Gothic novels in assigning only a marginal role to Roman Catholicism and monasticism; Adeline escapes with relative ease from the 'cruelty and superstition' of the convent in which she has been educated. There is another feature of its representation of the foreign, however, in which *The Romance of the Forest* exhibits a much sharper divergence from other works of Gothic fiction: the discussion of national character. Many Gothic novels reproduce the portrayal of unrestraint as a quality especially characteristic of southern Europe, of Italy, or even of particular parts of Italy, which is regularly found in eighteenth-century travel writings. (The account of the inhabitants of Naples in Henry Swinburne's *Travels in the Two Sicilies* (1783–5), for example, places a strong emphasis on

---

[10] Jane Austen, *Northanger Abbey, Lady Susan, The Watsons and Sanditon*, edited by John Davie, World's Classics (Oxford, 1980), p. 160.

'the violence of their passions and the enthusiasm of their character', whilst Piozzi's *Observations and Reflections* indicates an excess of both virtue and vice in southern Europe in the remark that 'in all hot countries . . . flowers and weeds shoot up to enormous growths'.)[11] In *The Mysteries of Udolpho*, as in *A Sicilian Romance* and *The Italian*, violent passions are presented as a well-known attribute of the Italians: Signora Laurentini suffers 'all the delirium of Italian love' for the Marquis de Villeroi, and the heroine lives in terror of the fury of 'Italian revenge'.[12] *The Monk*, though set in Spain rather than Italy, simply shifts the geographical location of excessive passion to this alternative southern setting: at one point, for example, the reader is reminded that 'the climate's heat, 'tis well known, operates with no small influence upon the constitutions of the Spanish Ladies'.[13]

In *The Romance of the Forest*, however, locations which may be defined as unequivocally southern are introduced only at the very end of the novel, in a journey through Piedmont and Nice and along the Mediterranean coast of France, followed by a visit to a town on the borders of France and Spain. Most of the action of the novel takes place in a relatively northern region, somewhere near Lyons, and even when Adeline flees from this area, she spends a large portion of her time in the mountainous country of Savoy.

This use of northern and Alpine settings is not in itself uncommon in Gothic novels: *The Mysterious Warning* and *The Orphan of the Rhine*, for example, are both set, primarily, in Germany, whilst interludes in the Alps play a part in very many works of Gothic fiction. In most cases, however, the traits of character usually attributed to southern Europeans are simply transferred to a northern setting; *The Romance of the Forest* is unusual in constructing its account of the indulgence

[11] Swinburne, 2 vols (London, 1783–5), II, 83; Piozzi, edited by Herbert Barrows (Ann Arbor, 1967), p. 66.

[12] Edited by Bonamy Dobrée, World's Classics (Oxford, 1980), p. 656, p. 225.

[13] Edited by James Kinsley and Howard Anderson, World's Classics (Oxford, 1980), p. 239.

of the passions to conform with an established national characterization quite distinct from that of the Italians, or of other southern European nations: the established characterization of the French.

The account of the French which is given in Smollett's *Travels through France and Italy* (1766), and which closely resembles that found in other eighteenth-century travel writings, describes them as 'a giddy people, engaged in the most frivolous pursuits', and emphasizes 'their volatility, prattle, and fondness for *bons mots*'.[14] A description of the French national character which is put forward in the course of a conversation in *The Romance of the Forest* lists a series of similar attributes, typifying the French, for example, by 'their sparkling, but sophistical discourse, frivolous occupations, and, withal, their gay animated air'. Such qualities might seem somewhat remote from the violence and unrestraint expected of the Gothic oppressor, but they are all, in fact, exhibited, in the course of the narrative, by the Marquis de Montalt. Not only does the Marquis display a Gallic 'animation' and Gallic powers of 'sophistry', but his excesses, in contrast to those of other Gothic villains, are characterized by an overt and relatively frivolous form of hedonism. Whereas the scenes of 'vice and violence' at which Montoni presides in *The Mysteries of Udolpho* take place within a somewhat comfortless castle, the Marquis de Montalt's château is portrayed as a dwelling in which everything is directed towards the gratification of the senses. (Even Adeline, held a prisoner there, asks as she gazes out onto the garden: 'Is this a charm to lure me to destruction?') The heroine is received, in this château, neither with threats nor with direct violence, but with enticements such as a song 'written with that sort of impotent art, by which some voluptuous poets believe they can at once conceal and recommend the principles of vice', and with such luxuries as 'a collation of fruits, ices and liquors'. (The Marquis is later discovered by Adeline 'flushed with drinking'.)

The prominent role which hedonism and frivolous

---

[14] Edited by Frank Felsenstein, World's Classics (Oxford, 1981), p. 57, p. 45.

dissipation assume in *The Romance of the Forest* does not, however—as the preceding account of the novel has made clear—preclude an accompanying fascination with the more grimly violent forms of unrestraint which are usually found in Gothic fiction. A speech by the Marquis, in fact, constructs an apparent continuity between 'French' hedonism and 'Italian' ruthlessness. The speech—a long and 'sophistical' one—begins by attacking the moral constraints which govern human behaviour in 'a civilized country', and praising the spontaneity with which 'the simple, uninformed American follows the impulse of his heart'. It soon becomes clear, however, that the Marquis is not merely advocating a carefree, pleasure-seeking existence, but is referring, in particular, to the lack of 'prejudice' attaching, in other societies, to the crime of murder. (This utilization by the oppressor of a primitivistic questioning of 'civilized' values, in order to justify any course of action which might be prompted by desire or expediency, is another feature which characterizes the portrayal of unrestraint not only in Gothic fiction but also in the novels of Sade.[15]) The impulsiveness of the savage is now equated with 'Italian' indulgence of violent passion (using the Turks as a point of mediation between the primitive and the 'polished'), and 'Italian' murderousness is thereby presented as a natural extension of the more frivolously Gallic form of impulsiveness which the Marquis at first appears to be advocating:

'Nature, uncontaminated by false refinement,' resumed the Marquis, 'every where acts alike in the great occurrences of life. The Indian discovers his friend to be perfidious, and he kills him; the wild Asiatic does the same; the Turk, when ambition fires, or revenge provokes, gratifies his passion at the expense of life, and does not call it murder. Even the polished Italian, distracted by jealousy, or tempted by a strong circumstance of advantage, draws his stilletto [*sic*] and accomplishes his purpose.'

[15] The affinity between the arguments assigned to feudal oppressors in these two different literary contexts is noted here not as part of an attempt to trace lines of authorial influence, but simply in order to emphasize that the intellectual and imaginative concerns of the Gothic novel were shared by other contemporary areas of writing, and should not be seen as isolated eccentricities.

One further aspect of the Gothic representation of unrestraint which should be noted here—and which provides yet another point of analogy with the works of Sade—is the use of the figure of a victim, and above all of the victim's body, to dramatize the untrammelled indulgence of lust and cruelty. The victims of Gothic fiction are frequently presented, weak, collapsing, or in chains, as emblems of oppression, and attention is focused particularly sharply on the body of the heroine, who always assumes the role of the main victim of 'vice and violence'. The heroine of *The Romance of the Forest*, like all Gothic heroines, appears throughout the narrative fainting, 'sinking with terror', tottering, trembling, and shuddering; at one point, the reader learns, 'the palpitations of terror were so strong, that she could with difficulty breathe'. On Adeline's first appearance in the novel, the terror and emotional suffering which mark her role as victim are defined as attributes which serve to display her body to particular advantage for the pleasure of the spectator, since they allow the usual requirements of decorum to be cast aside. The reader is implicitly invited to scrutinize her through the eyes of a male spectator, La Motte, who finds it impossible, as she sinks weeping at his feet, 'to contemplate the beauty and distress of the object before him with indifference'; he is later, the reader is told (without any apparent irony) 'interested . . . more warmly in her favour' by viewing her in another attitude of affliction and disarray: her 'habit of grey camlet', which 'shewed, but did not adorn, her figure', is described as 'thrown open at the bosom, upon which part of her hair had fallen in disorder, while the light veil hastily thrown on, had, in her confusion, been suffered to fall back.'

The heroines of Gothic fiction do not remain in a permanent state of decorative distress, however: their moments of collapse—like those of all other Gothic victims—alternate with moments of revival, when, sustained both by their characteristic virtues of fortitude and patience and by exterior sources of consolation, they recover sufficiently to face the horrors that remain in store for them. When Adeline emerges from a sleepless night in the vaults of the ruined abbey, for example, the reader is told that 'the cheerful beams of the sun played once more upon her sight, and re-animated her spirits'. Another sequence of collapse and revival in *The Romance of the Forest* describes the heroine 'reanimated with hope, and invigorated by a sense of the importance of the business before her', after a period in which, 'sinking under the influence of illness and despair', she 'could scarcely raise her languid head, or speak but in the faintest accents'.

One of the sources of inner sustainment which is named in these narratives of collapse and recovery is the heroine's pleasure in the landscape. When seated on 'some wild eminence' in Savoy, with 'a volume of Shakespear or Milton', Adeline is lulled into 'forgetfulness of grief', whilst the 'sweetly romantic' scenes of nature around the ruined abbey and the abundant fertility of the surroundings of Lyons are invested with similar powers to soothe, console, or distract her.

Descriptions of natural scenery, however, not only play a part in these accounts of the heroine's re-animation; they also assume another important role within the Gothic narrative structure. By delaying any resolution of a threat of impending danger, such descriptions often serve to keep the reader in a state of suspense—as in the episode in *The Romance of the Forest* in which Adeline, waiting to escape from the ruined abbey, and sharply aware of the necessity to leave the building before the Marquis arrives, sits at her window in contemplation of the 'uncommon splendour' of the sunset over the woods and ruins.

Landscape description is of importance, too, within the Gothic novel's mechanisms of self-definition. It is worth discussing these mechanisms in some detail, since an analysis of the literary and intellectual aspirations which are comprehended within them may help to elucidate a number of the characteristic features of the Gothic genre.

Contemporary accounts of Gothic novels often suggest, even when expressing an enthusiasm for these works, that their interest lies almost entirely in the excitement of the narrative; in less favourable commentaries, a strong emphasis is placed on the limitations of the genre. A review of *The*

Italian in the *Critical Review*, for example, classifies the Gothic novel, damningly, as a literary form which 'might for a time afford an acceptable variety to persons whose reading is confined to works of fiction', whilst Jane Austen's novel *Emma* assigns to *The Romance of the Forest* the rather undistinguished role of one of the literary works within the scope of the utterly ignorant Harriet Smith.[16] Gothic novels themselves, however, make a vigorous attempt to lay claim to a literary and intellectual status rather more elevated than that which is usually accorded to them. This attempt is evident, above all, in the wide range of references to other areas of writing which Gothic fiction establishes, and in the forms of authority to which it appeals in seeking to provide intellectual authentication for the narrative of horror and terror.

It has already been noted that the Gothic novel, in its portrayal of foreign society and manners, appropriates many of the themes and arguments which are found in eighteenth-century travel writing. In accounts of the landscape, references to travel books become yet more frequent: Gothic fiction derives from travel writing not only a range of general descriptive strategies (such as the strategy of constructing dramatic oppositions between wild and cultivated scenes of nature) but also a large number of precise descriptions of particular spots and of particular varieties of natural scenery. Many of the descriptions of landscape in *The Romance of the Forest*, for example, bear a very close resemblance to passages in works such as Smollett's *Travels through France and Italy*, Bourrit's *Relation of a Journey to the Glaciers, in the Dutchy of Savoy* (1775; translated from the original French edition of 1771) and Gray's letters from France and Savoy, as edited by Mason in *The Poems of Mr. Gray, to which are prefixed Memoirs of his Life and Writings* (1775).

References to travel writing, in Gothic fiction, are not usually proclaimed explicitly as such, but are used to suggest that each Gothic novel is itself the product of a personal experience of travel. The descriptions of the foreign which are found in Gothic fiction are, it is implied, uttered with the

---

[16] *Critical Review*, 23 (1798), 166–9 (p. 166); *Emma*, edited by James Kinsley and David Lodge, World's Classics (Oxford, 1980), p. 25.

authority of the traveller—a form of authority which is derived
not only from the traveller's claim to first-hand observation but
also from the status of the traveller as a participant, or ex-
participant, in the socially and culturally privileged practice of
travel on the Grand Tour. (In its flexibility, the Grand Tour
regularly included some or all of the regions described in *The
Romance of the Forest*.) The success of *The Romance of the Forest*
in defining at least some of its landscape descriptions as those of
a traveller who has actually visited the spots described is
indicated by the remark, in the *Critical Review*, that the
accounts of Savoy in this novel 'are often beautiful, and seem to
be drawn from personal experience'.[17] (This use of descriptive
language, in Gothic fiction, to indicate experience of travel need
not, of course, correspond to any actual experience of travel on
the part of the author; Ann Radcliffe, in fact, visited neither
Savoy nor any of the other regions described in her novels, but
only those areas of Europe named in the title of her *Journey
made in the Summer of 1794, through Holland and the Western
Frontier of Germany, with a return down the Rhine*, published in
1795.)

The self-definition of *The Romance of the Forest* as the product
of a personal acquaintance with the regions which the heroine
visits is reinforced by a great deal of discussion, towards the end
of the novel, of the actual practice of travel: the experiences of
two characters making their own versions of the Grand Tour—
M. Verneuil and M. Amand—are both recounted, specific
sightseeing expeditions (to the glaciers of Savoy and to Roman
remains near Nice) are described, and the novel even remarks on
the difficulties in finding furnished accommodation which the
traveller to Nice encounters. Such allusions to the experiences
of the traveller on the Grand Tour are, in fact, found very
frequently in almost every work of Gothic fiction: the heroine of
Montalbert, for example, is rescued from imprisonment in a
remote Italian fortress by an Englishman who discovers her by
chance whilst purchasing antiquities, 'of little value to them',
from the local peasantry.[18]

[17] *Critical Review*, 4 (1792), 458–60 (p. 459).
[18] Charlotte Smith, 3 vols (London, 1795), III, 34.

In its description of various different aspects of foreign countries, the Gothic novel introduces a range of different concepts of horror and terror. These concepts assume a rhetorical continuity with the horror and terror which are constantly promised within the narrative, not only by virtue of the fact that the same terms are used in both contexts, but also by virtue of the role which the horrors of the foreign assume in reinforcing the heroine's sense of dread, and so in encouraging the reader's expectation of future terrors. (Even the horrors of the wild landscape, which are usually described as aesthetically pleasurable, contribute, on occasion, to the heroine's apprehensions.) The horror and terror of the narrative, then, are invested with a certain intellectual authentication, through these apparent affiliations with concepts which form part of the privileged discourse of the traveller.

In descriptions of the foreign landscape, the Gothic genre's preoccupation with horror and terror is endorsed particularly strongly by the strategy of appealing to aesthetic theory—a strategy which also serves, moreover, to proclaim a general familiarity with current intellectual concerns, and to display a responsiveness towards the visual delights of the landscape, of a kind which is frequently exhibited in late eighteenth-century travel writings, and which readily suggests some degree of eyewitness experience of the varieties of scenery described. Gothic novels, in establishing multiple references to the aesthetic principles put forward in such writings as Edmund Burke's *Philosophical Enquiry into the Origin of our Ideas of the Sublime and Beautiful* (1757) and Hugh Blair's *Lectures on Rhetoric and Belles Lettres* (1783), appeal above all to the underlying association which is established in such writings between horror, terror, and the powerful and complex aesthetic effect of sublimity—an effect in which fear and pleasure both play a major part. In *The Romance of the Forest*, for example, the sight of a storm in the Alps is presented both as a source of terror and as a scene of 'dreadful sublimity', and the aesthetic delights which such a spectacle of terror and sublimity may offer are emphasized particularly strongly by a prefatory allusion to the heroine's desire to witness (from a position of safety) 'the tremendous effect of a thunder storm in these regions'.

The Gothic novel's concern with horror and terror is authenticated, too, by another form of reference which the genre establishes: reference to poetry. Epigraphs quoting from the works of Shakespeare, Milton, and a range of eighteenth-century poets (including, for example, Gray, Collins, Beattie, Thomson, and Mason) serve to make it clear that horror, terror, and similar concepts occupy a secure place within the tradition of English poetry, as the Gothic novel defines it. The title page of *The Romance of the Forest*, for example, quotes from *Macbeth* in order to indicate that 'a deed of dreadful note' will soon be recounted, and the epigraph to Chapter 7 cites the same play in its allusion to 'horrible imaginings', whilst two other epigraphs in this same novel quote lines from Collins's 'Ode to Fear'.

The attempt to affiliate the Gothic novel with an English literary tradition, moreover, goes far beyond this emphasis on a common concern with horror and terror. The events and dominant emotions of each chapter—emotions which include not only horror, terror, fear, awe, and dread but also, for example, melancholy and despair, and even joy and hope—are all defined as elements with a literary history of their own by the use of epigraphs, whilst quotations within the text—often short, and encapsulated within a sentence of the narrative, as though spontaneously springing to mind in the course of the narration—are used to suggest that the Gothic novel is composed with constant reference to English poetry. Yet further links with English poetry are established in poems by the novelist and in passages of description: in *The Romance of the Forest*, as in many other Gothic novels, indirect allusions are frequently made, for example, in both these contexts, to Collins's 'Ode to Evening', and to the many other eighteenth-century poems which, themselves referring back to Milton's 'Il Penseroso', dwell on such themes as twilight, obscurity, pensiveness, melancholy, and solemnity. The 'melancholy charm' of the hour 'when Twilight spreads her pensive shade', described in the poem 'To the Nightingale', is emphasized, too, in a large number of the other poems by

Radcliffe which are included within the text, and the account of Adeline's state of 'reverie' and 'still melancholy' as she contemplates the French coastline in the obscurity of evening is one of many descriptive passages in the novel which portrays the state of twilight as a source of similar emotional responses.

The Romance of the Forest, then, establishes the same range of reference to other areas of writing as that which is found in the Gothic novels which follow it. It also, however, includes many more allusions to contemporary intellectual concerns than most of these later works. Not only does the novel refer to the themes and arguments of eighteenth-century primitivism, in providing the Marquis with a theoretical defence of his pursuit of vice; it also incorporates a large number of references to Rousseau's *Emile* (1762), and especially to the 'Profession de foi du vicaire savoyard' which forms part of that work, in its account of La Luc, the benevolent Savoyard clergyman who takes Adeline into his family.

The aspirations which such references serve to emphasize are accompanied, however, by a strong element of unease. This unease stems, in part, from an uncertainty as to the kinds of authority which could be invoked within a work of fiction which explicitly proclaimed its female authorship on the title page—one of the tasks which the novel assumes is, in fact, that of negotiating the areas of discourse which might be considered as accessible to women. *The Romance of the Forest*, on the one hand, avoids any overt proclamation of literary or intellectual ambition by situating itself within the genre of romantic fiction. This acceptance of a relatively humble literary status has, on the other hand, the disadvantage that it makes it extremely difficult for the novel to introduce its more ambitious allusions to current intellectual concerns without producing a strong effect of incongruity.

The element of unease in *The Romance of the Forest* is, nevertheless, not entirely unwelcome, since it provides some relief from the unruffled complacency which is displayed, in this novel as in most other works of Gothic fiction, in the discussion of accepted social values and of established forms of authority. The description of the Gothic novel as complacent may sound unnecessarily dismissive; the genre might also be viewed as potentially subversive in its provision of a model for the criticism of oppression, and this view would find support in the use of a highly 'Gothic' setting to dramatize the oppression of women in Mary Wollstonecraft's *The Wrongs of Woman; or, Maria* (published posthumously in 1798). Most Gothic novels, however, far from questioning or attacking established social usages, employ their dramatizations of foreign 'vice and violence' to reaffirm, by contrast, the merits of the familiar values and customs of English society. *The Romance of the Forest*, moreover, is particularly cautious in the forms of authority which it attacks. The portrayal of France under the *ancien régime* in this novel carefully avoids any suggestion that the recent events of the French Revolution might be seen as a response to various forms of injustice: both the French monarch and the French courts are presented as, on the whole, just and benevolent (although accounts of the less politically sensitive areas of Savoy and Nice freely criticize the baneful effects of 'an arbitrary government'). The novel strongly resists the kind of transposition of the theme of oppression to the contemporary political situation which is found in the later Gothic novel *Hubert de Sevrac*. The heroine of this later work boldly ventures to suggest to her father, a French émigré marquis, that in pre-revolutionary days 'we lived amongst such as never felt for those, whose hard fortune placed them in poverty: all our friends, all our associates, were the enemies of the people'.[19]

[19] Mary Robinson, 3 vols (London, 1796), I, 13.

NOTE ON THE TEXT

The text of *The Romance of the Forest* is based on that of the first edition of 1791 (taken from a copy of this edition in the possession of Cambridge University Library, shelf-mark S727.d.79.7–9). A number of obvious misprints or mistakes in spelling or punctuation have been silently corrected, most of them in accordance with the text of the second edition of 1792, although four such errors, overlooked in this second edition, have been amended to conform instead with the text of the fourth edition of 1794. I have also followed the second edition in changing 'who had long *strove*', on p. 193, to 'who had long *tried*'.

I have retained, however, all but three of the discrepancies in spelling (between *Gulf* and *Gulph*, for example, and between *Montpellier* and *Montpelier*) which are found in the first edition. One of the exceptions is the discrepancy between *the Chatelet* [*sic*] (p. 316) and *the Chatalet* [*sic*]. The first edition contains two instances of the latter spelling, but one of these (p. 352) is changed to the former spelling in the second edition, and this same principle of correction has been applied here to the other instance as well (p. 345). The other two exceptions are the discrepancies between '*suite* of apartments' and '*suit* of apartments', and between *set* and *sat* (for the past tense or past participle of the verb 'to set'). Since most instances of the latter spellings are changed to the former in the second edition, the fourth edition, or both, these former spellings—*suite* and *set*—have been adopted throughout the text.

Finally, no attempt has been made to impose any uniformity on the variants of the family name *de la Motte*, *De la Motte* or *La Motte* which are adopted in the course of the narrative, and no corrections have been made to the various grammatical errors which are found in the first edition (and which, in every case, remain unaltered in the second edition).

SELECT BIBLIOGRAPHY

1. Bibliography

Arnaud, Pierre, *Ann Radcliffe et le fantastique: Essai de psycho-biographie* (Paris, 1976).

Cottom, Daniel, *The Civilized Imagination: A Study of Ann Radcliffe, Jane Austen, and Sir Walter Scott* (Cambridge, 1985).

Frank, Frederick S., *The First Gothics: A Critical Guide to the English Gothic Novel* (New York and London, 1987).

—— *Gothic Fiction: A Master List of Twentieth-Century Criticism and Research* (London, 1988).

MacIntyre, C. F., *Ann Radcliffe in Relation to her Time* (New Haven, 1920).

McNutt, D. J., *The Eighteenth-Century Gothic Novel: An Annotated Bibliography of Criticism and Selected Texts* (Folkestone, 1975).

Rogers, Deborah D., *Ann Radcliffe: A Bio-Bibliography* (Westport, Conn., and London, 1996).

Scott, Sir Walter, 'Mrs. Ann Radcliffe', in *The Lives of the Novelists*, with an Introduction by George Saintsbury (London, 1910), 211–45.

Spector, Robert Donald, *The English Gothic: A Bibliographic Guide to Writers from Horace Walpole to Mary Shelley* (London and Westport, Conn., 1984).

Summers, Montague, *A Gothic Bibliography* (New York, 1941).

Ware, Malcolm, *Sublimity in the Novels of Ann Radcliffe* (Uppsala and Copenhagen, 1963).

2. On Gothic Fiction

Baker, E. A., *The Novel of Sentiment and the Gothic Romance* (*The History of the English Novel*, v; New York, 1929).

Beer, Gillian, ' "Our unnatural no-voice": The Heroic Epistle, Pope, and Women's Gothic', *Yearbook of English Studies*, 12 (1982), 125–51.

Birkhead, Edith, *The Tale of Terror: A Study of the Gothic Romance* (London, 1921).

Carter, Margaret L., *Specter or Delusion? The Supernatural in Gothic Fiction* (Ann Arbor, 1987).

Doody, Margaret Anne, 'Deserts, Ruins, and Troubled Waters: Female Dreams in Fiction and the Development of the Gothic Novel', *Genre*, 10 (1977), 529–72.

Ellis, Kate F., *The Contested Castle: Gothic Novels and the Subversion of Domestic Ideology* (Urbana, Ill., and Chicago, 1989).

Fauchery, Pierre, *La Destinée féminine dans le roman européen du dix-huitième siècle, 1703–1807: Essai de gynécomythie romanesque* (Paris, 1972).

Fleenor, Juliann E. (ed.), *The Female Gothic* (Montreal and London, 1983).

Foucault, Michel, 'Le Langage à l'infini', *Tel Quel*, 15 (1963), 44–53, translated (by Donald F. Bouchard and Sherry Simon) as 'Language to Infinity', in *Language, Counter-Memory, Practice: Selected Essays and Interviews*, edited by Donald F. Bouchard (Oxford, 1977), 53–67.

Haggerty, George E., *Gothic Fiction/Gothic Form* (University Park, Pa., and London, 1989).

Harwell, Thomas Meade (ed.), *The English Gothic Novel: A Miscellany in Four Volumes* (Salzburg Studies in English Literature, 33/1–4; Salzburg, 1986).

Jackson, Rosemary, *Fantasy: The Literature of Subversion* (London, 1981).

Johnson, Claudia L., *Women, Politics, and the Novel* (Chicago, 1988).

Kelly, Gary, *English Fiction of the Romantic Period, 1789–1830* (London and New York, 1989).

Kiely, Robert, *The Romantic Novel in England* (Cambridge, Mass., 1972).

Lévy, Maurice, *Le Roman 'gothique' anglais, 1764–1824* (Toulouse, 1968).

Miles, Robert, *Gothic Writing 1750–1820: A Genealogy* (London, 1993).

Moers, Ellen, *Literary Women* (London, 1977).

Monk, Samuel H., *The Sublime: A Study of Critical Theories in Eighteenth-Century England* (Ann Arbor, 1960).

Morris, David B., 'Gothic Sublimity', *New Literary History*, 16 (1985), 299–319.

Napier, Elizabeth, *The Failure of Gothic: Problems of Disjunction in an Eighteenth-Century Literary Form* (Oxford, 1987).

Punter, David, *The Literature of Terror: A History of Gothic Fiction from 1765 to the Present Day* (London and New York, 1980).

Railo, Eino, *The Haunted Castle: A Study of the Elements of English Romanticism* (London and New York, 1927).

Sedgwick, Eve K., *The Coherence of Gothic Conventions* (New York, 1980).

Summers, Montague, *The Gothic Quest: A History of the Gothic Novel* (London, 1938).

Todorov, Tzvetan, *The Fantastic: A Structural Approach to a Literary Genre* (Ithaca, NY, 1975).

Tompkins, J. M. S., *The Popular Novel in England, 1770–1800* (London, 1932).

Varma, Devendra P., *The Gothic Flame* (London, 1957).

Ware, Malcolm, *Sublimity in the Novels of Ann Radcliffe* (Uppsala and Copenhagen, 1963).

A CHRONOLOGY OF ANN RADCLIFFE

1764 9 July, born in London, daughter of William Ward, a haberdasher, and Ann Ward (neé Oates).

1772 Moves to Bath, where she may have attended Sophia Lee's school for young ladies.

1787 Marries William Radcliffe, Oxford graduate, parliamentary reporter and proprietor of the *English Chronicle*. Encouraged by husband in first writing ventures.

1789 *The Castles of Athlin and Dunbayne* published anonymously.

1790 *A Sicilian Romance*, 2 vols., published anonymously.

1791 *The Romance of the Forest, Interspersed with some Pieces of Poetry*, 3 vols. First edition published anonymously; authorship acknowledged in advertisement to second edition the following year.

1794 *The Mysteries of Udolpho, A Romance, Interspersed with some Pieces of Poetry*, 4 vols. Literary reputation established with popular success of novel at home and abroad. Makes tour of war-torn Netherlands and Germany with husband, travelling down the Rhine as far as the Swiss border. Tour of the Lake District in autumn.

1795 *A Journey Made in the Summer of 1794, through Holland and the Western Frontier of Germany, With a Return Down the Rhine: To Which Are Added Observations During a Tour to the Lakes of Lancashire and Westmoreland, and Cumberland.*

1797 *The Italian, or the Confessional of the Black Penitents*, 3 vols. Ceases publishing, owing to new-found financial independence.

1798 Subject of laudatory essay (attributed to S. T. Coleridge) in the *Critical Review*.

1802 *Gaston de Blondeville* completed after visiting Kenilworth Castle, but 'laid aside, so disinclined had she become to publication' (Talfourd). Increasingly shuns literary society.

1810 Anonymous 'Ode to Terror' printed in which it is asserted that Radcliffe has gone mad and died of 'the horrors'.

1816   Publication of *The Poems of Ann Radcliffe*, an un-authorized reprint of poems from the novels.

1823   7 February, dies of asthmatic fever after bout of delirium.

1826   'On the Supernatural in Poetry', *New Monthly Magazine*, 7. *Gaston de Blondeville, or the Court of Henry III Keeping Festival in Ardenne, A Romance* and *St Alban's Abbey, A Metrical Tale* published posthumously in 4-vol. set prefaced by Thomas Talfourd's 'Memoir of the Life and Writings of Mrs Radcliffe'.

THE

Romance of the Foreſt:

INTERSPERSED WITH

SOME PIECES OF POETRY.

BY THE AUTHORESS OF

" A SICILIAN ROMANCE," &c.

———————

" Ere the bat hath flown
" His cloiſter'd flight ; ere to black Hecate's ſummons,
" The ſhard-born beetle, with his drowſy hums,
" Hath rung night's yawning peal, there ſhall be done
" A deed of dreadful note."

MACBETH.

———————

IN THREE VOLUMES.

VOL. I.

—————————

LONDON:

PRINTED FOR T. HOOKHAM AND CARPENTER,
NEW AND OLD BOND STREET.
M.DCC.XCI.

ADVERTISEMENT

IT is proper to mention that some of the little Poems inserted in the following Pages have appeared, by Permission of the Author, in the GAZETTEER.*

THE ROMANCE
OF THE FOREST

VOLUME I

CHAPTER I

I am a man,
So weary with disasters, tugg'd with fortune,
That I would set my life on any chance,
To mend it, or be rid on't.*

'WHEN once sordid interest seizes on the heart, it freezes up the source of every warm and liberal feeling; it is an enemy alike to virtue and to taste—*this* it perverts, and *that* it annihilates. The time may come, my friend, when death shall dissolve the sinews of avarice, and justice be permitted to resume her rights.'

Such were the words of the Advocate Nemours* to Pierre de la Motte,* as the latter stept at midnight into the carriage which was to bear him far from Paris, from his creditors and the persecution of the laws. De la Motte thanked him for this last instance of his kindness; the assistance he had given him in escape; and, when the carriage drove away, uttered a sad adieu! The gloom of the hour, and the peculiar emergency of his circumstances, sunk him in silent reverie.

Whoever has read Guyot de Pitaval, the most faithful of those writers who record the proceedings in the Parliamentary Courts of Paris, during the seventeenth century,* must surely remember the striking story of Pierre de la Motte, and the Marquis Phillipe de Montalt: let all such, therefore, be informed, that the person here introduced to their notice was that individual Pierre de la Motte.

As Madame de la Motte leaned from the coach window, and gave a last look to the walls of Paris—Paris, the scene of her former happiness, and the residence of many dear friends—the fortitude, which had till now supported her, yielded to the force of grief. 'Farewell all!' sighed she, 'this last look and we are separated for ever!' Tears followed her words, and, sinking back, she resigned herself to the stillness of sorrow. The recollection of former times pressed heavily upon her heart: a few months before and she was surrounded by friends, fortune, and consequence; now she was deprived of all, a miserable exile from her native place, without home, without comfort—almost without hope. It was not the least of her afflictions that she had been obliged to quit Paris without bidding adieu to her only son, who was now on duty with his regiment in Germany: and such had been the precipitancy of this removal, that had she even known where he was stationed, she had no time to inform him of it, or of the alteration in his father's circumstances.

Pierre de la Motte was a gentleman, descended from an ancient house of France. He was a man whose passions often overcame his reason, and, for a time, silenced his conscience;* but, though the image of virtue, which Nature had impressed upon his heart, was sometimes obscured by the passing influence of vice, it was never wholly obliterated. With strength of mind sufficient to have withstood temptation, he would have been a good man; as it was, he was always a weak, and sometimes a vicious member of society: yet his mind was active, and his imagination vivid, which, co-operating with the force of passion, often dazzled his judgement and subdued principle. Thus he was a man, infirm in purpose and visionary in virtue: in a word, his conduct was suggested by feeling, rather than principle; and his virtue, such as it was, could not stand the pressure of occasion.

Early in life he had married Constance Valentia, a beautiful and elegant woman, attached to her family and beloved by them. Her birth was equal, her fortune superior to his; and their nuptials had been celebrated under the auspices of an approving and flattering world. Her heart was devoted to La Motte, and, for some time, she found in him an affectionate husband; but, allured by the gaieties of Paris, he was soon devoted to its luxuries, and in a few years his fortune and affection were equally lost in dissipation. A false pride had still operated against his interest, and withheld him from honourable retreat while it was yet in his power: the habits, which he had acquired, enchained him to the scene of his former pleasure; and thus he had continued an expensive stile of life till the means of prolonging it were exhausted. He at length awoke from this lethargy of security; but it was only to plunge into new error, and to attempt schemes for the reparation of his fortune, which served to sink him deeper in destruction. The consequence of a transaction, in which he thus engaged, now drove him, with the small wreck of his property, into dangerous and ignominious exile.

It was his design to pass into one of the Southern Provinces, and there seek, near the borders of the kingdom, an asylum in some obscure village. His family consisted of his wife, and two faithful domestics, a man and woman, who followed the fortunes of their master.

The night was dark and tempestuous, and, at about the distance of three leagues from Paris, Peter, who now acted as postillion, having drove for some time over a wild heath where many ways crossed, stopped, and acquainted De la Motte with his perplexity. The sudden stopping of the carriage roused the latter from his reverie, and filled the whole party with the terror of pursuit; he was unable to supply the necessary direction, and the extreme darkness* made it dangerous to proceed without one. During this period of distress, a light was perceived at some distance, and after much doubt and hesitation, La Motte, in the hope of obtaining assistance, alighted and advanced towards it; he proceeded slowly, from the fear of unknown pits. The light issued from the window of a small and ancient house, which stood alone on the heath, at the distance of half a mile.

Having reached the door, he stopped for some moments, listening in apprehensive anxiety—no sound was heard but that of the wind, which swept in hollow gusts over the waste.* At length he ventured to knock, and, having waited some time, during which he indistinctly heard several voices in conversation, some one within inquired what he wanted? La Motte answered, that he was a traveller who had lost his way, and desired to be directed to the nearest town. 'That,' said the person, 'is seven miles off, and the road bad enough, even if you could see it: if you only want a bed, you may have it here, and had better stay.'

The 'pitiless pelting' of the storm,* which, at this time, beat with increasing fury upon La Motte, inclined him to give up the attempt of proceeding farther till day-light; but, desirous of seeing the person with whom he conversed, before he ventured to expose his family by calling up the carriage, he asked to be admitted. The door was now opened by a tall figure with a light, who invited La Motte to enter. He followed the man through a passage into a room almost unfurnished, in one corner of which a bed was spread upon the floor. The forlorn and desolate aspect of this apartment made La Motte shrink involuntarily, and he was turning to go out when the man suddenly pushed him back, and he heard the door locked upon him: his heart failed, yet he made a desperate, though vain, effort to force the door, and called loudly for release. No answer was returned; but he distinguished the voices of men in the room above, and, not doubting but their intention was to rob and murder him, his agitation, at first, overcame his reason. By the light of some almost-expiring embers, he perceived a window, but the hope, which this discovery revived, was quickly lost, when he found the aperture guarded by strong iron bars. Such preparation for security surprized him, and confirmed his worst apprehensions.—Alone, unarmed—beyond the chance of assistance, he saw himself in the power of people, whose trade was apparently rapine!—murder their means!—After revolving every possibility of escape, he endeavoured to await the event with fortitude; but La Motte could boast of no such virtue.

The voices had ceased, and all remained still for a quarter of an hour, when, between the pauses of the wind, he thought he distinguished the sobs and moaning of a female; he listened attentively and became confirmed in his conjecture; it was too evidently the accent of distress. At this conviction, the remains of his courage forsook him, and a terrible surmise darted, with the rapidity of lightning, cross his brain. It was probable that his carriage had been discovered by the people of the house, who, with a design of plunder, had secured his servant, and brought hither Madame de la Motte. He was the more inclined to believe this, by the stillness which had, for some time, reigned in the house, previous to the sounds he now heard. Or it was possible that the inhabitants were not robbers, but persons to whom he had been betrayed by his friend or servant, and who were appointed to deliver him into the hands of justice. Yet he hardly dared to doubt the integrity of his friend, who had been entrusted with the secret of his flight and the plan of his route, and had procured him the carriage in which he had escaped. 'Such depravity,' exclaimed La Motte, 'cannot surely exist in human nature; much less in the heart of Nemours!'

This ejaculation was interrupted by a noise in the passage leading to the room: it approached—the door was unlocked—and the man who had admitted La Motte into the house entered, leading, or rather forcibly dragging along, a beautiful girl, who appeared to be about eighteen. Her features were bathed in tears, and she seemed to suffer the utmost distress.* The man fastened the lock and put the key in his pocket. He then advanced to La Motte, who had before observed other persons in the passage, and pointing a pistol to his breast, 'You are wholly in our power,' said he, 'no assistance can reach you: if you wish to save your life, swear that you will convey this girl where I may never see her more; or rather consent to take her with you, for your oath I would not believe, and I can take care you shall not find me again.—Answer quickly, you have no time to lose.'

He now seized the trembling hand of the girl, who shrunk aghast with terror, and hurried her towards La Motte, whom surprize still kept silent. She sunk at his feet, and with supplicating eyes, that streamed with tears, implored him to have pity on her. Notwithstanding his present agitation, he found it impossible to contemplate the beauty and distress of the object before him with indifference. Her youth, her apparent innocence—the artless energy of her manner forcibly assailed his heart, and he was going to speak, when the ruffian, who mistook the silence of astonishment for that of hesitation, prevented him. 'I have a horse ready to take you from hence,' said he, 'and I will direct you over the heath. If you return within an hour, you die: after then, you are at liberty to come here when you please.'

La Motte, without answering, raised the lovely girl from the floor, and was so much relieved from his own apprehensions, that he had leisure to attempt dissipating hers. 'Let us be gone,' said the ruffian, 'and have no more of this nonsense; you may think yourself well off it's no worse. I'll go and get the horse ready.'

The last words roused La Motte, and perplexed him with new fears; he dreaded to discover his carriage, lest its appearance might tempt the banditti to plunder; and to depart on horseback with this man might produce a consequence yet more to be dreaded. Madame La Motte, wearied with apprehension, would, probably, send for her husband to the house, when all the former danger would be incurred, with the additional evil of being separated from his family, and the chance of being detected by the emissaries of justice in endeavouring to recover them. As these reflections passed over his mind in tumultuous rapidity, a noise was again heard in the passage, an uproar and scuffle ensued, and in the same moment he could distinguish the voice of his servant, who had been sent by Madame la Motte in search of him. Being now determined to disclose what could not long be concealed, he exclaimed aloud, that a horse was unnecessary, that he had a carriage at some distance which would convey them from the heath, the man, who was seized, being his servant.

The ruffian, speaking through the door, bid him be patient awhile and he should hear more from him. La Motte now turned his eyes upon his unfortunate companion, who, pale and exhausted, leaned for support against the wall. Her features, which were delicately beautiful, had gained from distress an expression of captivating sweetness: she had

         'An eye
As when the blue sky trembles thro' a cloud
   Of purest white.'*

A habit of grey camlet, with short slashed sleeves,* shewed, but did not adorn, her figure:* it was thrown open at the bosom, upon which part of her hair had fallen in disorder, while the light veil hastily thrown on, had, in her confusion, been suffered to fall back. Every moment of farther observation heightened the surprize of La Motte, and interested him more warmly in her favour. Such elegance and apparent refinement, contrasted with the desolation of the house, and the savage manners of its inhabitants, seemed to him like a romance of imagination, rather than an occurrence of real life. He endeavoured to comfort her, and his sense of compassion was too sincere to be misunderstood. Her terror gradually subsided into gratitude and grief. 'Ah, Sir,' said she, 'Heaven has sent you to my relief, and will surely reward you for your protection: I have no friend in the world, if I do not find one in you.'

La Motte assured her of his kindness, when he was interrupted by the entrance of the ruffian. He desired to be conducted to his family. 'All in good time,' replied the latter; 'I have taken care of one of them, and will of you, please Sr Peter, so be comforted.' These *comfortable* words renewed the terror of La Motte, who now earnestly begged to know if his family were safe. 'O! as for that matter they are safe enough, and you will be with them presently; but don't stand *parlying* here all night. Do you chuse to go or stay? you know the conditions.' They now bound the eyes of La Motte and of the young lady, whom terror had hitherto kept silent, and then placing them on two horses, a man mounted behind each, and they immediately gallopped off. They had proceeded in this way near half an hour, when La Motte entreated to know whither he was going? 'You will know that bye and bye,' said the ruffian, 'so be at peace.' Finding interrogatories useless, La Motte resumed silence till the horses stopped. His conductor then hallooed, and being answered by voices at some distance, in a few moments the sound of carriage wheels was heard, and, presently after, the words of a man directing

Peter which way to drive. As the carriage approached, La Motte called, and, to his inexpressible joy, was answered by his wife.

'You are now beyond the borders of the heath, and may go which way you will,' said the ruffian; 'if you return within an hour, you will be welcomed by a brace of bullets.' This was a very unnecessary caution to La Motte, whom they now released. The young stranger sighed deeply, as she entered the carriage; and the ruffian, having bestowed upon Peter some directions and more threats, waited to see him drive off. They did not wait long.

La Motte immediately gave a short relation of what had passed at the house, including an account of the manner in which the young stranger had been introduced to him. During this narrative, her deep convulsive sighs frequently drew the attention of Madame La Motte, whose compassion became gradually interested in her behalf, and who now endeavoured to tranquillize her spirits. The unhappy girl answered her kindness in artless and simple expressions, and then relapsed into tears and silence. Madame forbore for the present to ask any questions that might lead to a discovery of her connections, or seem to require an explanation of the late adventure, which now furnishing her with a new subject of reflection, the sense of her own misfortunes pressed less heavily upon her mind. The distress of La Motte was even for a while suspended; he ruminated on the late scene, and it appeared like a vision, or one of those improbable fictions that sometimes are exhibited in a romance: he could reduce it to no principles of probability, or render it comprehensible by any endeavour to analize it. The present charge, and the chance of future trouble brought upon him by this adventure, occasioned some dissatisfaction; but the beauty and seeming innocence of Adeline, united with the pleadings of humanity in her favour, and he determined to protect her.

The tumult of emotions which had passed in the bosom of Adeline, began now to subside; terror was softened into anxiety, and despair into grief. The sympathy so evident in the manners of her companions, particularly in those of

Madame La Motte, soothed her heart and encouraged her to hope for better days.

Dismally and silently the night passed on, for the minds of the travellers were too much occupied by their several sufferings to admit of conversation. The dawn, so anxiously watched for, at length appeared, and introduced the strangers more fully to each other. Adeline derived comfort from the looks of Madame La Motte, who gazed frequently and attentively at her, and thought she had seldom seen a countenance so interesting, or a form so striking. The languor of sorrow threw a melancholy grace upon her features, that appealed immediately to the heart; and there was a penetrating sweetness in her blue eyes, which indicated an intelligent and amiable mind.

La Motte now looked anxiously from the coach window, that he might judge of their situation, and observe whether he was followed. The obscurity of the dawn confined his views, but no person appeared. The sun at length tinted the eastern clouds and the tops of the highest hills, and soon after burst in full splendour on the scene. The terrors of La Motte began to subside, and the griefs of Adeline to soften. They entered upon a land confined by high banks and overarched by trees, on whose branches appeared the first green buds of spring glittering with dews. The fresh breeze of the morning animated the spirits of Adeline, whose mind was delicately sensible to the beauties of nature.* As she viewed the flowery luxuriance of the turf, and the tender green of the trees, or caught, between the opening banks, a glimpse of the varied landscape,* rich with wood, and fading into blue and distant mountains, her heart expanded in momentary joy. With Adeline the charms of external nature were heightened by those of novelty:* she had seldom seen the grandeur of an extensive prospect, or the magnificence of a wide horizon*— and not often the picturesque beauties of more confined scenery.* Her mind had not lost by long oppression that elastic energy, which resists calamity; else, however susceptible might have been her original taste, the beauties of nature would no longer have charmed her thus easily even to temporary repose.

The road, at length, wound down the side of a hill, and La Motte, again looking anxiously from the window, saw before him an open champaign country, through which the road, wholly unsheltered from observation, extended almost in a direct line. The danger of these circumstances alarmed him, for his flight might, without difficulty, be traced for many leagues from the hills he was now descending. Of the first peasant that passed, he inquired for a road among the hills, but heard of none. La Motte now sunk into his former terrors. Madame, notwithstanding her own apprehensions, endeavoured to re-assure him, but, finding her efforts ineffectual, she also retired to the contemplation of her misfortunes. Often, as they went on, did La Motte look back upon the country they had passed, and often did imagination suggest to him the sounds of distant pursuits.

The travellers stopped to breakfast in a village, where the road was at length obscured by woods, and La Motte's spirits again revived. Adeline appeared more tranquil than she had yet been, and La Motte now asked for an explanation of the scene he had witnessed on the preceding night. The inquiry renewed all her distress, and with tears she entreated for the present to be spared on the subject. La Motte pressed it no farther, but he observed that for the greater part of the day she seemed to remember it in melancholy and dejection. They now travelled among the hills and were, therefore, in less danger of observation; but La Motte avoided the great towns, and stopped in obscure ones no longer than to refresh the horses. About two hours after noon, the road wound into a deep valley, watered by a rivulet, and overhung with wood. La Motte called to Peter, and ordered him to drive to a thickly embowered spot, that appeared on the left. Here he alighted with his family, and Peter having spread the provisions on the turf, they seated themselves and partook of a repast, which, in other circumstances, would have been thought delicious. Adeline endeavoured to smile, but the languor of grief was now heightened by indisposition. The violent agitation of mind, and fatigue of body, which she had suffered for the last twenty-four hours, had overpowered her strength, and, when La Motte led her back to the carriage, her whole frame trembled with illness. But she uttered no complaint, and, having long observed the dejection of her companions, she made a feeble effort to enliven them.

They continued to travel throughout the day without any accident or interruption, and, about three hours after sunset, arrived at Monville, a small town where La Motte determined to pass the night. Repose was, indeed, necessary to the whole party, whose pale and haggard looks, as they alighted from the carriage, were but too obvious to pass unobserved by the people of the inn. As soon as beds could be prepared, Adeline withdrew to her chamber, accompanied by Madame La Motte, whose concern for the fair stranger made her exert every effort to soothe and console her. Adeline wept in silence, and taking the hand of Madame, pressed it to her bosom. These were not merely tears of grief—they were mingled with those which flow from the grateful heart, when, unexpectedly, it meets with sympathy. Madame La Motte understood them. After some momentary silence, she renewed her assurances of kindness, and entreated Adeline to confide in her friendship; but she carefully avoided any mention of the subject, which had before so much affected her. Adeline at length found words to express her sense of this goodness, which she did in a manner so natural and sincere, that Madame, finding herself much affected, took leave of her for the night.

In the morning, La Motte rose at an early hour, impatient to be gone. Every thing was prepared for his departure, and the breakfast had been waiting some time, but Adeline did not appear. Madame La Motte went to her chamber, and found her sunk in a disturbed slumber. Her breathing was short and irregular—she frequently started, or sighed, and sometimes she muttered an incoherent sentence. While Madame gazed with concern upon her languid countenance, she awoke, and, looking up, gave her hand to Madame La Motte, who found it burning with fever. She had passed a restless night, and, as she now attempted to rise, her head, which beat with intense pain, grew giddy, her strength failed, and she sunk back.

Madame was much alarmed, being at once convinced that it was impossible she could travel, and that a delay might prove fatal to her husband. She went to inform him of the truth, and his distress may be more easily imagined than described. He saw all the inconvenience and danger of delay, yet he could not so far divest himself of humanity, as to abandon Adeline to the care, or rather, to the neglect of strangers. He sent immediately for a physician, who pronounced her to be in a high fever, and said, a removal in her present state must be fatal. La Motte now determined to wait the event, and endeavoured to calm the transports of terror, which, at times, assailed him. In the mean while, he took such precautions as his situation admitted of, passing the greater part of the day out of the village, in a spot from whence he had a view of the road for some distance; yet to be exposed to destruction by the illness of a girl, whom he did not know, and who had actually been forced upon him, was a misfortune, to which La Motte had not philosophy enough to submit with composure.

Adeline's fever continued to increase during the whole day, and at night, when the physician took his leave, he told La Motte, the event would very soon be decided. La Motte received this intelligence with real concern. The beauty and innocence of Adeline had overcome the disadvantageous circumstances under which she had been introduced to him, and he now gave less consideration to the inconvenience she might hereafter occasion him, than to the hope of her recovery.

Madame La Motte watched over her with tender anxiety, and observed with admiration, her patient sweetness and mild resignation. Adeline amply repaid her, though she thought she could not. 'Young as I am,' she would say, 'and deserted by those upon whom I have a claim for protection, I can remember no connection to make me regret life so much, as that I hoped to form with you. If I live, my conduct will best express my sense of your goodness;—words are but feeble testimonies.'

The sweetness of her manners so much attracted Madame La Motte, that she watched the crisis of her disorder, with a solicitude which precluded every other interest. Adeline passed a very disturbed night, and, when the physician appeared in the morning, he gave orders that she should be indulged with whatever she liked, and answered the inquiries of La Motte with a frankness that left nothing to hope.

In the mean time, his patient, after drinking profusely of some mild liquids, fell asleep, in which she continued for several hours, and so profound was her repose, that her breath alone gave sign of existence. She awoke free from fever, and with no other disorder than weakness, which, in a few days, she overcame so well, as to be able to set out with La Motte for B——, a village out of the great road, which he thought it prudent to quit. There they passed the following night, and early the next morning commenced their journey upon a wild and woody tract of country. They stopped about noon at a solitary village, where they took refreshments, and obtained directions for passing the vast forest of Fontanville, upon the borders of which they now were. La Motte wished at first to take a guide, but he apprehended more evil from the discovery he might make of his route, than he hoped for benefit from assistance in the wilds of this uncultivated tract.

La Motte now designed to pass on to Lyons, where he could either seek concealment in its neighbourhood, or embark on the Rhone for Geneva, should the emergency of his circumstances hereafter require him to leave France. It was about twelve o'clock at noon, and he was desirous to hasten forward, that he might pass the forest of Fontanville, and reach the town on its opposite borders, before night fall. Having deposited a fresh stock of provisions in the carriage, and received such directions as were necessary concerning the roads, they again set forward, and in a short time entered upon the forest. It was now the latter end of April, and the weather was remarkably temperate and fine. The balmy freshness of the air, which breathed the first pure essence of vegetation; and the gentle warmth of the sun, whose beams vivified every hue of nature, and opened every floweret of spring, revived Adeline, and inspired her with life and health. As she inhaled the breeze, her strength seemed to return, and, as her eyes wandered through the romantic glades* that opened into the forest, her heart was gladdened with complacent delight: but when from these objects she turned her regard upon Monsieur and Madame La Motte, to whose tender attentions she owed her life, and in whose looks she now read esteem and kindness, her bosom glowed with sweet affections, and she experienced a force of gratitude which might be called sublime.

For the remainder of the day they continued to travel, without seeing a hut, or meeting a human being. It was now near sun-set, and, the prospect being closed on all sides by the forest, La Motte began to have apprehensions that his servant had mistaken the way. The road, if a road it could be called, which afforded only a slight track upon the grass, was sometimes over-run by luxuriant vegetation, and sometimes obscured by the deep shades, and Peter at length stopped, uncertain of the way. La Motte, who dreaded being benighted in a scene so wild and solitary as this forest, and whose apprehensions of banditti were very sanguine, ordered him to proceed at any rate, and, if he found no track, to endeavour to gain a more open part of the forest. With these orders, Peter again set forwards, but having proceeded some way, and his views being still confined by woody glades and forest walks, he began to despair of extricating himself, and stopped for further orders. The sun was now set, but, as La Motte looked anxiously from the window, he observed upon the vivid glow of the western horison, some dark towers rising from among the trees at a little distance, and ordered Peter to drive towards them. 'If they belong to a monastery,' said he, 'we may probably gain admittance for the night.'

The carriage drove along under the shade of 'melancholy boughs,'* through which the evening twilight, which yet coloured the air, diffused a solemnity that vibrated in thrilling sensations upon the hearts of the travellers.* Expectation kept them silent. The present scene recalled to Adeline a remembrance of the late terrific circumstances, and her mind responded but too easily to the apprehension of new misfortunes. La Motte alighted at the foot of a green knoll, where the trees again opening to light, permitted a nearer, though imperfect, view of the edifice.

CHAPTER II

'How these antique towers and vacant courts
Chill the suspended soul! Till expectation
Wears the face of fear: and fear, half ready
To become devotion, mutters a kind
Of mental orison, it knows not wherefore.
What a kind of being is circumstance!'
                    HORACE WALPOLE*

HE approached, and perceived the Gothic remains of an
abbey: it stood on a kind of rude lawn, overshadowed by high
and spreading trees, which seemed coeval with the building,
and diffused a romantic gloom* around. The greater part of
the pile appeared to be sinking into ruins, and that, which had
withstood the ravages of time, shewed the remaining features
of the fabric more awful in decay. The lofty battlements,*
thickly enwreathed with ivy, were half demolished, and
become the residence of birds of prey. Huge fragments of the
eastern tower, which was almost demolished, lay scattered
amid the high grass, that waved slowly to the breeze. 'The
thistle shook its lonely head; the moss whistled to the wind.'*
A Gothic gate, richly ornamented with fret-work, which
opened into the main body of the edifice, but which was now
obstructed with brush-wood, remained entire. Above the vast
and magnificent portal of this gate arose a window of the same
order, whose pointed arches still exhibited fragments of
stained glass, once the pride of monkish devotion. La Motte,
thinking it possible it might yet shelter some human being,
advanced to the gate and lifted a massy knocker. The hollow
sounds rung through the emptiness of the place. After waiting
a few minutes, he forced back the gate, which was heavy with
iron work, and creaked harshly on its hinges.

He entered what appeared to have been the chapel of the
abbey, where the hymn of devotion had once been raised, and
the tear of penitence had once been shed; sounds, which could
now only be recalled by imagination—tears of penitence,
which had been long since fixed in fate. La Motte paused a
moment, for he felt a sensation of sublimity rising into
terror—a suspension of mingled astonishment and awe!* He

surveyed the vastness of the place, and as he contemplated its ruins, fancy bore him back to past ages.* 'And these walls,' said he, 'where once superstition lurked, and austerity anticipated an earthly purgatory, now tremble over the mortal remains of the beings who reared them!'

The deepening gloom now reminded La Motte that he had no time to lose, but curiosity prompted him to explore farther, and he obeyed the impulse. As he walked over the broken pavement, the sound of his steps ran in echoes through the place, and seemed like the mysterious accents of the dead, reproving the sacrilegious mortal who thus dared to disturb their precincts.

From this chapel he passed into the nave of the great church, of which one window, more perfect than the rest, opened upon a long vista of the forest, through which was seen the rich colouring of evening, melting by imperceptible gradations into the solemn grey of upper air. Dark hills, whose outline appeared distinct upon the vivid glow of the horizon, closed the perspective. Several of the pillars, which had once supported the roof, remained the proud effigies of sinking greatness, and seemed to nod at every murmur of the blast over the fragments of those that had fallen a little before them. La Motte sighed. The comparison between himself and the gradation of decay, which these columns exhibited, was but too obvious and affecting. 'A few years,' said he, 'and I shall become like the mortals on whose reliques I now gaze, and, like them too, I may be the subject of meditation to a succeeding generation, which shall totter but a little while over the object they contemplate, ere they also sink into the dust.'*

Retiring from this scene, he walked through the cloisters, till a door, which communicated with the lofty part of the building, attracted his curiosity. He opened this and perceived, across the foot of the stair-case, another door;—but now, partly checked by fear, and partly by the recollection of the surprize his family might feel in his absence, he returned with hasty steps to his carriage, having wasted some of the precious moments of twilight, and gained no information.

Some slight answer to Madame La Motte's inquiries, and a

general direction to Peter to drive carefully on, and look for
a road, was all that his anxiety would permit him to utter. The
night shade fell thick around, which, deepened by the gloom
of the forest, soon rendered it dangerous to proceed. Peter
stopped, but La Motte, persisting in his first determination,
ordered him to go on. Peter ventured to remonstrate, Madame
La Motte entreated, but La Motte reproved—commanded,
and at length repented; for the hind wheel rising upon the
stump of an old tree, which the darkness had prevented Peter
from observing, the carriage was in an instant overturned.

The party, as may be supposed, were much terrified, but no
one was materially hurt, and having disengaged themselves
from their perilous situation, La Motte and Peter endeavoured
to raise the carriage. The extent of this misfortune was now
discovered, for they perceived that the wheel was broke. Their
distress was reasonably great, for not only was the coach
disabled from proceeding, but it could not even afford a
shelter from the cold dews of the night, it being impossible to
preserve it in an upright situation. After a few moment's
silence, La Motte proposed that they should return to the
ruins which they had just quitted, which lay at a very short
distance, and pass the night in the most habitable part of
them: that, when morning dawned, Peter should take one of
the coach horses, and endeavour to find a road and a town,
from whence assistance could be procured for repairing the
carriage. This proposal was opposed by Madame La Motte,
who shuddered at the idea of passing so many hours of
darkness in a place so forlorn as the monastery. Terrors,
which she neither endeavoured to examine, or combat,
overcame her, and she told La Motte she had rather remain
exposed to the unwholesome dews of night, than encounter
the desolation of the ruins. La Motte had at first felt an equal
reluctance to return to this spot, but having subdued his own
feelings, he resolved not to yield to those of his wife.

The horses being now disengaged from the carriage, the
party moved towards the edifice. As they proceeded, Peter,
who followed them, struck a light, and they entered the ruins
by the flame of sticks, which he had collected. The partial
gleams thrown across the fabric seemed to make its desolation

more solemn, while the obscurity of the greater part of the
pile heightened its sublimity, and led fancy on to scenes of
horror.* Adeline, who had hitherto remained in silence, now
uttered an exclamation of mingled admiration and fear. A kind
of pleasing dread thrilled her bosom, and filled all her soul.*
Tears started into her eyes:—she wished, yet feared, to go
on;—she hung upon the arm of La Motte, and looked at him
with a sort of hesitating interrogation.

He opened the door of the great hall, and they entered: its
extent was lost in gloom. 'Let us stay here,' said Madame de
la Motte, 'I will go no farther.' La Motte pointed to the
broken roof, and was proceeding, when he was interrupted by
an uncommon noise, which passed along the hall. They were
all silent—it was the silence of terror. Madame La Motte
spoke first. 'Let us quit this spot,' said she, 'any evil is
preferable to the feeling, which now oppresses me. Let us
retire instantly.' The stillness had for some time remained
undisturbed, and La Motte, ashamed of the fear he had
involuntarily betrayed, now thought it necessary to affect a
boldness, which he did not feel. He, therefore, opposed
ridicule to the terror of Madame, and insisted upon
proceeding. Thus compelled to acquiesce, she traversed the
hall with trembling steps. They came to a narrow passage, and
Peter's sticks being nearly exhausted, they awaited here, while
he went in search of more.

The almost expiring light flashed faintly upon the walls of
the passage, shewing the recess more horrible. Across the hall,
the greater part of which was concealed in shadow, the feeble
ray spread a tremulous gleam, exhibiting the chasm in the
roof, while many nameless objects were seen imperfectly
through the dusk. Adeline with a smile, inquired of La Motte,
if he believed in spirits. The question was ill-timed, for the
present scene impressed its terrors upon La Motte, and, in
spite of endeavour, he felt a superstitious dread stealing upon
him. He was now, perhaps, standing over the ashes of the
dead. If spirits were ever permitted to revisit the earth, this
seemed the hour and the place most suitable for their
appearance. La Motte remaining silent, Adeline said, 'Were I
inclined to superstition'—She was interrupted by a return of

the noise, which had been lately heard. It sounded down the passage, at whose entrance they stood, and sunk gradually away. Every heart palpitated, and they remained listening in silence. A new subject of apprehension seized La Motte:—the noise might proceed from banditti, and he hesitated whether it would be safe to proceed. Peter now came with the light: Madame refused to enter the passage—La Motte was not much inclined to it; but Peter, in whom curiosity was more prevalent than fear, readily offered his services. La Motte, after some hesitation, suffered him to go, while he awaited at the entrance the result of the inquiry. The extent of the passage soon concealed Peter from view, and the echoes of his footsteps were lost in a sound, which rushed along the avenue, and became fainter and fainter, till it sunk into silence. La Motte now call aloud to Peter, but no answer was returned; at length, they heard the sound of a distant footstep, and Peter soon after appeared, breathless, and pale with fear.

When he came within hearing of La Motte, he called out, 'An please your honour, I've done for them, I believe, but I've had a hard bout. I thought I was fighting with the devil.'— 'What are you speaking of?' said La Motte.

'They were nothing but owls and rooks after all,' continued Peter; 'but the light brought them all about my ears, and they made such a confounded clapping with their wings, that I thought at first I had been beset with a legion of devils. But I have drove them all out, master, and you have nothing to fear now.'

The latter part of the sentence, intimating a suspicion of his courage, La Motte could have dispensed with, and, to retrieve in some degree his reputation, he made a point of proceeding through the passage. They now moved on with alacrity, for, as Peter said, they had 'nothing to fear.'*

The passage led into a large area, on one side of which, over a range of cloisters, appeared the west tower, and a lofty part of the edifice; the other side was open to the woods. La Motte led the way to a door of the tower, which he now perceived was the same he had formerly entered; but he found some difficulty in advancing, for the area was overgrown with brambles and nettles, and the light, which Peter carried, afforded only an uncertain gleam. When he unclosed the door, the dismal aspect of the place revived the apprehensions of Madame La Motte, and extorted from Adeline an inquiry whither they were going. Peter held up the light to shew the narrow stair-case that wound round the tower; but La Motte, observing the second door, drew back the rusty bolts, and entered a spacious apartment, which, from its stile and condition, was evidently of a much later date than the other part of the structure: though desolate and forlorn, it was very little impaired by time; the walls were damp, but not decayed; and the glass was yet firm in the windows.

They passed on to a suite of apartments resembling the first they had seen, and expressed their surprise at the incongruous appearance of this part of the edifice with the mouldering walls they had left behind. These apartments conducted them to a winding passage, that received light and air through narrow cavities, placed high in the wall; and was at length closed by a door barred with iron, which being with some difficulty opened, they entered a vaulted room. La Motte surveyed it with a scrutinizing eye, and endeavoured to conjecture for what purpose it had been guarded by a door of such strength; but he saw little within to assist his curiosity. The room appeared to have been built in modern times upon a Gothic plan. Adeline approached a large window that formed a kind of recess raised by one step over the level of the floor; she observed to La Motte that the whole floor was inlaid with Mosaic work; which drew from him a remark, that the style of this apartment was not strictly Gothic.* He passed on to a door, which appeared on the opposite side of the apartment, and, unlocking it, found himself in the great hall, by which he had entered the fabric.

He now perceived, what the gloom had before concealed, a spiral stair-case, which led to a gallery above; and which, from its present condition, seemed to have been built with the more modern part of the fabric, though this also affected the Gothic mode of architecture: La Motte had little doubt that these stairs led to apartments, corresponding with those he had passed below, and hesitated whether to explore them; but the entreaties of Madame, who was much fatigued, prevailed with him to defer all farther examination. After some deliberation, in which of the rooms they should pass the night, they determined to return to that which opened from the tower.

A fire was kindled on a hearth, which it is probable had not for many years before afforded the warmth of hospitality; and Peter having spread the provision he had brought from the coach, La Motte and his family, encircled round the fire, partook of a repast, which hunger and fatigue made delicious. Apprehension gradually gave way to confidence, for they now found themselves in something like a human habitation, and they had leisure to laugh at their late terrors; but, as the blast shook the doors, Adeline often started, and threw a fearful glance around. They continued to laugh and talk cheerfully for a time; yet their merriment was transient, if not affected; for a sense of their peculiar and distressed circumstances pressed upon their recollection, and sunk each individual into langour and pensive silence. Adeline felt the forlornness of her condition with energy; she reflected upon the past with astonishment, and anticipated the future with fear. She found herself wholly dependent upon strangers, with no other claim than what distress demands from the common sympathy of kindred beings; sighs swelled her heart, and the frequent tear started to her eye; but she checked it, ere it betrayed on her cheek the sorrow, which she thought it would be ungrateful to reveal.

La Motte, at length, broke this meditative silence, by directing the fire to be renewed for the night, and the door to be secured: this seemed a necessary precaution, even in this solitude, and was effected by means of large stones piled against it, for other fastening there was none. It had frequently occurred to La Motte, that this apparently forsaken edifice might be a place of refuge to banditti. Here was solitude to conceal them; and a wild and extensive forest to assist their schemes of rapine, and to perplex, with its labyrinths, those who might be bold enough to attempt pursuit. These apprehensions, however, he hid within his own bosom, saving his companions from a share of the uneasiness they occasioned. Peter was ordered to watch at the door, and, having given the fire a rousing stir, our desolate party drew round it, and sought in sleep a short oblivion of care.

The night passed on without disturbance. Adeline slept, but uneasy dreams fleeted before her fancy, and she awoke at an early hour: the recollection of her sorrows arose upon her mind, and yielding to their pressure, her tears flowed silently and fast. That she might indulge them without restraint, she went to a window that looked upon an open part of the forest; all was gloom and silence; she stood for some time viewing the shadowy scene.

The first tender tints of morning now appeared on the verge of the horizon, stealing upon the darkness;—so pure, so fine, so ætherial! it seemed as if Heaven was opening to the view. The dark mists were seen to roll off to the west, as the tints of light grew stronger, deepening the obscurity of that part of the hemisphere, and involving the features of the country below; meanwhile, in the east, the hues become more vivid, darting a trembling lustre far around, till a ruddy glow, which fired all that part of the Heavens, announced the rising sun. At first, a small line of inconceivable splendour emerged on the horizon, which, quickly expanding, the sun appeared in all his glory, unveiling the whole face of nature, vivifying every colour of the landscape, and sprinkling the dewy earth with glittering light. The low and gentle responses of birds, awakened by the morning ray, now broke the silence of the hour; the soft warbling rising by degrees till they swelled the chorus of universal gladness. Adeline's heart swelled too with gratitude and adoration.

The scene before her soothed her mind, and exalted her thoughts to the great Author of Nature; she uttered an involuntary prayer: 'Father of good, who made this glorious scene! I resign myself to thy hands: thou wilt support me under my present sorrows, and protect me from future evil.'*

Thus confiding in the benevolence of God, she wiped the tears from her eyes, while the sweet union of conscience and reflection rewarded her trust; and her mind, losing the feelings which had lately oppressed it, became tranquil and composed.

La Motte awoke soon after, and Peter prepared to set out

on his expedition. As he mounted his horse, 'An' please you, Master,' said he, 'I think we had as good look no farther for an habitation till better times turn up; for nobody will think of looking for us here; and when one sees the place by day light, it's none so bad, but what a little patching up would make it comfortable enough.' La Motte made no reply, but he thought of Peter's words. During the intervals of the night, when anxiety had kept him waking, the same idea had occurred to him; concealment was his only security, and this place afforded it. The desolation of the spot was repulsive to his wishes; but he had only a choice of evils—a forest with liberty was not a bad home for one, who had too much reason to expect a prison. As he walked through the apartments, and examined their condition more attentively, he perceived they might easily be made habitable; and now surveying them under the cheerfulness of morning, his design strengthened; and he mused upon the means of accomplishing it, which nothing seemed so much to obstruct as the apparent difficulty of procuring food.

He communicated his thoughts to Madame la Motte, who felt repugnance to the scheme. La Motte, however, seldom consulted his wife till he had determined how to act; and he had already resolved to be guided in this affair by the report of Peter. If he could discover a town in the neighbourhood of the forest, where provisions and other necessaries could be procured, he would seek no farther a place of rest.

In the mean time, he spent the anxious interval of Peter's absence in examining the ruin, and walking over the environs; they were sweetly romantic, and the luxuriant woods, with which they abounded, seemed to sequester this spot from the rest of the world. Frequently a natural vista would yield a view of the country, terminated by hills, which retiring in distance, faded into the blue horizon. A stream, various* and musical in its course, wound at the foot of the lawn, on which stood the abbey; here it silently glided beneath the shades, feeding the flowers that bloomed on its banks, and diffusing dewy freshness around; there it spread in broad expanse to-day, reflecting the sylvan scene, and the wild deer that tasted its waves. La Motte observed every where a profusion of game;

the pheasants scarcely flew from his approach, and the deer gazed mildly at him as he passed. They were strangers to man!

On his return to the abbey, La Motte ascended the stairs that led to the tower. About half way up, a door appeared in the wall; it yielded, without resistance, to his hand; but, a sudden noise within, accompanied by a cloud of dust, made him step back and close the door. After waiting a few minutes, he again opened it, and perceived a large room of the more modern building. The remains of tapestry hung in tatters upon the walls, which were become the residence of birds of prey, whose sudden flight on the opening of the door had brought down a quantity of dust, and occasioned the noise. The windows were shattered, and almost without glass; but he was surprised to observe some remains of furniture; chairs, whose fashion and condition bore the date of their antiquity; a broken table, and an iron grate almost consumed by rust.

On the opposite side of the room was a door, which led to another apartment, proportioned like the first, but hung with arras somewhat less tattered. In one corner stood a small bedstead, and a few scattered chairs were placed round the walls. La Motte gazed with a mixture of wonder and curiosity. ''Tis strange,' said he, 'that these rooms, and these alone, should bear the marks of inhabitation: perhaps, some wretched wanderer, like myself, may have here sought refuge from a persecuting world; and here, perhaps, laid down the load of existence: perhaps, too, I have followed his footsteps, but to mingle my dust with his!' He turned suddenly, and was about to quit the room, when he perceived a small door near the bed; it opened into a closet, which was lighted by one small window, and was in the same condition as the apartments he had passed, except that it was destitute even of the remains of furniture. As he walked over the floor, he thought he felt one part of it shake beneath his steps, and, examining, found a trap door. Curiosity prompted him to explore farther, and with some difficulty he opened it. It disclosed a staircase which terminated in darkness. La Motte descended a few steps, but was unwilling to trust the abyss; and, after wondering for what purpose it was so secretly constructed, he closed the trap, and quitted this suite of apartments.

The stairs in the tower above were so much decayed, that he did not attempt to ascend them: he returned to the hall, and by the spiral stair-case, which he had observed the evening before, reached the gallery, and found another suite of apartments entirely unfurnished, very much like those below.

He renewed with Madame La Motte his former conversation respecting the abbey, and she exerted all her endeavours to dissuade him from his propose, acknowledging the solitary security of the spot, but pleading that other places might be found equally well adapted for concealment and more for comfort. This La Motte doubted: besides, the forest abounded with game, which would, at once, afford him amusement and food, a circumstance, considering his small stock of money, by no means to be overlooked: and he had suffered his mind to dwell so much upon the scheme, that it was become a favourite one. Adeline listened in silent anxiety to the discourse, and waited the issue of Peter's report.

The morning passed, but Peter did not return. Our solitary party took their dinner of the provision they had fortunately brought with them, and afterwards walked forth into the woods. Adeline, who never suffered any good to pass unnoticed, because it came attended with evil, forgot for a while the desolation of the abbey in the beauty of the adjacent scenery. The pleasantness of the shades soothed her heart, and the varied features of the landscape amused her fancy; she almost thought she could be contented to live here. Already she began to feel an interest in the concerns of her companions, and for Madame La Motte she felt more; it was the warm emotion of gratitude and affection.

The afternoon wore away, and they returned to the abbey. Peter was still absent, and his absence now began to excite surprize and apprehension. The approach of darkness also threw a gloom upon the hopes of the wanderers: another night must be passed under the same forlorn circumstances as the preceding one; and, what was still worse, with a very scanty stock of provisions. The fortitude of Madame La Motte now entirely forsook her, and she wept bitterly. Adeline's heart was as mournful as Madame's, but she rallied her drooping spirits, and gave the first instance of her kindness by endeavouring to revive those of her friend.

La Motte was restless and uneasy, and, leaving the abbey, he walked alone the way which Peter had taken. He had not gone far, when he perceived him between the trees, leading his horse. 'What news, Peter?' hallooed La Motte. Peter came on, panting for breath, and said not a word, till La Motte repeated the question in a tone of somewhat more authority. 'Ah, bless you, Master!' said he, when he had taken breath to answer, 'I am glad to see you; I thought I should never have got back again: I've met with a world of misfortunes.'

'Well, you may relate them hereafter; let me hear whether you have discovered—'

'Discovered!' interrupted Peter, 'Yes, I am discovered with a vengeance! If your Honour will look at my arms, you'll see how I am discovered.'

'Discoloured! I suppose you mean,'* said La Motte. 'But how came you in this condition?'

'Why, I'll tell you how it was, Sir; your Honour knows I learned a smack of boxing of that Englishman that used to come with his master to our house.'

'Well, well—tell me where you have been.'

'I scarcely know myself, Master; I've been where I got a sound drubbing,* but then it was in your business, and so I don't mind. But if ever I meet with that rascal again!'—

'You seem to like your first drubbing so well, that you want another, and unless you speak more to the purpose, you shall soon have one.'

Peter was now frightened into method, and endeavoured to proceed: 'When I left the old Abbey,' said he, 'I followed the way you directed, and, turning to the right of that grove of trees yonder, I looked this way and that to see if I could see a house, or a cottage, or even a man, but not a *soul* of them was to be seen, and so I jogged on, near the value of a league, I warrant, and then I came to a track; oh! oh! says I, we have you now; this will do—paths can't be made without feet. However, I was out in my reckoning, for the devil a bit of a *soul* could I see, and, after following the track this way and that way, for the third of a league, I lost it, and had to find out another.'

'Is it impossible for you to speak to the point?' said La Motte: 'omit these foolish particulars, and tell whether you have succeeded.'

'Well, then, Master, to be short, for that's the nearest way after all, I wandered a long while at random, I did not know where, all through a forest like this, and I took special care to note how the trees stood, that I might find my way back. At last I came to another path, and was sure I should find something now, though I had found nothing before, for I could not be mistaken twice; so, peeping between the trees, I spied a cottage, and I gave my horse a lash, that sounded through the forest, and I was at the door in a minute. They told me there was a town about half a league off, and bade me follow the track and it would bring me there, so it did; and my horse, I believe, smelt the corn in the manger by the rate he went at. I inquired for a wheel-wright, and was told there was but one in the place, and he could not be found. I waited and waited, for I knew it was in vain to think of returning without doing my business. The man at last came home from the country, and I told him how long I had waited; for, says I, I knew it was in vain to return without my business.'

'Do be less tedious,' said La Motte, 'if it is in thy nature.'

'It is in my nature,' answered Peter, 'and if it was more in my nature, your Honour should have it all. Would you think it, Sir, the fellow had the impudence to ask a louis-d'or for mending the coach wheel! I believe in my conscience he saw I was in a hurry and could not do without him. A louis-d'or! says I, my Master shall give no such price, he sha'n't be imposed upon by no such rascal as you. Whereupon, the fellow looked glum, and gave me a douse o' the chops:* with this, I up with my fist and gave him another, and should have beat him presently, if another man had not come in, and then I was obliged to give up.'

'And so you are returned as wise as you went?'

'Why, Master, I hope I have too much spirit to submit to a rascal, or let you submit to one either: besides, I have bought some nails to try if I can't mend the wheel myself—I had always a hand at carpentry.'

'Well, I commend your zeal in my cause, but on this occasion it was rather ill-timed. And what have you got in that basket?'

'Why, Master, I bethought me that we could not get away from this place till the carriage was ready to draw us, and in the mean time, says I, nobody can live without victuals, so I'll e'en lay out the little money I have and take a basket with me.'

'That's the only wise thing you have done yet, and this, indeed, redeems your blunders.'

'Why now, Master, it does my heart good to hear you speak; I knew I was doing for the best all the while: but I've had a hard job to find my way back; and here's another piece of ill luck, for the horse has got a thorn in his foot.'

La Motte made inquiries concerning the town, and found it was capable of supplying him with provision, and what little furniture was necessary to render the abbey habitable. This intelligence almost settled his plans, and he ordered Peter to return on the following morning and make inquiries concerning the abbey. If the answers were favourable to his wishes, he commissioned him to buy a cart and load it with some furniture, and some materials necessary for repairing the modern apartments. Peter stared: 'What, does your Honour mean to live here?'

'Why, suppose I do?'

'Why then your Honour has made a wise determination, according to my hint; for your Honour knows I said'—

'Well, Peter, it is not necessary to repeat what you said; perhaps, I had determined on the subject before.'

'Egad, Master, you're in the right, and I'm glad of it, for, I believe, we shall not quickly be disturbed here, except by the rooks and owls. Yes, yes—I warrant I'll make it a place fit for a king; and as for the town, one may get any thing, I'm sure of that; though they think no more about this place than they do about India or England, or any of those places.'

They now reached the abbey, where Peter was received with great joy; but the hopes of his mistress and Adeline were repressed, when they learned that he returned, without having executed his commission, and heard his account of the town. La Motte's orders to Peter were heard with almost equal concern by Madame and Adeline; but the latter concealed her uneasiness, and used all her efforts to overcome that of her friend. The sweetness of her behaviour, and the air of satisfaction she assumed, sensibly affected Madame, and discovered to her a source of comfort, which she had hitherto overlooked. The affectionate attentions of her young friend promised to console her for the want of other society, and her conversation to enliven the hours which might otherwise be passed in painful regret.

The observations and general behaviour of Adeline already bespoke a good understanding and an amiable heart, but she had yet more—she had genius. She was now in her nineteenth year; her figure of the middling size, and turned to the most exquisite proportion; her hair was dark auburn, her eyes blue, and whether they sparkled with intelligence, or melted with tenderness, they were equally attractive: her form had the airy lightness of a nymph, and, when she smiled, her countenance might have been drawn for the younger sister of Hebe:* the captivations of her beauty were heightened by the grace and simplicity of her manners, and confirmed by the intrinsic value of a heart

> 'That might be shrin'd in crystal,
> And have all its movements scann'd.'*

Annette now kindled the fire for the night: Peter's basket was opened, and supper prepared. Madame La Motte was still pensive and silent. 'There is scarcely any condition so bad,' said Adeline, 'but we may one time or other wish we had not quitted it. Honest Peter, when he was bewildered in the forest, or had two enemies to encounter instead of one, confesses he wished himself at the abbey. And I am certain, there is no situation so destitute, but comfort may be extracted from it. The blaze of this fire shines yet more cheerfully from the contrasted dreariness of the place; and this plentiful repast is made yet more delicious, from the temporary want we have suffered. Let us enjoy the good and forget the evil.'

'You speak, my dear,' replied Madame La Motte, 'like one,

whose spirits have not been often depressed by misfortune, (Adeline sighed) and whose hopes are, therefore, vigorous.'

'Long suffering,' said La Motte, 'has subdued in our minds that elastic energy, which repels the pressure of evil, and dances to the bound of joy. But I speak in rhapsody, though only from the remembrance of such a time. I once, like you, Adeline, could extract comfort from most situations.'

'And may now, my dear Sir,' said Adeline. 'Still believe it possible, and you will find it is so.'

'The illusion is gone—I can no longer deceive myself.'

'Pardon me, Sir, if I say, it is now only you deceive yourself, by suffering the cloud of sorrow to tinge every object you look upon.'

'It may be so,' said La Motte, 'but let us leave the subject.'

After supper, the doors were secured, as before, for the night, and the wanderers resigned themselves to repose.

On the following morning, Peter again set out for the little town of Auboine, and the hours of his absence were again spent by Madame La Motte and Adeline in much anxiety and some hope, for the intelligence he might bring concerning the abbey might yet release them from the plans of La Motte. Towards the close of the day he was descried coming slowly on; and the cart, which accompanied him, too certainly confirmed their fears. He brought materials for repairing the place, and some furniture.

Of the abbey he gave an account, of which the following is the substance:—It belonged, together with a large part of the adjacent forest, to a nobleman, who now resided with his family on a remote estate. He inherited it, in right of his wife, from his father-in-law, who had caused the more modern apartments to be erected, and had resided in them some part of every year, for the purpose of shooting and hunting. It was reported, that some person was, soon after it came to the present possessor, brought secretly to the abbey and confined in these apartments; who, or what he was, had never been conjectured, and what became of him nobody knew. The report died gradually away, and many persons entirely disbelieved the whole of it. But however this affair might be, certain it was, the present owner had visited the abbey only two summers, since his succeeding to it; and the furniture, after some time, was removed.

This circumstance had at first excited surprize, and various reports arose in consequence, but it was difficult to know what ought to be believed. Among the rest, it was said, that strange appearances had been observed at the abbey, and uncommon noises heard; and though this report had been ridiculed by sensible persons as the idle superstition of ignorance, it had fastened so strongly upon the minds of the common people, that for the last seventeen years none of the peasantry had ventured to approach the spot. The abbey was now, therefore, abandoned to decay.

La Motte ruminated upon this account. At first, it called up unpleasant ideas, but they were soon dismissed, and considerations more interesting to his welfare took place: he congratulated himself that he had now found a spot, where he was not likely to be either discovered or disturbed; yet it could not escape him that there was a strange coincidence between one part of Peter's narrative, and the condition of the chambers that opened from the tower above stairs. The remains of furniture, of which the other apartments were void—the solitary bed—the number and connection of the rooms, were circumstances that united to confirm his opinion. This, however, he concealed in his own breast, for he already perceived that Peter's account had not assisted in reconciling his family to the necessity of dwelling at the abbey.

But they had only to submit in silence, and whatever disagreeable apprehension might intrude upon them, they now appeared willing to suppress the expression of it. Peter, indeed, was exempt from any evil of this kind; he knew no fear, and his mind was now wholly occupied with his approaching business. Madame La Motte, with a placid kind of despair, endeavoured to reconcile herself to that, which no effort of understanding could teach her to avoid, and which, an indulgence in lamentation, could only make more intolerable. Indeed, though a sense of the immediate inconveniences to be endured at the abbey, had made her oppose the scheme of living there, she did not really know how their situation could be improved by removal: yet her thoughts often wandered towards Paris, and reflected the retrospect of past times, with the images of weeping friends left, perhaps, for ever. The affectionate endearments of her only son, whom, from the danger of his situation, and obscurity of hers, she might reasonably fear never to see again, arose upon her memory and overcame her fortitude. 'Why—why was I reserved for this hour?' would she say, 'and what will be my years to come?'

Adeline had no retrospect of past delight to give emphasis to present calamity—no weeping friends—no dear regretted objects to point the edge of sorrow, and throw a sickly hue upon her future prospects: she knew not yet the pangs of disappointed hope, or the acuter sting of self-accusation; she had no misery, but what patience could assuage, or fortitude overcome.

At the dawn of the following day Peter arose to his labour: he proceeded with alacrity, and, in a few days, two of the lower apartments were so much altered for the better, that La Motte began to exult, and his family to perceive that their situation would not be so miserable as they had imagined. The furniture Peter had already brought was disposed in these rooms, one of which was the vaulted apartment. Madame La Motte furnished this as a sitting room, preferring it for its large Gothic window, that descended almost to the floor, admitting a prosepect of the lawn, and the picturesque scenery of the surrounding woods.

Peter having returned to Auboine for a farther supply, all the lower apartments were in a few weeks not only habitable, but comfortable. These, however, being insufficient for the accommodation of the family, a room above stairs was prepared for Adeline: it was the chamber that opened immediately from the tower, and she preferred it to those beyond, because it was less distant from the family, and the windows fronting an avenue of the forest, afforded a more extensive prospect. The tapestry, that was decayed, and hung loosely from the walls, was now nailed up, and made to look less desolate; and, though the room had still a solemn aspect, from its spaciousness and the narrowness of the windows, it was not uncomfortable.

The first night that Adeline retired hither, she slept little: the solitary air of the place affected her spirits; the more so, perhaps, because she had, with friendly consideration, endeavoured to support them in the presence of Madame La Motte. She remembered the narrative of Peter, several circumstances of which had impressed her imagination in spite of her reason, and she found it difficult wholly to subdue apprehension. At one time, terror so strongly seized her mind, that she had even opened the door with an intention of calling Madame La Motte; but, listening for a moment on the stairs of the tower, every thing seemed still; at length, she heard the voice of La Motte speaking cheerfully, and the absurdity of her fears struck her forcibly; she blushed that she had for a moment submitted to them, and returned to her chamber wondering at herself.

CHAPTER III

'Are not these woods
More free from peril than the envious court?
Here feel we but the penalty of Adam,
The season's difference, as the icy fang
And churlish chiding of the winter's wind.'
SHAKESPEARE.*

LA Motte arranged his little plan of living. His mornings were usually spent in shooting, or fishing, and the dinner, thus provided by his industry, he relished with a keener appetite than had ever attended him at the luxurious tables of Paris. The afternoons he passed with his family: sometimes he would select a book from the few he had brought with him, and endeavour to fix his attention to the words his lips repeated:—but his mind suffered little abstraction from its own cares, and the sentiment he pronounced left no trace behind it. Sometimes he conversed, but oftener sat in gloomy silence, musing upon the past, or anticipating the future.

At these moments, Adeline, with a sweetness almost irresistible, endeavoured to enliven his spirits, and to withdraw him from himself. Seldom she succeeded, but when she did the grateful looks of Madame La Motte, and the benevolent feelings of her own bosom, realized the chearfulness she had at first only assumed. Adeline's mind had the happy art, or, perhaps, it were more just to say, the happy nature, of accommodating itself to her situation. Her present condition, though forlorn, was not devoid of comfort, and this comfort was confirmed by her virtues. So much she won upon the affections of her protectors, that Madame La Motte loved her as her child, and La Motte himself, though a man little susceptible of tenderness, could not be insensible to her solicitudes. Whenever he relaxed from the sullenness of misery, it was at the influence of Adeline.

Peter regularly brought a weekly supply of provisions from Auboine, and, on those occasions, always quitted the town by a route contrary to that leading to the abbey. Several weeks having passed without molestation, La Motte dismissed all apprehension of pursuit, and at length became tolerably reconciled to the complection of his circumstances. As habit and effort strengthened the fortitude of Madame La Motte, the features of misfortune appeared to soften. The forest, which at first seemed to her a frightful solitude, had lost its terrific aspect; and that edifice, whose half demolished walls and gloomy desolation had struck her mind with the force of melancholy and dismay, was now beheld as a domestic asylum, and a safe refuge from the storms of power.

She was a sensible and highly accomplished woman, and it became her chief delight to form the rising graces of Adeline, who had, as has been already shown, a sweetness of disposition, which made her quick to repay instruction with improvement, and indulgence with love. Never was Adeline so pleased as when she anticipated her wishes, and never so diligent as when she was employed in her business. The little affairs of the houshold she overlooked and managed with such admirable exactness, that Madame La Motte had neither anxiety, nor care, concerning them. And Adeline formed for herself in this barren situation, many amusements, that occasionally banished the remembrance of her misfortunes. La Motte's books were her chief consolation. With one of these she would frequently ramble into the forest, where the river, winding through a glade, diffused coolness, and with its murmuring accents, invited repose: there she would seat herself, and, resigned to the illusions of the page, pass many hours in oblivion of sorrow.

Here too, when her mind was tranquilized by the surrounding scenery, she wooed the gentle muse, and indulged in ideal happiness. The delight of these moments she commemorated in the following address

TO THE VISIONS OF FANCY

Dear, wild illusions of creative mind!
  Whose varying hues arise to Fancy's art,
And by her magic force are swift combin'd
  In forms that please, and scenes that touch the heart:
Oh! whether at her voice ye soft assume
  The pensive grace of sorrow drooping low;
Or rise sublime on terror's lofty plume,
  And shake the soul with wildly thrilling woe;
Or, sweetly bright, your gayer tints ye spread,
  Bid scenes of pleasure steal upon my view,
Love wave his purple pinions o'er my head,
  And wake the tender thought to passion true;
O! still—ye shadowy forms! attend my lonely hours,
Still chase my real cares with your illusive powers!*

Madame La Motte had frequently expressed curiosity concerning the events of Adeline's life, and by what circumstances she had been thrown into a situation so perilous and mysterious as that in which La Motte had found her. Adeline had given a brief account of the manner, in which she had been brought thither, but had always with tears intreated to be spared for that time from a particular relation of her history. Her spirits were not then equal to retrospection, but now that they were soothed by quiet, and strengthened by confidence, she one day gave Madame La Motte the following narration.

———————

I am the only child, said Adeline, of Louis de St. Pierre, a chevalier of reputable family, but of small fortune, who for many years resided at Paris. Of my mother I have a faint remembrance: I lost her when I was only seven years old, and this was my first misfortune. At her death, my father gave up housekeeping, boarded me in a convent, and quitted Paris. Thus was I, at this early period of my life, abandoned to strangers. My father came sometimes to Paris; he then visited me, and I well remember the grief I used to feel when he bade me farewell. On these occasions, which rung my heart with grief, he appeared unmoved; so that I often thought he had little tenderness for me. But he was my father, and the only person to whom I could look up for protection and love.

In this convent I continued till I was twelve years old. A thousand times I had entreated my father to take me home, but at first motives of prudence, and afterwards of avarice, prevented him. I was now removed from this convent, and placed in another, where I learned my father intended I should take the veil. I will not attempt to express my surprize and grief on this occasion. Too long I had been immured in the walls of a cloister, and too much had I seen of the sullen misery of its votaries, not to feel horror and disgust at the prospect of being added to their number.

The Lady Abbess was a woman of rigid decorum and severe devotion; exact in the observance of every detail of form, and never forgave an offence against ceremony. It was her method, when she wanted to make converts to her order, to denounce and terrify rather than to persuade and allure. Her's were the arts of cunning practised upon fear, not those of sophistication upon reason. She employed numberless stratagems to gain me to her purpose, and they all wore the complection of her character. But in the life to which she would have devoted me, I saw too many forms of real terror, to be overcome by the influence of her ideal host, and was resolute in rejecting the veil. Here I passed several years of miserable resistance against cruelty and superstition. My father I seldom saw; when I did, I entreated him to alter my destination, but he objected that his fortune was insufficient to support me in the world, and at length denounced vengeance on my head if I persisted in disobedience.

You, my dear Madam, can form little idea of the wretchedness of my situation, condemned to perpetual imprisonment, and imprisonment of the most dreadful kind, or to the vengeance of a father, from whom I had no appeal. My resolution relaxed—for some time I paused upon the choice of evils—but at length the horrors of the monastic life rose so fully to my view, that fortitude gave way before them. Excluded from the cheerful intercourse of society—from the pleasant view of nature—almost from the light of day—condemned to silence—rigid formality—abstinence and penance—condemned to forego the delights of a world, which imagination painted in the gayest and most alluring colours, and whose hues were, perhaps, not the less captivating because they were only ideal:—such was the state, to which I was destined. Again my resolution was invigorated: my father's cruelty subdued tenderness, and roused indignation. 'Since he can forget,' said I, 'the affection of a parent, and condemn his child without remorse to wretchedness and despair—the bond of filial and parental duty no longer subsists between us—he has himself dissolved it, and I will yet struggle for liberty and life.'

Finding me unmoved by menace, the Lady Abbess had now recourse to more subtle measures: she condescended to smile, and even to flatter; but her's was the distorted smile of cunning, not the gracious emblem of kindness; it provoked disgust, instead of inspiring affection. She painted the character of a vestal in the most beautiful tints of art—its holy innocence—its mild dignity—its sublime devotion. I sighed as she spoke. This she regarded as a favourable symptom, and proceeded on her picture with more animation. She described the serenity of a monastic life—its security from the seductive charms, restless passions, and sorrowful vicissitudes of the world—the rapturous delights of religion, and sweet reciprocal affection of the sisterhood.

So highly she finished the piece, that the lurking lines of cunning would, to an inexperienced eye, have escaped detection. Mine was too sorrowfully informed. Too often had I witnessed the secret tear and bursting sigh of vain regret, the sullen pinings of discontent, and the mute anguish of despair. My silence and my manner assured her of my incredulity, and it was with difficulty that she preserved a decent composure.

My father, as may be imagined, was highly incensed at my

perseverance, which he called obstinacy, but, what will not be so easily believed, he soon after relented, and appointed a day to take me from the convent. O! judge of my feelings when I received this intelligence. The joy it occasioned awakened all my gratitude; I forgot the former cruelty of my father, and that the present indulgence was less the effect of his kindness than of my resolution. I wept that I could not indulge his every wish.

What days of blissful expectation were those that preceded my departure! The world, from which I had been hitherto secluded—the world, in which my fancy had been so often delighted to roam—whose paths were strewn with fadeless roses—whose every scene smiled in beauty and invited to delight—where all the people were good, and all the good happy—Ah! *then* that world was bursting upon my view. Let me catch the rapturous remembrance before it vanish! It is like the passing lights of autumn, that gleam for a moment on a hill, and then leave it to darkness. I counted the days and hours that with-held me from this fairy land. It was in the convent only that people were deceitful and cruel: it was there only that misery dwelt. I was quitting it all! How I pitied the poor nuns that were to be left behind. I would have given half that world I prized so much, had it been mine, to have taken them out with me.

The long wished for day at last arrived. My father came, and for a moment my joy was lost in the sorrow of bidding farewell to my poor companions, for whom I had never felt such warmth of kindness as at this instant. I was soon beyond the gates of the convent. I looked around me, and viewed the vast vault of heaven no longer bounded by monastic walls, and the green earth extended in hill and dale to the round verge of the horizon! My heart danced with delight, tears swelled in my eyes, and for some moments I was unable to speak. My thoughts rose to Heaven in sentiments of gratitude to the Giver of all good!*

At length, I returned to my father; dear Sir, said I, how I thank you for my deliverance, and how I wish I could do every thing to oblige you.

Return, then, to your convent, said he, in a harsh accent. I shuddered; his look and manner jarred the tone of my feelings; they struck discord upon my heart, which had before responded only to harmony. The ardour of joy was in a moment repressed, and every object around me was saddened with the gloom of disappointment. It was not that I suspected my father would take me back to the convent; but that his feelings seemed so very dissonant to the joy and gratitude, which I had but a moment before felt and expressed to him.— Pardon, Madam, a relation of these trivial circumstances; the strong vicissitudes of feeling which they impressed upon my heart, make me think them important, when they are, perhaps, only disgusting.

'No, my dear,' said Madame La Motte, 'they are interesting to me; they illustrate little traits of character, which I love to observe. You are worthy of all my regards, and from this moment I give my tenderest pity to your misfortunes, and my affection to your goodness.'

These words melted the heart of Adeline; she kissed the hand which Madame held out, and remained a few minutes silent. At length she said, 'May I deserve this goodness! and may I ever be thankful to God, who, in giving me such a friend, has raised me to comfort and hope!

'My father's house was situated a few leagues on the other side of Paris, and in our way to it, we passed through that city. What a novel scene! Where were now the solemn faces, the demure manners I had been accustomed to see in the convent? Every countenance was here animated, either by business or pleasure; every step was airy, and every smile was gay. All the people appeared like friends; they looked and smiled at me; I smiled again, and wished to have told them how pleased I was. How delightful, said I, to live surrounded by friends!

'What crowded streets! What magnificent hotels! What splendid equipages! I scarcely observed that the streets were narrow, or the way dangerous. What bustle, what tumult, what delight! I could never be sufficiently thankful that I was removed from the convent. Again, I was going to express my gratitude to my father, but his looks forbad me, and I was silent. I am too diffuse; even the faint forms which memory reflects of passed delight are grateful to the heart. The shadow of pleasure is still gazed upon with a melancholy enjoyment, though the substance is fled beyond our reach.'

'Having quitted Paris, which I left with many sighs, and gazed upon till the towers of every church dissolved in distance from my view; we entered upon a gloomy and unfrequented road. It was evening when we reached a wild heath; I look round in search of a human dwelling, but could find none; and not a human being was to be seen. I experienced something of what I used to feel in the convent; my heart had not been so sad since I left it. Of my father, who still sat in silence, I inquired if we were near home; he answered in the affirmative. Night came on, however, before we reached the place of our destination; it was a lone house on the waste; but I need not describe it to you, Madam. When the carriage stopped, two men appeared at the door, and assisted us to alight; so gloomy were their countenances, and so few their words, I almost fancied myself again in the convent. Certain it is, I had not seen such melancholy faces since I quitted it. Is this a part of the world I have so fondly contemplated? said I.

'The interior appearance of the house was desolate and mean; I was surprised that my father had chosen such a place for his habitation, and also that no woman was to be seen; but I knew that inquiry would only produce a reproof, and was, therefore, silent. At supper, the two men I had before seen sat down with us; they said little, but seemed to observe me much. I was confused and displeased, which, my father noticing, frowned at them with a look, which convinced me he meant more than I comprehended. When the cloth was drawn, my father took my hand and conducted me to the door of my chamber; having set down the candle, and wished me good night, he left me to my own solitary thoughts.

'How different were they from those I had indulged a few hours before! then expectation, hope, delight, danced before me; now melancholy and disappointment chilled the ardour of my mind, and discoloured my future prospect. The appearance of every thing around conduced to depress me. On the floor lay a small bed without curtains, or hangings; two old chairs and a table were all the remaining furniture in the room. I went to the window, with an intention of looking out upon the surrounding scene, and found it was grated. I was shocked at this circumstance, and, comparing it with the lonely situation, and the strange appearance of the house, together with the countenances and behaviour of the men who had supped with us, I was lost in a labyrinth of conjecture.

'At length I laid down to sleep; but the anxiety of my mind prevented repose; gloomy unpleasing images flitted before my fancy, and I fell into a sort of waking dream: I thought that I was in a lonely forest with my father; his looks were severe, and his gestures menacing: he upbraided me for leaving the convent, and while he spoke, drew from his pocket a mirror, which he held before my face; I looked in it and saw, (my blood now thrills as I repeat it) I saw myself wounded, and bleeding profusely. Then I thought myself in the house again; and suddenly heard these words, in accents so distinct, that for some time after I awoke, I could scarcely believe them ideal, "Depart this house, destruction hovers here."

'I was awakened by a footstep on the stairs; it was my father retiring to his chamber; the lateness of the hour surprised me, for it was past midnight.

'On the following morning, the party of the preceding evening assembled at breakfast, and were as gloomy and silent as before. The table was spread by a boy of my father's; but the cook and the house-maid, whatever they might be, were invisible.'

'The next morning, I was surprized, on attemping to leave my chamber, to find the door locked; I waited a considerable time before I ventured to call; when I did, no answer was returned; I then went to the window, and called more loudly, but my own voice was still the only sound I heard. Near an hour I passed in a state of surprise and terror not to be described: at length, I heard a person coming up stairs, and I renewed the call; I was answered, that my father had that morning set off for Paris, whence he would return in a few days; in the meanwhile he had ordered me to be confined in my chamber. On my expressing surprise and apprehension at this circumstance, I was assured I had nothing to fear, and that I should live as well as if I was at liberty.'

'The latter part of this speech seemed to contain an odd kind of comfort; I made little reply, but submitted to necessity. Once more I was abandoned to sorrowful reflection; what a day was the one I now passed! alone, and agitated with grief and apprehension. I endeavoured to conjecture the cause of this harsh treatment; and, at length concluded it was designed by my father, as a punishment for my former disobedience. But why abandon me to the power of strangers, to men, whose countenances bore the stamp of villany so strongly as to impress even my inexperienced mind with terror! Surmise involved me only deeper in perplexity, yet I found it impossible to forbear pursuing the subject; and the day was divided between lamentation and conjecture. Night at length came, and such a night! Darkness brought new terrors: I looked round the chamber for some means of fastening my door on the inside, but could perceive none; at last I contrived to place the back of a chair in an oblique direction, so as to render it secure.

'I had scarcely done this, and laid down upon my bed in my cloaths, not to sleep, but to watch, when I heard a rap at the door of the house, which was opened and shut so quickly, that the person who had knocked, seemed only to deliver a letter or message. Soon after, I heard voices at intervals in a room below stairs, sometimes speaking very low, and sometimes rising, all together, as if in dispute. Something more excusable than curiosity made me endeavour to distinguish what was said, but in vain; now and then a word or two reached me, and once I heard my name repeated, but no more.'

'Thus passed the hours till midnight, when all became still. I had laid for some time in a state between fear and hope, when I heard he lock of my door gently moved backward and forward; I started up, and listened; for a moment it was still, then the noise returned, and I heard a whispering without; my spirits died away, but I was yet sensible. Presently an effort was made at the door, as if to force it; I shrieked aloud, and immediately heard the voices of the men I had seen at my father's table: they called loudly for the door to be opened, and on my returning no answer, uttered dreadful execrations. I had just strength sufficient to move to the window, in the desperate hope of escaping thence; but my feeble efforts could not even shake the bars. O! how can I recollect these moments of horror, and be sufficiently thankful that I am now in safety and comfort!

'They remained some time at the door, then they quitted it, and went down stairs. How my heart revived at every step of their departure; I fell upon my knees, thanked God that he had preserved me this time, and implored his farther protection. I was rising from this short prayer, when suddenly I heard a noise in a different part of the room, and, on looking round, I perceived the door of a small closet open, and two men enter the chamber.

'They seized me, and I sunk senseless in their arms; how long I remained in this condition I know not, but on reviving, I perceived myself again alone, and heard several voices from below stairs. I had presence of mind to run to the door of the closet, my only chance of escape; but it was locked! I then recollected it was possible, that the ruffians might have forgot to turn the key of the chamber door, which was held by the chair; but here, also, I was disappointed. I clasped my hands in an agony of despair, and stood for some time immoveable.

'A violent noise from below rouzed me, and soon after I heard people ascending the stairs: I gave myself up for lost. The steps approached, the door of the closet was again unlocked. I stood calmly, and again saw the men enter the chamber; I neither spoke, nor resisted: the faculties of my soul were wrought up beyond the power of feeling; as a violent blow on the body stuns for awhile the sense of pain. They led me down stairs; the door of a room below was thrown open, and I beheld a stranger; it was then that my senses returned; I shrieked, and resisted, but was forced along. It is un-necessary to say that this stranger was Monsieur La Motte, or to add, that I shall for ever bless him as my deliverer.'

Adeline ceased to speak; Madame La Motte remained silent. There were some circumstances in Adeline's narrative, which raised all her curiosity. She asked if Adeline believed her father to be a party in this mysterious affair. Adeline, though it was impossible to doubt that he had been principally and materially concerned in some part of it, thought, or said she thought, he was innocent of any intention against her life. 'Yet, what motive,' said Madame La Motte, 'could there be for a degree of cruelty so apparently unprofitable?' Here the inquiry ended; and Adeline confessed she had pursued it, till her mind shrunk from all farther research.

The sympathy which such uncommon misfortune excited, Madame La Motte now expressed without reserve, and this expression of it, strengthened the tye of mutual friendship. Adeline felt her spirits relieved by the disclosure she had made to Madame La Motte; and the latter acknowledged the value of the confidence, by an increase of affectionate attentions.

CHAPTER IV

'———My May of life
Is fall'n into the sear, the yellow leaf.'
MACBETH*

'Full oft, unknowing and unknown,
He wore his endless noons alone,
   Amid th' autumnal wood:
Oft was he wont in hasty fit,
Abrupt the social board to quit.'
WHARTON*

LA Motte had now passed above a month in this seclusion; and his wife had the pleasure to see him recover tranquillity and even cheerfulness. In this pleasure Adeline warmly participated ; and she might justly have congratulated herself, as one cause of his restoration; her cheerfulness and delicate attention had effected what Madame La Motte's greater anxiety had failed to accomplish. La Motte did not seem regardless of her amiable disposition, and sometimes thanked her in a manner more earnest than was usual with him. She, in her turn, considered him as her only protector, and now felt towards him the affection of a daughter.

The time she had spent in this peaceful retirement had softened the remembrance of past events, and restored her mind to its natural tone: and when memory brought back to her view her former short and romantic expectations of happiness, though she gave a sigh to the rapturous illusion, she less lamented the disappointment, than rejoiced in her present security and comfort.

But the satisfaction which La Motte's cheerfulness diffused around him was of short continuance; he became suddenly gloomy and reserved; the society of his family was no longer grateful to him; and he would spend whole hours in the most secluded parts of the forest, devoted to melancholy and secret grief. He did not, as formerly, indulge the humour of his sadness, without restraint, in the presence of others; he now evidently endeavoured to conceal it, and affected a cheerfulness that was too artificial to escape detection.

His servant Peter, either impelled by curiosity or kindness, sometimes followed him, unseen, into the forest. He observed him frequently retire to one particular spot, in a remote part, which having gained, he always disappeared, before Peter, who was obliged to follow at a distance, could exactly notice where. All his endeavours, now prompted by wonder and invigorated by disappointment, were unsuccessful, and he was at length compelled to endure the tortures of unsatisfied curiosity.

This change in the manners and habits of her husband was too conspicuous to pass unobserved by Madame La Motte, who endeavoured, by all the stratagems which affection could suggest, or female invention supply, to win him to her confidence. He seemed insensible to the influence of the first, and withstood the wiles of the latter. Finding all her efforts insufficient to dissipate the glooms which overhung his mind, or to penetrate their secret cause, she desisted from farther attempt, and endeavoured to submit to this mysterious distress.

Week after week elapsed, and the same unknown cause sealed the lips and corroded the heart of La Motte. The place of his visitation in the forest had not been traced. Peter had frequently examined round the spot where his master disappeared, but had never discovered any recess, which could be supposed to conceal him. The astonishment of the servant was at length raised to an insupportable degree, and he communicated to his mistress the subject of it.

The emotion, which this information excited, she disguised from Peter, and reproved him for the means he had taken to gratify his curiosity. But she revolved this circumstance in her thoughts, and comparing it with the late alteration in his temper, her uneasiness was renewed, and her perplexity considerably increased. After much consideration, being unable to assign any other motive for his conduct, she began to attribute it to the influence of illicit passion; and her heart, which now out-ran her judgement, confirmed the supposition, and roused all the torturing pangs of jealousy.

Comparatively speaking, she had never known affliction till now: she had abandoned her dearest friends and connections—had relinquished the gaieties, the luxuries, and almost the necessaries of life;—fled with her family into exile, an exile the most dreary and comfortless; experiencing the evils of reality, and those of apprehension, united: all these she had patiently endured, supported by the affection of him, for whose sake she suffered. Though that affection, indeed, had for some time appeared to be abated, she had borne its decrease with fortitude:. but the last stroke of calamity, hitherto withheld, now came with irresistible force—the love, of which she lamented the loss, she now believed was transferred to another.

The operation of strong passion confuses the powers of reason, and warps them to its own particular direction.* Her usual degree of judgement, unopposed by the influence of her heart, would probably have pointed out to Madame La Motte some circumstances upon the subject of her distress, equivocal, if not contradictory to her suspicions. No such circumstances appeared to her, and she did not long hesitate to decide, that Adeline was the object of her husband's attachment. Her beauty out of the question, who else, indeed, could it be in a spot thus secluded from the world?

The same cause destroyed, almost at the same moment, her only remaining comfort; and, when she wept that she could no longer look for happiness in the affection of La Motte, she wept also, that she could no longer seek solace in the friendship of Adeline. She had too great an esteem for her to doubt, at first, the integrity of her conduct, but, in spite of reason, her heart no longer expanded to her with its usual warmth of kindness. She shrunk from her confidence; and, as the secret broodings of jealousy cherished her her suspicions, she became less kind to her, even in manner.

Adeline, observing the change, at first attributed it to accident, and afterwards to a temporary displeasure, arising from some little inadvertency in her conduct. She, therefore, increased her assiduities; but, perceiving, contrary to all expectation, that her efforts to please failed of their usual consequence, and that the reserve of Madame's manner rather increased than abated, she became seriously uneasy, and resolved to seek an explanation. This Madame La Motte as sedulously avoided, and was for some time able to prevent. Adeline, however, too much interested in the event to yield to delicate scruples, pressed the subject so closely, that Madame, at first agitated and confused, at length invented some idle excuse, and laughed off the affair.

She now saw the necessity of subduing all appearance of reserve towards Adeline; and though her art could not conquer the prejudices of passion, it taught her to assume, with tolerable success, the aspect of kindness. Adeline was deceived, and was again at peace. Indeed, confidence in the sincerity and goodness of others was her weakness. But the pangs of stifled jealousy struck deeper to the heart of Madame La Motte, and she resolved, at all events, to obtain some certainty upon the subject of her suspicions.

She now condescended to a meanness, which she had before despised, and ordered Peter to watch the steps of his master, in order to discover, if possible, the place of his visitation! So much did passion win upon her judgement, by time and indulgence, that she sometimes ventured even to doubt the integrity of Adeline, and afterwards proceeded to believe it possible that the object of La Motte's rambles might be an assignation with her. What suggested this conjecture was, that Adeline frequently took long walks alone in the forest, and sometimes was absent from the abbey for many hours. This circumstance, which Madame La Motte had at first attributed to Adeline's fondness for the picturesque beauties of nature, now operated forcibly upon her imagination, and she could view it in no other light, than as affording an opportunity for secret conversation with her husband.

Peter obeyed the orders of his mistress with alacrity, for they were warmly seconded by his own curiosity. All his endeavours were, however, fruitless; he never dared to follow La Motte near enough to observe the place of his last retreat. Her impatience thus heightened by delay, and her passion stimulated by difficulty, Madame La Motte now resolved to apply to her husband for an explanation of his conduct.

After some consideration, concerning the manner most likely to succeed with him, she went to La Motte, but when she entered the room where he sat, forgetting all her concerted address, she fell at his feet, and was, for some moments, lost in tears. Surprized at her attitude and distress, he inquired the occasion of it, and was answered, that it was caused by his own conduct. 'My conduct! What part of it, pray?' inquired he.

'Your reserve, you secret sorrow, and frequent absence from the abbey.',

'Is it then so wonderful, that a man, who has lost almost every thing, should sometimes lament his misfortunes? or so criminal to attempt concealing his grief, that he must be blamed for it by those, whom he would save from the pain of sharing it?'

Having uttered these words, he quitted the room, leaving Madame La Motte lost in surprize, but somewhat relieved from the pressure of her former suspicions. Still, however, she pursued Adeline with an eye of scrutiny; and the mask of kindness would sometimes fall off, and discover the features of distrust. Adeline, without exactly knowing why, felt less at ease and less happy in her presence than formerly; her spirits drooped, and she would often, when alone, weep at the forlornness of her condition. Formerly, her remembrance of past sufferings was lost in the friendship of Madame La Motte; now, though her behaviour was too guarded to betray any striking instance of unkindness, there was something in her manner which chilled the hopes of Adeline, unable as she was to analyse it. But a circumstance, which soon occurred, suspended, for a while, the jealousy of Madame La Motte, and roused her husband from his state of gloomy stupefaction.

Peter, having been one day to Auboine, for the weekly supply of provisions, returned with intelligence that awakened in La Motte new apprehension and anxiety.

'Oh, Sir! I've heard something that has astonished me, as well it may,' cried Peter, 'and so it will you, when you come to know it. As I was standing in the blacksmith's shop, while the smith was driving a nail into the horse's shoe (by the bye, the horse lost it in an odd way, I'll tell you, Sir, how it was)'—

'Nay, prithee leave it till another time, and go on with your story.'

'Why then, Sir, as I was standing in the blacksmith's shop, comes in a man with a pipe in his mouth, and a large pouch of tobacco in his hand'—

'Well—what has the pipe to do with the story?'

'Nay, Sir, you put me out; I can't go on, unless you let me tell it my own way. As I was saying—with a pipe in his mouth—I think I was there, your Honour!'

'Yes, yes.'

'He sets himself down on the bench, and, taking the pipe from his mouth, says to the blacksmith—Neighbour, do you know any body of the name of La Motte hereabouts?—Bless your Honour, I turned all of a cold sweat in a minute!—Is not your Honour well, shall I fetch you any thing?'

'No—but be short in your narrative.'

'La Motte! La Motte! said the blacksmith, I think I've heard the name.'—'Have you?' said I, 'you're cunning then, for there's no such person hereabouts, to my knowledge.'

'Fool!—why did you say that?'

'Because I did not want them to know your Honour was here; and if I had not managed very cleverly, they would have found me out. There is no such person, hereabouts, to my knowledge, says I,'—'Indeed! says the blacksmith, you know more of the neighbourhood than I do then.'—'Aye, says the man with the pipe, that's very true. How came you to know so much of the neighbourhood? I came here twenty-six years ago, come next St. Michael, and you know more than I do. How came you to know so much?'

'With that he put his pipe in his mouth, and gave a whiff full in my face. Lord! your Honour, I trembled from head to foot. Nay, as for that matter, says I, I don't know more than other people, but I'm sure I never heard of such a man as that.'—'Pray, says the blacksmith, staring me full in the face, an't you the man that was inquiring some time since about Saint Clair's Abbey?'—'Well, what of that? says I, what does that prove?'—'Why, they say, somebody lives in the abbey now, said the man, turning to the other; and, for aught I know, it may be this same La Motte.'—'Aye, or for aught I know either, says the man with the pipe getting up from the bench, and you know more of this than you'll own. I'll lay my life on't, this Monsieur La Motte lives at the abbey.'—'Aye, says I, you are out there, for he does not live at the abbey now.'

'Confound your folly!' cried La Motte, 'but be quick—how did the matter end?'

'My master does not live there now, said I.—Oh! oh! said the man with the pipe; he is your master, then? And pray how long has he left the abbey—and where does he live now?' 'Hold, said I, not so fast—I know when to speak and when to hold my tongue—but who has been inquiring for him?'

'What! he expected somebody to inquire for him? says the man.'—'No, says I, he did not, but if he did, what does that prove?—that argues nothing.' With that, he looked at the blacksmith, and they went out of the shop together, leaving my horse's shoe undone. But I never minded that, for the moment they were gone, I mounted and rode away as fast as I could. But in my fright, your Honour, I forgot to take the round about way, and so came straight home.'

La Motte, extremely shocked at Peter's intelligence, made no other reply than by cursing his folly, and immediately went in search of Madame, who was walking with Adeline on the banks of the river. La Motte was too much agitated to soften his information by preface. 'We are discovered!' said he, 'the King's officers have been inquiring for me at Auboine, and Peter has blundered upon my ruin.' He then informed her of what Peter had related, and bade her prepare to quit the abbey.

'But whither can we fly?' said Madame La Motte, scarcely

able to support herself. 'Any where!' said he, 'to stay here is certain destruction. We must take refuge in Switzerland, I think. If any part of France would have concealed me, surely it had been this!'

'Alas, how are we persecuted!' rejoined Madame. 'This spot is scarcely made comfortable, before we are obliged to leave it, and go we know not whither.'

'I wish we may not yet know whither,' replied La Motte, 'that is the least evil that threatens us. Let us escape a prison, and I care not whither we go. But return to the abbey immediately, and pack up what moveables you can.' A flood of tears came to the relief of Madame La Motte, and she hung upon Adeline's arm, silent and trembling. Adeline, though she had no comfort to bestow, endeavoured to command her feelings and appear composed. 'Come,' said La Motte, 'we waste time; let us lament hereafter, but at present prepare for flight. Exert a little of that fortitude, which is so necessary for our preservation. Adeline does not weep, yet her state is as wretched as your own, for I know not how long I shall be able to protect her.'

Notwithstanding her terror, this reproof touched the pride of Madame La Motte, who dried her tears, but disdained to reply, and looked at Adeline with a strong expression of displeasure. As they moved silently toward the abbey, Adeline asked La Motte if he was sure they were the king's officers, who inquired for him. 'I cannot doubt it,' he replied, 'who else could possibly inquire for me? Besides, the behaviour of the man, who mentioned my name, puts the matter beyond a question.'

'Perhaps not,' said Madame La Motte: 'let us wait till morning ere we set off. We may then find it will be unnecessary to go.'

'We may, indeed; the king's officers would probably by that time have told us as much.' La Motte went to give orders to Peter. 'Set off in an hour,' said Peter, 'Lord bless you, master! only consider the coach wheel; it would take me a day at least to mend it, for your Honour knows I never mended one in my life.'

This was a circumstance which La Motte had entirely over-

looked. When they settled at the abbey, Peter had at first been
too busy in repairing the apartments, to remember the
carriage, and afterwards, believing it would not quickly be
wanted, he had neglected to do it. La Motte's temper now
entirely forsook him, and with many execrations he ordered
Peter to go to work immediately: but on searching for the
materials formerly bought, they were no where to be found,
and Peter at length remembered, though he was prudent
enough to conceal this circumstance that he had used the nails
in repairing the abbey.

It was now, therefore, impossible to quit the forest that
night, and La Motte had only to consider the most probable
plan of concealment, should the officers of justice visit the
ruin before the morning; a circumstance, which the thoughtlessness of Peter in returning from Auboine, by the straight
way, made not unlikely.

At first, indeed, it occurred to him, that, though his family
could not be removed, he might himself take one of the horses,
and escape from the forest before night. But he thought there
would still be some danger of detection in the towns through
which he must pass, and he could not well bear the idea of
leaving his family unprotected, without knowing when he
could return to them, or whither he could direct them to
follow him. La Motte was not a man of very vigorous
resolution, and he was, perhaps, rather more willing to suffer
in company than alone.

After much consideration, he recollected the trap-door of
the closet belonging to the chambers above. It was invisible to
the eye, and, whatever might be its direction, it would
securely shelter *him*, at least, from discovery. Having deliberated farther upon the subject, he determined to explore the
recess to which the stairs led, and thought it possible, that for
a short time his whole family might be concealed within it.
There was little time between the suggestion of the plan and
the execution of his purpose, for darkness was spreading
around, and, in every murmur of the wind, he thought he
heard the voices of his enemies.

He called for a light and ascended alone to the chamber.
When he came to the closet, it was some time before he could

find the trap-door, so exactly did it correspond with the boards of the floor. At length, he found and raised it. The chill damps of long confined air rushed from the aperture, and he stood for a moment to let them pass, ere he descended. As he stood looking down the abyss, he recollected the report, which Peter had brought concerning the abbey, and it gave him an uneasy sensation. But this soon yielded to more pressing interests.

The stairs were steep, and in many places trembled beneath his weight. Having continued to descend for some time, his feet touched the ground, and he found himself in a narrow passage; but as he turned to pursue it, the damp vapours curled round him and extinguished the light. He called aloud for Peter, but could make nobody hear, and, after some time, he endeavoured to find his way up the stairs. In this, with difficulty, he succeeded, and, passing the chambers with cautious steps, descended the tower.

The security, which the place he had just quitted seemed to promise, was of too much importance to be slightly rejected, and he determined immediately to make another experiment with the light:—having now fixed it in a lanthorn, he descended a second time to the passage. The current of vapours occasioned by the opening of the trap-door, was abated, and the fresh air thence admitted had began to circulate: La Motte passed on unmolested.

The passage was of considerable length, and led him to a door, which was fastened. He placed the lanthorn at some distance to avoid the current of air, and applied his strength to the door. It shook under his hands, but did not yield. Upon examining it more closely, he perceived the wood round the lock was decayed, probably by the damps, and this encouraged him to proceed. After some time it gave way to his effort, and he found himself in a square stone room.

He stood for some time to survey it. The walls, which were dripping with unwholesome dews, were entirely bare and afforded not even a window. A small iron grate alone admitted the air. At the further end, near a low recess, was another door. La Motte went towards it, and, as he passed, looked into the recess. Upon the ground within it, stood a large chest, which he went forward to examine, and, lifting the lid, he saw the remains of a human skeleton. Horror struck upon his heart, and he involuntarily stepped back. During a pause of some moments, his first emotions subsided. That thrilling curiosity, which objects of terror often excite in the human mind, impelled him to take a second view of this dismal spectacle.*

La Motte stood motionless as he gazed; the object before him seemed to confirm the report that some person had formerly been murdered in the abbey. At length he closed the chest, and advanced to the second door, which also was fastened, but the key was in the lock. He turned it with difficulty, and then found the door was held by two strong bolts. Having undrawn these, it disclosed a flight of steps, which he descended. They terminated in a chain of low vaults, or rather cells, that, from the manner of their construction and present condition, seemed to have been coeval with the most ancient parts of the abbey. La Motte, in his then depressed state of mind, thought them the burial places of the monks, who formerly inhabited the pile above; but they were more calculated for places of penance for the living, than of rest for the dead.

Having reached the extremity of these cells, the way was again closed by a door. La Motte now hesitated whether he should attempt to proceed any farther. The present spot seemed to afford the security he sought. Here he might pass the night unmolested by apprehension of discovery, and it was most probable, that if the officers arrived in the night, and found the abbey vacated, they would quit if before morning, or, at least, before he could have any occasion to emerge from concealment. These considerations restored his mind to a state of greater composure. His only immediate care was to bring his family, as soon as possible, to this place of security, lest the officers should come unawares upon them; and, while he stood thus musing, he blamed himself for delay.

But an irresistible desire of knowing to what this door led, arrested his steps, and he turned to open it. The door, however, was fastened, and, as he attempted to force it, he suddenly thought he heard a noise above. It now occurred to him, that the officers might already have arrived, and he quitted the cells with precipitation, intending to listen at the trap-door.

'There, said he, I may wait in security, and perhaps hear something of what passes. My family will not be known, or, at least, not hurt, and their uneasiness on my account, they must learn to endure.'

These were the arguments of La Motte, in which, it must be owned, selfish prudence was more conspicuous than tender anxiety for his wife. He had by this time reached the bottom of the stairs, when, on looking up, he perceived the trap-door was left open, and ascending in haste to close it, he heard footsteps advancing through the chambers above. Before he could descend entirely out of sight, he again looked up and perceived through the aperture the face of a man looking down upon him. 'Master,' cried Peter;—La Motte was somewhat relieved at the sound of his voice, though angry that he had occasioned him so much terror.*

'What brings you here, and what is the matter below?'

'Nothing, Sir, nothing's the matter, only my mistress sent me to see after your Honour.'

'There's nobody there then,' said La Motte, 'setting his foot upon the step.'

'Yes, Sir, there is my mistress and Mademoiselle Adeline and'—

'Well—well' said La Motte briskly—'go your ways, I am coming.'

He informed Madame La Motte where he had been, and of his intention of secreting himself, and deliberated upon the means of convincing the officers, should they arrive, that he had quitted the abbey. For this purpose, he ordered all the moveable furniture to be conveyed to the cells below. La Motte himself assisted in this business, and every hand was employed for dispatch. In a very short time, the habitable part of the fabric was left almost as desolate as he had found it. He then bade Peter take the horses to a distance from the abbey, and turn them loose. After farther consideration, he thought it might contribute to mislead them, if he placed in some conspicuous part of the fabric an inscription, signifying his condition, and mentioning the date of his departure from the abbey. Over the door of the tower, which led to the habitable part of the structure, he, therefore, cut the following lines.

'O ye! whom misfortune may lead to this spot,
Learn that there are others as miserable as yourselves.'

P— L— M— a wretched exile, sought within these walls a refuge from persecution, on the 27th of April 1658, and quitted them on the 12th of July in the same year, in search of a more convenient asylum.

After engraving these words with a knife, the small stock of provisions remaining from the week's supply (for Peter, in his fright, had returned unloaded from his last journey) was put into a basket, and, La Motte having assembled his family, they all ascended the stairs of the tower and passed through the chambers to the closet. Peter went first with a light, and with some difficulty found the trap-door. Madame La Motte shuddered as she surveyed the gloomy abyss; but they were all silent.

La Motte now took the light and led the way; Madame followed, and then Adeline. 'These old monks loved good wine, as well as other people,' said Peter, who brought up the rear, 'I warrant your Honour, now, this was their cellar; I smell the casks already.'

'Peace,' said La Motte, 'reserve your jokes for a proper occasion.'

'There is no harm in loving good wine, as your Honour knows.'

'Have done with this buffoonery,' said La Motte, in a tone more authoritative, 'and go first.' Peter obeyed.

They came to the vaulted room. The dismal spectacle he had seen here, deterred La Motte from passing the night in this chamber; and the furniture had, by his own order, been conveyed to the cells below. He was anxious that his family should not perceive the skeleton; an object, which would, probably, excite a degree of horror not to be overcome during their stay. La Motte now passed the chest in haste; and Madame La Motte and Adeline were too much engrossed by their own thoughts, to give minute attention to external circumstances.

When they reached the cells, Madame La Motte wept at the

necessity which condemned her to a spot so dismal. 'Alas,' said she, 'are we, indeed, thus reduced! The apartments above, formerly appeared to me a deplorable habitation; but they are a palace compared to these.'

'True, my dear,' said La Motte, 'and let the remembrance of what you once thought them, soothe your discontent now; these cells are also a palace, compared to the Bicêtre, or the Bastille,* and to the terrors of farther punishment, which would accompany them: let the apprehension of the greater evil teach you to endure the less: I am contented if we find here the refuge I seek.'

Madame La Motte was silent, and Adeline, forgetting her late unkindness, endeavoured as much as she could to console her; while her heart was sinking with the misfortunes, which she could not but anticipate, she appeared composed, and even cheerful. She attended Madame La Motte with the most watchful solicitude, and felt so thankful that La Motte was now secreted within this recess, that she almost lost her perception of its glooms and inconveniences.

This she artlessly expressed to him, who could not be insensible to the tenderness it discovered. Madame La Motte was also sensible of it, and it renewed a painful sensation. The effusions of gratitude she mistook for those of tenderness.

La Motte returned frequently to the trap door, to listen if any body was in the abbey; but no sound disturbed the stillness of night; at length they sat down to supper; the repast was a melancholy one. 'If the officers do not come hither to night,' said Madame La Motte, sighing, 'suppose, my dear, Peter returns to Auboine to-morrow. He may there learn something more of this affair; or, at least, he might procure a carriage to convey us hence.'

'To be sure he might,' said La Motte, peevishly, 'and people to attend it also. Peter would be an excellent person to shew the officers the way to the abbey, and to inform them of what they might else be in doubt about, my concealment here.'

'How cruel is this irony!' replied Madame La Motte, 'I proposed only what I thought would be for our mutual good; my judgement was, perhaps, wrong, but my intention was certainly right.' Tears swelled into her eyes as she spoke these words. Adeline wished to relieve her; but delicacy kept her silent. La Motte observed the effect of his speech, and something like remorse touched his heart. He approached, and taking her hand, 'You must allow for the perturbation of my mind,' said he, 'I did not mean to afflict you thus. The idea of sending Peter to Auboine, where he has already done so much harm by his blunders, teased me, and I could not let it pass unnoticed. No, my dear, our only chance of safety is to remain where we are while our provisions last. If the officers do not come here to-night, they probably will to-morrow, or, perhaps, the next day. When they have searched the abbey, without finding me, they will depart; we may then emerge from this recess, and take measures for removing to a distant country.'

Madame La Motte acknowledged the justice of his words, and her mind being relieved by the little apology he had made, she became tolerably cheerful. Supper being ended, La Motte stationed the faithful, though simple Peter, at the foot of the steps that ascended to the closet; there to keep watch during the night. Having done this, he returned to the lower cells, where he had left his little family. The beds were spread, and having mournfully bad each other good night, they laid down, and implored rest.

Adeline's thoughts were too busy to suffer her to repose, and when she believed her companions were sunk in slumbers, she indulged the sorrow which reflection brought. She also looked forward to the future with the most mournful apprehension. 'Should La Motte be seized, what was to become of her? She would then be a wanderer in the wide world; without friends to protect, or money to support her; the prospect was gloomy—was terrible!' She surveyed it and shuddered! The distresses too of Monsieur and Madame La Motte, whom she loved with the most lively affection, formed no inconsiderable part of her's.

Sometimes she looked back to her father; but in him she only saw an enemy, from whom she must fly: this remembrance heightened her sorrow; yet it was not the recollection of the suffering he had occasioned her, by which she was so much afflicted, as by the sense of his unkindness:

she wept bitterly. At length, with that artless piety, which innocence only knows, she addressed the Supreme Being, and resigned herself to his care. Her mind then gradually became peaceful and re-assured, and soon after she sunk to repose.

CHAPTER V

A Surprize—An Adventure—A Mystery

THE night passed without any alarm; Peter had remained upon his post, and heard nothing that prevented his sleeping. La Motte heard him, long before he saw him, most musically snoring; though it must be owned there was more of the bass, than of any other part of the gamut in his performance. He was soon roused by the *bravura* of La Motte, whose notes sounded discord to his ears, and destroyed the torpor of his tranquillity.

'God bless you, Master, what's the matter?' cried Peter, waking, 'are they come?'

'Yes, for aught you care, they might be come. Did I place you here to sleep, sirrah?'

'Bless you, Master,' returned Peter, 'sleep is the only comfort to be had here; I'm sure I would not deny it to a dog in such a place as this.'

La Motte sternly questioned him concerning any noise he might have heard in the night; and Peter full as solemnly protested he had heard none; an assertion which was strictly true, for he had enjoyed the comfort of being asleep the whole time.

La Motte ascended to the trap-door and listened attentively. No sounds were heard, and, as he ventured to lift it, the full light of the sun burst upon his sight, the morning being now far advanced; he walked softly along the chambers, and looked through a window; no person was to be seen. Encouraged by this apparent security, he ventured down the stairs of the tower, and entered the first apartment. He was proceeding towards the second, when, suddenly recollecting himself, he first peeped through the crevice of the door, which stood half open. He looked, and distinctly saw a person sitting near the window, upon which his arm rested.

The discovery so much shocked him, that for a moment he lost all presence of mind, and was utterly unable to move from the spot. The person, whose back was towards him, arose, and turned his head. La Motte now recovered himself, and quitting the apartment as quickly, and, at the same time, as silently as possible, ascended to the closet. He raised the trap-door, but before he closed it, heard the footsteps of a person entering the outer chamber. Bolts, or other fastening to the trap there was none; and his security depended solely upon the exact correspondence of the boards. The outer door of the stone room had no means of defence; and the fastenings of the inner one were on the wrong side to afford security, even till some means of escape could be found.

When he reached this room, he paused, and heard distinctly, persons walking in the closet above. While he was listening, he heard a voice call him by name, and he instantly fled to the cells below, expecting every moment to hear the trap lifted, and the footsteps of pursuit; but he was fled beyond the reach of hearing either. Having thrown himself on the ground, at the farthest extremity of the vaults, he lay for some time breathless with agitation. Madame La Motte and Adeline, in the utmost terror, inquired what had happened. It was some time before he could speak; when he did, it was almost unnecessary, for the distant noises, which sounded from above, informed his family of a part of the truth.

The sounds did not seem to approach, but Madame La Motte, unable to command her terror, shrieked aloud: this re-doubled the distress of La Motte. 'You have already destroyed me,' cried he; 'that shriek has informed them where I am.' He traversed the cells with clasped hands and quick steps. Adeline stood pale and still as death, supporting Madame La Motte, whom, with difficulty, she prevented from fainting. 'O! Dupras! Dupras! you are already avenged!' said he, in a voice that seemed to burst from his heart: there was a pause of silence. 'But why should I deceive myself with a hope of escaping?' he resumed, 'why do I wait here for their coming?

Let me rather end these torturing pangs by throwing myself into their hands at once.'

As he spoke, he moved towards the door, but the distress of Madame La Motte arrested his steps. 'Stay,' said she, 'for my sake, stay; do not leave me thus, nor throw yourself voluntarily into destruction!'

'Surely, Sir,' said Adeline, 'you are too precipitate; this despair is useless, as it is ill-founded. We hear no person approaching; if the officers had discovered the trap-door, they would certainly have been here before now.' The words of Adeline stilled the tumult of his mind: the agitation of terror subsided; and reason beamed a feeble ray upon his hopes. He listened attentively, and perceiving that all was silent, advanced with caution to the stone room; and hence to the foot of the stairs that led to the trap-door. It was closed: no sound was heard above.

He watched a long time, and the silence continuing, his hopes strengthened, and, at length, he began to believe that the officers had quitted the abbey; the day, however, was spent in anxious watchfulness. He did not dare to unclose the trap-door; and he frequently thought he heard distant noises. It was evident, however, that the secret of the closet had escaped discovery; and on this circumstance he justly founded his security. The following night was passed, like the day, in trembling hope, and incessant watching.

But the necessities of hunger now threatened them. The provisions, which had been distributed with the nicest economy, were nearly exhausted, and the most deplorable consequences might be expected from their remaining longer in concealment. Thus circumstanced, La Motte deliberated upon the most prudent method of proceeding. There appeared no other alternative, than to send Peter to Auboine, the only town from which he could return within the time prescribed by their necessities. There was game, indeed, in the forest; but Peter could neither handle a gun, or use a fishing rod to any advantage.

It was, therefore, agreed he should go to Auboine for a supply of provisions, and at the same time bring materials for mending the coach wheel, that they might have some ready conveyance from the forest. La Motte forbade Peter to ask any questions concerning the people who had inquired for him, or take any methods for discovering whether they had quitted the country, lest his blunders should again betray him. He ordered him to be entirely silent as to these subjects, and to finish his business, and leave the place with all possible dispatch.

A difficulty yet remained to be overcome—Who should first venture abroad into the abbey, to learn, whether it was vacated by the officers of justice? La Motte considered, that if he was again seen, he should be effectually betrayed; which would not be *so* certain, if one of his family was observed, for they were all unknown to the officers. It was necessary, however, that the person he sent should have courage enough to go through with the inquiry, and wit enough to conduct it with caution. Peter, perhaps, had the first; but was certainly destitute of the last. Annette had neither. La Motte looked at his wife, and asked her, if, for his sake, she dared to venture. Her heart shrunk from the proposal, yet she was unwilling to refuse, or appear indifferent upon a point so essential to the safety of her husband. Adeline observed in her countenance the agitation of her mind, and, surmounting the fears, which had hitherto kept her silent, she offered herself to go.

'They will be less likely to offend me,' said she, 'than a man.' Shame would not suffer La Motte to accept her offer; and Madame, touched by the magnanimity of her conduct, felt a momentary renewal of all her former kindness. Adeline pressed her proposal so warmly, and seemed so much in earnest, that La Motte began to hesitate. 'You, Sir,' said she, 'once preserved me from the most imminent danger, and your kindness has since protected me. Do not refuse me the satisfaction of deserving your goodness by a grateful return of it. Let me go into the abbey, and if, by so doing, I should preserve you from evil, I shall be sufficiently rewarded for what little danger I may incur, for my pleasure will be at least equal to yours.'

Madame La Motte could scarcely refrain from tears as Adeline spoke; and La Motte, sighing deeply, said, 'Well, be it so; go, Adeline, and from this moment consider me as your debtor.' Adeline stayed not to reply, but taking a light, quitted the cells, La Motte following to raise the trap-door, and cautioning her to look, if possible, into every apartment, before she entered it. 'If you *should* be seen,' said he, 'you must account for your appearance so as not to discover me. Your own presence of mind may assist you, I cannot.—God bless you!'

When she was gone, Madame La Motte's admiration of her conduct began to yield to other emotions. Distrust gradually undermined kindness, and jealousy raised suspicions. 'It must be a sentiment more powerful than gratitude,' thought she, 'that could teach Adeline to subdue her fears. What, but Love, could influence her to a conduct so generous!' Madame La Motte, when she found it impossible to account for Adeline's conduct, without alledging some interested motives for it, however her suspicions might agree with the practice of the world, had surely forgotten how much she once admired the purity and disinterestedness of her young friend.

Adeline, mean while, ascended to the chambers: the cheerful beams of the sun played once more upon her sight, and re-animated her spirits; she walked lightly through the apartments, nor stopped till she came to the stairs of the tower. Here she stood for some time, but no sounds met her ear, save the sighing of the wind among the trees, and, at length, she descended. She passed the apartments below, without seeing any person; and the little furniture that remained, seemed to stand exactly as she had left it. She now ventured to look out from the tower: the only animate objects, that appeared, were the deer, quietly grazing under the shade of the woods. Her favourite little fawn distinguished Adeline, and came bounding towards her with strong marks of joy. She was somewhat alarmed lest the animal, being observed, should betray her, and walked swiftly away through the cloisters.

She opened the door that led to the great hall of the abbey, but the passage was so gloomy and dark, that she feared to enter it, and started back. It was necessary, however, that she should examine farther, particularly on the opposite side of the ruin, of which she had hitherto had no view: but her fears returned when she recollected how far it would lead her from her only place of refuge, and how difficult it would be to retreat. She hesitated what to do; but when she recollected her obligations to La Motte, and considered this as, perhaps, her only opportunity of doing him a service, she determined to proceed.

As these thoughts passed rapidly over her mind, she raised her innocent looks to heaven, and breathed a silent prayer. With trembling steps she proceeded over fragments of the ruin, looking anxiously around, and often starting as the breeze rustled among the trees, mistaking it for the whisperings of men. She came to the lawn which fronted the fabric, but no person was to be seen, and her spirits revived. The great door of the hall she now endeavoured to open, but suddenly remembering that it was fastened by La Motte's orders, she proceeded to the north end of the abbey, and, having surveyed the prospect around, as far as the thick foliage of the trees would permit, without perceiving any person, she turned her steps to the tower from which she had issued.

Adeline was now light of heart, and returned with impatience to inform La Motte of his security. In the cloisters she was again met by her little favourite, and stopped for a moment to caress it. The fawn seemed sensible to the sound of her voice, and discovered new joy; but while she spoke, it suddenly started from her hand, and looking up, she perceived the door of the passage, leading to the great hall, open, and a man in the habit of a soldier issue forth.

With the swiftness of an arrow she fled along the cloisters, nor once ventured to look back; but a voice called her to stop, and she heard steps advancing quick in pursuit. Before she could reach the tower, her breath failed her, and she leaned against a pillar of the ruin, pale and exhausted. The man came up, and gazing at her with a strong expression of surprize and curiosity, he assumed a gentle manner, assured her she had nothing to fear, and inquired if she belonged to La Motte: observing that she still looked terrified and remained silent, he repeated his assurances and his question.

'I know that he is concealed within the ruin,' said the stranger; 'the occasion of his concealment I also know; but it is of the utmost importance I should see him, and he will then be convinced he has nothing to fear from me.' Adeline trembled so excessively, that it was with difficulty she could support herself—she hesitated, and knew not what to reply. Her manner seemed to confirm the suspicions of the stranger, and her consciousness of this increased her embarrassment: he took advantage of it to press her farther. Adeline, at length, replied, that 'La Motte had some time since resided at the abbey.' 'And does still, Madam,' said the stranger; 'lead me to where he may be found—I must see him, and'—

'Never, Sir,' replied Adeline, 'and I solemnly assure you, it will be in vain to search for him.'

'That I must try,' resumed he, 'since you, Madam, will not assist me. I have already followed him to some chambers above, where I suddenly lost him: thereabouts he must be concealed, and it's plain, therefore, they afford some secret passage.'

Without waiting Adeline's reply, he sprung to the door of the tower. She now thought it would betray a consciousness of the truth of his conjecture to follow him, and resolved to remain below. But, upon farther consideration, it occurred to her, that he might steal silently into the closet, and possibly surprise La Motte at the door of the trap. She, therefore, hastened after him, that her voice might prevent the danger she apprehended. He was already in the second chamber, when she overtook him; she immediately began to speak aloud.

This room he searched with the most scrupulous care, but finding no private door, or other outlet, he proceeded to the closet: then it was, that it required all her fortitude to conceal her agitation. He continued the search. 'Within these chambers, I know he is concealed,' said he, 'though hitherto I have not been able to discover how. It was hither I followed a man, whom I believe to be him, and he could not escape without a passage; I shall not quit the place till I have found it.'

He examined the walls and the boards, but without discovering the division of the floor, which, indeed, so exactly corresponded, that La Motte himself had not perceived it by the eye, but by the trembling of the floor beneath his feet. 'Here is some mystery,' said the stranger, 'which I cannot

comprehend, and perhaps never shall.' He was turning to quit
the closet, when, who can paint the distress of Adeline, upon
seeing the trap-door gently raised, and La Motte himself
appeared. 'Hah!' cried the stranger, advancing eagerly to him.
La Motte sprang forward, and they were locked in each
other's arms.*

The astonishment of Adeline, for a moment, surpassed even
her former distress; but a remembrance darted across her
mind, which explained the present scene, and before La Motte
could exclaim, 'My son!' she knew the stranger as such. Peter,
who stood at the foot of the stairs and heard what passed
above, flew to acquaint his mistress with the joyful discovery,
and, in a few moments, she was folded in the embrace of
her son. This spot, so lately the mansion of despair, seemed
metamorphosed into the palace of pleasure, and the walls
echoed only to the accents of joy and congratulation.

The joy of Peter on this occasion was beyond expression: he
acted a perfect pantomime—he capered about, clasped his
hands—ran to his young master—shook him by the hand, in
spite of the frowns of La Motte; ran every where, without
knowing for what, and gave no rational answer to any thing
that was said to him.

After their first emotions were subsided, La Motte, as if
suddenly recollecting himself, resumed his wonted solemnity:
'I am to blame,' said he, 'thus to give way to joy, when I am
still, perhaps, surrounded by danger. Let us secure a retreat
while it is yet in our power,' continued he, 'in a few hours the
King's officers may search for me again.'

Louis comprehended his father's words, and immediately
relieved his apprehensions by the following relation:

'A letter from Monsieur Nemours, containing an account of
your flight from Paris, reached me at Peronne, where I was
then upon duty with my regiment. He mentioned, that you
was gone towards the south of France, but as he had not since
heard from you, he was ignorant of the place of your refuge.
It was about this time that I was dispatched into Flanders;
and, being unable to obtain farther intelligence of you, I
passed some weeks of very painful solicitude. At the conclusion of the campaign, I obtained leave of absence, and

immediately set out for Paris, hoping to learn from Nemours, where you had found an asylum.

'Of this, however, he was equally ignorant with myself. He informed me that you had once before written to him from D——, upon your second day's journey from Paris, under an assumed name, as had been agreed upon; and that you then said the fear of discovery would prevent your hazarding another letter. He, therefore, remained ignorant of your abode, but said, he had no doubt you had continued your journey to the southward. Upon this slender information I quitted Paris in search of you, and proceeded immediately to V——, where my inquiries, concerning your farther progress, were successful as far as M——. There they told me you had staid some time, on account of the illness of a young lady; a circumstance which perplexed me much, as I could not imagine what young lady would accompany you. I proceeded, however, to L——; but there all traces of you seemed to be lost. As I sat musing at the window of the inn, I observed some scribbling on the glass, and the curiosity of idleness prompted me to read it. I thought I knew the characters, and the lines I read confirmed my conjecture, for I remembered to have heard you often repeat them.

'Here I renewed my inquiries concerning your route, and at length I made the people of the inn recollect you, and traced you as far as Auboine. There I again lost you, till upon my return from a fruitless inquiry in the neighbourhood, the landlord of the little inn where I lodged, told me he believed he had heard news of you, and immediately recounted what had happened at a blacksmith's shop a few hours before.

'His description of Peter was so exact, that I had not a doubt it was you who inhabited the abbey; and, as I knew your necessity for concealment, Peter's denial did not shake my confidence. The next morning, with the assistance of my landlord, I found my way hither, and, having searched every visible part of the fabric, I began to credit Peter's assertion: your appearance, however, destroyed this fear, by proving that the place was still inhabited, for you disappeared so instantaneously, that I was not certain it was you whom I had seen. I continued seeking you till near the close of day, and till then scarcely quitted the chambers whence you had disappeared. I called on you repeatedly, believing that my voice might convince you of your mistake. At length, I retired to pass the night at a cottage near the border of the forest.

'I came early this morning to renew my inquiries, and hoped that, believing yourself safe, you would emerge from concealment. But how was I disappointed to find the abbey as silent and solitary as I had left it the preceding evening! I was returning once more from the great hall, when the voice of this young lady caught my ear, and effected the discovery I had so anxiously sought.'

This little narrative entirely dissipated the late apprehensions of La Motte; but he now dreaded that the inquiries of his son, and his own obvious desire of concealment, might excite a curiosity amongst the people of Auboine, and lead to a discovery of his true circumstances. However, for the present he determined to dismiss all painful thoughts, and endeavour to enjoy the comfort which the presence of his son had brought him. The furniture was removed to a more habitable part of the abbey, and the cells were again abandoned to their own glooms.

The arrival of her son seemed to have animated Madame La Motte with new life, and all her afflictions were, for the present, absorbed in joy. She often gazed silently on him with a mother's fondness, and her partiality heightened every improvement which time had wrought in his person and manner. He was now in his twenty-third year; his person was manly and his air military; his manners were unaffected and graceful, rather than dignified; and though his features were irregular, they composed a countenance, which, having seen it once, you would seek again.

She made eager inquiries after the friends she had left at Paris, and learned, that within the few months of her absence, some had died and others quitted the place. La Motte also learned, that a very strenuous search for him had been prosecuted at Paris; and, though this intelligence was only what he had before expected, it shocked him so much, that he now declared it would be expedient to remove to a distant country. Louis did not scruple to say, that he thought he would be as safe at the abbey as at any other place; and repeated what Nemours had said, that the King's officers had been unable to trace any part of his route from Paris.

'Besides,' resumed Louis, 'this abbey is protected by a supernatural power, and none of the country people dare approach it.'

'Please you, my young master,' said Peter who was waiting in the room, 'we were frightened enough the first night we came here, and I, myself, God forgive me! thought the place was inhabited by devils, but they were only owls, and such like, after all.'

'Your opinion was not asked,' said La Motte, 'learn to be silent.'

Peter was abashed. When he had quitted the room, La Motte asked his son with seeming carelessness, what were the reports circulated by the country people? 'O! Sir,' replied Louis, 'I cannot recollect half of them. I remember, however, they said, that, many years ago, a person (but nobody had ever seen him, so we may judge how far the report ought to be credited) a person was privately brought to this abbey, and confined in some part of it, and that there were strong reasons to believe he came unfairly to his end.'

La Motte sighed. 'They farther said,' continued Louis, 'that the spectre of the deceased had ever since watched nightly among the ruins: and to make the story more wonderful, for the marvellous is the delight of the vulgar, they added, that there was a certain part of the ruin, from whence no person that had dared to explore it, had ever returned. Thus people, who have few objects of real interest to engage their thoughts, conjure up for themselves imaginary ones.'

La Motte sat musing. 'And what were the reasons,' said he, at length awaking from his reverie, 'they pretended to assign, for believing the person confined here was murdered?'

'They did not use a term so positive as that,' replied Louis.

'True,' said La Motte, recollecting himself, 'they only said he came unfairly to his end.'

'That is a nice distinction,' said Adeline.

'Why I could not well comprehend what these reasons were,' resumed Louis, 'the people indeed say, that the person, who was brought here, was never known to depart, but I do not find it certain that he ever arrived; that there was strange privacy and mystery observed, while he was here, and that the abbey has never since been inhabited by its owner. There seems, however, to be nothing in all this that deserves to be remembered.' La Motte raised his head, as if to reply, when the entrance of Madame turned the discourse upon a new subject, and it was not resumed that day.

Peter was now dispatched for provisions, while La Motte and Louis retired to consider how far it was safe for them to continue at the abbey. La Motte, notwithstanding the assurances lately given him, could not but think that Peter's blunders and his son's inquiries might lead to a discovery of his residence. He revolved this in his mind for some time, but at length a thought struck him, that the latter of these circumstances might considerably contribute to his security. 'If you,' said he to Louis, 'return to the inn at Auboine, from whence you were directed here, and without seeming to intend giving intelligence, *do* give the landlord an account of your having found the abbey uninhabited, and then add, that you had discovered the residence of the person you sought in some distant town, it would suppress any reports that may at present exist, and prevent the belief of any in future. And if, after all this, you can trust yourself for presence of mind and command of countenance, so far as to describe some dreadful apparition, I think these circumstances, together with the distance of the Abbey, and the intricacies of the forest, could entitle me to consider this place as my castle.'

Louis agreed to all that his father had proposed, and, on the following day executed his commission with such success, that the tranquillity of the abbey may be then said to have been entirely restored.

Thus ended this adventure, the only one that had occurred to disturb the family, during their residence in the forest. Adeline, removed from the apprehension of those evils, with which the late situation of La Motte had threatened her, and from the depression which her interest in his occasioned her, now experienced, a more than usual complacency of mind. She thought too that she observed in Madame La Motte a renewal of her former kindness, and this circumstance awakened all her gratitude, and imparted to her a pleasure as lively as it was innocent. The satisfaction with which the presence of her son inspired Madame La Motte, Adeline mistook for kindness to herself, and she exerted her whole attention in an endeavour to become worthy of it.

But the joy which his unexpected arrival had given to La Motte quickly began to evaporate, and the gloom of despondency again settled on his countenance. He returned frequently to his haunt in the forest—the same mysterious sadness tinctured his manner and revived the anxiety of Madame La Motte, who was resolved to acquaint her son with this subject of distress, and solicit his assistance to penetrate its source.

Her jealousy of Adeline, however, she could not communicate, though it again tormented her, and taught her to misconstrue with wonderful ingenuity every look and word of La Motte, and often to mistake the artless expressions of Adeline's gratitude and regard for those of warmer tenderness. Adeline had formerly accustomed herself to long walks in the forest, and the design Madame had formed of watching her steps, had been frustrated by the late circumstances, and was now entirely overcome by her sense of its difficulty and danger. To employ Peter in the affair, would be to acquaint him with her fears, and to follow her herself, would most probably betray her scheme, by making Adeline aware of her jealousy. Being thus restrained by pride and delicacy, she was obliged to endure the pangs of uncertainty concerning the greatest part of her suspicions.

To Louis, however, she related the mysterious change in his father's temper. He listened to her account with very earnest attention, and the surprize and concern impressed upon his countenance spoke how much his heart was interested. He was, however, involved in equal perplexity with herself upon this subject, and readily undertook to observe the motions of La Motte, believing his interference likely to be of equal service both to his father and his mother. He, saw in some degree, the suspicions of his mother, but as he thought she wished to disguise her feelings, he suffered her to believe that she succeeded.

He now inquired concerning Adeline, and listened to her little history, of which his mother gave a brief relation, with great apparent interest. So much pity did he express for her condition, and so much indignation at the unnatural conduct of her father, that the apprehensions which Madame La Motte began to form, of his having discovered her jealousy, yielded to those of a different kind. She perceived that the beauty of Adeline had already fascinated his imagination, and she feared that her amiable manners would soon impress his heart. Had her first fondness for Adeline continued, she would still have looked with displeasure upon their attachment, as an obstacle to the promotion and the fortune she hoped to see one day enjoyed by her son. On these she rested all her future hopes of prosperity, and regarded the matrimonial alliance which he might form as the only means of extricating his family from their present difficulties. She, therefore, touched lightly upon Adeline's merit, joined coolly with Louis in compassionating her misfortunes, and with her censure of the father's conduct, mixed an implied suspicion of that of Adeline's. The means she employed to repress the passions of her son, had a contrary effect. The indifference, which she expressed towards Adeline, increased his pity for her destitute condition, and the tenderness, with which she affected to judge the father, heightened his honest indignation at his character.

As he quitted Madame La Motte, he saw his father cross the lawn and enter the deep shade of the forest on the left. He judged this to be a good opportunity of commencing his plan, and, quitting the abbey, slowly followed at a distance. La Motte continued to walk straight forward, and seemed so deeply wrapt in thought, that he looked neither to the right or left, and scarcely lifted his head from the ground. Louis had followed him near half a mile, when he saw him suddenly strike into an avenue of the forest, which took a different direction from the way he had hitherto gone. He quickened his steps that he might not lose sight of him, but, having reached the avenue, found the trees so thickly interwoven, that La Motte was already hid from his view.

He continued, however, to pursue the way before him: it conducted him through the most gloomy part of the forest he had yet seen, till at length it terminated in an obscure recess, over-arched with high trees, whose interwoven branches secluded the direct rays of the sun, and admitted only a sort of solemn twilight. Louis looked around in search of La Motte, but he was no where to be seen. While he stood surveying the place, and considering what farther should be done, he observed, through the gloom, an object at some distance, but the deep shadow that fell around prevented his distinguishing what it was.

In advancing, he perceived the ruins of a small building, which, from the traces that remained, appeared to have been a tomb. As he gazed upon it, 'Here,' said he, 'are probably deposited the ashes of some ancient monk, once an inhabitant of the abbey; perhaps, of the founder, who, after having spent a life of abstinence and prayer, sought in heaven the reward of his forbearance upon earth.* Peace be to his soul! but did he think a life of mere negative virtue deserved an eternal reward? Mistaken man! reason, had you trusted to its dictates, would have informed you, that the active virtues, the adherence to the golden rule, "Do as you would be done unto," could alone deserve the favour of a Deity, whose glory is benevolence.'

He remained with his eyes fixed upon the spot, and presently saw a figure arise under the arch of the sepulchre. It started, as if on perceiving him, and immediately disappeared. Louis, though unused to fear, felt at that moment an uneasy sensation, but almost it immediately struck him that this was La Motte himself. He advanced to the ruin and called him. No answer was returned, and he repeated the call, but all was yet still as the grave. He then went up to the arch-way and endeavoured to examine the place where he had disappeared, but the shadowy obscurity rendered the attempt fruitless. He observed, however, a little to the right, an entrance to the ruin, and advanced some steps down a kind dark of passage, when, recollecting that this place might be the haunt of banditti, his danger alarmed him, and he retreated with precipitation.

He walked toward the abbey by the way he came, and finding no person followed him, and believing himself again in safety, his former surmise returned, and he thought it was La Motte he had seen. He mused upon this strange possibility, and endeavoured to assign a reason for so mysterious a conduct, but in vain. Notwithstanding this, his belief of it strengthened, and he entered the abbey under as full a conviction as the circumstances would admit of, that it was his father who had appeared in the sepulchre. On entering what was now used as a parlour, he was much surprised to find him quietly seated there with Madame La Motte and Adeline, and conversing as if he had been returned some time.

He took the first opportunity of acquainting his mother with his late adventure, and of inquiring how long La Motte had been returned before him, when, learning that it was near half an hour, his surprise increased, and he knew not what to conclude.

Meanwhile, a perception of the growing partiality of Louis co-operated with the canker of suspicion, to destroy in Madame La Motte that affection which pity and esteem had formerly excited for Adeline. Her unkindness was now too obvious to escape the notice of her to whom it was directed, and, being noticed, it occasioned an anguish which Adeline found it very difficult to endure. With the warmth and candour of youth, she sought an explanation of this change of behaviour, and an opportunity of exculpating herself from any intention of provoking it. But this Madame La Motte artfully evaded, while at the same time she threw out hints, that involved Adeline in deeper perplexity, and served to make her present affliction more intolerable.

'I have lost that affection,' she would say, 'which was my all. It was my only comfort—yet I have lost it—and this without even knowing my offence. But I am thankful I have not merited unkindness, and, though *she* has abandoned *me*, I shall always love *her*.'

Thus distressed, she would frequently leave the parlour, and, retiring to her chamber, would yield to a despondency, which she had never known till now.

One morning, being unable to sleep, she arose at a very early hour. The faint light of day now trembled through the clouds, and, gradually spreading from the horizon, announced the

rising sun. Every feature of the landscape was slowly un-
veiled, moist with the dews of night, and brightening with
the dawn, till at length the sun appeared and shed the full
flood of day. The beauty of the hour invited her to walk, and
she went forth into the forest to taste the sweets of morning.
The carols of new-waked birds saluted her as she passed, and
the fresh gale came scented with the breath of flowers, whose
tints glowed more vivid through the dew drops that hung on
their leaves.

She wandered on without noticing the distance, and,
following the windings of the river, came to a dewy glade,
whose woods, sweeping down to the very edge of the water,
formed a scene so sweetly romantic, that she seated herself at
the foot of a tree, to contemplate its beauty. These images
insensibly soothed her sorrow, and inspired her with that soft
and pleasing melancholy, so dear to the feeling mind.* For
some time she sat lost in a reverie, while the flowers that grew
on the banks beside her seemed to smile in new life, and drew
from her a comparison with her own condition. She mused
and sighed, and then, in a voice, whose charming melody was
modulated by the tenderness of her heart, she sung the
following words:

SONNET

TO THE LILLY

Soft silken flow'r! that in the dewy vale
   Unfolds thy modest beauties to the morn,
And breath'st thy fragrance on her wand'ring gale,
   O'er earth's green hills and shadowy vallies born;

When day has closed his dazzling eye,
   And dying gales sink soft away;
When eve steals down the western sky,
   And mountains, woods, and vales decay;

Thy tender cups, that graceful swell,
   Droop sad beneath her chilly dews;
Thy odours seek their silken cell,
   And twilight veils thy languid hues.

But soon, fair flow'r! the morn shall rise,
  And rear again thy pensive head;
Again unveil thy snowy dyes,
  Again thy velvet foliage spread.

Sweet child of Spring! like thee, in sorrow's shade,
  Full oft I mourn in tears, and droop forlorn:
And O! like thine, may light *my* glooms pervade,
  And Sorrow fly before Joy's living morn!*

A distant echo lengthened out her tones, and she sat listening to the soft response, till repeating the last stanza of the Sonnet, she was answered by a voice almost as tender, and less distant. She looked round in surprise, and saw a young man in a hunter's dress, leaning against a tree, and gazing on her with that deep attention, which marks an enraptured mind.

A thousand apprehensions shot athwart her busy thought; and she now first remembered her distance from the abbey. She rose in haste to be gone, when the stranger respectfully advanced; but, observing her timid looks and retiring steps, he paused. She pursued her way towards the abbey; and, though many reasons made her anxious to know whether she was followed, delicacy forbade her to look back. When she reached the abbey, finding the family was not yet assembled to breakfast, she retired to her chamber, where her whole thoughts were employed in conjectures concerning the stranger; believing that she was interested on this point, no farther than as it concerned the safety of La Motte, she indulged, without scruple, the remembrance of that dignified air and manner which so much distinguished the youth she had seen. After revolving the circumstance more deeply, she believed it impossible that a person of his appearance should be engaged in a stratagem to betray a fellow creature; and though she was destitute of a single circumstance that might assist her surmises of who he was, or what was his business in an unfrequented forest, she rejected, unconsciously, every suspicion injurious to his character. Upon farther deliberation, therefore, she resolved not to mention this little circumstance to La Motte; well knowing, that though his danger might be imaginary, his apprehensions would be real, and would renew all the sufferings and perplexity, from which he was but just released. She resolved, however, to refrain, for some time, walking in the forest.

When she came down to breakfast, she observed Madame La Motte to be more than usually reserved. La Motte entered the room soon after her, and made some trifling observations on the weather; and, having endeavoured to support an effort at cheerfulness, sunk into his usual melancholy. Adeline watched the countenance of Madame with anxiety; and when there appeared in it a gleam of kindness, it was as sunshine to her soul: but she very seldom suffered Adeline thus to flatter herself. Her conversation was restrained, and often pointed at something more than could be understood. The entrance of Louis was a very seasonable relief to Adeline, who almost feared to trust her voice with a sentence, lest its trembling accents should betray her uneasiness.

'This charming morning drew you early from your chamber,' said Louis, addressing Adeline. 'You had, no doubt, a pleasant companion too,' said Madame La Motte, 'a solitary walk is seldom agreeable.'

'I was alone, Madam,' replied Adeline.

'Indeed! your own thoughts must be highly pleasing then.'

'Alas!' returned Adeline, a tear, spite of her efforts, starting to her eye, 'there are now few subjects of pleasure left for them.'

'That is very surprising,' pursued Madame La Motte.

'Is it, indeed, surprising, Madam, for those who have lost their last friend to be unhappy?'

Madame La Motte's conscience acknowledged the rebuke, and she blushed. 'Well,' resumed she, after a short pause, 'that is not your situation, Adeline;' looking earnestly at La Motte. Adeline, whose innocence protected her from suspicion, did not regard this circumstance; but, smiling through her tears, said, she rejoiced to hear her say so. During this conversation, La Motte had remained absorbed in his own thoughts; and Louis, unable to guess at what it pointed, looked alternately at his mother and Adeline for an explanation. The latter he regarded with an expression so full of tender compassion, that it revealed at once to Madame La Motte the sentiments of his soul; and she immediately replied to the last words of Adeline with a very serious air; 'A friend is only estimable when our conduct deserves one; the friendship that survives the merit of its object, is a disgrace, instead of an honour, to both parties.'

The manner and emphasis with which she delivered these words, again alarmed Adeline, who mildly said, 'she hoped she should never deserve such censure.' Madame was silent; but Adeline was so much shocked by what had already passed, that tears sprung from her eyes, and she hid her face with her handkerchief.

Louis now rose with some emotion; and La Motte, roused from his reverie, inquired what was the matter; but, before he could receive an answer, he seemed to have forgot that he had asked the question. 'Adeline may give you her own account,' said Madame La Motte. 'I have not deserved this,' said Adeline, rising, 'but since my presence is displeasing, I will retire.'

She moved toward the door, when Louis, who was pacing the room in apparent agitation, gently took her hand, saying, 'Here is some unhappy mistake,' and would have led her to the seat; but her spirits were too much depressed to endure longer restraint; and, withdrawing her hand, 'Suffer me to go;' said she, 'if there is any mistake, I am unable to explain it.' Saying this, she quitted the room. Louis followed her with his eyes to the door; when, turning to his mother, 'Surely, Madam,' said he, 'you are to blame: my life on it, she deserves your warmest tenderness.'

'You are very eloquent in her cause, Sir,' said Madame, 'may I presume to ask what has interested you thus in her favour?'

'Her own amiable manners,' rejoined Louis, 'which no one can observe without esteeming them.'

'But you may presume too much on your own observations; it is possible these amiable manners may deceive you.'

'Your pardon, Madam; I may, without presumption, affirm they cannot deceive me.'

'You have, no doubt, good reasons for this assertion, and I

perceive, by your admiration of this artless *innocent*, she has succeeded in her design of entrapping your heart.'

'Without designing it, she has won my admiration, which would not have been the case, had she been capable of the conduct you mention.'

Madame La Motte was going to reply, but was prevented by her husband, who, again roused from his reverie, inquired into the cause of dispute; 'Away with this ridiculous behaviour,' said he, in a voice of displeasure. 'Adeline has omitted some household duty I suppose, and an offence so heinous deserves severe punishment, no doubt; but let me be no more disturbed with your petty quarrels; if you must be tyrannical, Madam, indulge your humour in private.'

Saying this, he abruptly quitted the room, and Louis immediately following, Madame was left to her own unpleasant reflections. Her ill-humour proceeded from the usual cause. She had heard of Adeline's walk; and La Motte having gone forth into the forest at an early hour, her imagination, heated by the broodings of jealousy, suggested that they had appointed a meeting. This was confirmed to her by the entrance of Adeline, quickly followed by La Motte; and her perceptions thus jaundiced by passion, neither the presence of her son, nor her usual attention to good manners, had been able to restrain her emotions. The behaviour of Adeline, in the late scene, she considered as a refined piece of art; and the indifference of La Motte as affected. So true is it, that

> ——'Trifles, light as air,
> Are, to the jealous, confirmations strong
> As proof of Holy Writ.'*

And so ingenious was she 'to twist the true cause the wrong way.'*

Adeline had retired to her chamber to weep. When her first agitations were subsided, she took an ample view of her conduct; and perceiving nothing of which she could accuse herself, she became more satisfied; deriving her best comfort from the integrity of her intentions. In the moment of accusation, innocence may sometimes be oppressed with the punishment due only to guilt; but reflection dissolves the illusion of terror, and brings to the aching bosom the consolations of virtue.

When La Motte quitted the room, he had gone into the forest, which Louis observing, he followed and joined him, with an intention of touching upon the subject of his melancholy. 'It is a fine morning, Sir,' said Louis, 'if you will give me leave, I will walk with you.' La Motte, though dissatisfied, did not object; and after they had proceeded some way, he changed the course of his walk, striking into a path, contrary to that which Louis had observed him take on the foregoing day.

Louis remarked, that the avenue they had quitted was 'more shady, and, therefore, more pleasant.' La Motte not seeming to notice this remark, 'It leads to a singular spot,' continued he, 'which I discovered yesterday.' La Motte raised his head; Louis proceeded to describe the tomb, and the adventure he had met with: during this relation, La Motte regarded him with attention, while his own countenance suffered various changes. When he had concluded, 'You were very daring,' said La Motte, 'to examine that place, particularly when you ventured down the passage: I would advise you to be more cautious how you penetrate the depths of this forest. I, myself, have not ventured beyond a certain boundary; and am, therefore, uninformed what inhabitants it may harbour. Your account has alarmed me,' continued he, 'for if banditti are in the neighbourhood, I am not safe from their depredations: 'tis true, I have but little to lose, except my life.'

'And the lives of your family,' rejoined Louis,—'Of course,' said La Motte.

'It would be well to have more certainty upon that head,' rejoined Louis, 'I am considering how we may obtain it.'

''Tis useless to consider that,' said La Motte, 'the inquiry itself brings danger with it; your life would, perhaps, be paid for the indulgence of your curiosity; our only chance of safety is by endeavouring to remain undiscovered. Let us move towards the abbey.'

Louis knew not what to think, but said no more upon the subject. La Motte soon after relapsed into a fit of musing; and his son now took occasion to lament that depression of spirits, which he had lately observed in him. 'Rather lament the cause of it,' said La Motte with a sigh; 'That I do, most sincerely, whatever it may be. May I venture to inquire, Sir, what is this cause?'

'Are, then, my misfortunes so little known to you,' rejoined La Motte, 'as to make that question necessary? Am I not driven from my home, from my friends, and almost from my country? And shall it be asked why I am afflicted?' Louis felt the justice of this reproof, and was a moment silent. 'That you are afflicted, Sir, does not excite my surprise;' resumed he, 'it would, indeed, be strange, were you not.'

'What then does excite your surprise?'

'The air of cheerfulness you wore when I first came hither.'

'You lately lamented that I was afflicted,' said La Motte, 'and now seem not very well pleased that I once was cheerful. What is the meaning of this?'

'You much mistake me,' said his son, 'nothing could give me so much satisfaction as to see that cheerfulness renewed: the same cause of sorrow existed at that time, yet you was then cheerful.'

'That I was then cheerful,' said La Motte, 'you might, without flattery, have attributed to yourself; your presence revived me, and I was relieved at the same time from a load of apprehensions.'

'Why, then, as the same cause exists, are you not still cheerful?'

'And why do you not recollect that it is your father you thus speak to?'

'I do, Sir, and nothing but anxiety for my father, could have urged me thus far: it is with inexpressible concern I perceive you have some secret cause of uneasiness; reveal it, Sir, to those who claim a share in all your affliction, and suffer them, by participation, to soften its severity.' Louis looked up, and observed the countenance of his father, pale as death: his lips trembled while he spoke. 'Your penetration, however, you may rely upon it, has, in the present instance, deceived you. I have no subject of distress, but what you are already acquainted with, and I desire this conversation may never be renewed.'

'If it is your desire, of course, I obey,' said Louis; 'but, pardon me, Sir, if'—

'I will *not* pardon you, Sir,' interrupted La Motte, 'let the discourse end here.' Saying this, he quickened his steps, and Louis, not daring to pursue, walked quietly on till he reached the abbey.

Adeline passed the greatest part of the day alone in her chamber, where, having examined her conduct, she endeavoured to fortify her heart against the unmerited displeasure of Madame La Motte. This was a task more difficult than that of self acquittance. She loved her, and had relied on her friendship, which, notwithstanding the conduct of Madame, still appeared valuable to her. It was true, she had not deserved to lose it, but Madame was so averse to explanation, that there was little probability of recovering it, however ill-founded might be the cause of her dislike. At length, she reasoned, or rather, perhaps, persuaded herself into tolerable composure; for to resign a real good with contentment, is less an effort of reason than of temper.

For many hours she busied herself upon a piece of work, which she had undertaken for Madame La Motte; and this she did, without the least intention of conciliating her favour, but because she felt there was something in thus repaying unkindness, which was suitable to her own temper, her sentiments, and her pride. Self-love *may* be the center, round which the human affections move, for whatever motive conduces to self-gratification may be resolved into self-love; yet some of these affections are in their nature so refined—that though we cannot deny their origin, they almost deserve the name of virtue.* Of this species was that of Adeline.

In this employment and in reading Adeline passed as much of the day as possible. From books, indeed, she had constantly derived her chief information and amusement: those belonging to La Motte were few, but well chosen; and Adeline could find pleasure in reading them more than once. When her mind was discomposed by the behaviour of Madame La Motte, or by a retrospection of her early misfortunes, a book was the opiate that lulled it to repose. La Motte had several of the best English poets, a language which Adeline had

learned in the convent; their beauties, therefore, she was
capable of tasting, and they often inspired her with
enthusiastic delight.*

At the decline of day, she quitted her chamber to enjoy the
sweet evening hour, but strayed no farther than an avenue
near the abbey, which fronted the west. She read a little, but,
finding it impossible any longer to abstract her attention from
the scene around, she closed the book, and yielded to the sweet
complacent melancholy which the hour inspired. The air was
still, the sun, sinking below the distant hill, spread a purple
glow over the landscape, and touched the forest glades with
softer light. A dewy freshness was diffused upon the air. As
the sun descended, the dusk came silently on, and the scene
assumed a solemn grandeur. As she mused, she recollected
and repeated the following stanzas:

NIGHT

Now Ev'ning fades! her pensive step retires,
  And Night leads on the dews, and shadowy hours;
Her awful pomp of planetary fires,
  And all her train of visionary pow'rs.

These paint with fleeting shapes the dream of sleep,
  These swell the waking soul with pleasing dread;
These through the glooms in forms terrific sweep,
  And rouse the thrilling horrors of the dead!

Queen of the solemn thought—mysterious Night!
  Whose step is darkness, and whose voice is fear!
Thy shades I welcome with severe delight,
  And hail thy hollow gales, that sigh so drear!

When, wrapt in clouds, and riding in the blast,
  Thou roll'st the storm along the sounding shore,
I love to watch the whelming billows cast
  On rocks below, and listen to the roar.

Thy milder terror, Night, I frequent woo,
  Thy silent lightnings, and thy meteor's glare,
Thy northern fires, bright with ensanguine hue,
  That light in heaven's high vault the fervid air.

But chief I love thee, when thy lucid car
  Sheds through the fleecy clouds a trembling gleam,
And shews the misty mountain from afar,
  The nearer forest, and the valley's stream:

And nameless objects in the vale below,
  That floating dimly to the musing eye,
Assume, at Fancy's touch, fantastic shew,
  And raise her sweet romantic visions high.

Then let me stand amidst thy glooms profound
  On some wild woody steep, and hear the breeze
That swells in mournful melody around,
  And faintly dies upon the distant trees.

What melancholy charm steals o'er the mind!
  What hallow'd tears the rising rapture greet!
While many a viewless spirit in the wind,
  Sighs to the lonely hour in accents sweet!

Ah! who the dear illusions pleas'd would yield,
  Which Fancy wakes from silence and from shades,
For all the sober forms of Truth reveal'd,
  For all the scenes that Day's bright eye pervades!

On her return to the abbey she was joined by Louis, who, after some conversation, said, 'I am much grieved by the scene to which I was witness this morning, and have longed for an opportunity of telling you so. My mother's behaviour is too mysterious to be accounted for, but it is not difficult to perceive she labours under some mistake. What I have to request is, what whenever I can be of service to you, you will command me.'

Adeline thanked him for this friendly offer, which she felt more sensibly than she chose to express. 'I am unconscious,' said she, 'of any offence that may have deserved Madame La Motte's displeasure, and am, therefore, totally unable to account for it. I have repeatedly sought an explanation, which she has as anxiously avoided; it is better, therefore, to press the subject no farther. At the same time, Sir, suffer me to assure you, I have a just sense of your goodness.' Louis sighed, and was silent. At length, 'I wish you would permit

me,' resumed he, 'to speak with my mother upon this subject.
I am sure I could convince her of her error.'

'By no means,' replied Adeline, 'Madame La Motte's
displeasure has given me inexpressible concern; but to compel
her to an explanation, would only increase this displeasure,
instead of removing it. Let me beg of you not to attempt it.'

'I submit to your judgement,' said Louis, 'but, for once, it
is with reluctance. I should esteem myself most happy, if I
could be of service to you.' He spoke this with an accent so
tender, that Adeline, for the first time, perceived the
sentiments of his heart. A mind more fraught with vanity than
her's would have taught her long ago to regard the attentions
of Louis, as the result of something more than well-bred
gallantry. She did not appear to notice his last words, but
remained silent, and involuntarily quickened her pace. Louis
said no more, but seemed sunk in thought; and this silence
remained uninterrupted, till they entered the abbey.

CHAPTER VI

'Hence, horrible shadow!
Unreal mockery, hence!'
MACBETH*

NEAR a month elapsed without any remarkable occurrence:
the melancholy of La Motte suffered little abatement; and the
behaviour of Madame to Adeline, though somewhat softened,
was still far from kind. Louis, by numberless little attentions,
testified his growing affection for Adeline, who continued to
treat them as passing civilities.

It happened, one stormy night, as they were preparing for
rest, that they were alarmed by a trampling of horses near the
abbey. The sound of several voices succeeded, and a loud
knocking at the great gate of the hall soon after confirmed the
alarm. La Motte had little doubt that the officers of justice had
at length discovered his retreat, and the perturbation of fear
almost confounded his senses; he, however, ordered the lights

to be extinguished, and a profound silence to be observed, unwilling to neglect even the slightest possibility of security. There was a chance, he thought, that the persons might suppose the place uninhabited, and believe they had mistaken the object of their search. His orders were scarcely obeyed, when the knocking was renewed, and with increased violence. La Motte now repaired to a small grated window in the portal of the gate, that he might observe the number and appearance of the strangers.

The darkness of the night baffled his purpose; he could only perceive a groupe of men on horseback; but, listening attentively, he distinguished a part of the discourse. Several of the men contended, that they had mistaken the place; till a person, who, from his authoritative voice, appeared to be their leader, affirmed, that the lights had issued from this spot, and he was positive there were persons within. Having said this, he again knocked loudly at the gate, and was answered only by hollow echoes. La Motte's heart trembled at the sound, and he was unable to move.

After waiting some time, the strangers seemed as if in consultation, but their discourse was conducted in such a low tone of voice, that La Motte was unable to distinguish its purport. They withdrew from the gate, as if to depart, but he presently thought he heard them amongst the trees on the other side of the fabric, and soon became convinced they had not left the abbey. A few minutes held La Motte in a state of torturing suspence; he quitted the grate, where Louis now stationed himself, for that part of the edifice which overlooked the spot where he supposed them to be waiting.

The storm was now loud, and the hollow blasts, which rushed among the trees, prevented his distinguishing any other sound.*Once, in the pauses of the wind, he thought he heard distinct voices; but he was not long left to conjecture, for the renewed knocking at the gate appalled him; and regardless of the terrors of Madame La Motte and Adeline, he ran to try his last chance of concealment, by means of the trap-door.

Soon after, the violence of the assailants seeming to increase with every gust of the tempest, the gate, which was old and decayed, burst from its hinges, and admitted them to the hall. At the moment of their entrance, a scream from Madame La Motte, who stood at the door of an adjoining apartment, confirmed the suspicions of the principal stranger, who continued to advance, as fast as the darkness would permit him.

Adeline had fainted, and Madame La Motte was calling loudly for assistance, when Peter entered with lights, and discovered the hall filled with men, and his young mistress senseless upon the floor. A chevalier now advanced, and soliciting pardon of Madame for the rudeness of his conduct, was attempting an apology, when perceiving Adeline, he hastened to raise her from the ground, but Louis, who now returned, caught her in his arms, and desired the stranger not to interfere.

The person, to whom he spoke this, wore the star of one of the first orders in France, and had an air of dignity, which declared him to be of superior rank. He appeared to be about forty, but, perhaps, the spirit and fire of his countenance made the impression of time upon his features less perceptible. His softened aspect and insinuating manners, while, regardless of himself, he seemed attentive only to the condition of Adeline, gradually dissipated the apprehensions of Madame La Motte, and subdued the sudden resentment of Louis. Upon Adeline, who was yet insensible, he gazed with an eager admiration, which seemed to absorb all the faculties of his mind. She was, indeed, an object not to be contemplated with indifference.

Her beauty, touched with the languid delicacy of illness, gained from sentiment what it lost in bloom. The negligence of her dress, loosened for the purpose of freer respiration, discovered those glowing charms, which her auburn tresses, that fell in profusion over her bosom, shaded, but could not conceal.

There now entered another stranger, a young Chevalier, who, having spoken hastily to the elder, joined the general groupe that surrounded Adeline. He was of a person, in which elegance was happily blended with strength, and had a countenance animated, but not haughty; noble, yet expressive of peculiar sweetness. What rendered it at present more interesting, was the compassion he seemed to feel for Adeline, who now revived and saw him, the first object that met her eyes, bending over her in silent anxiety.

On perceiving him, a blush of quick surprize passed over her cheek, for she knew him to be the stranger she had seen in the forest. Her countenance instantly changed to the paleness of terror, when she observed the room crowded with people. Louis now supported her into another apartment, where the two Chevaliers, who followed her, again apologized for the alarm they had occasioned. The elder, turning to Madame La Motte, said, 'You are, no doubt, Madam, ignorant that I am the proprietor of this abbey.' She started: 'Be not alarmed, Madam, you are safe and welcome. This ruinous spot has been long abandoned by me, and if it has afforded you a shelter I am happy.' Madame La Motte expressed her gratitude for this condescension, and Louis declared his sense of the politeness of the Marquis de Montalt, for that was the name of the noble stranger.

'My chief residence,' said the Marquis, 'is in a distant province, but I have a chateau near the borders of the forest, and in returning from an excursion, I have been benighted and lost my way. A light, which gleamed through the trees, attracted me hither, and, such was the darkness without, that I did not know it proceeded from the abbey till I came to the door.' The noble deportment of the strangers, the splendour of their apparel, and, above all, this speech, dissipated every remaining doubt of Madame's, and she was giving orders for refreshments to be set before them, when La Motte, who had listened, and was now convinced he had nothing to fear, entered the apartment.*

He advanced towards the Marquis with a complacent air, but, as he would have spoke, the words of welcome faultered on his lips, his limbs trembled, and a ghastly paleness overspread his countenance. The Marquis was little less agitated, and, in the first moment of surprize, put his hand upon his sword, but, recollecting himself, he withdrew it, and endeavoured to obtain a command of features. A pause of agonizing silence ensued. La Motte made some motion towards the door, but his agitated frame refused to support him, and he sunk into a chair, silent and exhausted. The horror of his countenance, together with his whole behaviour, excited the utmost surprize in Madame, whose eyes inquired of the Marquis more than he thought proper to answer: his looks increased, instead of explaining the mystery, and expressed a mixture of emotions, which she could not analyse. Meanwhile, she endeavoured to soothe and revive her husband, but he repressed her efforts, and, averting his face, covered it with his hands.

The Marquis, seeming to recover his presence of mind, stepped to the door of the hall where his people were assembled, when La Motte, starting from his seat, with a frantic air, called on him to return. The Marquis looked back and stopped, but still hesitating whether to proceed; the supplications of Adeline, who was now returned, added to those of La Motte, determined him, and he sat down. 'I request of you, my Lord,' said La Motte, 'that we may converse for a few moments by ourselves.'

'The request is bold, and the indulgence, perhaps, dangerous,' said the Marquis: 'it is more also than I will grant. You can having nothing to say, with which your family are not acquainted—speak your purpose and be brief.' La Motte's complection varied to every sentence of this speech. 'Impossible, my Lord,' said he; 'my lips shall close for ever, ere they pronounce before another human being the words reserved for you alone. I entreat—I supplicate of you a few moments private discourse.' As he pronounced these words, tears swelled into his eyes, and the Marquis, softened by his distress, consented, though with evident emotion and reluctance, to his request.

La Motte took a light and led the Marquis to a small room in a remote part of the edifice, where they remained near an hour. Madame, alarmed by the length of their absence, went in quest of them: as she drew near, a curiosity, in such circumstances, perhaps not unjustifiable, prompted her to listen. La Motte just then exclaimed—'The phrenzy of despair!'—some words followed, delivered in a low tone, which she could not understand—'I have suffered more than I can express,' continued he; 'the same image has pursued me in my midnight dream, and in my daily wanderings. There is no punishment, short of death, which I would not have endured, to regain the state of mind, with which I entered this forest. I again address myself to your compassion.'

A loud gust of wind, that burst along the passage where Madame La Motte stood, overpowered his voice and that of the Marquis, who spoke in reply: but she soon after distinguished these words,—'To-morrow, my Lord, if you return to these ruins, I will lead you to the spot.'

'That is scarcely necessary, and may be dangerous,' said the Marquis. From you, my Lord, I can excuse these doubts,' resumed La Motte; 'but I will swear whatever you shall propose. Yes,' continued he, 'whatever may be the consequence, I will swear to submit to your decree!' The rising tempest again drowned the sound of their voices, and Madame La Motte vainly endeavoured to hear those words, upon which, probably, hung the explanation of this mysterious conduct. They now moved towards the door, and she retreated with precipitation to the apartment where she had left Adeline, with Louis and the young Chevalier.

Hither the Marquis and La Motte soon followed, the first haughty and cool, the latter somewhat more composed than before, though the impression of horror was not yet faded from his countenance. The Marquis passed on to the hall where his retinue awaited: the storm was not yet subsided, but he seemed impatient to be gone, and ordered his people to be in readiness. La Motte observed a sullen silence, frequently pacing the room with hasty steps, and sometimes lost in reverie. Meanwhile, the Marquis, seating himself by Adeline, directed to her his whole attention, except when sudden fits of absence came over his mind and suspended him in silence: at these times the young Chevalier addressed Adeline, who, with diffidence and some agitation, shrunk from the observance of both.

The Marquis had been near two hours at the abbey, and the tempest still continuing, Madame La Motte offered him a bed. A look from her husband made her tremble for the consequence. Her offer was, however, politely declined, the Marquis being evidently as impatient to be gone, as his tenant appeared distressed by his presence. He often returned to the hall, and from the gates raised a look of impatience to the clouds. Nothing was to be seen through the darkness of night—nothing heard but the howlings of the storm.

The morning dawned before he departed. As he was preparing to leave the abbey, La Motte again drew him aside, and held him for a few moments in close conversation. His impassioned gestures, which Madame La Motte observed from a remote part of the room, added to her curiosity a degree of wild apprehension, derived from the obscurity of the subject.* Her endeavour to distinguish the corresponding words was baffled by the low voice in which they were uttered.

The Marquis and his retinue at length departed, and La Motte, having himself fastened the gates, silently and dejectedly withdrew to his chamber. The moment they were alone, Madame seized the opportunity of entreating her husband to explain the scene she had witnessed. 'Ask me no questions,' said La Motte sternly, 'for I will answer none. I have already forbade your speaking to me on this subject.'

'What subject?' said his wife. La Motte seemed to recollect himself—'No matter—I was mistaken—I thought you had repeated these questions before.'

'Ah!' said Madame La Motte, 'it is then as I suspected: your former melancholy, and the distress of this night, have the same cause.'

'And why should you either suspect or inquire? Am I always to be persecuted with conjectures?'

'Pardon me, I meant not to persecute you; but my anxiety for your welfare will not suffer me to rest under this dreadful uncertainty. Let me claim the privilege of a wife, and share the affliction which oppresses you. Deny me not.'—La Motte interrupted her, 'Whatever may be the cause of the emotions which you have witnessed, I swear that I will not now reveal it. A time may come, when I shall no longer judge concealment necessary; till then be silent, and desist from importunity; above all, forbear to remark to any one what you may have seen uncommon in me. Bury your surmise in your own bosom, as you would avoid my curse and my destruction.' The determined air with which he spoke this, while his countenance was overspread with a livid hue, made his wife shudder; and she forbore all reply.

Madame La Motte retired to bed, but not to rest. She ruminated on the past occurrence; and her surprize and curiosity, concerning the words and behaviour of her husband, were but more strongly stimulated by reflection. One truth, however, appeared; she could not doubt, but the mysterious conduct of La Motte, which had for so many months oppressed her with anxiety, and the late scene with the Marquis originated from the same cause. This belief, which seemed to prove how unjustly she had suspected Adeline, brought with it a pang of self-accusation. She looked forward to the morrow, which would lead the Marquis again to the abbey, with impatience. Wearied nature at length resumed her rights, and yielded a short oblivion of care.

At a late hour, the next day, the family assembled to breakfast. Each individual of the party appeared silent and abstracted, but very different was the aspect of their features, and still more the complection of their thoughts. La Motte seemed agitated by impatient fear, yet the sullenness of despair overspread his countenance. A certain wildness in his eye at times expressed the sudden start of horror, and again his features would sink into the gloom of despondency.

Madame La Motte seemed harrassed with anxiety; she watched every turn of her husband's countenance, and impatiently waited the arrival of the Marquis. Louis was composed and thoughtful. Adeline seemed to feel her full share of uneasiness. She had observed the behaviour of La Motte the preceding night with much surprize, and the happy confidence she had hitherto reposed in him, was shaken. She feared also, lest the exigency of his circumstances should precipitate him again into the world, and that he would be either unable or unwilling to afford her a shelter beneath his roof.

During breakfast, La Motte frequently rose to the window, from whence he cast many an anxious look. His wife understood too well the cause of his impatience, and endeavoured to repress her own. In these intervals, Louis attempted by whispers to obtain some information from his father, but La Motte always returned to the table, where the presence of Adeline prevented farther discourse.

After breakfast, as he walked upon the lawn, Louis would have joined him, but La Motte peremptorily declared he intended to be alone, and soon after, the Marquis having not yet arrived, proceeded to a greater distance from the abbey.

Adeline retired into their usual working room with Madame La Motte, who affected an air of cheerfulness, and even of kindness. Feeling the necessity of offering some reason for the striking agitation of La Motte, and of preventing the surprize, which the unexpected appearance of the Marquis would occasion Adeline, if she was left to connect it with his behaviour of the preceding night, she mentioned that the Marquis and La Motte had long been known to each other, and that this unexpected meeting, after an absence of many years, and under circumstances so altered and humiliating, on the part of the latter, had occasioned him much painful emotion. This had been heightened by a consciousness that the Marquis had formerly misinterpreted some circumstances in his conduct towards him, which had caused a suspension of their intimacy.

This account did not bring conviction to the mind of Adeline, for it seemed inadequate to the degree of emotion, the Marquis and La Motte had mutually betrayed. Her surprize was excited, and her curiosity awakened by the words, which were meant to delude them both. But she forbore to express her thoughts.

Madame proceeding with her plan, said, 'The Marquis was now expected, and she hoped whatever differences remained, would be perfectly adjusted.' Adeline blushed, and endeavouring to reply, her lips faltered. Conscious of this agitation, and of the observance of Madame La Motte, her confusion increased, and her endeavours to suppress served only to heighten it. Still she tried to renew the discourse, and still she found it impossible to collect her thoughts. Shocked lest Madame should apprehend the sentiment, which had till this moment been concealed almost from herself, her colour fled, she fixed her eyes on the ground, and, for some time, found it difficult to respire. Madame La Motte inquired if she was ill, when Adeline, glad of the excuse, withdrew to the indulgence of her own thoughts, which were now wholly engrossed by the expectation of seeing again the young Chevalier, who had accompanied the Marquis.

As she looked from her room, she saw the Marquis on horseback, with several attendants, advancing at a distance, and she hastened to apprize Madame La Motte of his approach. In a short time, he arrived at the gates, and Madame and Louis went out to receive him, La Motte being not yet returned. He entered the hall, followed by the young Chevalier, and accosting Madame with a sort of stately politeness, inquired for La Motte, whom Louis now went to seek.

The Marquis remained for a few minutes silent, and then asked of Madame La Motte 'how her fair daughter did?' Madame understood it was Adeline he meant, and having answered his inquiry, and slightly said that she was not related to them, Adeline, upon some indication of the Marquis's wish, was sent for. She entered the room with a modest blush and a timid air, which seemed to engage all his attention. His compliments she received with a sweet grace, but, when the younger Chevalier approached, the warmth of his manner rendered her's involuntarily more reserved, and she scarcely dared to raise her eyes from the ground, lest they should encounter his.

La Motte now entered and apologized for his absence, which the Marquis noticed only by a slight inclination of his head, expressing at the same time by his looks, both distrust and pride. They immediately quitted the abbey together, and the Marquis beckoned his attendants to follow at a distance. La Motte forbade his son to accompany him, but Louis observed he took the way into the thickest part of the forest. He was lost in a chaos of conjecture concerning this affair, but curiosity and anxiety for his father induced him to follow at some distance.

In the mean time, the young stranger, whom the Marquis addressed by the name of Theodore, remained at the abbey with Madame La Motte and Adeline. The former, with all her address, could scarcely conceal her agitation during this interval. She moved involuntarily to the door, whenever she heard a footstep, and several times she went to the hall door, in order to look into the forest, but as often returned, checked by disappointment. No person appeared. Theodore seemed to address as much of his attention to Adeline, as politeness would allow him to withdraw from Madame La Motte. His manners so gentle, yet dignified, insensibly subdued her timidity, and banished her reserve. Her conversation no longer suffered a painful constraint, but gradually disclosed the beauties of her mind, and seemed to produce a mutual confidence. A similarity of sentiment soon appeared, and Theodore, by the impatient pleasure which animated his countenance, seemed frequently to anticipate the thought of Adeline.

To them the absence of the Marquis was short, though long to Madame La Motte, whose countenance brightened, when she heard the trampling of horses at the gate.

The Marquis appeared but for a moment, and passed on with La Motte to a private room, where they remained for some time in conference, immediately after which he departed. Theodore took leave of Adeline, who, as well as La Motte and Madame, attended them to the gates, with an expression of tender regret, and, often as he went, looked back upon the abbey, till the intervening branches intirely excluded it from his view.

The transient glow of pleasure diffused over the cheek of Adeline disappeared with the young stranger, and she sighed as she turned into the hall. The image of Theodore pursued her to her chamber; she recollected with exactness every particular of his late conversation—his sentiments so congenial with her own—his manners so engaging—his countenance so animated—so ingenuous and so noble, in which manly dignity was blended with the sweetness of benevolence—these, and every other grace, she recollected, and a soft melancholy stole upon her heart. 'I shall see him no more,' said she. A sigh, that followed, told her more of her heart than she wished to know. She blushed, and sighed again, and then suddenly recollecting herself, she endeavoured to divert her thoughts to a different subject. La Motte's connection with the Marquis for some time engaged her attention, but, unable to develope the mystery that attended it, she sought a refuge from her own reflections in the more pleasing ones to be derived from books.

During this time, Louis, shocked and surprized at the extreme distress which his father had manifested upon the first appearance of the Marquis, addressed him upon the subject. He had no doubt that the Marquis was intimately concerned in the event which made it necessary for La Motte to leave Paris, and he spoke his thoughts without disguise, lamenting at the same time the unlucky chance, which had brought him to seek refuge in a place, of all others, the least capable of affording it—the estate of his enemy. La Motte did not contradict this opinion of his son's and joined in lamenting the evil fate which had conducted him thither.

The term of Louis's absence from his regiment, was now nearly expired, and he took occasion to express his sorrow, that he must soon be obliged to leave his father in circumstances so dangerous as the present. 'I should leave you, Sir, with less pain,' continued he, 'was I sure I knew the full extent of your misfortunes. At present I am left to conjecture evils, which, perhaps, do not exist. Relieve me, Sir, from this state of painful uncertainty, and suffer me to prove myself worthy of your confidence.'

'I have already answered you on this subject,' said La Motte, 'and forbade you to renew it. I am now obliged to tell you, I care not how soon you depart, if I am to be subjected to these inquiries.' La Motte walked abruptly away, and left his son to doubt and concern.

The arrival of the Marquis had dissipated the jealous fears of Madame La Motte, and she awoke to a sense of her cruelty towards Adeline. When she considered her orphan state—the uniform affection which had appeared in her behaviour—the mildness and patience with which she had borne her injurious treatment, she was shocked, and took an early opportunity of renewing her former kindness. But she could not explain this seeming inconsistency of conduct, without betraying her late suspicions, which she now blushed to remember, nor could she apologise for her former behaviour, without giving this explanation.

She contented herself, therefore, with expressing in her manner the regard which was thus revived. Adeline was at first surprized, but she felt too much pleasure at the change to be scrupulous in inquiring its cause.

But, notwithstanding the satisfaction which Adeline received from the revival of Madame La Motte's kindness, her thoughts frequently recurred to the peculiar and forlorn circumstances of her condition. She could not help feeling less confidence than she had formerly done in the friendship of Madame La Motte, whose character now appeared less amiable than her imagination had represented it, and seemed strongly tinctured with caprice. Her thoughts often dwelt upon the strange introduction of the Marquis at the abbey, and on the mutual emotions and apparent dislike of La Motte and himself; and, under these circumstances, it equally excited her surprize that La Motte should chuse, and that the Marquis should permit him, to remain in his territory.

Her mind returned the oftener, perhaps, to this subject, because it was connected with Theodore; but it returned unconscious of the idea which attracted it. She attributed the interest she felt in the affair to her anxiety for the welfare of La Motte, and for her own future destination, which was now so deeply involved in his. Sometimes, indeed, she caught herself busy in conjecture as to the degree of relationship in which Theodore stood to the Marquis, but she immediately checked her thoughts, and severely blamed herself for having suffered them to stray to an object, which she perceived was too dangerous to her peace.

CHAPTER VII

'Present ills
Are less than horrible imaginings.'*

A FEW days after the occurrence related in the preceding chapter, as Adeline was alone in her chamber, she was roused from a reverie by a trampling of horses near the gate, and, on looking from the casement, she saw the Marquis de Montalt enter the abbey. This circumstance surprized her, and an emotion, whose cause she did not trouble herself to inquire for, made her instantly retreat from the window. The same cause, however, led her thither again as hastily, but the object of her search did not appear, and she was in no haste to retire.

As she stood musing and disappointed, the Marquis came out with La Motte, and, immediately looking up, saw Adeline and bowed. She returned his compliment respectfully, and withdrew from the window, vexed at having been seen there. They went into the forest, but the Marquis's attendants did not, as before, follow them thither. When they returned, which was not till after a considerable time, the Marquis immediately mounted his horse and rode away.

For the remainder of the day, La Motte appeared gloomy and silent, and was frequently lost in thought. Adeline observed him with particular attention and concern; she perceived that he was always more melancholy after an interview with the Marquis, and was now surprized to hear that the latter had appointed to dine the next day at the abbey.

When La Motte mentioned this, he added some high eulogiums on the character of the Marquis, and particularly praised his generosity and nobleness of soul. At this instant, Adeline recollected the anecdotes she had formerly heard concerning the abbey, and they threw a shadow over the brightness of that excellence, which La Motte now celebrated. The account, however, did not appear to deserve much credit; a part of it, as far as a negative will admit of demonstration, having been already proved false; for it had been reported, that the abbey was haunted, and no supernatural appearance had ever been observed by the present inhabitants.

Adeline, however, ventured to inquire, whether it was the present Marquis of whom those injurious reports had been raised? La Motte answered her with a smile of ridicule; 'Stories of ghosts and hobgoblins have always been admired and cherished by the vulgar,' said he. 'I am inclined to rely upon my own experience, at least as much as upon the accounts of these peasants. If you have seen any thing to corroborate these accounts, pray inform me of it, that I may establish my faith.'

'You mistake me, Sir,' said she, 'it was not concerning supernatural agency that I would inquire: I alluded to a different part of the report, which hinted, that some person had been confined here, by order of the Marquis, who was said to have died unfairly. This was alledged as a reason for the Marquis's having abandoned the abbey.'

'All the mere coinage of idleness,' said La Motte; 'a romantic tale to excite wonder: to see the Marquis is alone sufficient to refute this; and if we credit half the number of those stories that spring from the same source, we prove ourselves little superior to the simpletons who invent them. Your good sense, Adeline, I think, will teach you the merit of disbelief.'

Adeline blushed and was silent; but La Motte's defence of the Marquis appeared much warmer and more diffuse than was consistent with his own disposition, or required by the occasion. His former conversation with Louis occurred to her, and she was the more surprised at what passed at present.

She looked forward to the morrow with a mixture of pain and pleasure; the expectation of seeing again the young Chevalier occupying her thoughts, and agitating them with a various emotion: now she feared his presence, and now she doubted whether he would come. At length she observed this, and blushed to find how much he engaged her attention. The morrow arrived—the Marquis came—but he came alone; and the sunshine of Adeline's mind was clouded, though she was able to wear her usual air of cheerfulness. The Marquis was polite, affable, and attentive: to manners the most easy and elegant, was added the last refinement of polished life. His conversation was lively, amusing, sometimes even witty;* and discovered great knowledge of the world; or, what is often mistaken for it, an acquaintance with the higher circles, and with the topics of the day.

Here La Motte was also qualified to converse with him, and they entered into a discussion of the characters and manners of the age with great spirit, and some humour. Madame La Motte had not seen her husband so cheerful since they left Paris, and sometimes she could almost fancy she was there. Adeline listened, till the cheerfulness, which she had at first only assumed, became real. The address of the Marquis was so insinuating and affable, that her reserve insensibly gave way before it, and her natural vivacity resumed its long lost empire.

At parting, the Marquis told La Motte he rejoiced at having found so agreeable a neighbour. La Motte bowed. 'I shall sometimes visit you,' continued he, 'and I lament that I cannot at present invite Madame La Motte, and her fair friend to my chateau, but it is undergoing some repairs, which make it but an uncomfortable residence.'

The vivacity of La Motte disappeared with his guest, and he soon relapsed into fits of silence and abstraction. 'The Marquis is a very agreeable man,' said Madame La Motte. 'Very agreeable,' replied he. 'And seems to have an excellent heart,' she resumed. 'An excellent one,' said La Motte.

'You seem discomposed, my dear; what has disturbed you?'

'Not in the least—I was only thinking, that with such agreeable talents, and such an excellent heart, it was a pity the Marquis should'—

'What? my dear,' said Madame with impatience: 'That the Marquis should—should suffer this abbey to fall into ruins,' replied La Motte.

'Is that all!' said Madame with disappointment.—'That is all, upon my honour,' said La Motte, and left the room.

Adeline's spirits, no longer supported by the animated conversation of the Marquis, sunk into languor, and, when he departed, she walked pensively into the forest. She followed a little romantic path that wound along the margin of the stream, and was overhung with deep shades. The tranquillity of the scene, which autumn now touched with her sweetest tints, softened her mind to a tender kind of melancholy, and she suffered a tear, which, she knew not wherefore, had stolen into her eye, to tremble there unchecked. She came to a little lonely recess, formed by high trees; the wind sighed mournfully among the branches, and as it waved their lofty heads scattered their leaves to the ground. She seated herself on a bank beneath, and indulged the melancholy reflections that pressed on her mind.

'O! could I dive into futurity and behold the events which

await me!' said she; 'I should, perhaps, by constant contemplation, be enabled to meet them with fortitude. An
orphan in this wide world—thrown upon the friendship of
strangers for comfort, and upon their bounty for the very
means of existence, what but evil have I to expect! Alas, my
father! how could you thus abandon your child—how leave
her to the storms of life—to sink, perhaps, beneath them?
Alas, I have no friend!'

She was interrupted by a rustling among the fallen leaves;
she turned her head, and perceiving the Marquis's young
friend, arose to depart. 'Pardon this intrusion,' said he, 'your
voice attracted me hither, and your words detained me: my
offence, however, brings with it its own punishment, having
learned your sorrows—how can I help feeling them myself?
would that my sympathy, or my suffering, could rescue you
from them!'—He hesitated—'Would that I could deserve the
title of your friend, and be thought worthy of it by yourself!'

The confusion of Adeline's thoughts could scarcely permit
her to reply; she trembled and gently withdrew her hand,
which he had taken, while he spoke. 'You have, perhaps,
heard, Sir, more than is true: I am, indeed, not happy, but a
moment of dejection has made me unjust, and I am less
unfortunate than I have represented. When I said I had no
friend, I was ungrateful to the kindness of Monsieur and
Madame La Motte, who have been more than friends—have
been as parents to me.'

'If so, I honour them,' cried Theodore with warmth; 'and
if I did not feel it to be presumption, I would ask why you are
unhappy?—But'—He paused. Adeline, raising her eyes, saw
him gazing upon her with intense and eager anxiety, and her
looks were again fixed upon the ground. 'I have pained you,'
said Theodore, 'by an improper request. Can you forgive me,
and also when I add, that it was an interest in your welfare,
which urged my inquiry?'

'Forgiveness, Sir, it is unnecessary to ask. I am certainly
obliged by the compassion you express. But the evening is
cold, if you please, we will walk towards the abbey.' As they
moved on, Theodore was for some time silent. At length, 'It
was but lately that I solicited your pardon,' said he, 'and I

shall now, perhaps, have need of it again; but you will do me
the justice to believe, that I have a strong, and, indeed, a
pressing reason to inquire how nearly you are related to
Monsieur La Motte.'

'We are not at all related,' said Adeline; 'but the service he
has done me I can never repay, and I hope my gratitude will
teach me never to forget it.'

'Indeed!' said Theodore, surprized: 'and may I ask how long
you have known him?'

'Rather, Sir, let me ask, why these questions should be
necessary?'

'You are just,' said he, with an air of self-condemnation, 'my
conduct has deserved this reproof; I should have been more
explicit.' He looked as if his mind was labouring with
something which he was unwilling to express. 'But you know
not how delicately I am circumstanced,' continued he, 'yet I
will aver, that my questions are prompted by the tenderest
interest in your happiness—and even by my fears for your
safety.' Adeline started. 'I fear you are deceived,' said he, 'I
fear there's danger near you.'

Adeline stopped, and, looking earnestly at him, begged he
would explain himself. She suspected that some mischief
threatened La Motte; and Theodore continuing silent, she
repeated her request. 'If La Motte is concerned in this
danger,' said she, 'let me entreat you to acquaint him with it
immediately. He has but too many misfortunes to apprehend.'

'Excellent Adeline!' cried Theodore, 'that heart must be
adamant that would injure you. How shall I hint what I fear
is too true, and how forbear to warn you of your danger
without'—He was interrupted by a step among the trees, and
presently after saw La Motte cross into the path they were in.
Adeline felt confused at being thus seen with the Chevalier,
and was hastening to join La Motte, but Theodore detained
her, and entreated a moment's attention. 'There is now no
time to explain myself,' said he; 'yet what I would say is of
the utmost consequence to *yourself*.'

'Promise, therefore, to meet me in some part of the forest
at about this time to-morrow evening, you will then, I hope,

be convinced, that my conduct is directed, neither by common circumstances, nor common regard.' Adeline shuddered at the idea of making an appointment; she hesitated, and at length entreated Theodore not to delay till to-morrow an explanation, which appeared to be so important, but to follow La Motte and inform him of his danger immediately. 'It is not with La Motte I would speak,' replied Theodore; 'I know of no danger that threatens him—but he approaches, be quick, lovely Adeline, and promise to meet me.'

'I do promise,' said Adeline, with a faltering voice; 'I will come to the spot where you found me this evening, an hour earlier to-morrow.' Saying this, she withdrew her trembling hand, which Theodore had pressed to his lips in token of acknowledgement, and he immediately disappeared.

La Motte now approached Adeline, who, fearing that he had seen Theodore, was in some confusion. 'Whither is Louis gone so fast?' said La Motte. She rejoiced to find his mistake, and suffered him to remain in it. They walked pensively towards the abbey, where Adeline, too much occupied by her own thoughts to bear company, retired to her chamber. She ruminated upon the words of Theodore, and, the more she considered them, the more she was perplexed. Sometimes she blamed herself for having made an appointment, doubting whether he had not solicited it for the purpose of pleading a passion; and now delicacy checked this thought, and made her vexed that she had presumed upon having inspired one. She recollected the serious earnestness of his voice and manner, when he entreated her to meet him; and as they convinced her of the importance of the subject, she shuddered at a danger, which she could not comprehend, looking forward to the morrow with anxious impatience.

Sometimes too a remembrance of the tender interest he had expressed for her welfare, and of his correspondent look and air, would steal across her memory, awakening a pleasing emotion and a latent hope that she was not indifferent to him. From reflections like these she was roused by a summons to supper: the repast was a melancholy one, it being the last evening of Louis's stay at the abbey. Adeline, who esteemed him, regretted his departure, while his eyes were often bent on her with a look, which seemed to express that he was about to leave the object of his affection. She endeavoured by her cheerfulness to re-animate the whole party, and especially Madame La Motte, who frequently shed tears. 'We shall soon meet again,' said Adeline, 'I trust, in happier circumstances.' La Motte sighed. The countenance of Louis brightened at her words, 'Do you wish it?' said he, with peculiar emphasis. 'Most certainly I do,' she replied. 'Can you doubt my regard for my best friends?'

'I cannot doubt any thing that is good of you,' said he.

'You forget you have left Paris,' said La Motte to his son, while a faint smile crossed his face, 'such a compliment would there be in character with the place—in these solitary woods it is quite *outré*.'

'The language of admiration is not always that of compliment, Sir,' said Louis. Adeline, willing to change the discourse, asked, to what part of France he was going. He replied, that his regiment was now at Peronne, and he should go immediately thither. After some mention of indifferent subjects, the family withdrew for the night to their several chambers.

The approaching departure of her son occupied the thoughts of Madame La Motte, and she appeared at breakfast with eyes swoln with weeping. The pale countenance of Louis seemed to indicate that he had rested no better than his mother. When breakfast was over, Adeline retired for a while, that she might not interrupt, by her presence, their last conversation. As she walked on the lawn before the abbey she returned in thought to the occurrence of yesterday evening, and her impatience for the appointed interview increased. She was soon joined by Louis. 'It was unkind of you to leave us,' said he, 'in the last moments of my stay. Could I hope that you would sometimes remember me, when I am far away, I should depart with less sorrow.' He then expressed his concern at leaving her, and though he had hitherto armed himself with resolution to forbear a direct avowal of an attachment, which must be fruitless, his heart now yielded to the force of passion, and he told what Adeline every moment feared to hear.

'This declaration,' said Adeline, endeavouring to overcome the agitation it excited, 'gives me inexpressible concern.'

'O, say not so!' interrupted Louis, 'but give me some slender hope to support me in the miseries of absence. Say that you do not hate me—Say'—

'That I do most readily say,' replied Adeline, in a tremulous voice; 'if it will give you pleasure to be assured of my esteem and friendship—receive this assurance:—as the son of my best benefactors, you are entitled to'——

'Name not benefits,' said Louis, 'your merits outrun them all: and suffer me to hope for a sentiment less cool than that of friendship, as well as to believe that I do not owe your approbation of me to the actions of others. I have long borne my passion in silence, because I foresaw the difficulties that would attend it, nay, I have even dared to endeavour to overcome it: I have dared to believe it possible, forgive the supposition, that I could forget you—and'——

'You distress me,' interrupted Adeline; 'this is a conversation which I ought not to hear. I am above disguise, and, therefore, assure you, that, though your virtues will always command my esteem, you have nothing to hope from my love. Were it even otherwise, our circumstances would effectually decide for us. If you are really my friend, you will rejoice that I am spared this struggle between affection and prudence. Let me hope also, that time will teach you to reduce love within the limits of friendship.'

'Never!' cried Louis vehemently: 'Were this possible, my passion would be unworthy of its object.' While he spoke, Adeline's favourite fawn came bounding towards her. This circumstance affected Louis even to tears. 'This little animal,' said he, after a short pause, 'first conducted me to you: it was witness to that happy moment when I first saw you, surrounded by attractions too powerful for my heart; that moment is now fresh in my memory, and the creature comes even to witness this sad one of my departure.' Grief interrupted his utterance.

When he recovered his voice, he said, 'Adeline! when you look upon your little favourite and caress it, remember the unhappy Louis, who will then be far—far from you. Do not deny me the poor consolation of believing this!'

'I shall not require such a monitor to remind me of you,' said Adeline with a smile; 'your excellent parents and your own merits have sufficient claim upon my remembrance. Could I see your natural good sense resume its influence over passion, my satisfaction would equal my esteem for you.'

'Do not hope it,' said Louis, 'nor will I wish it—for passion here is virtue.' As he spoke, he saw La Motte turn round an angle of the abbey. 'The moments are precious,' said he, 'I am interrupted. O! Adeline, farewell! and say, that you will sometimes think of me.'

'Farewell,' said Adeline, who was affected by his distress—'farewell! and peace attend you. I will think of you with the affection of a sister.'—He sighed deeply, and pressed her hand; when La Motte, winding round another projection of the ruin, again appeared. Adeline left them together, and withdrew to her chamber, oppressed by the scene. Louis's passion and her esteem were too sincere not to inspire her with a strong degree of pity for his unhappy attachment. She remained in her chamber till he had quitted the abbey, unwilling to subject him or herself to the pain of a formal parting.

As evening and the hour of appointment drew nigh, Adeline's impatience increased; yet, when the time arrived, her resolution failed, and she faltered from her purpose. There was something of indelicacy and dissimulation in an *appointed* interview, on her part, that shocked her. She recollected the tenderness of Theodore's manner, and several little circumstances which seemed to indicate that his heart was not unconcerned in the event. Again she was inclined to doubt, whether he had not obtained her consent to this meeting upon some groundless suspicion; and she almost determined not to go: yet it was possible Theodore's assertion might be sincere, and her danger real; the chance of this made her delicate scruples appear ridiculous; she wondered that she had for a moment suffered them to weigh against so serious an interest, and, blaming herself for the delay they had occasioned, hastened to the place of appointment.

The little path, which led to this spot, was silent and solitary, and when she reached the recess, Theodore had not arrived. A transient pride made her unwilling he should find that she was more punctual to his appointment than himself; and she turned from the recess into a track, which wound among the trees to the right. Having walked some way, without seeing any person, or hearing a footstep, she returned; but he was not come, and she again left the place. A second time she came back, and Theodore was still absent. Recollecting the time at which she had quitted the abbey, she grew uneasy, and calculated that the hour appointed was now much exceeded. She was offended and perplexed; but she seated herself on the turf, and was resolved to wait the event. After remaining here till the fall of twilight in fruitless expectation, her pride became more alarmed; she feared that he had discovered something of the partiality he had inspired, and believing that he now treated her with purposed neglect, she quitted the place with disgust and self-accusation.

When these emotions subsided, and reason resumed its influence, she blushed for what she termed this childish effervescence of self-love. She recollected, as if for the first time, these words of Theodore: 'I fear you are deceived, and that some danger is near you.' Her judgement now acquitted the offender, and she saw only the friend. The import of these words, whose truth she no longer doubted, again alarmed her. Why did he trouble himself to come from the chateau, on purpose to hint her danger, if he did not wish to preserve her? And if he wished to preserve her, what but necessity could have withheld him from the appointment?

These reflections decided her at once. She resolved to repair on the following day at the same hour to the recess, whither the interest, which she believed him to take in her fate, would no doubt conduct him in the hope of meeting her. That some evil hovered over her she could not disbelieve, but what it might be, she was unable to guess. Monsieur and Madame La Motte were her friends, and who else, removed, as she now thought herself, beyond the reach of her father, could injure her? But why did Theodore say she was deceived? She found it impossible to extricate herself from the labyrinth of conjecture, but endeavoured to command her anxiety till the following evening. In the mean time she engaged herself in efforts to amuse Madame La Motte, who required some relief, after the departure of her son.

Thus oppressed by her own cares and interested by those of Madame La Motte, Adeline retired to rest. She soon lost her recollection, but it was only to fall into harrassed slumbers, such as but too often haunt the couch of the unhappy. At length her perturbed fancy suggested the following dream.

She thought she was in a large old chamber belonging to the abbey, more ancient and desolate, though in part furnished, than any she had yet seen. It was strongly barricadoed, yet no person appeared. While she stood musing and surveying the apartment, she heard a low voice call her, and, looking towards the place whence it came, she perceived by the dim light of a lamp a figure stretched on a bed that lay on the floor. The voice called again, and, approaching the bed, she distinctly saw the features of a man who appeared to be dying. A ghastly paleness overspread his countenance, yet there was an expression of mildness and dignity in it, which strongly interested her.

While she looked on him, his features changed and seemed convulsed in the agonies of death. The spectacle shocked her, and she started back, but he suddenly stretched forth his hand, and seizing her's, grasped it with violence: she struggled in terror to disengage herself, and again looking on his face, saw a man, who appeared to be about thirty, with the same features, but in full health, and of a most benign countenance. He smiled tenderly upon her and moved his lips, as if to speak, when the floor of the chamber suddenly opened and he sunk from her view. The effort she made to save herself from following awoke her.—This dream had so strongly impressed her fancy, that it was some time before she could overcome the terror it occasioned, or even be perfectly convinced she was in her own apartment. At length, however, she composed herself to sleep; again she fell into a dream.

She thought she was bewilderd in some winding passages of the abbey; that it was almost dark, and that she wandered about a considerable time, without being able to find a door. Suddenly she heard a bell toll from above, and soon after a confusion of distant voices. She redoubled her efforts to extricate herself. Presently all was still, and, at length, wearied with the search, she sat down on a step that crossed the passage. She had not been long here, when she saw a light glimmer at a distance on the walls, but a turn in the passage, which was very long, prevented her seeing from what it proceeded. It continued to glimmer faintly for some time and then grew stronger, when she saw a man enter the passage, habited in a long black cloak, like those usually worn by attendants at funerals, and bearing a torch. He called to her to follow him, and led her through a long passage to the foot of a staircase. Here she feared to proceed, and was running back, when the man suddenly turned to pursue her, and with the terror, which this occasioned, she awoke.

Shocked by these visions, and more so by their seeming connection, which now struck her, she endeavoured to continue awake, lest their terrific images should again haunt her mind: after some time, however, her harrassed spirits again sunk into slumber, though not to repose.

She now thought herself in a large old gallery, and saw at one end of it a chamber door standing a little open and a light within: she went towards it, and perceived the man she had before seen, standing at the door and beckoning her towards him. With the inconsistency so common in dreams, she no longer endeavoured to avoid him, but advancing, followed him into a suite of very ancient apartments, hung with black, and lighted up as if for a funeral.* Still he led her on, till she found herself in the same chamber she remembered to have seen in her former dream: a coffin, covered with a pall, stood at the farther end of the room; some lights, and several persons surrounded it, who appeared to be in great distress.

Suddenly, she thought these persons were all gone, and that she was left alone; that she went up to the coffin, and while she gazed upon it, she heard a voice speak, as if from within, but saw nobody. The man she had before seen, soon after stood by the coffin, and, lifting the pall, she saw beneath it a dead person, whom she thought to be the dying Chevalier she had seen in her former dream: his features were sunk in death, but they were yet serene. While she looked at him, a stream of blood gushed from his side, and descending to the floor, the whole chamber was overflowed; at the same time some words were uttered in the voice she heard before; but the horror of the scene so entirely overcame her, that she started and awoke.

When she had recovered her recollection, she raised herself in the bed, to be convinced it was a dream she had witnessed, and the agitation of her spirits was so great, that she feared to be alone, and almost determined to call Annette. The features of the deceased person, and the chamber where he lay, were strongly impressed upon her memory, and she still thought she heard the voice and saw the countenance which her dream represented. The longer she considered these dreams, the more she was surprized: they were so very terrible, returned so often, and seemed to be so connected with each other, that she could scarcely think them accidental; yet, why they should be supernatural, she could not tell. She slept no more that night.

END OF VOLUME I

VOLUME II

CHAPTER VIII

———'When these prodigies
Do so conjointly meet, let not men say,
These are their reasons; they are natural;
For I believe they are portentous things.'
JULIUS CÆSAR*

WHEN Adeline appeared at breakfast, her harrassed and languid countenance struck Madame La Motte, who inquired if she was ill; Adeline, forcing a smile upon her features, said she had not rested well, for that she had had very disturbed dreams: she was about to describe them, but a strong and involuntary impulse prevented her. At the same time, La Motte ridiculed her concern so unmercifully, that she was almost ashamed to have mentioned it, and tried to overcome the remembrance of its cause.

After breakfast, she endeavoured to employ her thoughts by conversing with Madame La Motte; but they were really engaged by the incidents of the last two days; the circumstance of her dreams, and her conjectures concerning the information to be communicated to her by Theodore. They had thus sat for some time, when a sound of voices arose from the great gate of the abbey; and, on going to the casement, Adeline saw the Marquis and his attendants on the lawn below. The portal of the abbey concealed several people from her view, and among these it was possible might be Theodore, who had not yet appeared: she continued to look for him with great anxiety, till the Marquis entered the hall with La Motte, and some other persons, soon after which Madame went to receive him, and Adeline retired to her own apartment.

A message from La Motte, however, soon called her to join the party, where she vainly hoped to find Theodore. The

Marquis arose as she approached, and, having paid her some general compliments, the conversation took a very lively turn. Adeline, finding it impossible to counterfeit cheerfulness, while her heart was sinking with anxiety and disappointment, took little part in it: Theodore was not once named. She would have asked concerning him, had it been possible to inquire with propriety; but she was obliged to content herself with hoping, first, that he would arrive before dinner, and then before the departure of the Marquis.

Thus the day passed in expectation and disappointment. The evening was now approaching, and she was condemned to remain in the presence of the Marquis, apparently listening to a conversation, which, in truth, she scarcely heard, while the opportunity was, perhaps, escaping that would decide her fate. She was suddenly relieved from this state of torture, and thrown into one, if possible, still more distressing.

The Marquis inquired for Louis, and being informed of his departure, mentioned that Theodore Peyrou* had that morning set out for his regiment in a distant province. He lamented the loss he should sustain by his absence; and expressed some very flattering praise of his talents. The shock of this intelligence overpowered the long-agitated spirits of Adeline; the blood forsook her cheeks, and a sudden faintness came over her, from which she recovered only to a consciousness of having discovered her emotion, and the danger of relapsing into a second fit.

She retired to her chamber, where, being once more alone, her oppressed heart found relief from tears, in which she freely indulged. Ideas crowded so fast upon her mind, that it was long ere she could arrange them so as to produce any thing like reasoning. She endeavoured to account for the abrupt departure of Theodore. 'Is it possible,' said she, 'that he should take an interest in my welfare, and yet leave me exposed to the full force of a danger, which he himself foresaw? Or am I to believe that he has trifled with my simplicity for an idle frolic, and has now left me to the wondering apprehension he has raised? Impossible! a countenance so noble, and a manner so amiable, could never disguise a heart capable of forming so despicable a design.

No!—whatever is reserved for me, let me not relinquish the pleasure of believing that he is worthy of my esteem.'

She was awakened from thoughts like these by a peal of distant thunder, and now perceived that the gloominess of evening was deepened by the coming storm; it rolled onward, and soon after the lightning began to flash along the chamber. Adeline was superior to the affectation of fear, and was not apt to be terrified; but she now felt it unpleasant to be alone,* and, hoping that the Marquis might have left the abbey, she went down to the sitting room; but the threatening aspect of the Heavens had hitherto detained him, and now the evening tempest made him rejoice that he had not quitted a shelter. The storm continued, and night came on. La Motte pressed his guest to take a bed at the abbey, and he, at length, consented; a circumstance, which threw Madame La Motte into some perplexity, as to the accommodation to be afforded him; after some time, she arranged the affair to her satisfaction; resigning her own apartment to the Marquis, and that of Louis to two of his superior attendants; Adeline, it was farther settled, should give up her room to Monsieur and Madame La Motte, and remove to an inner chamber, where a small bed, usually occupied by Annette, was placed for her.

At supper, the Marquis was less gay than usual; he frequently addressed Adeline, and his look and manner seemed to express the tender interest, which her indisposition, for she still appeared pale and languid, had excited. Adeline, as usual, made an effort to forget her anxiety, and appear happy; but the veil of assumed cheerfulness was too thin to conceal the features of sorrow; and her feeble smiles only added a peculiar softness to her air. The Marquis conversed with her on a variety of subjects, and displayed an elegant mind. The observations of Adeline, which, when called upon, she gave with reluctant modesty, in words at once simple and forceful, seemed to excite his admiration, which he sometimes betrayed by an inadvertent expression.

Adeline retired early to her room, which adjoined on one side to Madame La Motte's, and on the other to the closet formerly mentioned. It was spacious and lofty, and what little furniture it contained was falling to decay; but, perhaps, the present tone of her spirits might contribute more than these circumstances to give that air of melancholy, which seemed to reign in it. She was unwilling to go to bed, lest the dreams that had lately pursued her should return; and determined to sit up till she found herself oppressed by sleep, when it was probable her rest would be profound. She placed the light on a small table, and, taking a book, continued to read for above an hour, till her mind refused any longer to abstract itself from its own cares, and she sat for some time leaning pensively on her arm.

The wind was high, and as it whistled through the desolate apartment, and shook the feeble doors, she often started, and sometimes even thought she heard sighs between the pauses of the gust; but she checked these illusions, which the hour of the night and her own melancholy imagination conspired to raise. As she sat musing, her eyes fixed on the opposite wall, she perceived the arras, with which the room was hung, wave backwards and forwards; she continued to observe it for some minutes, and then rose to examine it farther. It was moved by the wind; and she blushed at the momentary fear it had excited: but she observed that the tapestry was more strongly agitated in one particular place than elsewhere, and a noise that seemed something more than that of the wind issued thence. The old bedstead, which La Motte had found in this apartment, had been removed to accommodate Adeline, and it was behind the place where this had stood, that the wind seemed to rush with particular force: curiosity prompted her to examine still farther; she felt about the tapestry, and perceiving the wall behind shake under her hand, she lifted the arras, and discovered a small door, whose loosened hinges admitted the wind, and occasioned the noise she had heard.

The door was held only by a bolt, having undrawn which, and brought the light, she descended by a few steps into another chamber: she instantly remembered her dreams. The chamber was not much like that in which she had seen the dying Chevalier, and afterwards the bier; but it gave her a confused remembrance of one through which she had passed. Holding up the light to examine it more fully, she was convinced by its structure that it was part of the ancient foundation. A shattered casement, placed high from the floor, seemed to be the only opening to admit light. She observed a door on the opposite side of the apartment; and after some moments of hesitation, gained courage, and determined to pursue the inquiry. 'A mystery seems to hang over these chambers,' said she, 'which it is, perhaps, my lot to develope; I will, at least, see to what that door leads.'

She stepped forward, and having unclosed it, proceeded with faltering steps along a suite of apartments, resembling the first in style and condition, and terminating in one exactly like that where her dream had represented the dying person; the remembrance struck so forcibly upon her imagination, that she was in danger of fainting; and looking round the room, almost expected to see the phantom of her dream.

Unable to quit the place, she sat down on some old lumber to recover herself, while her spirits were nearly overcome by a superstitious dread, such as she had never felt before. She wondered to what part of the abbey these chambers belonged, and that they had so long escaped detection. The casements were all too high to afford any information from without. When she was sufficiently composed to consider the direction of the rooms, and the situation of the abbey, there appeared not a doubt that they formed an interior part of the original building.

As these reflections passed over her mind, a sudden gleam of moonlight fell upon some object without the casement. Being now sufficiently composed to wish to pursue the inquiry; and believing this object might afford her some means of learning the situation of these rooms, she combated her remaining terrors, and, in order to distinguish it more clearly, removed the light to an outer chamber; but before she could return, a heavy cloud was driven over the face of the moon, and all without was perfectly dark: she stood for some moments waiting a returning gleam, but the obscurity continued. As she went softly back for the light, her foot stumbled over something on the floor, and while she stooped to examine it, the moon again shone, so that she could distinguish, through the casement, the eastern towers of the abbey. This discovery confirmed her former conjectures concerning the interior situation of these apartments. The obscurity of the place prevented her discovering what it was that had impeded her steps, but having brought the light forward, she perceived on the floor an old dagger: with a trembling hand she took it up, and upon a closer view perceived, that it was spotted and stained with rust.

Shocked and surprised, she looked round the room for some object that might confirm or destroy the dreadful suspicion which now rushed upon her mind; but she saw only a great chair, with broken arms, that stood in one corner of the room, and a table in a condition equally shattered, except that in another part lay a confused heap of things, which appeared to be old lumber. She went up to it, and perceived a broken bedstead, with some decayed remnants of furniture, covered with dust and cobwebs, and which seemed, indeed, as if they had not been moved for many years. Desirous, however, of examining farther, she attempted to raise what appeared to have been part of the bedstead, but it slipped from her hand, and, rolling to the floor, brought with it some of the remaining lumber. Adeline started aside and saved herself, and when the noise it made had ceased, she heard a small rustling sound, and as she was about to leave the chamber, saw something falling gently among the lumber.

It was a small roll of paper, tied with a string, and covered with dust. Adeline took it up, and on opening it perceived an handwriting. She attempted to read it, but the part of the manuscript she looked at was so much obliterated, that she found this difficult, though what few words were legible impressed her with curiosity and terror, and induced her to return with it immediately to her chamber.

Having reached her own room, she fastened the private door, and let the arras fall over it as before. It was now midnight. The stillness of the hour, interrupted only at intervals by the hollow sighings of the blast, heightened the solemnity of Adeline's feelings. She wished she was not alone, and before she proceeded to look into the manuscript, listened whether Madame La Motte was yet in her chamber: not the least sound was heard, and she gently opened the door. The profound silence within almost convinced her that no person was there; but willing to be farther satisfied, she brought the light and found the room empty. The lateness of the hour made her wonder that Madame La Motte was not in her chamber, and she proceeded to the top of the tower stairs, to hearken if any person was stirring.

She heard the sound of voices from below, and, amongst the rest, that of La Motte speaking in his usual tone. Being now satisfied that all was well, she turned towards her room, when she heard the Marquis pronounce her name with very unusual emphasis. She paused. 'I adore her,' pursued he, 'and by heaven'—He was interrupted by La Motte, 'My Lord, remember your promise.'

'I do,' replied the Marquis, 'and I will abide by it. But we trifle. To-morrow I will declare myself, and I shall then know both what to hope and how to act.' Adeline trembled so excessively, that she could scarcely support herself: she wished to return to her chamber; yet she was too much interested in the words she had heard, not to be anxious to have them more fully explained. There was an interval of silence, after which they conversed in a lower tone. Adeline remembered the hints of Theodore, and determined, if possible, to be relieved from the terrible suspense she now suffered. She stole softly down a few steps, that she might catch the accents of the speakers, but they were so low, that she could only now and then distinguish a few words. 'Her father, say you?' said the Marquis. 'Yes, my Lord, her father. I am well informed of what I say.' Adeline shuddered at the mention of her father, a new terror seized her, and with increasing eagerness she endeavoured to distinguish their words, but for some time found this to be impossible. 'Here is no time to be lost,' said the Marquis, 'to-morrow then.'—She heard La Motte rise, and, believing it was to leave the room, she hurried up the steps, and having reached her chamber, sunk almost lifeless in a chair.

It was her father only of whom she thought. She doubted not that he had pursued and discovered her retreat, and, though this conduct appeared very inconsistent with his former behaviour in abandoning her to strangers, her fears suggested that it would terminate in some new cruelty. She did not hesitate to pronounce this the danger of which Theodore had warned her; but it was impossible to surmise how he had gained his knowledge of it, or how he had become sufficiently acquainted with her story, except through La Motte, her apparent friend and protector, whom she was thus, though unwillingly, led to suspect of treachery. Why, indeed, should La Motte conceal from her only his knowledge of her father's intention, unless he designed to deliver her into his hands? Yet it was long ere she could bring herself to believe this conclusion possible. To discover depravity in those whom we have loved, is one of the most exquisite tortures to a virtuous mind, and the conviction is often rejected before it is finally admitted.

The words of Theodore, which told her he was fearful she was deceived, confirmed this most painful apprehension of La Motte, with another yet more distressing, that Madame La Motte was also united against her. This thought, for a moment, subdued terror and left her only grief; she wept bitterly. 'Is this human nature?' cried she. 'Am I doomed to find every body deceitful?' An unexpected discovery of vice in those, whom we have admired, inclines us to extend our censure of the individual to the species; we henceforth contemn appearances, and too hastily conclude that no person is to be trusted.

Adeline determined to throw herself at the feet of La Motte, on the following morning, and implore his pity and protection. Her mind was now too much agitated, by her own interests, to permit her to examine the manuscripts, and she sat musing in her chair, till she heard the steps of Madame La Motte, when she retired to bed. La Motte soon after came up to his chamber, and Adeline, the mild, persecuted Adeline, who had now passed two days of torturing anxiety, and one night of terrific visions, endeavoured to compose her mind to sleep. In the present state of her spirits, she quickly caught alarm, and she had scarcely fallen into a slumber, when she was roused by a loud and uncommon noise. She listened, and thought the sound came from the apartments below, but in a few minutes there was a hasty knocking at the door of La Motte's chamber.

La Motte, who had just fallen asleep, was not easily to be roused, but the knocking increased with such violence, that Adeline, extremely terrified, arose and went to the door that opened from her chamber into his, with a design to call him.

She was stopped by the voice of the Marquis, which she now clearly distinguished at the door. He called to La Motte to rise immediately, and Madame La Motte endeavoured at the same time to rouse her husband, who, at length, awoke in much alarm, and soon after, joining the Marquis, they went down stairs together. Adeline now dressed herself, as well as her trembling hands would permit, and went into the adjoining chamber, where she found Madame La Motte extremely surprized and terrified.

The Marquis, in the mean time, told La Motte, with great agitation, that he recollected having appointed some persons to meet him upon business of importance, early in the morning, and it was, therefore, necessary for him to set off for his chateau immediately. As he said this, and desired that his servants might be called, La Motte could not help observing the ashy paleness of his countenance, or expressing some apprehension that his Lordship was ill. The Marquis assured him he was perfectly well, but desired that he might set out immediately. Peter was now ordered to call the other servants, and the Marquis, having refused to take any refreshment, bade La Motte a hasty adieu, and, as soon as his people were ready, left the abbey.

La Motte returned to his chamber, musing on the abrupt departure of his guest, whose emotion appeared much too strong to proceed from the cause assigned. He appeased the anxiety of Madame La Motte, and at the same time excited her surprize by acquainting her with the occasion of the late disturbance. Adeline, who had retired from the chamber, on the approach of La Motte, looked out from her window on hearing the trampling of horses. It was the Marquis and his people, who just then passed at a little distance. Unable to distinguish who the persons were, she was alarmed at observing such a party about the abbey at that hour, and, calling to inform La Motte of the circumstance, was made acquainted with what had passed.

At length she retired to her bed, and her slumbers were this night undisturbed by dreams.

When she arose in the morning, she observed La Motte walking alone in the avenue below, and she hastened to seize the opportunity which now offered of pleading her cause. She approached him with faltering steps, while the paleness and timidity of her countenance discovered the disorder of her mind. Her first words, without entering upon any explanation, implored his compassion. La Motte stopped, and, looking earnestly in her face, inquired whether any part of his conduct towards her merited the suspicion which her request implied. Adeline for a moment blushed that she had doubted his integrity, but the words she had overheard returned to her memory.

'Your behaviour, Sir,' said she, 'I acknowledge to have been kind and generous, beyond what I had a right to expect, but'—and she paused. She knew not how to mention what she blushed to believe. La Motte continued to gaze on her in silent expectation, and at length desired her to proceed and explain her meaning. She entreated that he would protect her from her father. La Motte looked surprised and confused. 'Your father!' said he. 'Yes, Sir,' replied Adeline; 'I am not ignorant that he has discovered my retreat. I have every thing to dread from a parent, who has treated me with such cruelty as you was witness of; and I again implore that you will save me from his hands.'

La Motte stood fixed in thought, and Adeline continued her endeavours to interest his pity. 'What reason have you to suppose, or, rather, how have you learned, that your father pursues you?' The question confused Adeline, who blushed to acknowledge that she had overheard his discourse, and disdained to invent, or utter a falsity: at length she confessed the truth. The countenance of La Motte instantly changed to a savage fierceness, and, sharply rebuking her for a conduct, to which she had been rather tempted by chance, than prompted by design, he inquired what she had overheard, that could so much alarm her. She faithfully repeated the substance of the incoherent sentences that had met her ear; while she spoke, he regarded her with a fixed attention. 'And was this all you heard? Is it from these few words that you draw such a positive conclusion? Examine them, and you will find they do not justify it.'

She now perceived, what the fervor of her fears had not

permitted her to observe before, that the words, unconnectedly as she heard them, imported little, and that her imagination had filled up the void in the sentences, so as to suggest the evil apprehended. Notwithstanding this, her fears were little abated. 'Your apprehensions are, doubtless, now removed,' resumed La Motte; 'but to give you a proof of the sincerity which you have ventured to question, I will tell you they were just. You seem alarmed, and with reason. Your father has discovered your residence, and has already demanded you. It is true, that from a motive of compassion I have refused to resign you, but I have neither authority to withhold, or means to defend you. When he comes to enforce his demand, you will perceive this. Prepare yourself, therefore, for the evil, which you see is inevitable.'

Adeline, for some time, could speak only by her tears. At length, with a fortitude which despair had roused, she said, 'I resign myself to the will of Heaven!' La Motte gazed on her in silence, and a strong emotion appeared in his countenance. He forbore, however, to renew the discourse, and withdrew to the abbey, leaving Adeline in the avenue, absorbed in grief.

A summons to breakfast hastened her to the parlour, where she passed the morning in conversation with Madame La Motte, to whom she told all her apprehensions, and expressed all her sorrow. Pity and superficial consolation was all that Madame La Motte could offer, though apparently much affected by Adeline's discourse. Thus the hours passed heavily away, while the anxiety of Adeline continued to increase, and the moment of her fate seemed fast approaching. Dinner was scarcely over, when Adeline was surprized to see the Marquis arrive. He entered the room with his usual ease, and, apologizing for the disturbance he had occasioned on the preceding night, repeated what he had before told La Motte.

The remembrance of the conversation she had overheard, at first gave Adeline some confusion, and withdrew her mind from a sense of the evils to be apprehended from her father. The Marquis, who was, as usual, attentive to Adeline, seemed affected by her apparent indisposition, and expressed much concern for that dejection of spirits, which, notwithstanding every effort, her manner betrayed. When Madame La Motte withdrew, Adeline would have followed her, but the Marquis entreated a few moments' attention, and led her back to her seat. La Motte immediately disappeared.

Adeline knew too well what would be the purport of the Marquis's discourse, and his words soon increased the confusion which her fears had occasioned. While he was declaring the ardour of his passion in such terms, as but too often make vehemence pass for sincerity, Adeline, to whom this declaration, if honourable, was distressing, and if dishonourable, was shocking, interrupted him and thanked him for the offer of a distinction, which, with a modest, but determined air, she said she must refuse. She rose to withdraw. 'Stay, too lovely Adeline!' said he, 'and if compassion for my sufferings will not interest you in my favour, allow a consideration of your own dangers to do so. Monsieur La Motte had informed me of your misfortunes, and of the evil that now threatens you; accept from me the protection which he cannot afford.'

Adeline continued to move towards the door, when the Marquis threw himself at her feet, and, seizing her hand, impressed it with kisses. She struggled to disengage herself. 'Hear me, charming Adeline! hear me,' cried the Marquis; 'I exist but for you. Listen to my entreaties and my fortune shall be yours. Do not drive me to despair by ill-judged rigour, or, because'—

'My Lord,' interrupted Adeline, with an air of ineffable dignity, and still affecting to believe his proposal honourable, 'I am sensible of the generosity of your conduct, and also flattered by the distinction you offer me. I will, therefore, say something more than is necessary to a bare expression of the denial which I must continue to give. *I can not* bestow my heart. *You can not* obtain more than my esteem, to which, indeed, nothing can so much contribute as a forbearance from any similar offers in future.'

She again attempted to go, but the Marquis prevented her, and, after some hesitation, again urged his suit, though in terms that would no longer allow her to misunderstand him. Tears swelled into her eyes, but she endeavoured to check them, and with a look, in which grief and indignation seemed to struggle for pre-eminence, she said, 'My Lord, this is unworthy of reply, let me pass.'

For a moment, he was awed by the dignity of her manner, and he threw himself at her feet to implore forgiveness. But she waved her hand in silence and hurried from the room. When she reached her chamber, she locked the door, and, sinking into a chair, yielded to the sorrow that pressed at her heart. And it was not the least of her sorrow, to suspect that La Motte was unworthy of her confidence; for it was almost impossible that he could be ignorant of the real designs of the Marquis. Madame La Motte, she believed, was imposed upon by a specious pretence of honourable attachment; and thus was she spared the pang which a doubt of her integrity would have added.

She threw a trembling glance upon the prospect around her. On one side was her father, whose cruelty had already been too plainly manifested; and on the other, the Marquis pursuing her with insult and vicious passion. She resolved to acquaint Madame La Motte with the purport of the late conversation, and, in the hope of her protection and sympathy, she wiped away her tears, and was leaving the room just as Madame La Motte entered it. While Adeline related what had passed, her friend wept, and appeared to suffer great agitation. She endeavoured to comfort her, and promised to use her influence in persuading La Motte to prohibit the addresses of the Marquis. 'You know, my dear,' added Madame, 'that our present circumstances oblige us to preserve terms with the Marquis, and you will, therefore, suffer as little resentment to appear in your manner towards him as possible; conduct yourself with your usual ease in his presence, and I doubt not this affair will pass over, without subjecting you to farther solicitation.'

'Ah, Madam!' said Adeline, 'how hard is the task you assign me! I entreat you that I may never more be subjected to the humiliation of being in his presence, that, whenever he visits the abbey, I may be suffered to remain in my chamber.'

'This,' said Madame La Motte, 'I would most readily consent to, would our situation permit it. But you well know our asylum in this abbey depends upon the good-will of the

Marquis, which we must not wantonly lose; and surely such a conduct as you propose would endanger this. Let us use milder measures, and we shall preserve his friendship, without subjecting you to any serious evil. Appear with your usual complacence: the task is not so difficult as you imagine.'

Adeline sighed. 'I obey you, Madam,' said she; 'it is my duty to do so; but I may be pardoned for saying—it is with extreme reluctance.' Madame La Motte promised to go immediately to her husband, and Adeline departed, though not convinced of her safety, yet somewhat more at ease.

She soon after saw the Marquis depart, and, as there now appeared to be no obstacle to the return of Madame La Motte, she expected her with extreme impatience. After thus waiting near an hour in her chamber, she was at length summoned to the parlour, and there found Monsieur La Motte alone. He arose upon her entrance, and for some minutes paced the room in silence. He then seated himself, and addressed her: 'What you have mentioned to Madame La Motte,' said he, 'would give me much concern, did I consider the behaviour of the Marquis in a light so serious as she does. I know that young ladies are apt to misconstrue the unmeaning gallantry of fashionable manners, and you, Adeline, can never be too cautious in distinguishing between a levity of this kind, and a more serious address.'

Adeline was surprized and offended that La Motte should think so lightly both of her understanding and disposition as his speech implied. 'Is it possible, Sir,' said she, 'that you have been apprized of the Marquis's conduct?'

'It is very possible, and very certain,' replied La Motte with some asperity; 'and very possible, also, that I may see this affair with a judgement less discoloured by prejudice than you do. But, however, I shall not dispute this point. I shall only request, that, since you are acquainted with the emergency of my circumstances, you will conform to them, and not, by an ill-timed resentment, expose me to the enmity of the Marquis. He is now my friend, and it is necessary to my safety that he should continue such; but if I suffer any part of my family to treat him with rudeness, I must expect to see him my enemy. You may surely treat him with complaisance.' Adeline thought the term *rudeness* a harsh one, as La Motte applied it, but she forebore from any expression of displeasure. 'I could have wished, Sir,' said she, 'for the privilege of retiring whenever the Marquis appeared; but since you believe this conduct would affect your interest, I ought to submit.'

'This prudence and good-will delight me,' said La Motte, 'and since you wish to serve me, know that you cannot more effectually do it, than by treating the Marquis as a friend.' The word *friend*, as it stood connected with the Marquis, sounded dissonantly to Adeline's ear; she hesitated and looked at La Motte. 'As *your* friend, Sir,' said she; 'I will endeavour to'—treat him as mine, she would have said, but she found it impossible to finish the sentence. She entreated his protection from the power of her father.

'What protection I can afford is your's,' said La Motte, 'but you know how destitute I am both of the right and the means of resisting him, and also how much I require protection myself. Since he has discovered your retreat, he is probably not ignorant of the circumstances which detain me here, and if I oppose him, he may betray me to the officers of the law, as the surest method of obtaining possession of you. We are encompassed with dangers,' continued La Motte; 'would I could see any method of extricating ourselves!'

'Quit this abbey,' said Adeline, 'and seek an asylum in Switzerland or Germany; you will then be freed from farther obligation to the Marquis and from the persecution you dread. Pardon me for thus offering advice, which is certainly, in some degree, prompted by a sense of my own safety, but which, at the same time, seems to afford the only means of ensuring your's.'

'Your plan is reasonable,' said La Motte, 'had I money to execute it. As it is I must be contented to remain here, as little known as possible, and defending myself by making those who know me my friends. Chiefly I must endeavour to preserve the favour of the Marquis. He may do much, should your father ever pursue desperate measures. But why do I talk thus? Your father may ere this have commenced these measures, and the effects of his vengeance may now be hanging over my head. My regard for you, Adeline, has exposed me to this; had I resigned you to his will, I should have remained secure.'

Adeline was so much affected by this instance of La Motte's kindness, which she could not doubt, that she was unable to express her sense of it. When she could speak, she uttered her gratitude in the most lively terms. 'Are you sincere in these expressions?' said La Motte.

'Is it possible I can be less than sincere?' replied Adeline, weeping at the idea of ingratitude.—'Sentiments are easily pronounced,' said La Motte, 'though they may have no connection with the heart; I believe them to be sincere so far only as they influence our actions.'

'What mean you, Sir?' said Adeline with surprize.

'I mean to inquire, whether, if an opportunity should ever offer of thus proving your gratitude, you would adhere to your sentiments?'

'Name one that I shall refuse,' said Adeline with energy.

'If, for instance, the Marquis should hereafter avow a serious passion for you, and offer you his hand, would no petty resentment, no lurking prepossession for some more happy lover prompt you to refuse it?'

Adeline blushed and fixed her eyes on the ground. 'You have, indeed, Sir, named the only means I should reject of evincing my sincerity. The Marquis I can never love, nor, to speak sincerely, ever esteem. I confess the peace of one's whole life is too much to sacrifice even to gratitude.'—La Motte looked displeased. ''Tis as I thought,' said he; 'these delicate sentiments make a fine appearance in speech, and render the person who utters them infinitely amiable; but bring them to the test of action, and they dissolve into air, leaving only the wreck of vanity behind.'

This unjust sarcasm brought tears to her eyes. 'Since your safety, Sir, depends upon my conduct,' said she, 'resign me to my father. I am willing to return to him, since my stay here must involve you in new misfortune. Let me not prove myself unworthy of the protection I have hitherto experienced, by preferring my own welfare to yours. When I am gone, you will have no reason to apprehend the Marquis's displeasure, which you may probably incur if I stay here: for I feel it impossible that I could even consent to receive his addresses, however honourable were his views.'

La Motte seemed hurt and alarmed. 'This must not be,' said he; 'let us not harrass ourselves by stating *possible* evils, and then, to avoid them, fly to those which are *certain*. No, Adeline, though you are ready to sacrifice yourself to my safety, I will not suffer you to do so. I will not yield you to your father, but upon compulsion. Be satisfied, therefore, upon this point. The only return I ask, is a civil deportment towards the Marquis.'

'I will endeavour to obey you, Sir,' said Adeline.—Madame La Motte now entered the room, and this conversation ceased. Adeline passed the evening in melancholy thoughts, and retired, as soon as possible, to her chamber, eager to seek in sleep a refuge from sorrow.

CHAPTER IX

'Full many a melancholy night
He watched the slow return of light,
And sought the powers of sleep;
To spread a momentary calm
O'er his sad couch, and in the balm
Of bland oblivion's dews his burning eyes to steep.'

WARTON*

THE MS. found by Adeline, the preceding night, had several times occurred to her recollection in the course of the day, but she had then been either too much interested by the events of the moment, or too apprehensive of interruption, to attempt a perusal of it. She now took it from the drawer in which it had been deposited, and, intending only to look cursorily over the few first pages, sat down with it by her bed-side.

She opened it with an eagerness of inquiry, which the discoloured and almost obliterated ink but slowly gratified. The first words on the page were entirely lost, but those that appeared to commence the narrative were as follows:

'O! ye, whoever ye are, whom chance, or misfortune, may

hereafter conduct to this spot—to ye I speak—to ye reveal the story of my wrongs, and ask ye to avenge them. Vain hope! yet it imparts some comfort to believe it possible that what I now write may one day meet the eye of a fellow creature; that the words, which tell my sufferings, may one day draw pity from the feeling heart.

'Yet stay your tears—your pity now is useless: long since have the pangs of misery ceased; the voice of complaining is passed away. It is weakness to wish for compassion which cannot be felt till I shall sink in the repose of death, and taste, I hope, the happiness of eternity!

'Know then, that on the night of the twelfth of October, in the year 1642, I was arrested on the road to Caux, and on the very spot where a column is erected to the memory of the immortal Henry,* by four ruffians, who, after disabling my servant, bore me through wilds and woods to this abbey. Their demeanour was not that of common banditti, and I soon perceived they were employed by a superior power to perpetrate some dreadful purpose. Entreaties and bribes were vainly offered them to discover their employer and abandon their design: they would not reveal even the least circumstance of their intentions.

'But when, after a long journey, they arrived at this edifice, their base employer was at once revealed, and his horrid scheme but too well understood. What a moment was that! All the thunders of Heaven seemed launched at this defence-less head! O fortitude! nerve my heart to'——

Adeline's light was now expiring in the socket, and the paleness of the ink, so feebly shone upon, baffled her efforts to discriminate the letters: it was impossible to procure a light from below, without discovering that she was yet up; a circumstance, which would excite surprize and lead to explanations, such as she did not wish to enter upon. Thus compelled to suspend the inquiry, which so many attendant circumstances had rendered awfully interesting, she retired to her humble bed.

What she had read of the MS. awakened a dreadful interest in the fate of the writer, and called up terrific images to her mind. 'In these apartments!'—said she, and she shuddered and closed her eyes. At length, she heard Madame La Motte enter her chamber, and the phantoms of fear beginning to dissipate, left her to repose.

In the morning, she was awakened by Madame La Motte, and found, to her disappointment, that she had slept so much beyond her usual time, as to be unable to renew the perusal of the MS.—La Motte appeared uncommonly gloomy, and Madame wore an air of melancholy, which Adeline attributed to the concern she felt for her. Breakfast was scarcely over, when the sound of horses feet announced the arrival of a stranger; and Adeline, from the oriel recess of the hall, saw the Marquis alight. She retreated with precipitation, and, forgetting the request of La Motte, was hastening to her chamber; but the Marquis was already in the hall, and seeing her leaving it, turned to La Motte with a look of inquiry. La Motte called her back, and by a frown too intelligent, reminded her of her promise. She summoned all her spirits to her aid, but advanced, notwithstanding, in visible emotion, while the Marquis addressed her as usual, the same easy gaiety playing upon his countenance and directing his manner.

Adeline was surprized and shocked at this careless confidence, which, however, by awakening her pride, communicated to her an air of dignity that abashed him. He spoke with hesitation, and frequently appeared abstracted from the subject of discourse. At length arising, he begged Adeline would favour him with a few moments conversation. Monsieur and Madame La Motte were now leaving the room, when Adeline, turning to the Marquis, told him, 'she would not hear any conversation, except in the presence of her friends.' But she said it in vain, for they were gone; and La Motte, as he withdrew, expressed by his looks how much an attempt to follow would displease him.

She sat for some time in silence, and trembling expectation. 'I am sensible,' said the Marquis at length, 'that the conduct to which the ardour of my passion lately betrayed me, has injured me in your opinion, and that you will not easily restore me to your esteem; but, I trust, the offer which I now make you, both of my *title* and fortune, will sufficiently prove the sincerity of my attachment, and atone for the transgression which love only prompted.'

After this specimen of common place verbosity, which the Marquis seemed to consider as a prelude to triumph, he attempted to impress a kiss upon the hand of Adeline, who, withdrawing it hastily, said, 'You are already, my Lord, acquainted with my sentiments upon this subject, and it is almost unnecessary for me now to repeat, that I cannot accept the honour you offer me.'

'Explain yourself, lovely Adeline! I am ignorant that till now, I ever made you this offer.'

'Most true, Sir,' said Adeline, 'and you do well to remind me of this, since, after having heard your former proposal, I cannot listen for a moment to any other.' She rose to quit the room. 'Stay, Madam,' said the Marquis, with a look, in which offended pride struggled to conceal itself; 'do not suffer an extravagant resentment to operate against your true interests; recollect the dangers that surround you, and consider the value of an offer, which may afford you at least an honourable asylum.'

'My misfortunes, my Lord, whatever they are, I have never obtruded upon you; you will therefore, excuse my observing, that your present mention of them conveys a much greater appearance of insult that compassion.' The Marquis, though with evident confusion, was going to reply; but Adeline would not be detained, and retired to her chamber. Destitute as she was, her heart revolted from the proposal of the Marquis, and she determined never to accept it. To her dislike of his general disposition, and the aversion excited by his late offer, was added, indeed, the influence of a prior attachment, and of a remembrance, which she found it impossible to erase from her heart.

The Marquis stayed to dine, and, in consideration of La Motte, Adeline appeared at table, where the former gazed upon her with such frequent and silent earnestness, that her distress became insupportable, and when the cloth was drawn, she instantly retired. Madame La Motte soon followed, and it was not till evening that she had an opportunity of returning to the MS. When Monsieur and Madame La Motte were in their chamber, and all was still, she drew forth the narrative, and, trimming her lamp, sat down to read as follows:

'The ruffians unbound me from my horse, and led me through the hall up the spiral staircase of the abbey: resistance was useless, but I looked around in the hope of seeing some person less obdurate than the men who brought me hither; some one who might be sensible to pity, and capable, at least, of civil treatment. I looked in vain; no person appeared: and this circumstance confirmed my worst apprehensions. The secrecy of the business foretold a horrible conclusion. Having passed some chambers, they stopped in one hung with old tapestry. I inquired why we did not go on, and was told, I should soon know.

'At that moment, I expected to see the instrument of death uplifted, and silently recommended myself to God. But death was not then designed for me; they raised the arras, and discovered a door, which they then opened. Seizing my arms, they led me through a suite of dismal chambers beyond. Having reached the farthest of these, they again stopped: the horrid gloom of the place seemed congenial to murder, and inspired deadly thoughts. Again I looked round for the instrument of destruction, and again I was respited. I supplicated to know what was designed me; it was now unnecessary to ask who was the author of the design. They were silent to my question, but at length told me, this chamber was my prison. Having said this, and set down a jug of water, they left the room, and I heard the door barred upon me.

'O sound of despair! O moment of unutterable anguish! The pang of death itself is, surely, not superior to that I then suffered. Shut out from day, from friends, from life—*for such I must foretell it*—in the prime of my years, in the height of my transgressions, and left to imagine horrors more terrible than any, perhaps, which certainty could give*—I sink beneath the'—

Here several pages of the manuscript were decayed with damp and totally illegible. With much difficulty Adeline made out the following lines:

'Three days have now passed in solitude and silence: the

horrors of death are ever before my eyes, let me endeavour to
prepare for the dreadful change! When I awake in the morning
I think I shall not live to see another night; and, when night
returns, that I must never more unclose my eyes on morning.
Why am I brought hither—why confined thus rigorously—but
for death! Yet what action of my life has deserved this at the
hand of a fellow creature?—Of——   *   *   *   *

*   *   *   *   *   *   *   *   *
*   *   *   *   *   *   *   *   *

'O my children! O friends far distant! I shall never see you
more—never more receive the parting look of kindness—never
bestow a parting blessing!—Ye know not my wretched state—
alas! ye cannot know it by human means. Ye believe me
happy, or ye would fly to my relief. I know that what I now
write cannot avail me, yet there is comfort in pouring forth my
griefs; and I bless that man, less savage than his fellows, who
has supplied me these means of recording them. Alas! he
knows full well, that from this indulgence he has nothing to
fear. My pen can call no friends to succour me, nor reveal my
danger ere it is too late. O! ye, who may hereafter read what
I now write, give a tear to my sufferings: I have wept often
for the distresses of my fellow creatures!'

Adeline paused. Here the wretched writer appealed directly
to her heart; he spoke in the energy of truth, and, by a strong
illusion of fancy, it seemed as if his past sufferings were at this
moment present. She was for some time unable to proceed,
and sat in musing sorrow. 'In these very apartments,' said she,
'this poor sufferer was confined—here he'—Adeline started,
and thought she heard a sound; but the stillness of night was
undisturbed.—'In these very chambers,' said she, 'these lines
were written—these lines, from which he then derived a
comfort in believing they would hereafter be read by some
pitying eye: this time is now come. Your miseries, O injured
being! are lamented, where they were endured. *Here*, where
you suffered, I weep for your sufferings!'

Her imagination was now strongly impressed, and to her
distempered senses the suggestions of a bewildered mind
appeared with the force of reality. Again she started and
listened, and thought she heard '*Here*' distinctly repeated by

a whisper immediately behind her. The terror of the thought, however, was but momentary, she knew it could not be; convinced that her fancy had deceived her, she took up the MS. and again began to read.

'For what am I reserved! Why this delay? If I am to die—why not quickly? Three weeks have I now passed within these walls, during which time, no look of pity has softened my afflictions; no voice, save my own, has met my ear. The countenances of the ruffians who attend me, are stern and inflexible, and their silence is obstinate. This stillness is dreadful! O! ye, who have known what it is to live in the depths of solitude, who have passed your dreary days without one sound to cheer you; ye, and ye only, can tell what now I feel; and ye may know how much I would endure to hear the accents of a human voice.

'O dire extremity! O state of living death! What dreadful stillness! All around me is dead; and do I really exist, or am I but a statue? Is this a vision? Are these things real? Alas, I am bewildered!—this deathlike and perpetual silence—this dismal chamber—the dread of farther sufferings have disturbed my fancy. O for some friendly breast to lay my weary head on! some cordial accents to revive my soul! *

* * * * * * * * *

* * * * * * * * *

* 'I write by stealth. He who furnished me with the means, I fear, has suffered for some symptoms of pity he may have discovered for me; I have not seen him for several days: perhaps he is inclined to help me, and for that reason is forbid to come. O that hope! but how vain. Never more must I quit these walls while life remains. Another day is gone, and yet I live; at this time to-morrow night my sufferings may be sealed in death. I will continue my journal nightly, till the hand that writes shall be stopped by death: when the journal ceases, the reader will know I am no more. Perhaps, these are the last lines I shall ever write'   *   *   *   *

* * * * * * * * *

* * * * * * * * *

Adeline paused, while her tears fell fast. 'Unhappy man!' she exclaimed, 'and was there no pitying soul to save thee!

Great God! thy ways are wonderful!' While she sat musing, her fancy, which now wandered in the regions of terror, gradually subdued reason. There was a glass before her upon the table, and she feared to raise her looks towards it, lest some other face than her own should meet her eyes: other dreadful ideas, and strange images of fantastic thought now crossed her mind.

A hollow sigh seemed to pass near her. 'Holy Virgin, protect me!' cried she, and threw a fearful glance round the room; 'this is surely something more than fancy.' Her fears so far overcame her, that she was several times upon the point of calling up part of the family, but unwillingness to disturb them, and a dread of ridicule, withheld her. She was also afraid to move and almost to breathe. As she listened to the wind, that murmured at the casements of her lonely chamber, she again thought she heard a sigh. Her imagination refused any longer the controul of reason, and, turning her eyes, a figure, whose exact form she could not distinguish, appeared to pass along an obscure part of the chamber: a dreadful chillness came over her, and she sat fixed in her chair. At length a deep sigh somewhat relieved her oppressed spirits, and her senses seemed to return

All remaining quiet, after some time she began to question whether her fancy had not deceived her, and she so far conquered her terror as to desist from calling Madame La Motte: her mind was, however, so much disturbed, that she did not venture to trust herself that night again with the MS.; but, having spent some time in prayer, and in endeavouring to compose her spirits, she retired to bed.

When she awoke in the morning, the cheerful sun-beams played upon the casements, and dispelled the illusions of darkness: her mind, soothed and invigorated by sleep, rejected the mystic and turbulent promptings of imagination. She arose refreshed and thankful; but, upon going down to breakfast, this transient gleam of peace fled upon the appearance of the Marquis, whose frequent visits at the abbey, after what had passed, not only displeased, but alarmed her. She saw that he was determined to persevere in addressing her, and the boldness and insensibility of this conduct, while it excited her indignation, increased her disgust. In pity to La Motte, she endeavoured to conceal these emotions, though she now thought that he required too much from her complaisance, and began seriously to consider how she might avoid the necessity of continuing it. The Marquis behaved to her with the most respectful attention; but Adeline was silent and reserved, and seized the first opportunity of withdrawing.

As she passed up the spiral staircase, Peter entered the hall below, and, seeing Adeline, he stopped and looked earnestly at her: she did not observe him, but he called her softly, and she then saw him make a signal as if he had something to communicate. In the next instant La Motte opened the door of the vaulted room, and Peter hastily disappeared. She proceeded to her chamber, ruminating upon this signal, and the cautious manner in which Peter had given it.

But her thoughts soon returned to their wonted subjects. Three days were now passed, and she heard no intelligence of her father; she began to hope that he had relented from the violent measures hinted at by La Motte, and that he meant to pursue a milder plan: but when she considered his character, this appeared improbable, and she relapsed into her former fears. Her residence at the abbey was now become painful, from the perseverance of the Marquis, and the conduct which La Motte obliged her to adopt; yet she could not think without dread of quitting it to return to her father.

The image of Theodore often intruded upon her busy thoughts, and brought with it a pang, which his strange departure occasioned. She had a confused notion, that his fate was somehow connected with her own; and her struggles to prevent the remembrance of him, served only to shew how much her heart was his.

To divert her thoughts from these subjects, and gratify the curiosity so strongly excited on the preceding night, she now took up the MS. but was hindered from opening it by the entrance of Madame La Motte, who came to tell her the Marquis was gone. They passed their morning together in work and general conversation; La Motte not appearing till dinner, when he said little, and Adeline less. She asked him, however, if he had heard from her father? 'I have not heard from him,' said La Motte; 'but there is good reason, as I am informed by the Marquis, to believe he is not far off.'

Adeline was shocked, yet she was able to reply with becoming firmness. 'I have already, Sir, involved you too much in my distress, and now see that resistance will destroy you, without serving me; I am, therefore, contented to return to my father, and thus spare you farther calamity.'

'This is a rash determination,' replied La Motte, 'and if you pursue it, I fear you will severely repent. I speak to you as a friend, Adeline, and desire you will endeavour to listen to me without prejudice. The Marquis, I find, has offered you his hand. I know not which circumstance most excites my surprize, that a man of his rank and consequence should solicit a marriage with a person without fortune, or ostensible connections; or that a person so circumstanced should even for a moment reject the advantages thus offered her. You weep, Adeline, let me hope that you are convinced of the absurdity of this conduct, and will no longer trifle with your good fortune. The kindness I have shewn you must convince you of my regard, and that I have no motive for offering you this advice but your advantage. It is necessary, however, to say, that, should your father not insist upon your removal, I know not how long my circumstances may enable me to afford even the humble pittance you receive here. Still you are silent.'

The anguish which this speech excited, suppressed her utterance, and she continued to weep. At length she said, 'Suffer me, Sir, to go back to my father; I should, indeed, make an ill return for the kindness you mention, could I wish to stay, after what you now tell me; and to accept the Marquis, I feel to be impossible.' The remembrance of Theodore arose to her mind, and she wept aloud.

La Motte sat for some time musing. 'Strange infatuation,' said he; 'is it possible that you can persist in this heroism of romance, and prefer a father so inhuman as yours, to the Marquis de Montalt! A destiny so full of danger to a life of splendour and delight!'

'Pardon me,' said Adeline, 'a marriage with the Marquis would be splendid, but never happy. His character excites my aversion, and I entreat, Sir, that he may no more be mentioned.'

CHAPTER X

'Nor are those empty hearted, whose low sound
Reverbs no hollowness.'   LEAR*

THE conversation related in the last chapter was interrupted
by the entrance of Peter, who, as he left the room, looked
significantly at Adeline and almost beckoned. She was anxious
to know what he meant, and soon after went into the hall,
where she found him loitering. The moment he saw her, he
made a sign of silence and beckoned her into the recess. 'Well,
Peter, what is it you would say?' said Adeline.

'Hush, Ma'mselle; for Heaven's sake speak lower: if we
should be overheard, we are all blown up.'* Adeline begged
him to explain what he meant. 'Yes, Ma'mselle, that is what
I have wanted all day long. I have watched and watched for
an opportunity, and looked and looked, till I was afraid my
master himself would see me: but all would not do; you would
not understand.'

Adeline entreated he would be quick. 'Yes, Ma'am, but I'm
so afraid we shall be seen; but I would do much to serve such
a good young lady, for I could not bear to think of what
threatened you, without telling you of it.'

'For God's sake,' said Adeline, 'speak quickly, or we shall
be interrupted.'

'Well, then; but you must first promise by the Holy Virgin
never to say it was I that told you. My master would'—

'I do, I do!' said Adeline.

'Well, then—on Monday evening as I—hark! did not I hear
a step? do, Ma'mselle, just step this way to the cloisters. I
would not for the world we should be seen. I'll go out at the
hall door and you can go through the passage. I would not for
the world we should be seen.'—Adeline was much alarmed by
Peter's words, and hurried to the cloisters. He quickly

appeared, and, looking cautiously round, resumed his discourse. 'As I was saying, Ma'mselle, Monday night, when the Marquis slept here, you know he sat up very late, and I can guess, perhaps, the reason of that. Strange things came out, but it is not my business to tell all I think.'

'Pray do speak to the purpose,' said Adeline impatiently, 'what is this danger which you say threatens me? Be quick, or we shall be observed.'

'Danger enough, Ma'mselle,' replied Peter, 'if you knew all, and when you do, what will it signify, for you can't help yourself. But that's neither here nor there: I was resolved to tell you, though I may repent it.'

'Or rather you are resolved not to tell me,' said Adeline; 'for you have made no progress towards it. But what do you mean? You was speaking of the Marquis.'

'Hush, Ma'am, not so loud. The Marquis, as I said, sat up very late and my master sat up with him. One of his men went to bed in the oak room, and the other stayed to undress his Lord. So as we were sitting together—Lord have mercy! it made my hair stand on end! I tremble yet. So as we were sitting together,—but as sure as I live yonder is my master: I caught a glimpse of him between the trees, if he sees me it is all over with us. I'll tell you another time.' So saying, he hurried into the abbey, leaving Adeline in a state of alarm, curiosity, and vexation. She walked out into the forest, ruminating upon Peter's words, and endeavouring to guess to what they alluded; there Madame La Motte joined her, and they conversed on various topics till they reached the abbey.

Adeline watched in vain through that day for an opportunity of speaking with Peter. While he waited at supper, she occasionally observed his countenance with great anxiety, hoping it might afford her some degree of intelligence on the subject of her fears. When she retired, Madame La Motte accompanied her to her chamber, and continued to converse with her for a considerable time, so that she had no means of obtaining an interview with Peter.—Madame La Motte appeared to labour under some great affliction, and when Adeline, noticing this, entreated to know the cause of her dejection, tears started into her eyes, and she abruptly left the room.

This behaviour of Madame La Motte concurred with Peter's discourse, to alarm Adeline, who sat pensively upon her bed, given up to reflection, till she was roused by the sound of a clock which stood in the room below, and which now struck twelve. She was preparing for rest, when she recollected the MS. and was unable to conclude the night without reading it. The first words she could distinguish were the following:

'Again I return to this poor consolation—again I have been permitted to see another day. It is now midnight! My solitary lamp burns beside me; the time is awful, but to me the silence of noon is as the silence of midnight: a deeper gloom is all in which they differ. The still, unvarying hours are numbered only by my sufferings! Great God! when shall I be released!

*　　*　　*　　*　　*　　*　　*　　*　　*

*　　*　　*　　*　　*　　*　　*　　*　　*

'But whence this strange confinement? I have never injured him. If death is designed me, why this delay; and for what but death am I brought hither? This abbey—alas!'—Here the MS. was again illegible, and for several pages Adeline could only make out disjointed sentences.

'O bitter draught! when, when shall I have rest! O my friends! will none of ye fly to aid me; will none of ye avenge my sufferings? Ah! when it is too late—when I am gone for ever, ye will endeavour to avenge them. *　　*　　*

*　　*　　*　　*　　*　　*　　*　　*　　*

*　　*　　*　　*　　*　　*　　*　　*　　*

'Once more is night returned to me. Another day has passed in solitude and misery. I have climbed to the casement, thinking the view of nature would refresh my soul, and somewhat enable me to support these afflictions. Alas! even this small comfort is denied me, the windows open towards other parts of this abbey, and admit only a portion of that day which I must never more fully behold. Last night! last night! O scene of horror!'

*　　*　　*　　*　　*　　*　　*　　*　　*

*　　*　　*　　*　　*　　*　　*　　*　　*

Adeline shuddered. She feared to read the coming sentence, yet curiosity prompted her to proceed. Still she paused: an unaccountable dread came over her. 'Some horrid deed has been done here,' said she; 'the reports of the peasants are true. Murder has been committed.' The idea thrilled her with horror. She recollected the dagger which had impeded her steps in the secret chamber, and this circumstance served to confirm her most terrible conjectures. She wished to examine it, but it lay in one of these chambers, and she feared to go in quest of it.

'Wretched, wretched victim!' she exclaimed, 'could no friend rescue thee from destruction! O that I had been near! yet what could I have done to save thee? Alas! nothing. I forget that even now, perhaps, I am like thee abandoned to dangers, from which I have no friend to succour me. Too surely I guess the author of my miseries!' she stopped, and thought she heard a sigh, such as, on the preceding night, had passed along the chamber. Her blood was chilled and she sat motionless. The lonely situation of her room, remote from the rest of the family, (for she was now in her old apartment, from which Madame La Motte had removed) who were almost beyond call, struck so forcibly upon her imagination, that she with difficulty preserved herself from fainting. She sat for a considerable time, but all was still. When she was somewhat recovered, her first design was to alarm the family; but farther reflection again withheld her.

She endeavoured to compose her spirits, and addressed a short prayer to that Being who had hitherto protected her in every danger. While she was thus employed, her mind gradually became elevated and re-assured; a sublime complacency filled her heart, and she sat down once more to pursue the narrative.

Several lines that immediately followed were obliterated.—

*   *   *   *   *   *   *   *   *

*   * 'He had told me I should not be permitted to live long, not more than three days, and bade me chuse whether I would die by poison or the sword. O the agonies of that moment! Great God! thou seest my sufferings! I often viewed, with a momentary hope of escaping, the high grated windows of my prison—all things within the compass of possibility I was resolved to try, and with an eager desperation I climbed

towards the casements, but my foot slipped, and falling back to the floor, I was stunned by the blow. On recovering, the first sounds I heard were the steps of a person entering my prison. A recollection of the past returned, and deplorable was my condition. I shuddered at what was to come. The same man approached; he looked at me at first with pity, but his countenance soon recovered its natural ferocity. Yet he did not then come to execute the purposes of his employer: I am reserved to another day—Great God, thy will be done!'

Adeline could not go on. All the circumstances that seemed to corroborate the fate of this unhappy man, crowded upon her mind. The reports concerning the abbey—the dreams, which had forerun her discovery of the private apartments— the singular manner in which she had found the MS. and the apparition, which she now believed she had really seen. She blamed herself for having not yet mentioned the discovery of the manuscript and chambers to La Motte, and resolved to delay the disclosure no longer than the following morning. The immediate cares that had occupied her mind, and a fear of losing the manuscript before she had read it, had hitherto kept her silent.

Such a combination of circumstances she believed could only be produced by some supernatural power, operating for the retribution of the guilty. These reflections filled her mind with a degree of awe, which the loneliness of the large old chamber in which she sat, and the hour of the night, soon heightened into terror. She had never been superstitious, but circumstances so uncommon had hitherto conspired in this affair, that she could not believe them accidental. Her imagination, wrought upon by these reflections, again became sensible to every impression, she feared to look round, lest she should again see some dreadful phantom, and she almost fancied she heard voices swell in the storm, which now shook the fabric.

Still she tried to command her feelings so as to avoid disturbing the family, but they became so painful, that even the dread of La Motte's ridicule had hardly power to prevent her quitting the chamber. Her mind was now in such a state, that she found it impossible to pursue the story in the MS.

though, to avoid the tortures of suspense, she had attempted it. She laid it down again, and tried to argue herself into composure. 'What have I to fear?' said she, 'I am at least innocent, and I shall not be punished for the crime of another.'

The violent gust of wind that now rushed through the whole suite of apartments, shook the door that led from her late bedchamber to the private rooms so forcibly, that Adeline, unable to remain longer in doubt, ran to see from whence the noise issued. The arras, which concealed the door, was violently agitated, and she stood for a moment observing it in indescribable terror, till believing it was swayed by the wind, she made a sudden effort to overcome her feelings, and was stooping to raise it. At that instant, she thought she heard a voice. She stopped and listened, but every thing was still; yet apprehension so far overcame her, that she had no power, either to examine, or to leave the chambers.

In a few moments the voice returned, she was now convinced she had not been deceived, for, though low, she heard it distinctly, and was almost sure it repeated her own name. So much was her fancy affected, that she even thought it was the same voice she had heard in her dreams. This conviction entirely subdued the small remains of her courage, and, sinking into a chair, she lost all recollection.

How long she remained in this state she knew not, but when she recovered, she exerted all her strength, and reached the winding staircase, where she called aloud. No one heard her, and she hastened, as fast as her feebleness would permit, to the chamber of Madame La Motte. She tapped gently at the door, and was answered by Madame, who was alarmed at being awakened at so unusual an hour, and believed that some danger threatened her husband. When she understood that it was Adeline, and that she was unwell, she quickly came to her relief. The terror that was yet visible in Adeline's countenance excited her inquiries, and the occasion of it was explained to her.

Madame was so much discomposed by the relation that she called La Motte from his bed, who, more angry at being disturbed than interested for the agitation he witnessed, reproved Adeline for suffering her fancies to overcome her reason. She now mentioned the discovery she had made of the inner chambers and the manuscript, circumstances, which roused the attention of La Motte so much, that he desired to see the MS. and resolved to go immediately to the apartments described by Adeline.

Madame La Motte endeavoured to dissuade him from his purpose; but La Motte, with whom opposition had always an effect contrary to the one designed, and who wished to throw farther ridicule upon the terrors of Adeline, persisted in his intention. He called to Peter to attend with a light, and insisted that Madame La Motte and Adeline should accompany him; Madame La Motte desired to be excused, and Adeline, at first, declared she could not go; but he would be obeyed.

They ascended the tower, and entered the first chambers together, for each of the party was reluctant to be the last; in the second chamber all was quiet and in order. Adeline presented the MS. and pointed to the arras which concealed the door: La Motte lifted the arras, and opened the door; but Madame La Motte and Adeline entreated to go no farther—again he called to them to follow. All was quiet in the first chamber; he expressed his surprise that the rooms should so long have remained undiscovered, and was proceeding to the second, but suddenly stopped. 'We will defer our examination till to-morrow,' said he, 'the damps of these apartments are unwholesome at any time; but they strike one more sensibly at night. I am chilled. Peter, remember to throw open the windows early in the morning, that the air may circulate.'

'Lord bless your honour,' said Peter, 'don't you see, I can't reach them? Besides, I don't believe they are made to open; see what strong iron bars there are; the room looks, for all the world, like a prison; I suppose this is the place the people meant, when they said, nobody that had been in ever came out.' La Motte, who, during this speech, had been looking attentively at the high windows, which, if he had seen them at first, he had certainly not observed; now interrupted the eloquence of Peter, and bade him carry the light before them. They all willingly quitted these chambers, and returned to the room below, where a fire was lighted, and the party remained together for some time.

La Motte, for reasons best known to himself, attempted to ridicule the discovery and fears of Adeline, till she, with a seriousness that checked him, entreated he would desist. He was silent, and soon after, Adeline, encouraged by the return of day-light, ventured to her chamber, and, for some hours, experienced the blessing of undisturbed repose.

On the following day, Adeline's first care was to obtain an interview with Peter, whom she had some hopes of seeing as she went down stairs; he, however, did not appear, and she proceeded to the sitting room, where she found La Motte, apparently much disturbed. Adeline asked him if he had looked at the MS. 'I have run my eye over it,' said he, 'but it is so much obscured by time that it can scarcely be decyphered. It appears to exhibit a strange romantic story; and I do not wonder, that after you had suffered its terrors to impress your imagination, you fancied you saw spectres, and heard wondrous noises.'

Adeline thought La Motte did not chuse to be convinced, and she, therefore, forbore reply. During breakfast, she often looked at Peter, (who waited) with anxious inquiry; and, from his countenance, was still more assured, that he had something of importance to communicate. In the hope of some conversation with him, she left the room as soon as possible, and repaired to her favourite avenue, where she had not long remained when he appeared. 'God bless you! Ma'amselle,' said he, 'I'm sorry I frighted you so last night.'

'Frighted me,' said Adeline; 'how was you concerned in that?'

He then informed her, that when he thought Monsieur and Madame La Motte were asleep, he had stole to her chamber door, with an intention of giving her the sequel of what he had begun in the morning; that he had called several times as loudly as he dared, but receiving no answer, he believed she was asleep, or did not chuse to speak with him, and he had, therefore, left the door. This account of the voice she had heard relieved Adeline's spirits;* she was even surprised that she did not know it, till remembering the perturbation of her mind for some time preceding, this surprise disappeared.

She entreated Peter to be brief in explaining the danger with which she was threatened. 'If you'll let me go on my own way, Ma'am, you'll soon know it; but if you hurry me, and ask me questions, here and there, out of their places, I don't know what I am saying.'

'Be it so;' said Adeline, 'only remember that we may be observed.'

'Yes, Ma'amselle, I'm as much afraid of that as you are, for I believe I should be almost as ill off; however, that is neither here nor there, but I'm sure, if you stay in this old abbey another night, it will be worse for you; for, as I said before, I know all about it.'

'What mean you, Peter?'

'Why, about this scheme that's going on.'

'What, then, is my father?'——'Your father,' interrupted Peter; 'Lord bless you, that is all fudge,* to frighten you; your father, *nor nobody* else has ever sent after you; I dare say, he knows no more of you than the Pope does—not he.' Adeline looked displeased. 'You trifle,' said she, 'if you have any thing to tell, say it quickly; I am in haste.'

'Bless you, young Lady, I meant no harm, I hope you're not angry; but I'm sure you can't deny that your father is cruel. But, as I was saying, the Marquis de Montalt likes you; and he and my master (Peter looked round) have been laying their heads together about you.' Adeline turned pale—she comprehended a part of the truth, and eagerly entreated him to proceed.

'They have been laying their heads together about you. This is what Jacques, the Marquis's man, tells me: Says he, Peter, you little know what is going on—I could tell all if I chose it, but it is not for those who are trusted to tell again. I warrant now your master is close enough with you. Upon which I was piqued, and resolved to make him believe I could be trusted as well as he. Perhaps not, says I, perhaps I know as much as you, though I do not chuse to brag on't; and I winked.—Do you so? says he, then you are closer than I thought for. She is a fine girl, says he, meaning you, Ma'amselle; but she is

nothing but a poor foundling after all—so it does not much
signify. I had a mind to know farther what he meant—so I
did not knock him down. By seeming to know as much as he,
I at last made him discover all, and he told me—but you look
pale, Ma'amselle, are you ill?'

'No,' said Adeline, in a tremulous accent, and scarcely able
to support herself, 'pray proceed.'

'And he told me, that the Marquis had been courting you
a good while, but you would not listen to him, and had even
pretended he would marry you, and all would not do. As for
marriage, says I, I suppose she knows the Marchioness is
alive; and I'm sure she is not one for his turn upon other
terms.'

'The Marchioness is really living then!' said Adeline.

'O yes, Ma'amselle! we all know that, and I thought you had
known it too.'—'We shall see that, replies Jacques; at least, I
believe, that our master will outwit her.'—I stared; I could not
help it.—'Aye, says he, you know your master has agreed to
give her up to my Lord.'

'Good God! what will become of me?' exclaimed Adeline.

'Aye, Ma'amselle, I am sorry for you; but hear me out.
When Jacques said this, I quite forgot myself. I'll never
believe it, said I; I'll never believe my master would be guilty
of such a base action: he'll not give her up, or I'm no
Christian.'—'Oh! said Jacques, for that matter, I thought
you'd known all, else I should not have said a word about it.
However, you may soon satisfy yourself by going to the
parlour door, as I have done; they're in consultation about it
now, I dare say.'

'You need not repeat any more of this conversation,' said
Adeline; 'but tell me the result of what you heard from the
parlour.'

'Why, Ma'amselle, when he said this, I took him at his word
and went to the door, where, sure enough, I heard my master
and the Marquis talking about you. They said a great deal,
which I could make nothing of; but, at last, I heard the
Marquis say, You know the terms; on these terms only will
I consent to bury the past in ob---ob---oblivion——that was the
word. Monsieur La Motte then told the Marquis, if he would

return to the abbey upon such a night, meaning this very
night, Ma'amselle, every thing should be prepared according
to his wishes; Adeline shall then be yours, my Lord, said
he,—you are already acquainted with her chamber.'

At these words, Adeline clasped her hands and raised her
eyes to Heaven in silent despair.—Peter went on. 'When I
heard this, I could not doubt what Jacques had said.—'Well,
said he, what do you think of it now?'—'Why, that my
master's a rascal, says I.'—'It's well you don't think mine one
too, says he.'—'Why, as for that matter, says I'——Adeline, interrupting him, inquired if he had heard any thing farther.
'Just then,' said Peter, 'we heard Madame La Motte come out
from another room, and so we made haste back to the kitchen.'

'She was not present at this conversation then?' said
Adeline. 'No, Ma'amselle, but my master has told her of it,
I warrant.' Adeline was almost as much shocked by this
apparent perfidy of Madame La Motte, as by a knowledge of
the destruction that threatened her. After musing a few
moments in extreme agitation, 'Peter,' said she, 'you have a
good heart, and feel a just indignation at your master's
treachery—will you assist me to escape?'

'Ah, Ma'amselle! said he, 'how can I assist you; besides,
where can we go? I have no friends about here, no more than
yourself.'

'O!' replied Adeline, in extreme emotion, 'we fly from
enemies; strangers may prove friends: assist me but to escape
from this forest, and you will claim my eternal gratitude: I
have no fears beyond it.'

'Why, as for this forest,' replied Peter, 'I am weary of it
myself; though, when we first came, I thought it would be fine
living here, at least, I thought it was very different from any
life I had ever lived before. But these ghosts that haunt the
abbey, I am no more a coward than other men, but I don't like
them; and then there *is* so many strange reports abroad; and
my master—I thought I could have served him to the end of
the world, but now I care not how soon I leave him, for his
behaviour to you, Ma'amselle.'

'You consent, then, to assist me in escaping?' said Adeline
with eagerness.

'Why as to that, Ma'amselle, I would willingly if I knew where to go. To be sure, I have a sister lives in Savoy, but that is a great way off: and I have saved a little money out of my wages, but that won't carry us such a long journey.'

'Regard not that,' said Adeline, 'if I was once beyond this forest, I would then endeavour to take care of myself, and repay you for your kindness.'

'O! as for that, Madam'——'Well, well, Peter, let us consider how we may escape. This night, say you, this night—the Marquis is to return?'

'Yes, Ma'amselle, to-night, about dark. I have just thought of a scheme: My master's horses are grazing in the forest, we may take one of them, and send it back from the first stage; but how shall we avoid being seen? besides, if we go off in the day-light, he will soon pursue and overtake us; and if you stay till night, the Marquis will be come, and then there is no chance. If they miss us both at the same time too, they'll guess how it is, and set off directly. Could not you contrive to go first and wait for me till the hurly-burly's over? Then, while they're searching in the place under ground for you, I can slip away, and we should be out of their reach, before they thought of pursuing us.'

Adeline agreed to the truth of all this, and was somewhat surprized at Peter's sagacity. She inquired if he knew of any place in the neighbourhood of the abbey, where she could remain concealed till he came with a horse. 'Why yes, Madam, there is a place, now I think of it, where you may be safe enough, for nobody goes near: but they say it's haunted, and, perhaps, you would not like to go there.' Adeline, remembering the last night, was somewhat startled at this intelligence; but a sense of her present danger pressed again upon her mind, and overcame every other apprehension. 'Where is this place?' said she, 'if it will conceal me, I shall not hesitate to go.'

'It is an old tomb that stands in the thickest part of the forest about a quarter of a mile off the nearest way, and almost a mile the other. When my master used to hide himself so much in the forest, I have followed him somewhere thereabouts, but I did not find out the tomb till t'other day. However, that's neither here nor there; if you dare venture it, Ma'amselle, I'll shew you the nearest way.' So saying, he pointed to a winding path on the right. Adeline, having looked round, without perceiving any person near, directed Peter to lead her to the tomb: they pursued the path, till turning into a gloomy romantic part of the forest, almost impervious to the rays of the sun, they came to the spot whither Louis had formerly traced his father.

The stillness and solemnity of the scene struck awe upon the heart of Adeline, who paused and surveyed it for some time in silence. At length, Peter led her into the interior part of the ruin, to which they descended by several steps. 'Some old Abbot,' said he, 'was formerly buried here, as the Marquis's people say; and it's like enough that he belonged to the abbey yonder. But I don't see why he should take it in his head to walk; *he* was not murdered, surely?'

'I hope not,' said Adeline.

'That's more than can be said for all that lies buried at the abbey though, and'——Adeline interrupted him; 'Hark! surely, I hear a noise;' said she, 'Heaven protect us from discovery!' They listened, but all was still, and they went on. Peter opened a low door, and they entered upon a dark passage, frequently obstructed by loose fragments of stone, and along which they moved with caution. 'Whither are we going!' said Adeline—'I scarcely know myself,' said Peter, 'for I never was so far before; but the place seems quiet enough.' Something obstructed his way; it was a door, which yielded to his hand, and discovered a kind of cell, obscurely seen by the twilight admitted through a grate above. A partial gleam shot athwart the place, leaving the greatest part of it in shadow.

Adeline sighed as she surveyed it. 'This is a frightful spot,' said she, 'but if it will afford me a shelter, it is a palace. Remember, Peter, that my peace and honour depend upon your faithfulness; be both discrete and resolute. In the dusk of the evening I can pass from the abbey with least danger of being observed, and in this cell I will wait your arrival. As soon as Monsieur and Madame La Motte are engaged in searching the vaults, you will bring here a horse; three knocks upon the tomb shall inform me of your arrival. For Heaven's sake be cautious, and be punctual.'

'I will, Ma'amselle, let come what may.'

They re-ascended to the forest, and Adeline, fearful of observation, directed Peter to run first to the abbey, and invent some excuse for his absence, if he had been missed. When she was again alone, she yielded to a flood of tears, and indulged the excess of her distress. She saw herself without friends, without relations, destitute, forlorn, and abandoned to the worst of evils. Betrayed by the very persons, to whose comfort she had so long administered, whom she had loved as her protectors, and revered as her parents! These reflections touched her heart with the most afflicting sensations, and the sense of her immediate danger was for a while absorbed in the grief occasioned by a discovery of such guilt in others.

At length she roused all her fortitude, and turning towards the abbey, endeavoured to await with patience the hour of evening, and to sustain an appearance of composure in the presence of Monsieur and Madame La Motte. For the present she wished to avoid seeing either of them, doubting her ability to disguise her emotions: having reached the abbey, she, therefore, passed on to her chamber. Here she endeavoured to direct her attention to indifferent subjects, but in vain; the danger of her situation, and the severe disappointment she had received, in the character of those whom she had so much esteemed, and even loved, pressed hard upon her thoughts. To a generous mind few circumstances are more afflicting than a discovery of perfidy in those whom we have trusted, even though it may fail of any absolute inconvenience to ourselves. The behaviour of Madame La Motte in thus, by concealment, conspiring to her destruction, particularly shocked her.

'How had my imagination deceived me!' said she; 'what a picture did it draw of the goodness of the world! And must I then believe that every body is cruel and deceitful? No—let me still be deceived, and still suffer, rather than be condemned to a state of such wretched suspicion.' She now endeavoured to extenuate the conduct of Madame La Motte, by attributing it to a fear of her husband. 'She dare not oppose his will,' said she, 'else she would warn me of my danger, and assist me to escape from it. No—I will never believe her capable of conspiring my ruin. Terror alone keeps her silent.'

Adeline was somewhat comforted by this thought. The benevolence of her heart taught her, in this instance, to sophisticate. She perceived not, that by ascribing the conduct of Madame La Motte to terror, she only softened the degree of her guilt, imputing it to a motive less depraved, but not less selfish. She remained in her chamber till summoned to dinner, when, drying her tears, she descended with faltering steps and a palpitating heart to the parlour. When she saw La Motte, in spite of all her efforts, she trembled and grew pale: she could not behold, even with apparent indifference, the man who she knew had destined her to destruction. He observed her emotion, and inquiring if she was ill, she saw the danger to which her agitation exposed her. Fearful lest La Motte should suspect its true cause, she rallied all her spirits, and, with a look of complacency, answered she was well.

During dinner she preserved a degree of composure, that effectually concealed the varied anguish of her heart. When she looked at La Motte, terror and indignation were her predominant feelings; but when she regarded Madame La Motte, it was otherwise; gratitude for her former tenderness had long been confirmed into affection, and her heart now swelled with the bitterness of grief and disappointment. Madame La Motte appeared depressed, and said little. La Motte seemed anxious to prevent thought, by assuming a fictitious and unnatural gaiety: he laughed and talked, and threw off frequent bumpers of wine:* it was the mirth of desperation. Madame became alarmed, and would have restrained him, but he persisted in his libations to Bacchus* till reflection seemed to be almost overcome.

Madame La Motte, fearful that in the carelessness of the present moment he might betray himself, withdrew with Adeline to another room. Adeline recollected the happy hours she once passed with her, when confidence banished reserve, and sympathy and esteem dictated the sentiments of friendship: now those hours were gone for ever; she could no longer unbosom her griefs to Madame La Motte; no longer even esteem her. Yet, notwithstanding all the danger to which she was exposed by the criminal silence of the latter, she could not converse with her, consciously for the last time, without feeling a degree of sorrow, which wisdom may call weakness, but to which benevolence will allow a softer name.

Madame La Motte, in her conversation, appeared to labour under an almost equal oppression with Adeline: her thoughts were abstracted from the subject of discourse, and there were long and frequent intervals of silence. Adeline more than once caught her gazing with a look of tenderness upon her, and saw her eyes fill with tears. By this circumstance she was so much affected, that she was several times upon the point of throwing herself at her feet, and imploring her pity and protection. Cooler reflection shewed her the extravagance and danger of this conduct: she suppressed her emotions, but they at length compelled her to withdraw from the presence of Madame La Motte.

CHAPTER XI*

Thou! to whom the world unknown
With all its·shadowy shapes is shown;
Who seest appall'd th' unreal scene,
While fancy lifts the veil between;
Ah, Fear! ah, frantic Fear!
I see, I see thee near!
I know thy hurry'd step, thy haggard eye!
Like thee I start, like thee disordered fly!

COLLINS*

ADELINE anxiously watched from her chamber window the sun set behind the distant hills, and the time of her departure draw nigh: it set with uncommon splendour, and threw a fiery gleam athwart the woods, and upon some scattered fragments of the ruins, which she could not gaze upon with indifference.* 'Never, probably, again shall I see the sun sink below those hills,' said she, 'or illumine this scene! Where shall I be when next it sets—where this time to-morrow? sunk, perhaps, in misery!' She wept to the thought. 'A few hours,' resumed Adeline, 'and the Marquis will arrive—a few hours, and this abbey will be a scene of confusion and tumult: every eye will be in search of me, every recess will be explored.' These reflections inspired her with new terror, and increased her impatience to be gone.

Twilight gradually came on, and she now thought it sufficiently dark to venture forth; but, before she went, she kneeled down and addressed herself to Heaven. She implored support and protection, and committed herself to the care of the God of mercies. Having done this, she quitted her chamber, and passed with cautious steps down the winding staircase. No person appeared, and she proceeded through the door of the tower into the forest. She looked around; the gloom of the evening obscured every object.

With a trembling heart she sought the path pointed out by Peter, which led to the tomb; having found it, she passed along forlorn and terrified. Often did she start as the breeze shook the light leaves of the trees, or as the bat flitted by, gamboling in the twilight; and often, as she looked back towards the abbey, thought she distinguished, amid the deepening gloom, the figures of men. Having proceeded some way, she suddenly heard the feet of horses, and soon after a sound of voices, among which she distinguished that of the Marquis: they seemed to come from the quarter she was approaching, and evidently advanced. Terror for some minutes arrested her steps; she stood in a state of dreadful hesitation: to proceed was to run into the hands of the Marquis; to return was to fall into the power of La Motte.

After remaining for some time uncertain whither to fly, the sounds suddenly took a different direction, and wheeled towards the abbey. Adeline had a short cessation of terror. She now understood that the Marquis had passed this spot only in his way to the abbey, and she hastened to secrete herself in the ruin. At length, after much difficulty, she reached it, the deep shades almost concealing it from her search. She paused at the entrance, awed by the solemnity that reigned within, and the utter darkness of the place; at length she determined to watch without till Peter should arrive. 'If any person approaches,' said she, 'I can hear them before they can see me, and I can then secrete myself in the cell.'

She leaned against a fragment of the tomb in trembling expectation, and, as she listened, no sound broke the silence of the hour. The state of her mind can only be imagined, by considering that upon the present time turned the crisis of her fate. 'They have now,' thought she, 'discovered my flight; even now they are seeking me in every part of the abbey. I hear their dreadful voices call me; I see their eager looks.' The power of imagination almost overcame her. While she yet looked around, she saw lights moving at a distance; and sometimes they glimmered between the trees, and sometimes they totally disappeared.

They seemed to be in a direction with the abbey; and she now remembered, that in the morning she had seen a part of the fabric through an opening in the forest. She had, therefore, no doubt that the lights she saw proceeded from people in search of her; who, she feared, not finding her at the abbey, might direct their steps towards the tomb. Her place of refuge now seemed too near her enemies to be safe, and she would have fled to a more distant part of the forest, but recollected that Peter would not know where to find her.

While these thoughts passed over her mind, she heard distant voices in the wind, and was hastening to conceal herself in the cell when she observed the lights suddenly disappear. All was soon after hushed in silence and darkness, yet she endeavoured to find the way to the cell, She remembered the situation of the outer door and of the passage, and having passed these she unclosed the door of the cell. Within it was utterly dark. She trembled violently, but entered; and, having felt about the walls, at length seated herself on a projection of stone.

She here again addressed herself to Heaven, and endeavoured to re-animate her spirits till Peter should arrive. Above half an hour elapsed in this gloomy recess, and no sound foretold his approach. Her spirits sunk, she feared some part of their plan was discovered, or interrupted, and that he was detained by La Motte. This conviction operated sometimes so strongly upon her fears, as to urge her to quit the cell alone, and seek in flight her only chance of escape.

While this design was fluctuating in her mind, she distinguished through the grate above a clattering of hoofs. The noise approached, and at length stopped at the tomb. In the succeeding moment she heard three strokes of a whip; her heart beat, and for some moments her agitation was such, that she made no effort to quit the cell. The strokes were repeated: she now roused her spirits, and, stepping forward, ascended to the forest. She called 'Peter;' for the deep gloom would not permit her to distinguish either man or horse. She was quickly answered, 'Hush! Ma'amselle, our voices will betray us.'

They mounted and rode off as fast as the darkness would permit. Adeline's heart revived at every step they took. She inquired what had passed at the abbey, and how he had contrived to get away. 'Speak softly, Ma'amselle; you'll know all by and bye, but I can't tell you now.' He had scarcely spoke ere they saw lights move along at a distance; and coming now to a more open part of the forest, he set off on a full gallop, and continued the pace till the horse could hold it no longer. They looked back, and no lights appearing, Adeline's terror subsided. She inquired again what had passed at the abbey, when her flight was discovered. 'You may speak without fear of being heard,' said she, 'we are gone beyond their reach I hope.'

'Why, Ma'amselle,' said he, 'you had not been gone long before the Marquis arrived, and Monsieur La Motte then found out you was fled. Upon this a great rout there was, and he talked a great deal with the Marquis.'

'Speak louder,' said Adeline, 'I cannot hear you.'

'I will, Ma'amselle.'—

'Oh! Heavens!' interrupted Adeline, 'What voice is this? It is not Peter's. For God's sake tell me who you are, and whither I am going?'

'You'll know that soon enough, young lady,' answered the stranger, for it was indeed not Peter; 'I am taking you where my master ordered.' Adeline, not doubting he was the Marquis's servant, attempted to leap to the ground, but the man, dismounting, bound her to the horse. One feeble ray of hope at length beamed upon her mind: she endeavoured to soften the man to pity, and pleaded with all the genuine eloquence of distress; but he understood his interest too well to yield even for a moment to the compassion, which, in spite of himself, her artless supplication inspired.

She now resigned herself to despair, and, in passive silence, submitted to her fate. They continued thus to travel, till a storm of rain, accompanied by thunder and lightning, drove them to the covert of a thick grove. The man believed this a safe situation, and Adeline was now too careless of life to attempt convincing him of his error. The storm was violent and long, but as soon as it abated they set off on full gallop, and having continued to travel for about two hours, they came to the borders of the forest, and, soon after, to a high lonely wall, which Adeline could just distinguish by the moon-light, which now streamed through the parting clouds.

Here they stopped; the man dismounted, and having opened a small door in the wall, he unbound Adeline, who shrieked, though involuntarily and in vain, as he took her from the horse. The door opened upon a narrow passage, dimly lighted by a lamp, which hung at the farther end. He led her on; they came to another door; it opened and disclosed a magnificent saloon,* splendidly illuminated, and fitted up in the most airy and elegant taste.

The walls were painted in fresco, representing scenes from Ovid,* and hung above with silk drawn up in festoons and richly fringed. The sofas were of a silk to suit the hangings. From the centre of the ceiling, which exhibited a scene from the Armida of Tasso,* descended a silver lamp of Etruscan form:* it diffused a blaze of light, that, reflected from large pier glasses,* completely illuminated the saloon. Busts of Horace, Ovid, Anacreon, Tibullus, and Petronius Arbiter,* adorned the recesses, and stands of flowers, placed in Etruscan vases, breathed the most delicious perfume. In the middle of the apartment stood a small table, spread with a collation of fruits, ices, and liquors.* No person appeared. The whole seemed the works of enchantment, and rather resembled the palace of a fairy than any thing of human conformation.

Adeline was astonished, and inquired where she was, but

the man refused to answer her questions, and, having desired her
to take some refreshment, left her. She walked to the windows,
from which a gleam of moon-light discovered to her an extensive
garden, where groves and lawns, and water glittering in the moon-
beam, composed a scenery of varied* and romantic beauty.
'What can this mean!' said she: 'Is this a charm to lure me to
destruction?'* She endeavoured, with a hope of escaping, to
open the windows, but they were all fastened; she next
attempted several doors, and found them also secured.

Perceiving all chance of escape was removed, she remained
for some time given up to sorrow and reflection; but was at
length drawn from her reverie by the notes of soft music,
breathing such dulcet and entrancing sounds, as suspended
grief, and waked the soul to tenderness and pensive pleasure.
Adeline listened in surprize, and insensibly became soothed and
interested; a tender melancholy stole upon her heart, and
subdued every harsher feeling: but the moment the strain
ceased, the enchantment dissolved, and she returned to a sense
of her situation.

Again the music sounded—'music such as charmeth
sleep'*—and again she gradually yielded to its sweet magic. A
female voice, accompanied by a lute, a hautboy,* and a few
other instruments, now gradually swelled into a tone so
exquisite, as raised attention into ecstacy. It sunk by degrees,
and touched a few simple notes with pathetic softness, when the
measure was suddenly changed, and in a gay and airy melody
Adeline distinguished the following words:

SONG

Life's a varied, bright illusion,
  Joy and sorrow—light and shade;
Turn from sorrow's dark suffusion,
  Catch the pleasures ere they fade.

Fancy paints with hues unreal,
  Smile of bliss, and sorrow's mood;
If they both are but ideal,
  Why reject the seeming good?

Hence! no more! 'tis Wisdom calls ye,
  Bids ye court Time's present aid;
The future trust not—hope enthrals ye,
  'Catch the pleasures ere they fade.'

The music ceased, but the sound still vibrated on her imagination, and she was sunk in the pleasing languor they had inspired, when the door opened, and the Marquis de Montalt appeared. He approached the sofa where Adeline sat, and addressed her, but she heard not his voice—she had fainted. He endeavoured to recover her, and at length succeeded; but when she unclosed her eyes, and again beheld him, she relapsed into a state of insensibility, and having in vain tried various methods to restore her, he was obliged to call assistance. Two young women entered, and, when she began to revive, he left them to prepare her for his reappearance. When Adeline perceived that the Marquis was gone, and that she was in the care of women, her spirits gradually returned; she looked at her attendants, and was surprised to see so much elegance and beauty.

Some endeavour she made to interest their pity, but they seemed wholly insensible to her distress, and began to talk of the Marquis in terms of the highest admiration. They assured her it would be her own fault if she was not happy, and advised her to appear so in his presence. It was with the utmost difficulty that Adeline forebore to express the disdain which was rising to her lips, and that she listened to their discourse in silence. But she saw the inconvenience and fruitlessness of opposition, and she commanded her feelings.

They were thus proceeding in their praises of the Marquis, when he himself appeared, and, waving his hand, they immediately quitted the apartment. Adeline beheld him with a kind of mute despair, while he approached and took her hand, which she hastily withdrew, and turning from him with a look of unutterable distress, burst into tears. He was for some time silent, and appeared softened by her anguish. But again approaching, and addressing her in a gentle voice, he entreated her pardon for the step, which despair, and, as he called it, love had prompted. She was too much absorbed in

grief to reply, till he solicited a return of his love, when her
sorrow yielded to indignation, and she reproached him with
his conduct. He pleaded that he had long loved and sought her
upon honourable terms, and his offer of those terms he began
to repeat, but, raising his eyes towards Adeline, he saw in her
looks the contempt which he was conscious he deserved.

For a moment he was confused, and seemed to understand
both that his plan was discovered and his person despised; but
soon resuming his usual command of feature, he again pressed
his suit, and solicited her love. A little reflection shewed
Adeline the danger of exasperating his pride, by an avowal of
the contempt which his pretended offer of marriage excited;
and she thought it not improper, upon an occasion in which
the honour and peace of her life was concerned, to yield
somewhat to the policy of dissimulation. She saw that her only
chance of escaping his designs depended upon delaying them,
and she now wished him to believe her ignorant that the
Marchioness was living, and that his offers were delusive.

He observed her pause, and, in the eagerness to turn her
hesitation to his advantage, renewed his proposal with
increased vehemence.—'To-morrow shall unite us, lovely
Adeline; to-morrow you shall consent to become the
Marchioness de Montalt. You will then return my love
and'——

'You must first deserve my esteem, my Lord.'

'I will—I do deserve it. Are you not now in my power, and
do I not forbear to take advantage of your situation? Do I
not make you the most honourable proposals?'—Adeline
shuddered: 'if you wish I should esteem you, my Lord,
endeavour, if possible, to make me forget by what means I
came into your power; if your views are, indeed, honourable,
prove them so by releasing me from my confinement.'

'Can you then wish, lovely Adeline, to fly from him who
adores you?' replied the Marquis, with a studied air of
tenderness. 'Why will you exact so severe a proof of my
disinterestedness, a disinterestedness which is not consistent
with love? No, charming Adeline, let me at least have the
pleasure of beholding you, till the bonds of the church shall
remove every obstacle to my love. To-morrow'——

Adeline saw the danger to which she was now exposed, and interrupted him. '*Deserve* my esteem, Sir, and then you will *obtain* it: as a first step towards which, liberate me from a confinement that obliges me to look on you only with terror and aversion. How can I believe your professions of love, while you shew that you have no interest in my happiness?' Thus did Adeline, to whom the arts and the practice of dissimulation were hitherto equally unknown, condescend to make use of them in disguising her indignation and contempt. But though these arts were adopted only for the purpose of self-preservation, she used them with reluctance, and almost with abhorrence; for her mind was habitually impregnated with the love of virtue, in thought, word, and action, and, while her end in using them was certainly good, she scarcely thought that end could justify the means.

The Marquis persisted in his sophistry.* 'Can you doubt the reality of that love, which, to obtain you, has urged me to risque your displeasure? But have I not consulted your happiness, even in the very conduct which you condemn? I have removed you from a solitary and desolate ruin to a gay and splendid villa, where every luxury is at your command, and where every person shall be obedient to your wishes.'

'My first wish is to go hence,' said Adeline; 'I entreat, I conjure you, my Lord, no longer to detain me. I am a friendless and wretched orphan, exposed to many evils, and, I fear, abandoned to misfortune: I do not wish to be rude; but allow me to say, that no misery can exceed that I shall feel in remaining here, or, indeed, in being any where pursued by the offers you make me!' Adeline had now forgot her policy: tears prevented her from proceeding, and she turned away her face to hide her emotion.

'By Heaven! Adeline, you do me wrong,' said the Marquis, rising from his seat, and seizing her hand; 'I love, I adore you; yet you doubt my passion, and are insensible to my vows. Every pleasure possible to be enjoyed within these walls you shall partake, but beyond them you shall not go.' She disengaged her hand, and in silent anguish walked to a distant part of the saloon; deep sighs burst from her heart, and, almost fainting, she leaned on a window-frame for support.

The Marquis followed her; 'Why thus obstinately persist in refusing to be happy?' said he; 'recollect the proposal I have made you, and accept it, while it is yet in your power. To-morrow a priest shall join our hands—Surely, being, as you are, in my power, it must be your interest to consent to this?' Adeline could answer only by tears; she despaired of softening his heart to pity, and feared to exasperate his pride by disdain. He now led her, and she suffered him, to a seat near the banquet,* at which he pressed her to partake of a variety of confectionaries, particularly of some liquors, of which he himself drank freely: Adeline accepted only of a peach.

And now the Marquis, who interpreted her silence into a secret compliance with his proposal, resumed all his gaiety and spirit, while the long and ardent regards he bestowed on Adeline, overcame her with confusion and indignation. In the midst of the banquet, soft music again sounded the most tender and impassioned airs; but its effect on Adeline was now lost, her mind being too much embarrassed and distressed by the presence of the Marquis, to admit even the soothings of harmony. A song was now heard, written with that sort of impotent art, by which some voluptuous poets believe they can at once conceal and recommend the principles of vice. Adeline received it with contempt and displeasure, and the Marquis, perceiving its effect, presently made a sign for another composition, which adding the force of poetry to the charms of music, might withdraw her mind from the present scene, and enchant it in sweet delirium.

SONG OF A SPIRIT

In the sightless air I dwell,
  On the sloping sun-beams play;
Delve the cavern's inmost cell,
  Where never yet did day-light stray:

Dive beneath the green sea waves,
  And gambol in briny deeps;
Skim ev'ry shore that Neptune laves,
  From Lapland's plains to India's steeps.

Oft I mount with rapid force
  Above the wide earth's shadowy zone;

Follow the day-star's flaming course
   Through realms of space to thought unknown:

And listen oft celestial sounds
   That swell the air unheard of men,
As I watch my nightly rounds
   O'er woody steep, and silent glen.

Under the shade of waving trees,
   On the green bank of fountain clear,
At pensive eve I sit at ease,
   While dying music murmurs near.

And oft, on point of airy clift,
   That hangs upon the western main,
I watch the gay tints passing swift,
   And twilight veil the liquid plain.

Then, when the breeze has sunk away,
   And ocean scarce is heard to lave,
For me the sea-nymphs softly play
   Their dulcet shells beneath the wave.

Their dulcet shells! I hear them now,
   Slow swells the strain upon mine ear;
Now faintly falls—now warbles low,
   Till rapture melts into a tear.

The ray that silvers o'er the dew,
   And trembles through the leafy shade,
And tints the scene with softer hue,
   Calls me to rove the lonely glade;

Or hie me to some ruin'd tower,
   Faintly shewn by moon-light gleam,
Where the lone wanderer owns my power
   In shadows dire that substance seem;

In thrilling sounds that murmur woe,
   And pausing silence make more dread;
In music breathing from below
   Sad solemn strains, that wake the dead.

Unseen I move—unknown am fear'd!
   Fancy's wildest dreams I weave;
And oft by bards my voice is heard
   To die along the gales of eve.

When the voice ceased, a mournful strain, played with exquisite expression, sounded from a distant horn; sometimes the notes floated on the air in soft undulations—now they swelled into full and sweeping melody, and now died faintly into silence: when again they rose and trembled in sounds so sweetly tender, as drew tears from Adeline, and exclamations of rapture from the Marquis; he threw his arm round her, and would have pressed her towards him, but she liberated herself from his embrace, and with a look, on which was impressed the firm dignity of virtue, yet touched with sorrow, she awed him to forbearance. Conscious of a superiority, which he was ashamed to acknowledge, and endeavouring to despise the influence which he could not resist, he stood for a moment the slave of virtue, though the votary of vice. Soon, however, he recovered his confidence, and began to plead his love; when Adeline, no longer animated by the spirit she had lately shewn, and sinking beneath the languor and fatigue which the various and violent agitations of her mind produced, entreated he would leave her to repose.

The paleness of her countenance, and the tremulous tone of her voice, were too expressive to be misunderstood; and the Marquis, bidding her remember to-morrow, with some hesitation, withdrew. The moment she was alone, she yielded to the bursting anguish of her heart, and was so absorbed in grief, that it was some time before she perceived she was in the presence of the young women, who had lately attended her, and had entered the saloon soon after the Marquis quitted it: they came to conduct her to her chamber. She followed them for some time in silence, till, prompted by desperation, she again endeavoured to awaken their compassion: but again the praises of the Marquis were repeated, and perceiving that all attempts to interest them in her favour were in vain, she dismissed them. She secured the door through which they had departed, and then, in the languid hope of discovering some means of escape, she surveyed her chamber. The airy elegance with which it was fitted up, and the luxurious accommodations with which it abounded, seemed designed to fascinate the imagination, and to seduce the heart. The hangings were of straw-coloured silk, adorned with a variety of landscapes and historical paintings, the subjects of which partook of the voluptuous character of the owner; the chimney-piece, of Parian marble,* was ornamented with several reposing figures from the antique. The bed was of silk the colour of the hangings, richly fringed with purple and silver, and the head made in form of a canopy. The steps, which were placed near the bed to assist in ascending it, were supported by Cupids, apparently of solid silver. China vases, filled with perfume, stood in several of the recesses, upon stands of the same structure as the toilet,* which was magnificent, and ornamated with a variety of trinkets.

Adeline threw a transient look upon these various objects, and proceeded to examine the windows, which descended to the floor, and opened into balconies towards the garden she had seen from the saloon. They were now fastened, and her efforts to move them were ineffectual; at length she gave up the attempt. A door next attracted her notice, which she found was not fastened; it opened upon a dressing closet, to which she descended by a few steps: two windows appeared, she hastened towards them; one refused to yield, but her heart beat with sudden joy when the other opened to her touch.

In the transport of the moment, she forgot that its distance from the ground might yet deny the escape she meditated. She returned to lock the door of the closet, to prevent a surprize, which, however, was unnecessary, that of the bedroom being already secured. She now looked out from the window; the garden lay before her, and she perceived that the window, which descended to the floor, was so near the ground, that she might jump from it with ease: almost in the moment she perceived this, she sprang forward and alighted safely in an extensive garden, resembling more an English pleasure ground, than a series of French parterres.*

Thence she had little doubt of escaping, either by some broken fence, or low part of the wall; she tripped lightly along, for hope played round her heart. The clouds of the late storm were now dispersed, and the moon-light, which slept on the lawns and spangled the flowerets, yet heavy with rain-drops, afforded her a distinct view of the surrounding scenery: she followed the direction of the high wall that adjoined the

chateau, till it was concealed from her sight by a thick
wilderness, so entangled with boughs and obscured by
darkness, that she feared to enter, and turned aside into a walk
on the right; it conducted her to the margin of a lake overhung
with lofty trees.

The moon-beams dancing upon the waters, that with gentle
undulation played along the shore, exhibited a scene of tranquil beauty, which would have soothed an heart less agitated
than was that of Adeline: she sighed as she transiently surveyed it, and passed hastily on in search of the garden wall,
from which she had now strayed a considerable way. After
wandering for some time through alleys and over lawns, without meeting with any thing like a boundary to the grounds,
she again found herself at the lake, and now traversed its
border with the footsteps of despair:—tears rolled down her
cheeks. The scene around exhibited only images of peace and
delight; every object seemed to repose; not a breath waved the
foliage, not a sound stole through the air: it was in her bosom
only that tumult and distress prevailed. She still pursued the
windings of the shore, till an opening in the woods conducted
her up a gentle ascent: the path now wound along the side of
a hill, where the gloom was so deep, that it was with some
difficulty she found her way: suddenly, however, the avenue
opened to a lofty grove, and she perceived a light issue from
a recess at some distance.

She paused, and her first impulse was to retreat, but
listening and hearing no sound, a faint hope beamed upon her
mind, that the person to whom the light belonged, might be
won to favour her escape. She advanced, with trembling and
cautious steps, towards the recess, that she might secretly
observe the person, before she ventured to enter it. Her
emotion increased as she approached, and having reached the
bower, she beheld, through an open window, the Marquis,
reclining on a sofa, near which stood a table, covered with
fruit and wine. He was alone, and his countenance was flushed
with drinking.

While she gazed, fixed to the spot by terror, he looked up
towards the casement; the light gleamed full upon her face,
but she stayed not to learn whether he had observed her, for,

with the swiftness of sound, she left the place and ran, without knowing whether she was pursued. Having gone a considerable way, fatigue, at length, compelled her to stop, and she threw herself upon the turf, almost fainting with fear and languor. She knew if the Marquis detected her in an attempt to escape, he would, probably, burst the bounds which he had hitherto prescribed to himself, and that she had the most dreadful evils to expect. The palpitations of terror were so strong, that she could with difficulty breathe.

She watched and listened in trembling expectation, but no form met her eye, no sound her ear; in this state she remained a considerable time. She wept, and the tears she shed relieved her oppressed heart. 'O my father!' said she, 'why did you abandon your child? If you knew the dangers to which you have exposed her, you would, surely, pity and relieve her. Alas! shall I never find a friend; am I destined still to trust and be deceived?—Peter too, could he be treacherous?' She wept again, and then returned to a sense of her present danger, and to a consideration of the means of escaping it—but no means appeared.

To her imagination the grounds were boundless; she had wandered from lawn to lawn, and from grove to grove, without perceiving any termination to the place; the garden wall she could not find, but she resolved neither to return to the chateau, nor to relinquish her search. As she was rising to depart, she perceived a shadow move along at some distance; she stood still to observe it. It slowly advanced and then disappeared, but presently she saw a person emerge from the gloom, and approach the spot where she stood. She had no doubt that the Marquis had observed her, and she ran with all possible speed to the shade of some woods on the left. Footsteps pursued her, and she heard her name repeated, while she in vain endeavoured to quicken her pace.

Suddenly the sound of pursuit turned, and sunk away in a different direction: she paused to take breath; she looked around and no person appeared. She now proceeded slowly along the avenue, and had almost reached its termination, when she saw the same figure emerge from the woods and dart across the avenue; it instantly pursued her and approached. A voice called her, but she was gone beyond its reach, for she had sunk senseless upon the ground: it was long before she revived, when she did, she found herself in the arms of a stranger, and made an effort to disengage herself.

'Fear nothing, lovely Adeline,' said he, 'fear nothing: you are in the arms of a friend, who will encounter any hazard for your sake; who will protect you with his life.' He pressed her gently to his heart. 'Have you then forgot me?' continued he. She looked earnestly at him, and was now convinced that it was Theodore who spoke.* Joy was her first emotion; but, recollecting his former abrupt departure, at a time so critical to her safety, and that he was the friend of the Marquis, a thousand mingled sensations struggled in her breast, and overwhelmed her with mistrust, apprehension, and disappointment.

Theodore raised her from the ground, and while he yet supported her, 'Let us immediately fly from this place,' said he; 'a carriage waits to receive us; it shall go wherever you direct, and convey you to your friends.' This last sentence touched her heart: 'Alas, I have no friends!' said she, 'nor do I know whither to go.' Theodore gently pressed her hand between his, and, in a voice of the softest compassion, said, '*My* friends then shall be yours; suffer me to lead you to them. But I am in agony while you remain in this place; let us hasten to quit it.' Adeline was going to reply, when voices were heard among the trees, and Theodore, supporting her with his arm, hurried her along the avenue: they continued their flight till Adeline, panting for breath, could go no farther.

Having paused a while, and heard no footsteps in pursuit, they renewed their course: Theodore knew that they were now not far from the garden wall; but he was also aware, that in the intermediate space several paths wound from remote parts of the grounds into the walk he was to pass, from whence the Marquis's people might issue and intercept him. He, however, concealed his apprehensions from Adeline, and endeavoured to soothe and support her spirits.

At length they reached the wall, and Theodore was leading her towards a low part of it, near which stood the carriage, when again they heard voices in the air. Adeline's spirits and strength were nearly exhausted, but she made a last effort to proceed, and she now saw the ladder at some distance by which Theodore had descended to the garden. 'Exert yourself yet a little longer,' said he, 'and you will be in safety.' He held the ladder while she ascended; the top of the wall was broad and level, and Adeline, having reached it, remained there till Theodore followed and drew the ladder to the other side.

When they had descended, the carriage appeared in waiting, but without the driver. Theodore feared to call, lest his voice should betray him; he, therefore, put Adeline into the carriage, and went himself in search of the postillion, whom he found asleep under a tree at some distance; having awakened him, they returned to the vehicle, which soon drove furiously away. Adeline did not yet dare to believe herself safe, but, after proceeding a considerable time without interruption, joy burst upon her heart, and she thanked her deliverer in terms of the warmest gratitude. The sympathy expressed in the tone of his voice and manner, proved that his happiness, on this occasion, almost equalled her own.

As reflection gradually stole upon her mind, anxiety superseded joy: in the tumult of the late moments, she thought only of escape, but the circumstances of her present situation now appeared to her, and she became silent and pensive: she had no friends to whom she could fly, and was going with a young Chevalier, almost a stranger to her, she knew not whither. She remembered how often she had been deceived and betrayed where she trusted most, and her spirits sunk: she remembered also the former attention which Theodore had shewn her, and dreaded lest his conduct might be prompted by a selfish passion. She saw this to be possible, but she disdained to believe it probable, and felt that nothing could give her greater pain than to doubt the integrity of Theodore.

He interrupted her reverie, by recurring to her late situation at the abbey. 'You would be much surprised,' said he, 'and I fear, offended, that I did not attend my appointment at the abbey, after the alarming hints I had given you in our last interview. That circumstance has, perhaps, injured me in your esteem, if, indeed, I was ever so happy as to possess it: but my designs were over-ruled by those of the Marquis de

Montalt; and I think I may venture to assert, that my distress upon this occasion was, at least, equal to your apprehensions.'

Adeline said, 'She had been much alarmed by the hints he had given her, and by his failing to afford farther information, concerning the subject of her danger; and'—She checked the sentence that hung upon her lips, for she perceived that she was unwarily betraying the interest he held in her heart. There were a few moments of silence, and neither party seemed perfectly at ease. Theodore, at length, renewed the conversation: 'Suffer me to acquaint you,' said he, 'with the circumstances that withheld me from the interview I solicited; I am anxious to exculpate myself.' Without waiting her reply, he proceeded to inform her, that the Marquis had, by some inexplicable means, learned or suspected the subject of their last conversation, and, perceiving his designs were in danger of being counteracted, had taken effectual means to prevent her obtaining farther intelligence of them. Adeline immediately recollected that Theodore and herself had been seen in the forest by La Motte, who had, no doubt, suspected their growing intimacy, and had taken care to inform the Marquis how likely he was to find a rival in his friend.

'On the day following that, on which I last saw you,' said Theodore, 'the Marquis, who is my colonel, commanded me to prepare to attend my regiment, and appointed the following morning for my journey. This sudden order gave me some surprise, but I was not long in doubt concerning the motive for it: a servant of the Marquis, who had been long attached to me, entered my room soon after I had left his Lord, and expressing concern at my abrupt departure, dropped some hints respecting it, which excited my surprise. I inquired farther, and was confirmed in the suspicions I had for some time entertained of the Marquis's designs upon you.

'Jacques farther informed me, that our late interview had been noticed and communicated to the Marquis. His information had been obtained from a fellow servant, and it alarmed me so much, that I engaged him to send me intelligence from time to time, concerning the proceedings of the Marquis. I now looked forward to the evening which would bring me again to your presence with increased impatience:

but the ingenuity of the Marquis effectually counteracted my
endeavours and wishes; he had made an engagement to pass
the day at the villa of a nobleman some leagues distant, and,
notwithstanding all the excuses I could offer, I was obliged to
attend him. Thus compelled to obey, I passed a day of more
agitation and anxiety than I had ever before experienced. It
was midnight before we returned to the Marquis's chateau. I
arose early in the morning to commence my journey, and
resolved to seek an interview with you before I left the
province.

'When I entered the breakfast room, I was much surprized
to find the Marquis there already, who, commending the
beauty of the morning, declared his intention of accompanying me as far as Chineau. Thus unexpectedly deprived of
my last hope, my countenance, I believe, expressed what I
felt, for the scrutinizing eye of the Marquis instantly changed
from seeming carelessness to displeasure. The distance from
Chineau to the abbey was, at least, twelve leagues; yet I had
once some intention of returning from thence, when the
Marquis should leave me, till I recollected the very remote
chance there would even then be of seeing you alone, and also,
that if I was observed by La Motte, it would awaken all his
suspicions, and caution him against any future plan I might
see it expedient to attempt: I, therefore, proceeded to join my
regiment.

'Jacques sent me frequent accounts of the operations of the
Marquis, but his manner of relating them was so very confused, that they only served to perplex and distress me. His
last letter, however, alarmed me so much, that my residence
in quarters became intolerable; and, as I found it impossible
to obtain leave of absence, I secretly left the regiment, and
concealed myself in a cottage about a mile from the chateau,
that I might obtain the earliest intelligence of the Marquis's
plans. Jacques brought me daily information, and, at last, an
account of the horrible plot which was laid for the following
night.

'I saw little probability of warning you of your danger. If I
ventured near the abbey, La Motte might discover me, and
frustrate every attempt on my part to save you: yet I de-

termined to encounter this risk for the chance of seeing you, and towards evening I was preparing to set out for the forest, when Jacques arrived and informed me, that you was to be brought to the chateau. My plan was thus rendered less difficult. I learned also, that the Marquis, by means of those refinements in luxury, with which he is but too well acquainted, designed, now that his apprehension of losing you was no more, to seduce you to his wishes, and impose upon you by a fictitious marriage. Having obtained information concerning the situation of the room allotted you, I ordered a chaise to be in waiting, and with a design of scaling your window, and conducting you thence, I entered the garden at midnight.'

Theodore having ceased to speak, 'I know not how words can express my sense of the obligations I owe you,' said Adeline, 'or my gratitude for your generosity.'

'Ah! call it not generosity,' he replied, 'it was love.' He paused. Adeline was silent. After some moments of expressive emotion, he resumed; 'But pardon this abrupt declaration; yet why do I call it abrupt, since my actions have already disclosed what my lips have never, till this instant, ventured to acknowledge.' He paused again. Adeline was still silent. 'Yet do me the justice to believe, that I am sensible of the impropriety of pleading my love at present, and have been surprized into this confession. I promise also to forbear from a renewal of the subject, till you are placed in a situation, where you may freely accept or refuse, the sincere regards I offer you. If I could, however, now be certain that I possess your esteem, it would relieve me from much anxiety.'

Adeline felt surprized that he should doubt her esteem for him, after the signal and generous service he had rendered her; but she was not yet acquainted with the timidity of love. 'Do you then,' said she, in a tremulous voice, 'believe me ungrateful? It is impossible I can consider your friendly interference in my behalf without esteeming you.' Theodore immediately took her hand and pressed it to his lips in silence. They were both too much agitated to converse, and continued to travel for some miles without exchanging a word.

CHAPTER XII

'And Hope enchanted smil'd, and wav'd her golden hair;
And longer had she sung—but with a frown,
Revenge impatient rose.'

ODE TO THE PASSIONS*

THE dawn of morning now trembled through the clouds,* when the travellers stopped at a small town to change horses. Theodore entreated Adeline to alight and take some refreshment, and to this she at length consented. But the people of the inn were not yet up, and it was some time before the knocking and roaring of the postillion could rouse them.

Having taken some slight refreshment, Theodore and Adeline returned to the carriage. The only subject upon which Theodore could have spoke with interest, delicacy forbade him at this time to notice; and after pointing out some beautiful scenery on the road, and making other efforts to support a conversation, he relapsed into silence. His mind, though still anxious, was now relieved from the apprehension that had long oppressed it. When he first saw Adeline, her loveliness made a deep impression on his heart: there was a sentiment in her beauty, which his mind immediately acknowledged, and the effect of which, her manners and conversation had afterwards confirmed. Her charms appeared to him like those since so finely described by an English poet:

'Oh! have you seen, bath'd in the morning dew,
   The budding rose its infant bloom display;
When first its virgin tints unfold to view,
   It shrinks and scarcely trusts the blaze of day?

So soft, so delicate, so sweet she came,
   Youth's damask glow just dawning on her cheek.
I gaz'd, I sigh'd, I caught the tender flame,
   Felt the fond pang, and droop'd with passion weak.'*

A knowledge of her destitute condition, and of the dangers with which she was environed, had awakened in his heart the tenderest touch of pity, and assisted the change of admiration into love. The distress he suffered, when compelled to leave her exposed to these dangers, without being able to warn her of them, can only be imagined. During his residence with his regiment, his mind was the constant prey of terrors, which he saw no means of combating, but by returning to the neighbourhood of the abbey, where he might obtain early intelligence of the Marquis's schemes, and be ready to give his assistance to Adeline.

Leave of absence he could not request, without betraying his design where most he dreaded it should be known, and, at length, with a generous rashness, which, though it defied law, was impelled by virtue, he secretly quitted his regiment. The progress of the Marquis's plan he had observed, with trembling anxiety, till, the night that was to decide the fate of Adeline and himself roused all his mind to action, and involved him in a tumult of hope and fear—horror and expectation.

Never, till the present hour, had he ventured to believe she was in safety. Now the distance they had gained from the chateau, without perceiving any pursuit, increased his best hopes. It was impossible he could sit by the side of his beloved Adeline, and receive assurances of her gratitude and esteem, without venturing to hope for her love. He congratulated himself as her preserver, and anticipated scenes of happiness when she should be under the protection of his family. The clouds of misery and apprehension disappeared from his mind, and left it to the sunshine of joy. When a shadow of fear would sometimes return, or when he recollected, with compunction, the circumstances under which he had left his regiment, stationed, as it was, upon the frontiers, and in a time of war, he looked at Adeline, and her countenance, with instantaneous magic, beamed peace upon his heart.

But Adeline had a subject of anxiety from which Theodore was exempt; the prospect of her future days was involved in darkness and uncertainty. Again she was going to claim the bounty of strangers—again going to encounter the uncertainty of their kindness; exposed to the hardships of dependance, or to the difficulty of earning a precarious livelihood. These anticipations obscured the joy occasioned by her escape, and by the affection which the conduct and avowal of Theodore had exhibited. The delicacy of his behaviour, in forbearing to take advantage of her present situation to plead his love, increased her esteem, and flattered her pride.

Adeline was lost in meditation upon subjects like these, when the postillion stopped the carriage; and pointing to part of a road, which wound down the side of a hill they had passed, said there were several horsemen in pursuit! Theodore immediately ordered him to proceed with all possible speed, and to strike out of the great road into the first obscure way that offered. The postillion cracked his whip in the air, and set off as if he was flying for life. In the mean while Theodore endeavoured to re-animate Adeline, who was sinking with terror, and who now thought, if she could only escape from the Marquis, she could defy the future.

Presently they struck into a bye lane, screened and overshadowed by thick trees; Theodore again looked from the window, but the closing boughs prevented his seeing far enough to determine whether the pursuit continued. For his sake Adeline endeavoured to disguise her emotions. 'This lane,' said Theodore, 'will certainly lead to a town or village, and then we have nothing to apprehend; for, though my single arm could not defend you against the number of our pursuers, I have no doubt of being able to interest some of the inhabitants in our behalf.'

Adeline appeared to be comforted by the hope this reflection suggested, and Theodore again looked back, but the windings of the road closed his view, and the rattling of the wheels overcame every other sound. At length he called to the postillion to stop, and having listened attentively, without perceiving any sound of horses, he began to hope they were now in safety. 'Do you know where this road leads?' said he. The postillion answered that he did not, but he saw some houses through the distance, and believed it led to them. This was most welcome intelligence to Theodore, who looked forward and perceived the houses. The postillion set off, 'Fear nothing, my adored Adeline,' said he, 'you are now safe; I will part with you but with life.' Adeline sighed, not for herself only, but for the danger to which Theodore might be exposed.

They had continued to travel in this manner for near half an hour, when they arrived at a small village, and soon after stopped at an inn, the best the place afforded. As Theodore lifted Adeline from the chaise, he again entreated her to dismiss her apprehensions, and spoke with a tenderness, to which she could reply only by a smile that ill concealed her anxiety. After ordering refreshments, he went out to speak with the landlord, but had scarcely left the room, when Adeline observed a party of horsemen enter the inn-yard, and she had no doubt these were the persons from whom they fled. The faces of two of them only were turned towards her, but she thought the figure of one of the others not unlike that of the Marquis.

Her heart was chilled, and for some moments the powers of reason forsook her. Her first design was to seek concealment; but while she considered the means one of the horsemen looked up to the window near which she stood, and speaking to his companions, they entered the inn. To quit the room, without being observed, was impossible; to remain there, alone and unprotected as she was, would almost be equally dangerous. She paced the room in an agony of terror, often secretly calling on Theodore, and often wondering he did not return. These were moments of indescribable suffering. A loud and tumultuous sound of voices now arose from a distant part of the house, and she soon distinguished the words of the disputants. 'I arrest you in the King's name,' said one; 'and bid you, at your peril, attempt to go from hence, except under a guard.'

The next minute Adeline heard the voice of Theodore in reply. 'I do not mean to dispute the King's orders,' said he, 'and give you my word of honour not to go without you; but first unhand me, that I may return to that room; I have a friend there whom I wish to speak with.' To this proposal they at first objected, considering it merely as an excuse to obtain an opportunity of escaping; but, after much altercation and entreaty, his request was granted. He sprang forwards towards the room where Adeline remained, and while a serjeant and corporal followed him to the door, the two soldiers went out into the yard of the inn, to watch the windows of the apartment.

With an eager hand he unclosed the door, but Adeline hastened not to meet him, for she had fainted almost at the beginning of the dispute. Theodore called loudly for assistance, and the mistress of the inn soon appeared with her stock of remedies, which were administered in vain to Adeline, who remained insensible, and by breathing alone gave signs of her existence. The distress of Theodore was in the mean time heightened by the appearance of the officers, who, laughing at the discovery of his pretended friend, declared they could·wait no longer. Saying this, they would have forced him from the inanimate form of Adeline, over whom he hung in unutterable anguish, when fiercely turning upon them, he drew his sword, and swore no power on earth should force him away before the lady recovered.

The men, enraged by the action and the determined air of Theodore, exclaimed, 'Do you oppose the King's orders?' and advanced to seize him, but he presented the point of his sword, and bid them at their peril approach. One of them immediately drew, Theodore kept his guard, but did not advance. 'I demand only to wait here till the lady recovers,' said he; 'you understand the alternative.' The man, already exasperated by the opposition of Theodore, regarded the latter part of his speech as a threat, and became determined not to give up the point; he pressed forward, and while his comrade called the men from the yard, Theodore wounded him slightly in the shoulder, and received himself the stroke of a sabre on his head.

The blood gushed furiously from the wound; Theodore, staggering to a chair, sunk into it, just as the remainder of the party entered the room, and Adeline unclosed her eyes to see him ghastly pale, and covered with blood. She uttered an involuntary scream, and exclaiming, 'they have murdered him,' nearly relapsed. At the sound of her voice he raised his head, and smiling held out his hand to her. 'I am not much hurt,' said he faintly, 'and shall soon be better, if indeed you are recovered.' She hastened towards him, and gave her hand. 'Is nobody gone for a surgeon?' said she, with a look of agony. 'Do not be alarmed,' said Theodore, 'I am not so ill as you imagine.' The room was now crowded with people, whom the report of the affray had brought together; among these was a man, who acted as physician, apothecary, and surgeon to the village, and who now stepped forward to the assistance of Theodore.

Having examined the wound, he declined giving his opinion, but ordered the patient to be immediately put to bed, to which the officers objected, alledging that it was their duty to carry him to the regiment. 'That cannot be done without great danger to his life,' replied the doctor; 'and'—

'Oh! his life,' said the serjeant; 'we have nothing to do with that, we must do our duty.' Adeline, who had hitherto stood in trembling anxiety, could now no longer be silent. 'Since the surgeon,' said she, 'has declared it his opinion, that this gentleman cannot be removed in his present condition, without endangering his life, you will remember, that if he dies, yours will probably answer it.'

'Yes,' rejoined the surgeon, who was unwilling to relinquish his patient, 'I declare before these witnesses, that he cannot be removed with safety: you will do well, therefore, to consider the consequences. He has received a very dangerous wound, which requires the most careful treatment, and the event is even then doubtful; but, if he travels, a fever may ensue, and the wound will then be mortal.' Theodore heard this sentence with composure, but Adeline could with difficulty conceal the anguish of her heart: she roused all her fortitude to suppress the tears that struggled in her eyes; and though she wished to interest the humanity, or to awaken the fears of the men, in behalf of their unfortunate prisoner, she dared not to trust her voice with utterance.

From this internal struggle she was relieved by the compassion of the people who filled the room, and becoming clamorous in the cause of Theodore, declared the officers would be guilty of murder if they removed him. 'Why he must die at any rate,' said the serjeant, 'for quitting his post, and drawing upon me in the execution of the King's orders.' A faint sickness seized the heart of Adeline, and she leaned for support against Theodore's chair, whose concern for himself was for a while suspended in his anxiety for her. He supported her with his arm, and forcing a smile, said in a low voice, which she only could hear, 'This is a misrepresentation; I doubt not, when the affair is inquired into, it will be settled without any serious consequences.'

Adeline knew these words were uttered only to console her, and therefore did not give much credit to them, though Theodore continued to give her similar assurances of his safety. Meanwhile the mob, whose compassion for him had been gradually excited by the obduracy of the officer, were now roused to pity and indignation by the seeming certainty of his punishment, and the unfeeling manner in which it had been denounced. In a short time they became so much enraged, that, partly from a dread of farther consequences, and partly from the shame which their charges of cruelty occasioned, the serjeant consented that he should be put to bed, till his commanding officer might direct what was to be done. Adeline's joy at this circumstance overcame for a moment the sense of her misfortunes, and of her situation.

She waited in an adjoining room the sentence of the surgeon, who was now engaged in examining the wound; and though the accident would in any other circumstances have severely afflicted her, she now lamented it the more, because she considered herself as the cause of it, and because the misfortune, by illustrating more fully the affecion of her lover, drew him closer to her heart, and seemed, therefore, to sharpen the poignancy of her affliction. The dreadful assertion that Theodore, should he recover, would be punished with death, she scarcely dared to consider, but endeavoured to believe that it was no more than a cruel exaggeration of his antagonist.

Upon the whole, Theodore's present danger, together with the attendant circumstances, awakened all her tenderness, and discovered to her the true state of her affections. The graceful form, the noble, intelligent countenance, and the engaging manners which she had at first admired in Theodore, became afterwards more interesting by that strength of thought, and elegance of sentiment, exhibited in his conversation. His conduct, since her escape, had excited her warmest gratitude, and the danger which he had now encountered in her behalf, called forth her tenderness, and heightened it into love. The veil was removed from her heart, and she saw, for the first time, its genuine emotions.

The surgeon at length came out of Theodore's chamber into the room where Adeline was waiting to speak with him. She inquired concerning the state of his wound. 'You are a relation of the gentleman's, I presume, Madam; his sister, perhaps.' The question vexed and embarrassed her, and, without answering it, she repeated her inquiry. 'Perhaps, Madam, you are more nearly related,' pursued the surgeon, seeming also to disregard her question, 'perhaps you are his wife.' Adeline blushed, and was about to reply, but he continued his speech. 'The interest you take in his welfare is, at least, very flattering, and I would almost consent to exchange conditions with him, were I sure of receiving such tender compassion from so charming a lady.' Saying this, he bowed to the ground. Adeline assuming a very reserved air, said, 'Now, Sir, that you have concluded your compliment, you will, perhaps, attend to my question; I have inquired how you left your patient.'

'That, Madam, is, perhaps, a question very difficult to be resolved; and it is likewise a very disagreeable office to pronounce ill news—I fear he will die.' The surgeon opened his snuff-box and presented it to Adeline. 'Die!' she exclaimed in a faint voice, 'Die!'

'Do not be alarmed, Madam,' resumed the surgeon, observing her grow pale, 'do not be alarmed. It is possible that the wound may not have reached the——,' he stammered; 'in that case the——,' stammering again, 'is not affected; and if so, the interior membranes of the brain are not touched: in this case the wound may, perhaps, escape inflammation, and the patient may possibly recover. But if, on the other hand,——'

'I beseech you, Sir, to speak intelligibly,' interrupted Adeline, 'and not to trifle with my anxiety. Do you really believe him in danger?'

'In danger, Madam,' exclaimed the surgeon, 'in danger! yes, certainly, in very great danger.' Saying this, he walked away with an air of chagrin and displeasure. Adeline remained for some moments in the room, in an excess of sorrow, which she found it impossible to restrain, and then drying her tears, and endeavouring to compose her countenance, she went to inquire for the mistress of the inn, to whom she sent a waiter. After expecting her in vain for some time, she rang the bell, and sent another message somewhat more pressing. Still the hostess did not appear, and Adeline, at length, went herself down stairs, where she found her, surrounded by a number of people, relating, with a loud voice and various gesticulations, the particulars of the late accident. Perceiving Adeline, she called out, 'Oh! here is Mademoiselle herself,' and the eyes of the assembly were immediately turned upon her. Adeline, whom the crowd prevented from approaching the hostess, now beckoned her, and was going to withdraw, but the landlady, eager in the pursuit of her story, disregarded the signal. In vain did Adeline endeavour to catch her eye; it glanced every where but upon her, who was unwilling to attract the farther notice of the crowd by calling out.

'It is a great pity, to be sure, that he should be shot,' said the landlady, 'he's such a handsome man; but they say he certainly will if he recovers. Poor gentleman! he will very likely not suffer though, for the doctor says he will never go out of this house alive.' Adeline now spoke to a man who stood near, and desiring he would tell the hostess she wished to speak with her, left the place.

In about ten minutes the landlady appeared. 'Alas! Madamoiselle,' said she, 'your brother is in a sad condition; they fear he won't get over it.' Adeline inquired whether there was any other medical person in the town than the surgeon whom she had seen. 'Lord, Madam, this is a rare healthy place; we have little need of *medicine* people here; such an accident never happened in it before. The doctor has been here ten years, but there's very bad encouragement for his trade, and I believe he's poor enough himself. One of the sort's quite enough for us.' Adeline interrupted her to ask some questions concerning Theodore, whom the hostess had attended to his chamber. She inquired how he had borne the dressing of the wound, and whether he appeared to be easier after the operation; questions to which the hostess gave no very satisfactory answers. She now inquired whether there was any surgeon in the neighbourhood of the town, and was told there was not.

The distress visible in Adeline's countenance, seemed to excite the compassion of the landlady, who now endeavoured to console her in the best manner she was able. She advised her to send for her friends, and offered to procure a messenger. Adeline sighed and said it was unnecessary. 'I don't know, Ma'amselle, what you may think necessary,' continued the hostess, 'but I know I should think it very hard to die in a strange place with no relations near me, and I dare say the poor gentleman thinks so himself; and, besides, who is to pay for his funeral if he dies?' Adeline begged she would be silent, and, desiring that every proper attention might be given, she promised her a reward for her trouble, and requested pen and ink immediately. 'Ay, to be sure, Ma'amselle, that is the proper way; why your friends would never forgive you if you did not acquaint them; I know it by myself. And as for taking care of him, he shall have every thing the house affords, and I warrant there is never a better inn in the province, though the town is none of the biggest.' Adeline was obliged to repeat her request for pen and ink, before the loquacious hostess would quit the room.

The thought of sending for Theodore's friends had, in the tumult of the late scenes, never occurred to her, and she was now somewhat consoled by the prospect of comfort which it opened for him. When the pen and ink were brought, she wrote the following note to Theodore.

'In your present condition, you have need of every comfort that can be procured you, and surely there is no cordial more valuable in illness, than the presence of a friend: suffer me, therefore, to acquaint your family with your situation; it will be a satisfaction to me, and, I doubt not, a consolation to you.'

In a short time after she had sent the note, she received a message from Theodore, entreating most respectfully, but earnestly, to see her for a few minutes. She immediately went to his chamber, and found her worst apprehensions confirmed, by the languor expressed in his countenance, while the shock she received, together with her struggle to disguise her emotions, almost overcame her. 'I thank you for this goodness,' said he, extending his hand, which she received, and, sitting down by the bed, burst into a flood of tears. When her agitation had somewhat subsided, and, removing her handkerchief from her eyes, she again looked on Theodore, a smile of the tenderest love expressed his sense of the interest she took in his welfare, and administered a temporary relief to her heart.

'Forgive this weakness,' said she; 'my spirits have of late been so variously agitated'—Theodore interrupted her—'These tears are most flattering to my heart. But, for my sake, endeavour to support yourself: I doubt not I shall soon be better; the surgeon'—

'I do not like him,' said Adeline, 'but tell me how you find yourself?' He assured her that he was now much easier than he had yet been, and mentioning her kind note, he led to the subject, on account of which he had solicited to see her. 'My family,' said he, 'reside at a great distance from hence, and I well know their affection is such, that, were they informed of my situation, no consideration, however reasonable, could prevent their coming to my assistance; but before they can arrive, their presence will probably be unnecessary,' (Adeline looked earnestly at him) 'I should probably be well,' pursued he, smiling, 'before a letter could reach them; it would, therefore, occasion them unnecessary pain, and, moreover, a fruitless journey. For your sake, Adeline, I could wish they were here, but a few days will more fully shew the consequences of my wound: let us wait, at least, till then, and be directed by circumstances.'

Adeline forbore to press the subject farther, and turned to one more immediately interesting. 'I much wish,' said she, 'that you had a more able surgeon; you know the geography of the province better than I do; are we in the neighbourhood of any town likely to afford you other advice?'

'I believe not,' said he, 'and this is an affair of little consequence, for my wound is so inconsiderable, that a very moderate share of skill may suffice to cure it. But why, my beloved Adeline, do you give way to this anxiety? Why suffer yourself to be disturbed by this tendency to forbode the worst? I am willing, perhaps presumptuously so, to attribute it to your kindness, and suffer me to assure you, that, while it excites my gratitude, it increases my tenderest esteem. O

Adeline! since you wish my speedy recovery, let me see you composed: while I believe you to be unhappy I cannot be well.'—She assured him she would endeavour to be, at least, tranquil, and fearing the conversation, if prolonged, would be prejudicial to him, she left him to repose.

As she turned out of the gallery, she met the hostess, upon whom certain words of Adeline had operated as a talisman, transforming neglect and impertinence into officious civility. She came to inquire whether the gentleman above stairs had every thing that he liked, for she was sure it was her endeavour that he should. 'I have got him a nurse, Ma'amselle, to attend him, and I dare say she will do very well, but I will look to that, for I shall not mind helping him myself sometimes. Poor gentleman! how patiently he bears it! One would not think now that he believes he is going to die; yet the doctor told him so himself, or, at least as good.' Adeline was extremely shocked at this imprudent conduct of the surgeon, and dismissed the landlady, after ordering a slight dinner.

Towards evening the surgeon again made his appearance, and, having passed some time with his patient, returned to the parlour, according to the desire of Adeline, to inform her of his condition. He answered Adeline's inquiries with great solemnity. 'It is impossible to determine positively, at present, Madam, but I have reason to adhere to the opinion I gave you this morning. I am not apt, indeed, to form opinions upon uncertain grounds. I will give you a singular instance of this:

'It is not above a fortnight since I was sent for to a patient at some leagues distance. I was from home when the messenger arrived, and the case being urgent, before I could reach the patient, another physician was consulted,* who had ordered such medicines as he thought proper, and the patient had been apparently relieved by them. His friends were congratulating themselves upon his improvement when I arrived, and had agreed in opinion with the physician, that there was no danger in his case. Depend upon it, said I, you are mistaken; these medicines cannot have relieved him; the patient is in the utmost danger. The patient groaned, but my brother physician persisted in affirming that the remedies he had prescribed would not only be certain, but speedy, some good effect having been already produced by them. Upon this I lost all patience, and adhering to my opinion, that these effects were fallacious and the case desperate, I assured the patient himself that his life was in the utmost danger. I am not one of those, Madam, who deceive their patients to the last moment; but you shall hear the conclusion.

'My brother physician was, I suppose, enraged by the firmness of my opposition, for he assumed a most angry look, which did not in the least affect me, and turning to the patient, desired he would decide, upon which of our opinions to rely, for he must decline acting with me. The patient did me the honour,' pursued the surgeon, with a smile of complacency, and smoothing his ruffles, 'to think more highly of me than, perhaps, I deserved, for he immediately dismissed my opponent. I could not have believed, said he, as the physician left the room, I could not have believed that a man, who has been so many years in the profession, could be so wholly ignorant of it.

'I could not have believed it either, said I.—I am astonished that he was not aware of my danger, resumed the patient.—I am astonished likewise, replied I—I was resolved to do what I could for the patient, for he was a man of understanding, as you perceive, and I had a regard for him. I, therefore, altered the prescriptions, and myself administered the medicines; but all would not do, my opinion was verified, and he died even before the next morning.'——Adeline, who had been compelled to listen to this long story, sighed at the conclusion of it. 'I don't wonder that you are affected, Madam,' said the surgeon, 'the instance I have related is certainly a very affecting one. It distressed me so much, that it was some time before I could think, or even speak concerning it. But you must allow, Madam,' continued he, lowering his voice and bowing with a look of self-congratulation, 'that this was a striking instance of the infallibility of my judgement.'

Adeline shuddered at the infallibility of his judgement, and made no reply. 'It was a shocking thing for the poor man,' resumed the surgeon.—'It was, indeed, very shocking,' said Adeline.—'It affected me a good deal when it happened,' continued he.—'Undoubtedly, Sir,' said Adeline.

'But time wears away the most painful impressions.'

'I think you mentioned it was about a fortnight since this happened.'

'Somewhere thereabouts,' replied the surgeon, without seeming to understand the observation.—'And will you permit me, Sir, to ask the name of the physician, who so ignorantly opposed you?'

'Certainly, Madam, it is Lafance.'

'He lives in the obscurity he deserves, no doubt,' said Adeline.

'Why no, Madam, he lives in a town of some note, at about the distance of four leagues from hence, and affords one instance, among many others, that the public opinion is generally erroneous. You will hardly believe it, but I assure you it is a fact, that this man comes into a great deal of practice, while I am suffered to remain here, neglected, and, indeed, very little known.'

During his narrative, Adeline had been considering by what means she could discover the name of the physician, for the instance that had been produced to prove his *ignorance*, and the *infallibility* of his opponent, had completely settled her opinion concerning them both. She now, more than ever, wished to deliver Theodore from the hands of the surgeon, and was musing on the possibility, when he, with so much self-security, developed the means.

She asked him a few more questions, concerning the state of Theodore's wound, and was told it was much as it had been, but that some degree of fever had come on. 'But I have ordered a fire to be made in the room,' continued the surgeon, 'and some additional blankets to be laid on the bed; these, I doubt not, will have a proper effect. In the mean time, they must be careful to keep from him every kind of liquid, except some cordial draughts, which I shall send. He will naturally ask for drink, but it must, on no account, be given to him.'

'You do not approve, then, of the method, which I have somewhere heard of,' said Adeline, 'of attending to nature in these cases.'

'Nature, Madam!' pursued he, 'Nature is the most improper guide in the world. I always adopt a method directly contrary to what she would suggest; for what can be the use of Art, if she is only to follow Nature? This was my first opinion on setting out in life, and I have ever since strictly adhered to it. From what I have said, indeed, Madam, you may, perhaps, perceive that my opinions may be depended on; what they once are they always are, for my mind is not of that frivolous kind to be affected by circumstances.'

Adeline was fatigued by this discourse, and impatient to impart to Theodore her discovery of a physician, but the surgeon seemed by no means disposed to leave her, and was expatiating upon various topics, with new instances of his surprising sagacity, when the waiter brought a message that some person desired to see him. He was, however, engaged upon too agreeable a topic to be easily prevailed upon to quit it, and it was not till after a second message was brought that he made his bow to Adeline and left the room. The moment he was gone she sent a note to Theodore, entreating his permission to call in the assistance of the physician.

The conceited manners of the surgeon had by this time given Theodore a very unfavourable opinion of his talents, and the last prescription had so fully confirmed it, that he now readily consented to have other advice. Adeline immediately inquired for a messenger, but recollecting that the residence of the physician was still a secret, she applied to the hostess, who being really ignorant of it, or pretending to be so, gave her no information. What farther inquiries she made were equally ineffectual, and she passed some hours in extreme distress, while the disorder of Theodore rather increased than abated.

When supper appeared, she asked the boy who waited, if he knew a physician of the name of Lafance, in the neighbourhood. 'Not in the neighbourhood, Madam, but I know Doctor Lafance of Chancy, for I come from the town.'—Adeline inquired farther, and received very satisfactory answers. But the town was at some leagues distance, and the delay this circumstance must occasion again alarmed her; she, however, ordered a messenger to be immediately dispatched, and, having sent again to inquire concerning Theodore, retired to her chamber for the night.

The continued fatigue she had suffered for the last fourteen hours overcame anxiety, and her harrassed spirits sunk to repose. She slept till late in the morning, and was then awakened by the landlady, who came to inform her, that Theodore was much worse, and to inquire what should be done. Adeline, finding that the physician was not arrived, immediately arose, and hastened to inquire farther concerning Theodore. The hostess informed her, that he had passed a very disturbed night; that he had complained of being hot, and desired that the fire in his room might be extinguished; but that the nurse knew her duty too well to obey him, and had strictly followed the doctor's orders.

She added, that he had taken the cordial draughts regularly, but had, notwithstanding, continued to grow worse, and at last became light-headed. In the mean time the boy, who had been sent for the physician, was still absent:—'And no wonder,' continued the hostess; 'why, only consider, it's eight leagues off, and the lad had to find the road, bad as it is, in the dark. But, indeed, Ma'amselle, you might as well have trusted our doctor, for we never want any body else, not we, in the town here; and if I might speak my mind, Jacques had better have been sent off for the young gentleman's friends than for this strange doctor that no body knows.'

After asking some farther questions concerning Theodore, the answers to which rather increased than diminished her alarm, Adeline endeavoured to compose her spirits, and await in patience the arrival of the physician. She was now more sensible than ever of the forlornness of her own condition, and of the danger of Theodore's, and earnestly wished that his friends could be informed of his situation; a wish which could not be gratified, for Theodore, who alone could acquaint her with their place of residence, was deprived of recollection.

When the surgeon arrived and perceived the situation of his patient, he expressed no surprise; but having asked some questions, and given a few general directions, he went down to Adeline. After paying her his usual compliments, he suddenly assumed an air of importance, 'I am sorry, Madam,' said he, 'that it is my office to communicate disagreeable intelligence, but I wish you to be prepared for the event, which, I fear, is approaching.' Adeline comprehended his meaning, and though she had hitherto given little faith to his judgement, she could not hear him hint at the immediate danger of Theodore without yielding to the influence of fear.

She entreated him to acquaint her with all he apprehended; and he then proceeded to say, that Theodore was, as he had foreseen, much worse this morning than he had been the preceding night; and the disorder having now affected his head, there was every reason to fear it would prove fatal in a few hours. 'The worst consequences may ensue,' continued he; 'if the wound becomes inflamed, there will be very little chance of his recovery.'

Adeline listened to this sentence with a dreadful calmness, and gave no utterance to grief, either by words or tears. 'The gentleman, I suppose, Madam, has friends, and the sooner you inform them of his condition the better. If they reside at any distance, it is indeed too late; but there are other necessary——you are ill, Madam.'

Adeline made an effort to speak, but in vain, and the surgeon now called loudly for a glass of water; she drank it, and a deep sigh that she uttered, seemed somewhat to relieve her oppressed heart: tears succeeded. In the mean time, the surgeon perceiving she was better, though not well enough to listen to his conversation, took his leave, and promised to return in an hour. The physician was not yet arrived, and Adeline awaited his appearance with a mixture of fear and anxious hope.

About noon he came, and having been informed of the accident by which the fever was produced, and of the treatment which the surgeon had given it, he ascended to Theodore's chamber: in a quarter of an hour he returned to the room where Adeline expected him. 'The gentleman is still delirious,' said he, 'but I have ordered him a composing draught.'——'Is there any hope, Sir?' inquired Adeline. 'Yes, Madam, certainly there is hope; the case at present is somewhat doubtful, but a few hours may enable me to judge with more certainty. In the mean time, I have directed that he shall be kept quiet, and be allowed to drink freely of some diluting liquids.'

He had scarcely, at Adeline's request, recommended a
surgeon, instead of the one at present employed, when the
latter gentleman entered the room, and, perceiving the
physician, threw a glance of mingled surprize and anger at
Adeline, who retired with him to another apartment, where
she dismissed him with a politeness, which he did not deign
to return, and which he certainly did not deserve.

Early the following morning the surgeon arrived, but either
the medicines, or the crisis of the disorder, had thrown
Theodore into a deep sleep, in which he remained for several
hours. The physician now gave Adeline reason to hope for a
favourable issue, and every precaution was taken to prevent
his being disturbed. He awoke perfectly sensible and free from
fever, and his first words inquired for Adeline, who soon
learned that he was out of danger.

In a few days he was sufficiently recovered to be removed
from his chamber to a room adjoining, where Adeline met him
with a joy, which she found it impossible to repress; and the
observance of this lighted up his countenance with pleasure:
indeed Adeline, sensible to the attachment he had so nobly
testified, and softened by the danger he had encountered, no
longer attempted to disguise the tenderness of her esteem, and
was at length brought to confess the interest his first
appearance had impressed upon her heart.

After an hour of affecting conversation, in which the happiness of a young and mutual attachment occupied all their
minds, and excluded every idea not in unison with delight,
they returned to a sense of their present embarrassments:
Adeline recollected that Theodore was arrested for disobedience of orders, and deserting his post; and Theodore,
that he must shortly be torn away from Adeline, who would
be left exposed to all the evils from which he had so lately
rescued her. This thought overwhelmed his heart with
anguish; and, after a long pause, he ventured to propose, what
his wishes had often suggested, a marriage with Adeline
before he departed from the village: this was the only means
of preventing, perhaps, an eternal separation; and though he
saw the many dangerous inconveniences to which she would
be exposed, by a marriage with a man circumstanced like

himself, yet these appeared so unequal to those she would otherwise be left to encounter alone, that his reason could no longer scruple to adopt what his affection had suggested.

Adeline was, for some time, too much agitated to reply; and though she had little to oppose to the arguments and pleadings of Theodore; though she had no friends to control, and no contrariety of interests to perplex her, she could not bring herself to consent thus hastily to a marriage with a man, of whom she had little knowledge, and to whose family and connections she had no sort of introduction. At length, she entreated he would drop the subject, and the conversation for the remainder of the day was more general, yet still interesting.

That similarity of taste and opinion, which had at first attracted them, every moment now more fully disclosed. Their discourse was enriched by elegant literature, and endeared by mutual regard. Adeline had enjoyed few opportunities of reading, but the books to which she had access, operating upon a mind eager for knowledge, and upon a taste peculiarly sensible of the beautiful and the elegant, had impressed all their excellencies upon her understanding. Theodore had received from nature many of the qualities of genius, and from education all that it could bestow; to these were added, a noble independency of spirit, a feeling heart, and manners, which partook of a happy mixture of dignity and sweetness.

In the evening, one of the officers, who, upon the representation of the serjeant, was sent by the persons employed to prosecute military criminals, arrived at the village, and entering the apartment of Theodore, from which Adeline immediately withdrew, informed him, with an air of infinite importance, that he should set out on the following day for head-quarters. Theodore answered, that he was not able to bear the journey, and referred him to his physician; but the officer replied, that he should take no such trouble, it being certain that the physician might be instructed what to say, and that he should begin his journey on the morrow. 'Here has been delay enough,' said he, 'already, and you will have sufficient business on your hands when you reach head-quarters; for the serjeant, whom you have severely wounded, intends to appear against you; and this, with the offence you have committed by deserting your post.'——

Theodore's eyes flashed fire, 'Deserting!' said he, rising from his scat, and darting a look of menace at his accuser, 'who dares to brand me with the name of deserter?' But instantly recollecting how much his conduct had appeared to justify the accusation, he endeavoured to stifle his emotions, and, with a firm voice and composed manner, said, that when he reached head-quarters, he should be ready to answer whatever might be brought against him, but that till then he should be silent. The boldness of the officer was repressed by the spirit and dignity with which Theodore spoke these words, and muttering a reply, that was scarcely audible, he left the room.

Theodore sat musing on the danger of his situation: he knew that he had much to apprehend from the peculiar circumstances attending his abrupt departure from his regiment, it having been stationed in a garrison town upon the Spanish frontiers; where the discipline was very severe, and from the power of his colonel, the Marquis de Montalt, whom pride and disappointment would now rouse to vengeance, and, probably, render indefatigable in the accomplishment of his destruction. But his thoughts soon fled from his own danger to that of Adeline, and, in the consideration of this, all his fortitude forsook him: he could not support the idea of leaving her exposed to the evils he foreboded, nor, indeed, of a separation so sudden as that which now threatened him; and when she again entered the room, he renewed his solicitations for a speedy marriage, with all the arguments that tenderness and ingenuity could suggest.

Adeline, when she learned that he was to depart on the morrow, felt as if bereaved of her last comfort. All the horrors of his situation arose to her mind, and she turned from him in unutterable anguish. Considering her silence as a favourable presage, he repeated his entreaties that she would consent to be his, and thus give him a surety that their separation should not be eternal. Adeline sighed deeply to these words: 'And who can know that our separation will *not* be eternal,' said she, 'even if I could consent to the marriage you propose? But while you hear my determination, forbear to accuse me of indifference, for indifference towards you would, indeed, be a crime, after the services you have rendered me.'

'And is a cold sentiment of gratitude all that I must expect from you?' said Theodore. 'I know that you are going to distress me with a proof of your indifference, which you mistake for the suggestions of prudence; and that I shall be compelled to look, without reluctance, upon the evils that may shortly await me. Ah, Adeline! if you mean to reject this, perhaps, the last proposal which I can ever make to you, cease, at least, to deceive yourself with an idea that you love me; that delirium is fading even from my mind.'

'Can you then so soon forget our conversation of this morning?' replied Adeline; 'and can you think so lightly of me as to believe I would profess a regard, which I do not feel? If, indeed, you can believe this, I shall do well to forget that I ever made such an acknowledgement, and you, that you heard it.'

'Forgive me, Adeline, forgive the doubts and inconsistencies I have betrayed: let the anxieties of love, and the emergency of my circumstances, plead for me.' Adeline, smiling faintly through her tears, held out her hand, which he seized and pressed to his lips. 'Yet do not drive me to despair by a rejection of my suit,' continued Theodore; 'think what I must suffer to leave you here destitute of friends and protection.'

'I am thinking how I may avoid a situation so deplorable,' said Adeline. 'They say there is a convent, which receives boarders, within a few miles, and thither I wish to go.'

'A convent!' rejoined Theodore, 'would you go to a convent? Do you know the persecutions you would be liable to; and that if the Marquis should discover you, there is little probability the superior would resist his authority, or, at least, his bribes?'

'All this I have considered,' said Adeline, 'and am prepared to encounter it, rather than enter into an engagement, which, at this time, can be productive only of misery to us both.'

'Ah, Adeline! could you think thus, if you truly loved? I see myself about to be separated, and that, perhaps, for ever, from the object of my tenderest affections—and I cannot but express all the anguish I feel—I cannot forbear to repeat every argument that may afford even the slightest possibility of altering your determination. But *you*, Adeline, *you* look with complacency upon a circumstance which tortures *me* with despair.'

Adeline, who had long tried to support her spirits in his presence, while she adhered to a resolution which reason suggested, but which the pleadings of her heart powerfully opposed, was unable longer to command her distress, and burst into tears. Theodore was in the same moment convinced of his error, and shocked at the grief he had occasioned. He drew his chair towards her, and, taking her hand, again entreated her pardon, and endeavoured in the tenderest accents to soothe and comfort her.— 'What a wretch was I to cause you this distress, by questioning that regard with which I can no longer doubt you honour me! Forgive me, Adeline; say but you forgive me, and, whatever may be the pain of this separation, I will no longer oppose it.'

'You have given me some pain,' said Adeline, 'but you have not offended me.'—She then mentioned some farther particulars concerning the convent. Theodore endeavoured to conceal the distress which the approaching separation occasioned him, and to consult with her on these plans with composure. His judgement by degrees prevailed over his passions, and he now perceived that the plan she suggested would afford her best chance of security. He considered, what in the first agitation of his mind had escaped him, that he might be condemned upon the charges brought against him, and that his death, should they have been married, would not only deprive her of her protector, but leave her more immediately exposed to the designs of the Marquis, who would, doubtless, attend his trial. Astonished that he had not noticed this before, and shocked at the unwariness by which he might have betrayed her into so dangerous a situation, he became at once reconciled to the idea of leaving her in a convent. He could have wished to place her in the asylum of his own family, but the circumstances under which she must be introduced were so awkward and painful, and, above all, the distance at which they resided, would render a journey so highly dangerous for her, that he forbore to propose it. He entreated only that she would allow him to write to her; but recollecting that his letters might be a means of betraying the place of her residence to the Marquis, he checked himself: 'I must deny myself even this melancholy pleasure,' said he, 'lest my letters should discover your abode; yet how shall I be able to endure the impatience and uncertainty to which prudence condemns me! If you are in danger, I shall be ignorant of it; though, indeed, did I know it,' said he with a look of despair, 'I could not fly to save you. O exquisite misery! 'tis now only I perceive all the horrors of confinement—'tis now only that I understand the value of liberty!'

His utterance was interrupted by the violent agitation of his mind; he rose from his chair, and walked with quick paces about the room. Adeline sat, overcome by the description which Theodore had given of his approaching situation, and by the consideration that she might remain in the most terrible suspense concerning his fate. She saw him in a prison—pale—emaciated, and in chains:—she saw all the vengeance of the Marquis descending upon him; and this for his noble exertions in her cause. Theodore, alarmed by the placid despair expressed in her countenance, threw himself into a chair by her's, and, taking her hand, attempted to speak comfort to her, but the words faltered on his lips, and he could only bathe her hand with tears.

This mournful silence was interrupted by the arrival of the carriage at the inn, and Theodore, arising, went to the window that opened into the yard. The darkness of the night prevented his distinguishing the objects without, but a light now brought from the house shewed him a carriage and four, attended by several servants. Presently he saw a gentleman, wrapped up in a roquelaure,* alight and enter the inn, and the next moment he heard the voice of the Marquis.

He had flown to support Adeline, who was sinking with terror, when the door opened, and the Marquis, followed by the officers and several servants, entered. Fury flashed from his eyes, as they glanced upon Theodore, who hung over Adeline with a look of fearful solicitude—'Seize that traitor,' said he turning to the officers; 'why have you suffered him to remain here so long?'

'I am no traitor,' said Theodore, with a firm voice, and the dignity of conscious worth, 'but a defender of innocence, of one whom the treacherous Marquis de Montalt would destroy.'

'Obey your orders,' said the Marquis to the officers. Adeline shrieked, held faster by Theodore's arm, and entreated the men not to part them. 'Force only can effect it,' said Theodore, as he looked round for some instrument of defence, but he could see none, and in the same moment they surrounded and seized him. 'Dread every thing from my vengeance,' said the Marquis to Theodore, as he caught the hand of Adeline, who had lost all power of resistance, and was scarcely sensible of what passed; 'dread every thing from my vengeance; you know you have deserved it.'

'I defy your vengeance,' cried Theodore, 'and dread only the pangs of conscience, which your power cannot inflict upon me, though your vices condemn you to its tortures.'

'Take him instantly from the room, and see that he is strongly fettered,' said the Marquis; 'he shall soon know what a criminal, who adds insolence to guilt, may suffer.'— Theodore, exclaiming, 'Oh Adeline! farewell!' was now forced out of the room; while Adeline, whose torpid senses were roused by his voice and his last looks, fell at the feet of the Marquis, and with tears of agony implored compassion for Theodore: but her pleadings for his rival served only to irritate the pride and exasperate the hatred of the Marquis. He denounced vengeance on his head, and imprecations too dreadful for the spirits of Adeline, whom he compelled to rise; and then, endeavouring to stifle the emotions of rage, which the presence of Theodore had excited, he began to address her with his usual expressions of admiration.

The wretched Adeline, who, regardless of what he said, still continued to plead for her unhappy lover, was at length alarmed by the returning rage which the countenance of the Marquis expressed, and, exerting all her remaining strength, she sprung from his grasp towards the door of the room; but he seized her hand before she could reach it, and, regardless of her shrieks, bringing her back to her chair, was going to speak, when voices were heard in the passage, and immediately the landlord and his wife, whom Adeline's cries had alarmed, entered the apartment. The Marquis, turning furiously to them, demanded what they wanted; but not waiting for their answer, he bade them attend him, and quitting the room, she heard the door locked upon her.

Adeline now ran to the windows, which were unfastened, and opened into the inn-yard. All was dark and silent. She called aloud for help, but no person appeared; and the windows were so high, that it was impossible to escape unassisted. She walked about the room in an agony of terror and distress, now stopping to listen, and fancying she heard voices disputing below, and now quickening her steps, as suspense increased the agitation of her mind.

She had continued in this state for near half an hour, when she suddenly heard a violent noise in the lower part of the house, which increased till all was uproar and confusion. People passed quickly through the passages, and doors were frequently opened and shut. She called, but received no answer. It immediately occurred to her, that Theodore, having heard her screams, had attempted to come to her assistance, and that the bustle had been occasioned by the opposition of the officers. Knowing their fierceness and cruelty, she was seized with dreadful apprehensions for the life of Theodore.

A confused uproar of voices now sounded from below, and the screams of women convinced her there was fighting; she even thought she heard the clashing of swords; the image of Theodore, dying by the hands of the Marquis, now rose to her imagination, and the terrors of suspense became almost insupportable. She made a desperate effort to force the door, and again called for help, but her trembling hands were powerless, and every person in the house seemed to be too much engaged even to hear her. A loud shriek now pierced her ears, and, amidst the tumult that followed, she clearly distinguished deep groans. This confirmation of her fears deprived her of all her remaining spirits, and growing faint, she sunk almost lifeless into a chair near the door. The uproar gradually subsided till all was still, but nobody returned to her. Soon after she heard voices in the yard, but she had no power to walk across the room, even to ask the questions she wished, yet feared, to have answered.

About a quarter of an hour elapsed, when the door was unlocked, and the hostess appeared with a countenance as pale as death. 'For God's sake,' said Adeline, 'tell me what has happened? Is he wounded? Is he killed?'

'He is not dead, Ma'amselle, but—'.

'He is dying then?—tell me where he is—let me go.'

'Stop, Ma'amselle,' cried the hostess, 'you are to stay here, I only want the hartshorn out of that cupboard there.' Adeline tried to escape by the door, but the hostess, pushing her aside, locked it, and went down stairs.

Adeline's distress now entirely overcame her, and she sat motionless, and scarcely conscious that she existed, till roused by a sound of footsteps near the door, which was again opened and three men, whom she knew to be the Marquis's servants, entered. She had sufficient recollection to repeat the questions she had asked the landlady, but they answered only that she must come with them, and that a chaise was waiting for her at the door. Still she urged her questions. 'Tell me if he lives,' cried she.—'Yes, Ma'amselle, he is alive, but he is terribly wounded, and the surgeon is just come to him.' As they spoke they hurried her along the passage, and without noticing her entreaties and supplications to know whither she was going, they had reached the foot of the stairs, when her cries brought several people to the door. To these the hostess related, that the lady was the wife of a gentleman just arrived, who had overtaken her in her flight with a gallant; an account which the Marquis's servants corroborated. ''Tis the gentleman who has just fought the duel,' added the hostess, 'and it was on her account.'

Adeline, partly disdaining to take any notice of this artful story, and partly from her desire to know the particulars of what had happened, contented herself with repeating her inquiries; to which one of the spectators at last replied, that the gentleman was desperately wounded. The Marquis's people would now have hurried her into the chaise, but she sunk lifeless in their arms, and her condition so interested the humanity of the spectators, that, notwithstanding their belief of what had been said, they opposed the effort made to carry her, senseless as she was, into the carriage.

She was at length taken into a room, and, by proper applications, restored to her senses. There she so earnestly besought an explanation of what had happened, that the hostess acquainted her with some particulars of the late rencounter. 'When the gentleman that was ill heard your screams, Madam,' said she, 'he became quite outrageous, as they tell me, and nothing could pacify him. The Marquis, for they say he is a Marquis, but you know best, was then in the room with my husband and I, and when he heard the uproar, he went down to see what was the matter; and when he came into the room where the Captain was, he found him struggling with the serjeant. Then the Captain was more outrageous than ever; and notwithstanding he had one leg chained, and no sword, he contrived to get the serjeant's cutlass out of the scabbard, and immediately flew at the Marquis, and wounded him desperately; upon which he was secured.'—'It is the Marquis then who is wounded,' said Adeline; 'the other gentleman is not hurt?'

'No, not he,' replied the hostess; 'but he will smart for it by and bye, for the Marquis swears he will do for him.' Adeline, for a moment, forgot all her misfortunes and all her her danger in thankfulness for the immediate escape of Theodore; and she was proceeding to make some farther inquiries concerning him, when the Marquis's servants entered the room, and declared they could wait no longer. Adeline, now awakened to a sense of the evils with which she was threatened, endeavoured to win the pity of the hostess, who, however, was, or affected to be, convinced of the truth of the Marquis's story, and, therefore, insensible to all she could urge. Again she addressed his servants, but in vain; they would neither suffer her to remain longer at the inn, or inform her whither she was going; but, in the presence of several persons, already prejudiced by the injurious assertions of the hostess, Adeline was hurried into the chaise, and her conductors mounting their horses, the whole party was very soon beyond the village.

Thus ended Adeline's share of an adventure, begun with a

prospect not only of security, but of happiness; an adventure, which had attached her more closely to Theodore, and shewn him to be more worthy of her love; but which, at the same time, had distressed her by new disappointment, produced the imprisonment of her generous and now-adored lover, and delivered both himself and her into the power of a rival, irritated by delay, contempt, and opposition.

CHAPTER XIII

'Nor sea, nor shade, nor shield, nor rock, nor cave,
   Nor silent desarts, nor the sullen grave,
Where flame-ey'd Fury means to frown—can save.'*

THE surgeon of the place, having examined the Marquis's wound, gave him an immediate opinion upon it, and ordered that he should be put to bed: but the Marquis, ill as he was, had scarcely any other apprehension than that of losing Adeline, and declared he should be able to begin his journey in a few hours. With this intention, he had begun to give orders for keeping horses in readiness, when the surgeon persisting most seriously, and even passionately to exclaim, that his life would be the sacrifice of his rashness, he was carried to a bed-chamber, where his valet alone was permitted to attend him.

This man, the convenient confidant of all his intrigues, had been the chief instrument in assisting his designs concerning Adeline, and was indeed the very person who had brought her to the Marquis's villa on the borders of the forest. To him the Marquis gave his farther directions concerning her; and, foreseeing the inconvenience, as well as the danger of detaining her at the inn, he had ordered him, with several other servants, to carry her away immediately in a hired carriage. The valet having gone to execute his orders, the Marquis was left to his own reflections, and to the violence of contending passions.

The reproaches and continued opposition of Theodore, the favoured lover of Adeline, exasperated his pride, and roused all his malice. He could not for a moment consider this opposition, which was in some respects successful, without feeling an excess of indignation and inveteracy, such as the prospect of a speedy revenge could alone enable him to support.

When he had discovered Adeline's escape from the villa, his surprize at first equalled his disappointment; and; after exhausting the paroxysms of his rage upon his domestics, he dispatched them all different ways in pursuit of her, going himself to the abbey, in the faint hope, that, destitute as she was of other succour, she might have fled thither. La Motte, however, being as much surprized as himself, and as ignorant of the route which Adeline had taken, he returned to the villa, impatient of intelligence, and found some of his servants arrived, without any news of Adeline, and those who came afterwards were as successless as the first.

A few days after, a letter from the Lieutenant-Colonel of the regiment informed him, that Theodore had quitted his company, and had been for some time absent, nobody knew where. This information, confirming a suspicion which had frequently occurred to him, that Theodore had been by some means, or other, instrumental in the escape of Adeline, all his other passions became, for a time, subservient to his revenge, and he gave orders for the immediate pursuit and apprehension of Theodore: but Theodore, in the mean time, had been overtaken and secured.

It was in consequence of having formerly observed the growing partiality between him and Adeline, and of intelligence received from La Motte, who had noticed their interview in the forest, that the Marquis had resolved to remove a rival so dangerous to his love, and so likely to be informed of his designs. He had therefore told Theodore, in a manner as plausible as he could, that it would be necessary for him to join the regiment; a notice which affected him only as it related to Adeline, and which seemed the less extraordinary, as he had already been at the villa a much longer time than was usual with the officers invited by the Marquis. Theodore, indeed, very well knew the character of the Marquis, and had accepted his invitation rather from an unwillingness to shew any disrespect of his Colonel by a refusal, than from a sanguine expectation of pleasure.

From the men who had apprehended Theodore, the Marquis received the information, which had enabled him to pursue and recover Adeline; but, though he had now effected this, he was internally a prey to the corrosive effects of disappointed passion and exasperated pride. The anguish of his wound was almost forgotten in that of his mind, and every pang he felt seemed to increase his thirst of revenge, and to recoil with new torture upon his heart. While he was in this state, he heard the voice of the innocent Adeline imploring protection; but her cries excited in him neither pity or remorse; and when, soon after, the carriage drove away, and he was certain both that she was secured, and Theodore was wretched, he seemed to feel some cessation of mental pain.

Theodore, indeed, did suffer all that a virtuous mind, labouring under oppression so severe, could feel; but he was, at least, free from those inveterate and malignant passions which tore the bosom of the Marquis, and which inflict upon the possessor a punishment more severe than any they can prompt him to imagine for another. What indignation he might feel towards the Marquis, was at this time secondary to his anxiety for Adeline. His captivity was painful, as it prevented his seeking a just and honourable revenge; but it was dreadful, as it withheld him from attemping the rescue of her whom he loved more than life.

When he heard the wheels of the carriage that contained her drive off, he felt an agony of despair which almost overcame his reason. Even the stern hearts of the soldiers who attended him were not wholly insensible to his wretchedness, and by venturing to blame the conduct of the Marquis, they endeavoured to console their prisoner. The physician, who was just arrived, entered the room during this paroxysm of his distress, and, both feeling and expressing much concern at his condition, inquired with strong surprize why he had been thus precipitately removed to a room so very unfit for his reception?

Theodore explained to him the reason of this, of the distress he suffered, and of the chains by which he was disgraced; and perceiving the physician listened to him with attention and compassion, he became desirous of acquainting him with some farther particulars, for which purpose he desired the soldiers to leave the room. The men, complying with his request, stationed themselves on the outside of the door.

He then related all the particulars of the late transaction, and of his connection with the Marquis. The physician attended to his narrative with deep concern, and his countenance frequently expressed strong agitation. When Theodore concluded, he remained for some time silent and lost in thought; at length, awaking from his reverie, he said, 'I fear your situation is desperate. The character of the Marquis is too well known to suffer him either to be loved or respected; from such a man you have nothing to hope, for he has scarcely any thing to fear. I wish it was in my power to serve you, but I see no possibility of it.'

'Alas!' said Theodore, 'my situation is indeed desperate, and—for that suffering angel'—deep sobs interrupted his voice, and the violence of his agitation would not allow him to proceed. The physician could only express the sympathy he felt for his distress, and entreat him to be more calm, when a servant entered the room from the Marquis, who desired to see the physician immediately. After some time, he said he would attend the Marquis, and having endeavoured to attain a degree of composure, which he found it difficult to assume, he wrung the hand of Theodore and quitted the room, promising to return before he left the house.

He found the Marquis much agitated both in body and mind, and rather more apprehensive for the consequences of the wound than he had expected. His anxiety for Theodore now suggested a plan, by the execution of which he hoped he might be able to serve him. Having felt the patient's pulse, and asked some questions, he assumed a very serious look, when the Marquis, who watched every turn of his countenance, desired he would, without hesitation, speak his opinion.

'I am sorry to alarm you, my Lord, but here is some reason for apprehension: how long is it since you received the wound?'

'Good God! there is danger then!' cried the Marquis, adding some bitter execrations against Theodore.—'There certainly *is* danger;' replied the physician, 'a few hours may enable me to determine its degree.'

'A few hours, Sir!' interrupted the Marquis; 'a few hours!' The physician entreated him to be more calm. 'Confusion!' cried the Marquis, 'A man in health may, with great composure, entreat a dying man to be calm. Theodore will be broke upon the wheel for it, however.'

'You mistake me, Sir,' said the physician, 'if I believed you a dying man, or, indeed, *very* near death, I should not have spoken as I did. But it is of consequence I should know how long the wound has been inflicted.' The Marquis's terror now began to subside, and he gave a circumstantial account of the affray with Theodore, representing that he had been badly used in an affair, where his own conduct had been perfectly just and humane. The physician heard this relation with great coolness, and when it concluded, without making any comment upon it, told the Marquis he would prescribe a medicine, which he wished him to take immediately.

The Marquis, again alarmed by the gravity of his manner, entreated he would declare most seriously, whether he thought him in immediate danger. The physician hesitated, and the anxiety of the Marquis increased: 'It is of consequence,' said he, 'that I should know my exact situation.' The physician then said, that if he had any worldly affairs to settle, it would be as well to attend to them, for that it was impossible to say what might be the event.

He then turned the discourse and said, he had just been with the young officer under arrest, who, he hoped, would not be removed at present, as such a procedure must endanger his life. The Marquis uttered a dreadful oath, and, cursing Theodore for having brought him to his present condition, said, he should depart with the guard that very night. Against the cruelty of this sentence, the physician ventured to expostulate; and endeavouring to awaken the Marquis to a sense of humanity, pleaded earnestly for Theodore. But these entreaties and arguments seemed, by displaying to the

Marquis a part of his own character, to rouse his resentment, and re-kindle all the violence of his passions.

The physician at length withdrew in despondency, after promising, at the Marquis's request, not to leave the inn. He had hoped, by aggravating his danger, to obtain some advantages, both for Adeline and Theodore, but the plan had quite a contrary effect; for the apprehension of death, so dreadful to the guilty mind of the Marquis, instead of awakening penitence, increased his desire of vengeance against the man, who had brought him to such a situation. He determined to have Adeline conveyed, where Theodore, should he by any accident escape, could never obtain her; and thus to secure to himself, at least, some means of revenge. He knew, however, that when Theodore was once safely conveyed to his regiment, his destruction was certain, for should he even be acquitted of the intention of deserting, he would be condemned for having assaulted his superior officer.

The physician returned to the room where Theodore was confined. The violence of his distress was now subsided into a stern despair, more dreadful than the vehemence which had lately possessed him. The guard, in compliance with his request, having left the room, the physician repeated to him some part of his conversation with the Marquis. Theodore, after expressing his thanks, said, he had nothing more to hope. For himself he felt little; it was for his family, and for Adeline he suffered. He inquired what route she had taken, and though he had no prospect of deriving advantage from the information, desired the physician to assist him in obtaining it; but the landlord and his wife either were, or affected to be, ignorant of the matter, and it was in vain to apply to any other person.

The serjeant now entered with orders from the Marquis for the immediate departure of Theodore, who heard the message with composure, though the physician could not help expressing his indignation at this precipitate removal, and his dread of the consequences that might attend it. Theodore had scarcely time to declare his gratitude for the kindness of this valuable friend, before the soldiers entered room to conduct him to the carriage in waiting. As he bade him farewell,

Theodore slipped his purse into his hand, and turning abruptly away told the soldiers to lead on; but the physician stopped him, and refused the present with such serious warmth, that he was compelled to resume it: he wrung the hand of his new friend, and, being unable to speak, hurried away. The whole party immediately set off, and the unhappy Theodore was left to the remembrance of his past hopes and sufferings, to his anxiety for the fate of Adeline, the contemplation of his present wretchedness, and the apprehension of what might be reserved for him in future. For himself, indeed, he saw nothing but destruction, and was only relieved from total despair, by a feeble hope that she, whom he loved better than himself, might one time enjoy that happiness, of which he did not venture to look for a participation.

CHAPTER XIV

'Have you the heart? When your head did but ach,
  I knit my handkerchief about your brows,
And with my hand at midnight held up your head;
And, like the watchful minutes to the hour,
Still and anon cheer'd up the heavy time.'
                                        KING JOHN*

              'If the midnight bell
Did, with his iron tongue, and brazen mouth,
Sound one unto the drowsy race of night;
If this same were a church-yard where we stand,
And thou possessed with a thousand wrongs;
Or if that surly spirit melancholy,
Had baked thy blood and made it heavy, thick;
Then, in despite of broad-eyed watchful day,
I would into thy bosom pour my thoughts.'
                                        KING JOHN*

MEANWHILE the persecuted Adeline continued to travel, with little interruption, all night. Her mind suffered such a tumult of grief, regret, despair, and terror, that she could not be said to think. The Marquis's valet, who had placed himself in the chaise with her, at first seemed inclined to talk, but her inattention soon silenced him, and left her to the indulgence of her own misery.

They seemed to travel through obscure lanes and bye-ways, along which the carriage drove as furiously as the darkness would permit: when the dawn appeared, she perceived herself on the borders of a forest, and renewed her entreaties to know whither she was going. The man replied, he had no orders to tell, but she would soon see. Adeline, who had hitherto supposed they were carrying her to the villa, now began to doubt it; and as every place appeared less terrible to her imagination than that, her despair began to abate, and she thought only of the devoted Theodore, whom she knew to be the victim of malice and revenge.

They now entered upon the forest, and it occurred to her that she was going to the abbey; for though she had no remembrance of the scenery, through which she passed, it was not the less probable that this was the forest of Fontangville, whose boundaries were by much too extensive to have come within the circle of her former walks. This conjecture revived a terror, little inferior to that occasioned by the idea of going to the villa, for at the abbey she would be equally in the power of the Marquis, and also in that of her cruel enemy, La Motte. Her mind revolted at the picture her fancy drew, and as the carriage moved under the shades, she threw from the window a look of eager inquiry for some object which might confirm, or destroy her present surmise: she did not long look, before an opening in the forest shewed her the distant towers of the abbey—'I am, indeed, lost then!' said she, bursting into tears.

They were soon at the foot of the lawn, and Peter was seen running to open the gate, at which the carriage stopped. When he saw Adeline, he looked surprized and made an effort to speak, but the chaise now drove up to the abbey, where, at the door of the hall, La Motte himself appeared. As he advanced to take her from the carriage, an universal trembling seized her; it was with the utmost difficulty she supported herself, and for some moments she neither observed his countenance, nor heard his voice. He offered his arm to assist her into the abbey, which she at first refused, but having tottered a few paces, was obliged to accept; they then entered the vaulted room, where, sinking into a chair, a flood of tears came to her relief. La Motte did not interrupt the silence, which continued for some time, but paced the room in seeming agitation. When Adeline was sufficiently recovered to notice external objects, she observed his countenance, and there read the tumult of his soul, while he was struggling to assume a firmness, which his better feelings opposed.

La Motte now took her hand, and would have led her from the room, but she stopped, and, with a kind of desperate courage, made an effort to engage him to pity, and to save her. He interrupted her; 'It is not in my power,' said he, in a voice of emotion; 'I am not master of myself, or my conduct; inquire no farther—it is sufficient for you to know that I pity you; more I cannot do.' He gave her no time to reply, but, taking her hand, led her to the stairs of the tower, and from thence to the chamber she had formerly occupied.

'Here you must remain for the present,' said he, 'in a confinement, which is, perhaps, almost as involuntary on my part as it can be on yours. I am willing to render it as easy as possible, and have, therefore, ordered some books to be brought you.'

Adeline made an effort to speak, but he hurried from the room, seemingly ashamed of the part he had undertaken, and unwilling to trust himself with her tears. She heard the door of the chamber locked, and then, looking towards the windows, perceived they were secured: the door that led to the other apartments was also fastened. Such preparation for security shocked her, and, hopeless as she had long believed herself, she now perceived her mind sink deeper in despair. When the tears she shed had somewhat relieved her, and her thoughts could turn from the subjects of her immediate concern, she was thankful for the total seclusion allotted her, since it would spare her the pain she must feel in the presence of Monsieur and Madame La Motte, and allow the unrestrained indulgence of her own sorrow and reflection; reflection which, however distressing, was preferable to the agony inflicted on the mind, when agitated by care and fear, it is obliged to assume an appearance of tranquillity.

In about a quarter of an hour, her chamber door was unlocked, and Annette appeared with refreshments and books: she expressed satisfaction at seeing Adeline again, but seemed fearful of speaking, knowing, probably, that it was contrary to the orders of La Motte, who, she said, was waiting at the bottom of the stairs. When Annette was gone, Adeline took some refreshment, which was indeed necessary; for she had tasted nothing since she left the inn. She was pleased, but not surprized, that Madame La Motte did not appear, who, it was evident, shunned her from a consciousness of her own ungenerous conduct, a consciousness, which offered some presumption, that she was still not wholly unfriendly to her. She reflected upon the words of La Motte, 'I am not master of myself, or my conduct,' and though they afforded her no hope, she derived some comfort, poor as it was, from the belief that he pitied her. After some time spent in miserable reflection and various conjectures, her long-agitated spirits seemed to demand repose, and she laid down to sleep.

Adeline slept quietly for several hours, and awoke with a mind refreshed and tranquillized. To prolong this temporary peace, and to prevent, therefore, the intrusion of her own thoughts, she examined the books La Motte had sent her: among these she found some that in happier times had elevated her mind and interested her heart; their effect was now weakened, they were still, however, able to soften for a time the sense of her misfortunes.

But this Lethean* medicine to a wounded mind was but a temporary blessing; the entrance of La Motte dissolved the illusions of the page, and awakened her to a sense of her own situation. He came with food, and having placed it on the table, left the room without speaking. Again she endeavoured to read, but his appearance had broken the enchantment—bitter reflection returned to her mind, and brought with it the image of Theodore—of Theodore lost to her for ever!

La Motte, mean while, experienced all the terrors that could be inflicted by a conscience not wholly hardened to guilt. He had been led on by passion to dissipation—and from dissipation to vice; but having once touched the borders of infamy, the progressive steps followed each other fast, and he now saw himself the pander of a villain, and the betrayer of an innocent girl, whom every plea of justice and humanity called upon him to protect. He contemplated his picture—he shrunk from it, but he could change its deformity only by an effort too nobly daring for a mind already effeminated by vice. He viewed the dangerous labyrinth into which he was led, and perceived, as if for the first time, the progression of his guilt; from this labyrinth he weakly imagined farther guilt could alone extricate him. Instead of employing his mind upon the means of saving Adeline from destruction, and himself from being instrumental to it, he endeavoured only to lull the pangs of conscience and to persuade himself into a belief that he must proceed in the course he had begun. He knew himself to be in the power of the Marquis, and he dreaded that power more than the sure, though distant punishment that awaits upon guilt. The honour of Adeline and the quiet of his own conscience he consented to barter for a few years of existence.

He was ignorant of the present illness of the Marquis, or he would have perceived that there was a chance of escaping the threatened punishment at a price less enormous than infamy, and he would, perhaps, have endeavoured to save Adeline and himself by flight. But the Marquis, foreseeing the possibility of this, had ordered his servants carefully to conceal the circumstance which detained him, and to acquaint La Motte that he should be at the abbey in a few days, at the same time directing his valet to await him there. Adeline, as he expected, had neither inclination nor opportunity to mention it, and thus La Motte remained ignorant of the circumstance, which might have preserved him from farther guilt and Adeline from misery.

Most unwillingly had La Motte made his wife acquainted with the action, which had made him absolutely dependent upon the will of the Marquis, but the perturbation of his mind partly betrayed him: frequently in his sleep he muttered incoherent sentences, and frequently would start from his slumber and call, in passionate exclamation, upon Adeline. These instances of a disturbed mind had alarmed and terrified Madame La Motte, who watched while he slept and soon gathered from his words a confused idea of the Marquis's designs.

She hinted her suspicions to La Motte, who reproved her for having entertained them, but his manner, instead of repressing, increased her fears for Adeline; fears, which the conduct of the Marquis soon confirmed. On the night that he slept at the abbey, it had occurred to her, that whatever scheme was in agitation would now almost probably be discussed, and anxiety for Adeline made her stoop to a meanness, which, in other circumstances, would have been despicable. She quitted her room, and, concealing herself in an apartment adjoining that in which she had left the Marquis and her husband, listened to their discourse. It turned upon the subject she had expected, and disclosed to her the full extent of their designs. Terrified for Adeline, and shocked at the guilty weakness of La Motte, she was for some time incapable of thinking, or determining how to proceed. She knew her husband to be under great obligation to the Marquis, whose territory thus afforded him a shelter from the world, and that it was in the power of the former to betray him into the hands of his enemies. She believed also that the Marquis would do this, if provoked, yet she thought; upon such an occasion, La Motte might find some way of appeasing the Marquis, without subjecting himself to dishonour. After some farther reflection, her mind became more composed, and she returned to her chamber, where La Motte soon followed. Her spirits, however, were not now in a state to encounter either his displeasure, or his opposition, which she had too much reason to expect, whenever she should mention the subject of her concern, and she, therefore, resolved not to notice it till the morrow.

On the morrow, she told La Motte all he had uttered in his dreams, and mentioned other circumstances, which convinced him it was in vain any longer to deny the truth of her apprehensions. His wife then represented to him how possible it was to avoid the infamy, into which he was about to plunge, by quitting the territories of the Marquis, and pleaded so warmly for Adeline, that La Motte, in sullen silence, appeared to meditate upon the plan. His thoughts were, however, very differently engaged. He was conscious of having deserved from the Marquis a dreadful punishment, and knew that if he exasperated him by refusing to acquiesce with his wishes, he had little to expect from flight, for the eye of justice and revenge would pursue him with indefatigable research.

La Motte meditated how to break this to his wife, for he perceived that there was no other method of counteracting her virtuous compassion for Adeline, and the dangerous consequences to be expected from it, than by opposing it with terror for his safety, and this could be done only by shewing her the full extent of the evils that must attend the resentment of the Marquis. Vice had not yet so entirely darkened his conscience, but that the blush of shame stained his cheek, and his tongue faltered when he would have told his guilt. At length, finding it impossible to mention particulars, he told her that, on account of an affair, which no entreaties should ever induce him to explain, his life was in the power of the Marquis. 'You see the alternative,' said he, 'take your choice of evils, and, if you can, tell Adeline of her danger, and sacrifice my life to save her from a situation, which many would be ambitious to obtain.'—Madame La Motte, condemned to the horrible alternative of permitting the seduction of innocence, or of dooming her husband to destruction, suffered a distraction of thought, which defied all controul. Perceiving, however, that an opposition to the designs of the Marquis would ruin La Motte and avail Adeline little, she determined to yield and endure in silence.

At the time when Adeline was planning her escape from the abbey, the significant looks of Peter had led La Motte to suspect the truth and to observe them more closely. He had seen them separate in the hall in apparent confusion, and had afterwards observed them conversing together in the cloisters. Circumstances so unusual left him not a doubt that Adeline had discovered her danger, and was concerting with Peter some means of escape. Affecting, therefore, to be informed of the whole affair, he charged Peter with treachery towards himself, and threatened him with the vengeance of the Marquis if he did not disclose all he knew. The menace intimidated Peter, and, supposing that all chance of assisting Adeline was gone, he made a circumstantial confession, and promised to forbear acquainting Adeline with the discovery of the scheme. In this promise he was seconded by inclination, for he feared to meet the displeasure, which Adeline, believing he had betrayed her, might express.

On the evening of the day, on which Adeline's intended escape was discovered, the Marquis designed to come to the abbey, and it had been agreed that he should then take Adeline to his villa. La Motte had immediately perceived the advantage of permitting Adeline to repair, in the belief of being undiscovered, to the tomb. It would prevent much disturbance and opposition, and spare himself the pain he must feel in her presence, when she should know that he had betrayed her. A servant of the Marquis might go, at the appointed hour, to the tomb, and wrapt in the disguise of night, might take her quietly thence in the character of Peter. Thus, without resistance, she would be carried to the villa, nor discover her mistake till it was too late to prevent its consequence.

When the Marquis did arrive, La Motte, who was not so much intoxicated by the wine he had drank, as to forget his prudence, informed him of what had happened and what he had planned, and the Marquis approving it, his servant was made acquainted with the signal, which afterwards betrayed Adeline to his power.

A deep consciousness of the unworthy neutrality she had observed in Adeline's concerns, made Madame La Motte anxiously avoid seeing her now that she was again in the abbey. Adeline understood this conduct, and she rejoiced that she was spared the anguish of meeting her as an enemy, whom she had once considered as a friend. Several days now passed in solitude, in miserable retrospection, and dreadful expectation. The perilous situation of Theodore was almost the constant subject of her thoughts. Often did she breathe an agonizing wish for his safety, and often look round the sphere of possibility in search of hope: but hope had almost left the horizon of her prospect, and when it did appear, it sprung only from the death of the Marquis, whose vengeance threatened most certain destruction.

The Marquis, mean while, lay at the inn at Caux, in a state of very doubtful recovery. The physician and surgeon, neither of whom he would dismiss, nor suffer to leave the village, proceeded upon contrary principles, and the good effect of what the one prescribed, was frequently counteracted by the injudicious treatment of the other. Humanity alone prevailed on the physician to continue his attendance. The malady of the Marquis was also heightened by the impatience of his temper, the terrors of death, and the irritation of his passions. One moment he believed himself dying, another he could scarcely be prevented from attempting to follow Adeline to the abbey. So various were the fluctuations of his mind, and so rapid the schemes that succeeded each other, that his passions were in a continual state of conflict. The physician attempted to persuade him, that his recovery greatly depended upon tranquillity, and to prevail upon him to attempt, at least, some command of his feelings, but he was soon silenced, in hopeless disgust, by the impatient answers of the Marquis.

At length the servant, who had carried off Adeline, returned, and the Marquis having ordered him into his chamber, asked so many questions in a breath, that the man knew not which to answer. At length he pulled a folded paper from his pocket, which he said had been dropped in the chaise by Mademoiselle Adeline, and as he thought his lordship would like to see it, he had taken care of it. The Marquis stretched forth his hand with eagerness and received a note addressed to Theodore. On perceiving the superscription, the agitation of jealous rage for a moment overcame him, and he held it in his hand unable to open it.

He, however, broke the seal, and found it to be a note of inquiry, written by Adeline to Theodore during his illness, and which, from some accident she had been prevented from sending him. The tender solicitude it expressed for his recovery stung the soul of the Marquis, and drew from him a comparison of her feelings on the illness of his rival and that of himself. 'She could be solicitous for his recovery,' said he, 'but for mine, she only dreads it.' As if willing to prolong the pain this little billet had excited, he then read it again. Again he cursed his fate and execrated his rival, giving himself up, as usual, to the transports of his passion. He was going to throw it from him, when his eyes caught the seal, and he looked earnestly at it. His anger seemed now to have subsided, he deposited the note carefully in his pocket-book, and was, for some time, lost in thought.

After many days of hopes and fears, the strength of his constitution overcame his illness, and he was well enough to write several letters, one of which he immediately sent off to prepare La Motte for his reception. The same policy, which had prompted him to conceal his illness from La Motte, now urged him to say, what he knew would not happen, that he should reach the abbey on the day after his servant. He repeated this injunction, that Adeline should be strictly guarded, and renewed his promises of reward for the future services of La Motte.

La Motte, to whom each succeeding day had brought new surprize and perplexity concerning the absence of the Marquis, received this notice with uneasiness, for he had begun to hope that the Marquis had altered his intentions concerning Adeline, being either engaged in some new adventure, or obliged to visit his estates in some distant province: he would have been willing thus to have got rid of an affair, which was to reflect so much dishonour on himself.

This hope was now vanished, and he directed Madame to prepare for the reception of the Marquis. Adeline passed these days in a state of suspense, which was now cheered by hope, and now darkened by despair. This delay, so much exceeding her expectation, seemed to prove that the illness of the Marquis was dangerous; and when she looked forward to the consequences of his recovery, she could not be sorry that it was so. So odious was the idea of him to her mind, that she would not suffer her lips to pronounce his name, nor make the inquiry of Annette, which was of such consequence to her peace.

It was about a week after the receipt of the Marquis's letter, that Adeline one day saw from her window a party of horsemen enter the avenue, and knew them to be the Marquis and his attendants. She retired from the window in a state of mind not to be described, and, sinking into a chair, was for some time scarcely conscious of the objects around her. When she had recovered from the first terror, which his appearance excited, she again tottered to the window; the party was not in sight, but she heard the trampling of horses, and knew that the Marquis had wound round to the great gate of the abbey. She addressed herself to Heaven for support and protection, and her mind being now somewhat composed, sat down to wait the event.

La Motte received the Marquis with expressions of surprize at his long absence, and the latter, merely saying he had been detained by illness, proceeded to inquire for Adeline. He was told she was in her chamber, from whence she might be summoned if he wished to see her. The Marquis hesitated, and at length excused himself, but desired she might be strictly watched. 'Perhaps, my Lord,' said La Motte smiling, 'Adeline's obstinacy has been too powerful for your passion; you seem less interested concerning her than formerly.'

'O! by no means,' replied the Marquis; 'she interests me, if possible, more than ever; so much, indeed, that I cannot have her too closely guarded; and I, therefore, beg La Motte, that you will suffer no body to attend her, but when you can observe them yourself. Is the room where she is confined sufficiently secure?' La Motte assured him it was; but at the same time expressed his wish that she was removed to the villa. 'If by any means,' said he, 'she should contrive to escape, I know what I must expect from your displeasure; and this reflection keeps my mind in continual anxiety.'

'This removal cannot be at present,' said the Marquis; 'she is safer here, and you do wrong to disturb yourself with an apprehension of her escape, if her chamber is really so secure, as you represent it.'

'I can have no motive for deceiving you, my Lord, in this point.'

'I do not suspect you of any,' said the Marquis; 'guard her carefully, and trust me, she will not escape. I can rely upon my valet, and if you wish it, he shall remain here.' La Motte thought there could be no occasion for him, and it was agreed that the man should go home.

The Marquis, after remaining about half an hour in conversation with La Motte, left the abbey, and Adeline saw him depart with a mixture of surprize and thankfulness that almost overcame her. She had waited in momentary expectation of being summoned to appear, and had been endeavouring to arm herself with resolution to support his presence. She had listened to every voice that sounded from below, and at every step that crossed the passage, her heart had palpitated with dread, lest it should be La Motte coming to lead her to the Marquis. This state of suffering had been prolonged almost beyond her power of enduring it, when she heard voices under her window, and rising, saw the Marquis ride away. After giving way to the joy and thankfulness that swelled her heart, she endeavoured to account for this circumstance, which, considering what had passed, was certainly very strange. It appeared, indeed, wholly inexplicable, and, after much fruitless inquiry, she quitted the subject, endeavouring to persuade herself that it could only portend good.

The time of La Motte's usual visitation now drew near, and Adeline expected it in the trembling hope of hearing that the Marquis had ceased his persecution; but he was, as usual, sullen and silent, and it was not till he was about to quit the room, that Adeline had the courage to inquire, when the Marquis was expected again? La Motte, opening the door to depart, replied, 'On the following day,' and Adeline, whom fear and delicacy embarrassed, saw she could obtain no intelligence of Theodore but by a direct question; she looked earnestly, as if she would have spoke, and he stopped, but she blushed and was still silent, till upon his again attempting to leave the room, she faintly called him back.

'I would ask,' said she, 'after that unfortunate chevalier who has incurred the resentment of the Marquis by endeavouring to serve me. Has the Marquis mentioned him?'

'He has,' replied La Motte; 'and your indifference towards the Marquis is now fully explained.'

'Since I must feel resentment towards those whose injure me,' said Adeline, 'I may surely be allowed to be grateful towards those who serve me. Had the Marquis deserved my esteem, he would, probably, have possessed it.'

'Well, well,' said La Motte, 'this young hero, who, it seems, has been brave enough to lift his arm against his Colonel, is taken care of, and, I doubt not, will soon be sensible of the value of his quixotism.' Indignation, grief, and fear, struggled in the bosom of Adeline; she disdained to give La Motte an opportunity of again pronouncing the name of Theodore; yet the uncertainty under which she laboured, urged her to inquire, whether the Marquis had heard of him since he left Caux? 'Yes,' said La Motte, 'he has been safely carried to his regiment, where he is confined till the Marquis can attend to appear against him.'

Adeline had neither power nor inclination to inquire farther, and La Motte quitting the chamber, she was left to the misery he had renewed. Though this information contained no new circumstance of misfortune, (for she now heard confirmed what she had always expected) a weight of new sorrow seemed to fall upon her heart, and she perceived that she had unconsciously cherished a latent hope of Theodore's escape before he reached the place of his destination. All hope was now, however, gone; he was suffering the miseries of a prison, and the tortures of apprehension both for his own life and her safety. She pictured to herself the dark damp dungeon where he lay, loaded with chains, and pale with sickness and grief; she heard him, in a voice that thrilled her heart, call upon her name, and raise his eyes to Heaven in silent supplication: she saw the anguish of his countenance, the tears that fell slowly on his cheek, and remembering, at the same time, the generous conduct that had brought him to this abyss of misery, and that it was for her sake he suffered, grief resolved itself into despair, her tears ceased to flow, and she sunk silently into a state of dreadful torpor.

On the morrow the Marquis arrived, and departed as before. Several days then elapsed, and he did not appear, till one evening, as La Motte and his wife were in their usual sitting-room, he entered, and conversed for some time upon general subjects, from which, however, he by degrees fell into a reverie, and, after a pause of silence, he rose and drew La Motte to the window. 'I would speak with you alone,' said he, 'if you are at leisure; if not, another time will do.' La Motte, assuring him he was perfectly so, would have conducted him to another room, but the Marquis proposed a walk in the forest. They went out together, and when they had reached a solitary glade, where the spreading branches of the beech and oak deepened the shades of twilight, and threw a solemn obscurity around, the Marquis turned to La Motte, and addressed him:

'Your condition, La Motte, is unhappy; this abbey is a melancholy residence for a man like you fond of society, and like you also qualified to adorn it.' La Motte bowed. 'I wish it was in my power to restore you to the world,' continued the Marquis; 'perhaps, if I knew the particulars of the affair which has driven you from it, I might perceive that my interest could effectually serve you. I think I have heard you hint it was an affair of honour.' La Motte was silent. 'I mean not to distress you, however; nor is it common curiosity that prompts this inquiry, but a sincere desire to befriend you. You have already informed me of some particulars of your misfortunes. I think the liberality of your temper led you into expences which you afterwards endeavoured to retrieve by gaming.'

'Yes, my Lord,' said La Motte, ''tis true that I dissipated the greater part of an affluent fortune in luxurious indulgences, and that I afterwards took unworthy means to recover it: but I wish to be spared upon this subject. I would, if possible, lose the remembrance of a transaction which must for ever stain my character, and the rigorous effect of which, I fear, it is not in your power, my Lord, to soften.'

'You may be mistaken on this point,' replied the Marquis; 'my interest at Court is by no means inconsiderable. Fear not from me any severity of censure; I am not at all inclined to judge harshly of the faults of others. I well know how to allow for the emergency of circumstances; and, I think, La Motte, you have hitherto found me your friend.'

'I have, my Lord.'

'And when you recollect, that I have forgiven a certain transaction of late date——'

'It is true, my Lord; and allow me to say, I have a just sense of your generosity. The transaction you allude to is by far the worst of my life; and what I have to relate cannot, therefore, lower me in your opinion. When I had dissipated the greatest part of my property in habits of voluptuous pleasure, I had recourse to gaming to supply the means of continuing them. A run of good luck, for some time, enabled me to do this, and encouraging my most sanguine expectations, I continued in the same career of success.

Soon after this a sudden turn of fortune destroyed my hopes, and reduced me to the most desperate extremity. In one night my money was lowered to the sum of two hundred louis. These I resolved to stake also, and with them my life; for it was my resolution not to survive their loss. Never shall I forget the horrors of that moment on which hung my fate, nor the deadly anguish that seized my heart when my last stake was gone. I stood for some time in a state of stupefaction, till roused to a sense of my misfortune, my passion made me pour forth execrations on my more fortunate rivals, and act all the frenzy of despair. During this paroxysm of madness, a gentleman, who had been a silent observer of all that passed, approached me.—You are unfortunate, Sir, said he.—I need not be informed of that, Sir, I replied.

'You have, perhaps, been ill used, resumed he.—Yes, Sir, I am ruined, and, therefore, it may be said, I am ill used.

'Do you know the people you have played with?

'No; but I have met them in the first circles.

'Then I am, probably, mistaken, said he, and walked away. His last words roused me, and raised a hope that my money had not been fairly lost. Wishing for farther information, I went in search of the gentleman, but he had left the rooms; I, however, stifled my transports, returned to the table where I had lost my money, placed myself behind the chair of one of the persons who had won it, and closely watched the game. For some time I saw nothing that could confirm my suspicions, but was at length convinced they were just.

'When the game was ended I called one of my adversaries out of the room, and telling him what I had observed, threatened instantly to expose him if he did not restore my property. The man was, for some time, as positive as myself; and, assuming the bully, threatened me with chastisement for my scandalous assertions. I was not, however, in a state of mind to be frightened, and his manner served only to exasperate my temper, already sufficiently inflamed by misfortune. After retorting his threats, I was about to return to the apartment we had left, and expose what had passed, when, with an insidious smile and a softened voice, he begged I would favour him with a few moments attention, and allow him to speak with the gentleman his partner. To the latter part of his request I hesitated, but, in the mean time, the gentleman himself entered the room. His partner related to him, in few words, what had passed between us, and the terror that appeared in his countenance sufficiently declared his consciouness of guilt.

'They then drew aside, and remained a few minutes in conversation together, after which they approached me with an offer, as they phrased it, of a compromise. I declared, however, against any thing of this kind, and swore, nothing less than the whole sum I had lost should content me.—Is it not possible, Monsieur, that you may be offered something as advantageous as the whole?—I did not understand their meaning, but, after they had continued for some time to give distant hints of the same sort, they proceeded to explain.

'Perceiving their characters wholly in my power, they wished to secure my interest to their party, and, therefore, informing me, that they belonged to an association of persons, who lived upon the folly and inexperience of others, they offered me a share in their concern. My fortunes were desperate, and the proposal now made me would not only produce an immediate supply, but enable me to return to those scenes of dissipated pleasure, to which passion had at first, and long habit afterwards, attached me. I closed with the offer, and thus sunk from dissipation into infamy.'

La Motte paused, as if the recollection of these times filled him with remorse. The Marquis understood his feelings. 'You judge too rigorously of yourself,' said he; 'there are few persons, let their appearance of honesty be what it may, who, in such circumstances, would have acted better than you have done. Had I been in your situation, I know not how I might have acted. That rigid virtue which shall condemn you, may dignify itself with the appellation of wisdom, but I wish not to possess it; let it still reside, where it generally is to be found, in the cold bosoms of those, who, wanting feeling to be men, dignify themselves with the title of philosophers. But pray proceed.'

'Our success was for some time unlimited, for we held the wheel of fortune, and trusted not to her caprice. Thoughtless and voluptuous by nature, my expences fully kept pace with my income. An unlucky discovery of the practices of our party was at length made by a young nobleman, which obliged us to act for some time with the utmost circumspection. It would be tedious to relate the particulars, which made us at length so suspected, that the distant civility and cold reserve of our acquaintance rendered the frequenting public assemblies both painful and unprofitable. We turned our thoughts to other modes of obtaining money, and a swindling transaction, in which I engaged, to a very large amount, soon compelled me to leave Paris. You know the rest, my Lord.'

La Motte was now silent, and the Marquis continued for some time musing. 'You perceive, my Lord,' at length resumed La Motte, 'you perceive that my case is hopeless.'

'It is bad, indeed, but not entirely hopeless. From my soul I pity you. Yet, if you should return to the world, and incur the danger of prosecution, I think my interest with the Minister might save you from any severe punishment. You seem, however, to have lost your relish for society, and, perhaps, do not wish to return to it.'

'Oh! my Lord, can you doubt this?—But I am overcome with the excess of your goodness; would to Heaven it were in my power to prove the gratitude it inspires.'

'Talk not of goodness,' said the Marquis; 'I will not pretend that my desire of serving you is unalloyed by any degree of self-interest. I will not affect to be more than man, and trust me those who do are less. It is in your power to testify your gratitude, and bind me to your interest for ever.' He paused. 'Name but the means,' cried La Motte, 'name but the means, and if they are within the compass of possibility they shall be executed.' The Marquis was still silent. 'Do you doubt my sincerity, my Lord, that you are yet silent? Do you fear to repose a confidence in the man whom you have already loaded with obligation? who lives by your mercy, and almost by your means.' The Marquis looked earnestly at him, but did not speak. 'I have not deserved this of you, my Lord; speak, I entreat you.'

'There are certain prejudices attached to the human mind,' said the Marquis in a slow and solemn voice, 'which it requires all our wisdom to keep from interfering with our happiness; certain set notions, acquired in infancy, and cherished involuntarily by age, which grow up and assume a gloss so plausible, that few minds, in what is called a civilized country, can afterwards overcome them. Truth is often perverted by education. While the refined Europeans boast a standard of honour, and a sublimity of virtue, which often leads them from pleasure to misery, and from nature to error, the simple, uninformed American follows the impulse of his heart, and obeys the inspiration of wisdom.'* The Marquis paused, and La Motte continued to listen in eager expectation.

'Nature, uncontaminated by false refinement,' resumed the Marquis, 'every where acts alike in the great occurrences of life. The Indian discovers his friend to be perfidious, and he kills him; the wild Asiatic does the same; the Turk, when ambition fires, or revenge provokes, gratifies his passion at the expence of life, and does not call it murder.* Even the polished Italian, distracted by jealousy, or tempted by a strong circumstance of advantage, draws his stilletto, and accomplishes his purpose.* It is the first proof of a superior mind to liberate itself from prejudices of country, or of education. You are silent, La Motte; are you not of my opinion?'

'I am attending, my Lord, to your *reasoning*.'

'There are, I repeat it,' said the Marquis, 'people of minds so weak, as to shrink from acts they have been accustomed to hold wrong, however advantageous. They never suffer themselves to be guided by circumstances, but fix for life upon a certain standard, from which they will, on no account, depart. Self-preservation is the great law of nature; when a reptile hurts us, or an animal of prey threatens us, we think no farther, but endeavour to annihilate it. When my life, or what may be essential to my life, requires the sacrifice of another, or even if some passion, wholly unconquerable, requires it, I should be a madman to hesitate. La Motte, I think I may confide in you—there are ways of doing certain things—you understand me. There are times, and circumstances, and opportunities—you comprehend my meaning.'

'Explain yourself, my Lord.'

'Kind services that—in short there are services, which excite all our gratitude, and which we can never think repaid. It is in your power to place me in such a situation.'

'Indeed! my Lord, name the means.'

'I have already named them. This abbey well suits the purpose; it is shut up from the eye of observation; any transaction may be concealed within its walls; the hour of midnight may witness the deed, and the morn shall not dawn to disclose it; these woods tell no tales. Ah! La Motte, am I right in trusting this business with you; may I believe you are desirous of serving me, and of preserving yourself?' The Marquis paused, and looked stedfastly at La Motte, whose countenance was almost concealed by the gloom of evening.

'My Lord, you may trust me in any thing; explain yourself more fully.'

'What security will you give me for your faithfulness?'

'My life, my Lord; is it not already in your power?' The Marquis hesitated, and then said, 'To-morrow, about this time, I shall return to the abbey, and will then explain my meaning, if, indeed, you shall not already have understood it. You, in the mean time, will consider your own powers of resolution, and be prepared either to adopt the purpose I shall suggest, or to declare you will not.' La Motte made some confused reply. 'Farewell till to-morrow,' said the Marquis; 'remember that freedom and affluence are now before you.' He moved towards the abbey, and, mounting his horse, rode off with his attendants. La Motte walked slowly home, musing on the late conversation.

END OF VOLUME II

VOLUME III

CHAPTER XV

'Danger, whose limbs of giant mold
What mortal eye can fix'd behold?
Who stalks his round, an hideous form!
Howling amidst the midnight storm!—
And with him thousand phantoms join'd,
Who prompt to deeds accurs'd the mind!—
On whom that rav'ning brood of Fate,
Who lap the blood of Sorrow wait;
Who, Fear! this ghastly train can see,
And look not madly wild like thee!'

COLLINS*

THE Marquis was punctual to the hour. La Motte received him at the gate, but he declined entering, and said he preferred a walk in the forest. Thither, therefore, La Motte attended him. After some general conversation, 'Well,' said the Marquis, 'have you considered what I said, and are you prepared to decide?'

'I have, my Lord, and will quickly decide, when you shall farther explain yourself. Till then I can form no resolution.' The Marquis appeared dissatisfied, and was a moment silent. 'Is it then possible,' he at length resumed, 'that you do not understand? This ignorance is surely affected. La Motte, I expect sincerity. Tell me, therefore, is it necessary I should say more?'

'It is, my Lord,' said La Motte immediately. 'If you fear to confide in me freely, how can I fully accomplish your purpose?'

'Before I proceed farther,' said the Marquis, 'let me administer some oath which shall bind you to secrecy. But this

is scarcely necessary; for, could I even doubt your word of
honour, the remembrance of a certain transaction would point
out to you the necessity of being as silent yourself as you must
wish me to be.' There was now a pause of silence, during which
both the Marquis and La Motte betrayed some confusion. 'I
think, La Motte,' said he, 'I have given you sufficient proof that
I can be grateful: the services you have already rendered me
with respect to Adeline have not been unrewarded.'

'True, my Lord, I am ever willing to acknowledge this, and
am sorry it has not been in my power to serve you more
effectually. Your farther views respecting her I am ready to
assist.'

'I thank you.—Adeline'——the Marquis hesitated.—
'Adeline,' rejoined La Motte, eager to anticipate his wishes,
'has beauty worthy of your pursuit. She has inspired a passion
of which she ought to be proud, and, at any rate, she shall
soon be yours. Her charms are worthy of'——

'Yes, yes,' interrupted the Marquis; 'but'——he paused.—
'But they have given you too much trouble in the pursuit,'
said La Motte; 'and to be sure, my Lord, it must be confessed
they have; but this trouble is all over—you may now consider
her as your own.'

'I would do so,' said the Marquis, fixing an eye of earnest
regard upon La Motte—'I would do so.'

'Name your hour, my Lord; you shall not be interrupted.—
Beauty such as Adeline's'——

'Watch her closely,' interrupted the Marquis, 'and on no
account suffer her to leave her apartment. Where is she now?'

'Confined in her chamber.'

'Very well. But I am impatient.'

'Name your time, my Lord—to-morrow night.'

'*To-morrow* night,' said the Marquis—'to-morrow night. Do
you understand me now?'

'Yes, my Lord, this night, if you wish it so. But had you not
better dismiss your servants, and remain yourself in the forest.
You know the door that opens upon the woods from the west
tower. Come thither about twelve—I will be there to conduct
you to her chamber. Remember, then, my Lord, that to-
night'——

'Adeline dies!' interrupted the Marquis, in a low voice scarcely human. 'Do you understand me now?'——La Motte shrunk aghast—'My Lord!'

'La Motte!' said the Marquis.—There was a silence of several minutes, in which La Motte endeavoured to recover himself.—'Let me ask, my Lord, the meaning of this?' said he, when he had breath to speak. 'Why should you wish the death of Adeline—of Adeline whom so lately you loved?'

'Make no inquiries for my motive,' said the Marquis; 'but it is as certain as that I live that she you name must die. This is sufficient.' The surprise of La Motte equalled his horror. 'The means are various,' resumed the Marquis. 'I could have wished that no blood might be spilt; and there are drugs sure and speedy in their effect, but they cannot be soon or safely procured. I also wish it over—it must be done quickly—this night.'

'This night, my Lord!'

'Aye, this night, La Motte; if it is to be, why not soon. Have you no convenient drug at hand?'

'None, my Lord.'

'I feared to trust a third person, or I should have been provided,' said the Marquis. 'As it is, take this poignard; use it as occasion offers, but be resolute.' La Motte received the poignard with a trembling hand, and continued to gaze upon it for some time, scarcely knowing what he did. 'Put it up,' said the Marquis, 'and endeavour to recollect yourself.' La Motte obeyed, but continued to muse in silence.

He saw himself entangled in the web which his own crimes had woven. Being in the power of the Marquis, he knew he must either consent to the commission of a deed, from the enormity of which, depraved as he was, he shrunk in horror, or sacrifice fortune, freedom, probably life itself, to the refusal. He had been led on by slow gradations from folly to vice, till he now saw before him an abyss of guilt which startled even the conscience that so long had slumbered. The means of retreating were desperate—to proceed was equally so.

When he considered the innocence and the helplessness of Adeline, her orphan state, her former affectionate conduct, and her confidence in his protection, his heart melted with compassion for the distress he had already occasioned her, and shrunk in terror from the deed he was urged to commit. But when, on the other hand, he contemplated the destruction that threatened him from the vengeance of the Marquis, and then considered the advantages that were offered him of favour, freedom, and probably fortune, terror and temptation contributed to overcome the pleading of humanity, and silence the voice of conscience. In this state of tumultuous uncertainty he continued for some time silent, until the voice of the Marquis roused him to a conviction of the necessity of at least appearing to acquiesce in his designs.

'Do you hesitate?' said the Marquis.—'No, my Lord, my resolution is fixed—I will obey you. But methinks it would be better to avoid bloodshed. Strange secrets have been revealed by'——

'Aye, but how avoid it?' interrupted the Marquis.—'Poison *I* will not venture to procure. I have given you one sure instrument of death. You also may find it dangerous to inquire for a drug.' La Motte perceived that he could not purchase poison without incurring a discovery much greater than that he wished to avoid. 'You are right, my Lord, and I will follow your orders implicitly.' The Marquis now proceeded, in broken sentences to give farther directions concerning this dreadful scheme.

'In her sleep,' said he, 'at midnight; the family will then be at rest.' Afterwards they planned a story, which was to account for her disappearance, and by which it was to seem that she had sought an escape in consequence of her aversion to the addresses of the Marquis. The doors of her chamber and of the west tower were to be left open to corroborate this account, and many other circumstances were to be contrived to confirm the suspicion. They farther consulted how the Marquis was to be informed of the event; and it was agreed that he should come as usual to the Abbey on the following day. '*To-night, then,*' said the Marquis, 'I may rely upon your resolution.'

'You may, my Lord.'

'Farewell, then. When we meet again'——

'When we meet again,' said La Motte, 'it will be done.' He followed the Marquis to the Abbey, and having seen him mount his horse and wished him a good night, he retired to his chamber, where he shut himself up.

Adeline, mean while, in the solitude of her prison, gave way to the despair which her condition inspired. She tried to arrange her thoughts, and to argue herself into some degree of resignation; but reflection, by representing the past, and reason, by anticipating the future, brought before her mind the full picture of her misfortunes, and she sunk in despondency. Of Theodore, who, by a conduct so noble, had testified his attachment and involved himself in ruin, she thought with a degree of anguish infinitely superior to any she had felt upon any other occasion.

That the very exertions which had deserved all her gratitude, and awakened all her tenderness, should be the cause of his destruction, was a circumstance so much beyond the ordinary bounds of misery, that her fortitude sunk at once before it. The idea of Theodore suffering—Theodore dying—was for ever present to her imagination, and frequently excluding the sense of her own danger, made her conscious only of his. Sometimes the hope he had given her of being able to vindicate his conduct, or at least to obtain a pardon, would return; but it was like the faint beam of an April morn, transient and cheerless. She knew the Marquis, stung with jealousy, and exasperated to revenge, would pursue him with unrelenting malice.

Against such an enemy what could Theodore oppose? Conscious rectitude would not avail him to ward off the blow which disappointed passion and powerful pride directed. Her distress was considerably heightened by reflecting that no intelligence of him could reach her at the Abbey, and that she must remain she knew not how long in the most dreadful suspense concerning his fate. From the Abbey she saw no possibility of escaping. She was a prisoner in a chamber inclosed at every avenue: she had no opportunity of conversing with any person who could afford her even a chance of relief; and she saw herself condemned to await in passive silence the impending destiny, infinitely more dreadful to her imagination than death itself.

Thus circumstanced, she yielded to the pressure of her misfortunes, and would sit for hours motionless and given up to thought. 'Theodore!' she would frequently exclaim, 'you cannot hear my voice, you cannot fly to help me; yourself a prisoner and in chains.' The picture was too horrid. The swelling anguish of her heart would subdue her utterance—tears bathed her—and she became insensible to every thing but the misery of Theodore.

On this evening her mind had been remarkably tranquil; and as she watched from her window, with a still and melancholy pleasure, the setting sun, the fading splendour of the western horizon, and the gradual approach of twilight, her thoughts bore her back to the time when, in happier circumstances, she had watched the same appearances. She recollected also the evening of her temporary escape from the Abbey, when from this same window she had viewed the declining sun—how anxiously she had awaited the fall of twilight—how much she had endeavoured to anticipate the events of her future life—with what trembling fear she had descended from the tower and ventured into the forest. These reflections produced others that filled her heart with anguish and her eyes with tears.

While she was lost in her melancholy reverie she saw the Marquis mount his horse and depart from the gates. The sight of him revived, in all its force, a sense of the misery he inflicted on her beloved Theodore, and a consciousness of the evils which more immediately threatened herself. She withdrew from the window in an agony of tears, which continuing for a considerable time, her frame was, at length, quite exhausted, and she retired early to rest.

La Motte remained in his chamber till supper obliged him to descend. At table his wild and haggard countenance, which, in spite of all his endeavours, betrayed the disorder of his mind, and his long and frequent fits of abstraction surprised as well as alarmed Madame La Motte. When Peter left the room she tenderly inquired what had disturbed him, and he with a distorted smile tried to be gay, but the effort was beyond his art, and he quickly relapsed into silence; or when Madame La Motte spoke, and he strove to conceal the absence of his thoughts, he answered so entirely from the purpose, that his abstraction became still more apparent. Observing this, Madame La Motte appeared to take no notice of his present temper; and they continued to sit in uninterrupted silence till the hour of rest, when they retired to their chamber.

La Motte lay in a state of disturbed watchfulness for some time, and his frequent starts awoke Madame, who, however, being pacified by some trifling excuse, soon went to sleep again. This agitation continued till near midnight, when, recollecting that the time was now passing in idle reflection which ought to be devoted to action, he stole silently from his bed, wrapped himself in his night gown, and, taking the lamp which burned nightly in his chamber, passed up the spiral staircase. As he went he frequently looked back, and often started and listened to the hollow sighings of the blast.

His hand shook so violently, when he attempted to unlock the door of Adeline's chamber, that he was obliged to set the lamp on the ground, and apply both his hands. The noise he made with the key induced him to suppose he must have awakened her; but when he opened the door, and perceived the stillness that reigned within, he was convinced she was asleep. When he approached the bed he heard her gently breathe, and soon after sigh—and he stopped;* but silence returning, he again advanced, and then heard her sing in her sleep. As he listened he distinguished some notes of a melancholy little air which, in her happier days, she had often sung to him. The low and mournful accent in which she now uttered them expressed too well the tone of her mind.

La Motte now stepped hastily towards the bed, when, breathing a deep sigh, she was again silent. He undrew the curtain, and saw her laying in a profound sleep, her cheek yet wet with tears, resting upon her arm. He stood a moment looking at her; and as he viewed her innocent and lovely countenance, pale in grief, the light of the lamp, which shone strong upon her eyes, awoke her, and, perceiving a man, she uttered a scream. Her recollection returning, she knew him to be La Motte, and it instantly recurring to her that the Marquis was at hand, she raised herself in bed, and implored pity and protection. La Motte stood looking eagerly at her, but without replying.

The wildness of his looks and the gloomy silence he preserved increased her alarm, and with tears of terror she renewed her supplication. 'You once saved me from destruction,' cried she; 'O save me now! Have pity upon me—I have no protector but you.'

'What is it you fear?' said La Motte in a tone scarcely articulate.—'O save me—save me from the Marquis!'

'Rise then,' said he, 'and dress yourself quickly—I shall be back again in a few minutes.' He lighted a candle that stood on the table, and left the chamber. Adeline immediately arose and endeavoured to dress, but her thoughts were so bewildered that she scarcely knew what she did, and her whole frame so violently agitated that it was with the utmost difficulty she preserved herself from fainting. She threw her clothes hastily on, then sat down to await the return of La Motte. A considerable time elapsed, yet he did not appear, and, having in vain endeavoured to compose her spirits, the pain of suspence at length became so insupportable, that she opened the door of her chamber, and went to the top of the staircase to listen. She thought she heard voices below; but, considering that if the Marquis was there her appearance could only increase her danger, she checked the step she had almost involuntarily taken to descend. Still she listened, and still thought she distinguished voices. Soon after she heard a door shut, and then footsteps, and she hastened back to her chamber.

Near a quarter of an hour elapsed and La Motte did not appear. When again she thought she heard a murmur of voices below, and also passing steps, and at length her anxiety not suffering her to remain in her room, she moved through the passage that communicated with the spiral staircase; but all was now still. In a few moments, however, a light flashed across the hall, and La Motte appeared at the door of the vaulted room. He looked up, and seeing Adeline in the gallery, beckoned her to descend.

She hesitated and looked towards her chamber; but La Motte now approached the stairs, and, with faultering steps, she went to meet him. 'I fear the Marquis may see me,' said she, whispering; 'where is he?' La Motte took her hand, and led her on, assuring her she had nothing to fear from the Marquis. The wildness of his looks, however, and the trembling of his hand, seemed to contradict this assurance, and she inquired whither he was leading her. 'To the forest,' said La Motte, 'that you may escape from the Abbey—a horse waits for you without. I can save you by no other means.' New terror seized her. She could scarcely believe that La Motte, who had hitherto conspired with the Marquis, and had so closely confined her, should now himself undertake her escape, and she at this moment felt a dreadful presentiment, which it was impossible to account for, that he was leading her out to murder her in the forest. Again shrinking back, she supplicated his mercy. He assured her he meant only to protect her, and desired she would not waste time.

There was something in his manner that spoke sincerity, and she suffered him to conduct her to a side door that opened into the forest, where she could just distinguish through the gloom a man on horseback. This brought to her remembrance the night in which she had quitted the tomb, when trusting to the person who appeared she had been carried to the Marquis's villa. La Motte called, and was answered by Peter, whose voice somewhat re-assured Adeline.

He then told her that the Marquis would return to the Abbey on the following morning, and that this could be her only opportunity of escaping his designs; that she might rely upon his (La Motte's) word, that Peter had orders to carry her wherever she chose; but as he knew the Marquis would be indefatigable in search of her, he advised her by all means to leave the kingdom, which she might do with Peter, who was a native of Savoy,* and would convey her to the house of his sister. There she might remain till La Motte himself, who did not now think it would be safe to continue much longer in France, should join her. He intreated her whatever might happen, never to mention the events which had passed at the Abbey. 'To save you, Adeline, I have risked my life; do not increase my danger and your own by any unnecessary discoveries. We may never meet again, but I hope you will be happy; and remember, when you think of me, that I am not quite so bad as I have been tempted to be.'

Having said this, he gave her some money, which he told her would be necessary to defray the expences of her journey.

Adeline could no longer doubt his sincerity, and her transports of joy and gratitude would scarcely permit her to thank him. She wished to have bid Madame La Motte farewell, and indeed earnestly requested it; but he again told her she had no time to lose, and, having wrapped her in a large cloak, he lifted her upon the horse. She bade him adieu with tears of gratitude, and Peter set off as fast as the darkness would permit.

When they were got some way, 'I am glad with all my heart, Ma'amselle,' said he, 'to see you again. Who would have thought, after all, that my master himself would have bid me take you away!—Well, to be sure, strange things come to pass: but I hope we shall have better luck this time.' Adeline, not chusing to reproach him with the treachery of which she feared he had been formerly guilty, thanked him for his good wishes, and said she hoped they should be more fortunate; but Peter, in his usual strain of eloquence, proceeded to undeceive her in this point, and to acquaint her with every circumstance which his memory, and it was naturally a strong one, could furnish.

Peter expressed such an artless interest in her welfare, and such a concern for her disappointment, that she could no longer doubt his faithfulness; and this conviction not only strengthened her confidence in the present undertaking, but made her listen to his conversation with kindness and pleasure. 'I should never have staid at the Abbey till this time,' said he, 'if I could have got away; but my master frighted me so about the Marquis, and I had not money enough to carry me into my own country, so that I was forced to stay. It's well we have got some solid louis-d'ors now; for I question, Ma'amselle, whether the people on the road would have taken those trinkets you formerly talked of for money.'

'Possibly not,' said Adeline: 'I am thankful to Monsieur La Motte that we have more certain means of procuring conveniences. What route shall you take when we leave the forest, Peter?'—Peter mentioned very correctly a great part of the road to Lyons: 'and then,' said he, 'we can easily get to Savoy, and that will be nothing. My sister, God bless her! I hope is living; I have not seen her many a year; but if she is not, all the people will be glad to see me, and you will easily get a lodging, Ma'amselle, and every thing you want.'

Adeline resolved to go with him to Savoy. La Motte, who knew the character and designs of the Marquis, had advised her to leave the kingdom, and had told her, what her fears would have suggested, that the Marquis would be indefatigable in search of her. His motive for this advice must be a desire of serving her; why else, when she was already in his power, should he remove her to another place, and even furnish her with money for the expences of a journey?

At Leloncourt, where Peter said he was well known, she would be most likely to meet with protection and comfort, even should his sister be dead; and its distance and solitary situation were circumstances that pleased her. These reflections would have pointed out to her the prudence of proceeding to Savoy, had she been less destitute of resources in France; in her present situation they proved it to be necessary.

She inquired farther concerning the route they were to take, and whether Peter was sufficiently acquainted with the road. 'When once I get to Thiers, I know it well enough,' said Peter, 'for I have gone it many a time in my younger days, and any body will tell us the way there.' They travelled for several hours in darkness and silence, and it was not till they emerged from the forest that Adeline saw the morning light streak the eastern clouds. The sight cheered and revived her; and as she travelled silently along her mind revolved the events of the past night, and meditated plans for the future. The present kindness of La Motte appeared so very different from his former conduct that it astonished and perplexed her, and she could only account for it by attributing it to one of those sudden impulses of humanity which sometimes operate even upon the most depraved hearts.

But when she recollected his former words 'that he was not master of himself,' she could scarcely believe that mere pity could induce him to break the bonds which had hitherto so strongly held him, and then, considering the altered conduct of the Marquis, she was inclined to think that she owed her liberty to some change in his sentiments towards her; yet the advice La Motte had given her to quit the kingdom, and the money with which he had supplied her for that purpose, seemed to contradict this opinion, and involved her again in doubt.

Peter now got directions to Thiers, which place they reached without any accident, and there stopped to refresh themselves. As soon as Peter thought the horse sufficiently rested, they again set forward, and from the rich plains of the Lyonnois Adeline, for the first time, caught a view of the distant alps, whose majestic heads, seeming to prop the vault of heaven, filled her mind with sublime emotions.*

In a few hours they reached the vale, in which stands the city of Lyons, whose beautiful environs, studded with villas, and rich with cultivation, withdrew Adeline from the melancholy contemplation of her own circumstances,* and her more painful anxiety for Theodore.

When they reached that busy city,* her first care was to inquire concerning the passage of the Rhone; but she forbore to make these inquiries of the people of the inn, considering that if the Marquis should trace her thither they might enable him to pursue her route. She, therefore, sent Peter to the quays to hire a boat, while she herself took a slight repast, it being her intention to embark immediately. Peter presently returned, having engaged a boat and men to take them up the Rhone to the nearest part of Savoy, from whence they were to proceed by land to the village of Leloncourt.

Having taken some refreshment, she ordered him to conduct her to the vessel. A new and striking scene presented itself to Adeline, who looked with surprise upon the river gay with vessels, and the quay crowded with busy faces,* and felt the contrast which the cheerful objects around bore to herself—to her an orphan, desolate, helpless, and flying from persecution and her country. She spoke with the master of the boat, and having sent Peter back to the inn for the horse, (La Motte's gift to Peter in lieu of some arrears of wages) they embarked.

As they slowly passed up the Rhone, whose steep banks, crowned with mountains, exhibited the most various, wild, and romantic scenery,* Adeline sat in pensive reverie. The novelty* of the scene through which she floated, now frowning with savage grandeur, and now smiling in fertility,* and gay with towns and villages,* soothed her mind, and her sorrow gradually softened into a gentle and not unpleasing melancholy.* She had seated herself at the head of the boat, where she watched its sides cleave the swift stream, and listened to the dashing of the waters.

The boat, slowly opposing the current, passed along for some hours, and at length the veil of evening was stretched over the landscape. The weather was fine, and Adeline, regardless of the dews that now fell, remained in the open air, observing the objects darken round her, the gay tints of the horizon fade away, and the stars gradually appear, trembling upon the lucid mirror of the waters. The scene was now sunk in deep shadow, and the silence of the hour was broken only by the measured dashing of the oars, and now and then by the voice of Peter speaking to the boatmen. Adeline sat lost in thought: the forlornness of her circumstances came heightened to her imagination.

She saw herself surrounded by the darkness and stillness of night, in a strange place, far distant from any friends, going she scarcely knew whither, under the guidance of strangers, and pursued, perhaps, by an inveterate enemy. She pictured to herself the rage of the Marquis now that he had discovered her flight, and though she knew it very unlikely he should follow her by water, for which reason she had chosen that manner of travelling, she trembled at the portrait her fancy drew. Her thoughts then wandered to the plan she should adopt after reaching Savoy; and much as her experience had prejudiced her against the manners of a convent, she saw no place more likely to afford her a proper asylum. At length she retired to the little cabin for a few hours repose.

She awoke with the dawn, and her mind being too much disturbed to sleep again, she rose and watched the gradual approach of day. As she mused, she expressed the feelings of the moment in the following

SONNET*

> Morn's beaming eyes at length unclose,
> And wake the blushes of the rose,
> That all night long oppress'd with dews,
> And veil'd in chilling shade its hues,
> Reclin'd, forlorn, the languid head,

And sadly sought its parent bed;
Warmth from her ray the trembling flow'r derives,
And, sweetly blushing through its tears, revives.

'Morn's beaming eyes at length unclose,'
And melt the tears that bend the rose;
But can their charms suppress the sigh,
Or chace the tear from Sorrow's eye?
Can all their lustrous light impart
One ray of peace to Sorrow's heart?
Ah! no; their fires her fainting soul oppress—
Eve's pensive shades more soothe her meek distress!

When Adeline left the Abbey, La Motte had remained for some time at the gate, listening to the steps of the horse that carried her, till the sound was lost in distance; he then turned into the hall with a lightness of heart to which he had long been a stranger. The satisfaction of having thus preserved her, as he hoped, from the designs of the Marquis, overcame for a while all sense of danger in which this step must involve him. But when he returned entirely to his own situation, the terrors of the Marquis's resentment struck their full force upon his mind, and he considered how he might best escape it.

It was now past midnight—the Marquis was expected early on the following day; and in this interval it at first appeared probable to him that he might quit the forest. There was only one horse; but he considered whether it would be best to set off immediately for Auboine, where a carriage might be procured to convey his family and his moveables from the Abbey, or quietly to await the arrival of the Marquis, and endeavour to impose upon him by a forged story of Adeline's escape.

The time which must elapse before a carriage could reach the Abbey would leave him scarcely sufficient to escape from the forest; what money he had remaining from the Marquis's bounty would not carry him far; and when it was expended he must probably be at a loss for subsistence, should he not before then be detected. By remaining at the Abbey it would appear that he was unconscious of deserving the Marquis's resentment, and though he could not expect to impress a belief upon him that his orders had been executed, he might make it appear that Peter only had been accessary to the escape of Adeline; an account which would seem the more probable from Peter's having been formerly detected in a similiar scheme. He believed also that if the Marquis should threaten to deliver him into the hands of justice, he might save himself by a menace of disclosing the crime he had commissioned him to perpetrate.

Thus arguing, La Motte resolved to remain at the Abbey and await the event of the Marquis's disappointment.

When the Marquis did arrive, and was informed of Adeline's flight, the strong workings of his soul, which appeared in his countenance, for a while alarmed and terrified La Motte. He cursed himself and her in terms of such coarseness and vehemence as La Motte was astonished to hear from a man whose *manners* were generally amiable, whatever might be the violence and criminality of his passions. To invent and express these terms seemed to give him not only relief, but delight; yet he appeared more shocked at the circumstance of her escape than exasperated at the carelessness of La Motte and recollecting at length that he wasted time, he left the Abbey, and dispatched several of his servants in pursuit of her.

When he was gone, La Motte, believing his story had succeeded, returned to the pleasure of considering that he had done his duty, and to the hope that Adeline was now beyond the reach of pursuit. This calm was of short continuance. In a few hours the Marquis returned, accompanied by the officers of justice. The affrighted La Motte, perceiving him approach, endeavoured to conceal himself but was seized and carried to the Marquis, who drew him aside.

'I am not to be imposed upon,' said he, 'by such a superficial story as you have invented; you know your life is in my hands; tell me instantly where you have secreted Adeline, or I will charge you with the crime you have committed against me; but, upon your disclosing the place of her concealment, I will dismiss the officers, and, if you wish it, assist you to leave the kingdom. You have no time to hesitate, and may know that I will not be trifled with.' La Motte attempted to appease the Marquis, and affirmed that Adeline was really fled he knew not whither. 'You will remember, my Lord, that your character is also in my power; and that, if you proceed to extremities, you will compel me to reveal in the face of day that you would have made me a murderer.'

'And who will believe you?' said the Marquis. 'The crimes that banished you from society will be no testimony of your veracity, and that with which I now charge you will bring with it a sufficient presumption that your accusation is malicious. Officers, do your duty.'

They entered the room and seized La Motte, whom terror now deprived of all power of resistance, could resistance have availed him, and in the perturbation of his mind he informed the Marquis that Adeline had taken the road to Lyons. This discovery, however, was made too late to serve himself; the Marquis seized the advantage it offered, but the charge had been given, and, with the anguish of knowing that he had exposed Adeline to danger, without benefiting himself, La Motte submitted in silence to his fate. Scarcely allowing him time to collect what little effects might easily be carried with him, the officers conveyed him from the Abbey; but the Marquis, in consideration of the extreme distress of Madame La Motte, directed one of his servants to procure a carriage from Auboine that she might follow her husband.

The Marquis, in the mean time, now acquainted with the route Adeline had taken, sent forward his faithful valet to trace her to her place of concealment, and return immediately with intelligence to the villa.

Abandoned to despair, La Motte and his wife quitted the forest of Fontangville, which had for so many months afforded them an asylum, and embarked once more upon the tumultuous world, where justice would meet La Motte in the form of destruction. They had entered the forest as a refuge, rendered necessary by the former crimes of La Motte, and for some time found in it the security they sought; but other offences, for even in that sequestered spot there happened to be temptation, soon succeeded, and his life, already sufficiently marked by the punishment of vice, now afforded him another instance of this great truth, 'That where guilt is, there peace cannot enter.'*

CHAPTER XVI

'Hail awful scenes, that calm the troubled breast,
And woo the weary to profound repose!'
                                        BEATTIE.*

ADELINE, mean while, and Peter proceeded on their voyage, without any accident, and landed in Savoy, where Peter placed her upon the horse, and himself walked beside her. When he came within sight of his native mountains, his extravagant joy burst forth into frequent exclamations, and he would often ask Adeline if she had ever seen such *hills* in France. 'No, no,' said he, 'the hills there are very well for French hills, but they are not to be named on the same day with ours.'* Adeline, lost in admiration of the astonishing and tremendous scenery around her, assented very warmly to the truth of Peter's assertion, which encouraged him to expatiate more largely upon the advantages of his country; its disadvantages he totally forgot; and though he gave away his last sous to the children of the peasantry that run barefooted by the side of the horse, he spoke of nothing but the happiness and content of the inhabitants.*

His native village, indeed, was an exception to the general character of the country, and to the usual effects of an arbitrary government;* it was flourishing, healthy, and happy; and these advantages it chiefly owed to the activity and attention of the benevolent clergyman whose cure it was.

Adeline, who now began to feel the effects of long anxiety and fatigue, much wished to arrive at the end of her journey, and inquired impatiently of Peter concerning it. Her spirits, thus weakened, the gloomy grandeur of the scenes which had so lately awakened emotions of delightful sublimity, now awed her into terror;* she trembled at the sound of the torrents rolling among the clifts and thundering in the vale below, and shrunk from the view of the precipices, which sometimes overhung the road, and at others appeared beneath it. Fatigued as she was, she frequently dismounted to climb on foot the steep flinty road, which she feared to travel on horseback.

The day was closing when they drew near a small village at the foot of the Savoy Alps, and the sun, in all his evening splendour, now sinking behind their summits, threw a farewell gleam athwart the landscape, so soft and glowing as drew from Adeline, languid as she was, an exclamation of rapture.

The romantic situation of the village next attracted her notice. It stood at the foot of several stupendous mountains, which formed a chain round a lake at some little distance, and the woods that swept from their summits almost embosomed the village. The lake, unruffled by the lightest air, reflected the vermil tints of the horizon with the sublime scenery on its borders,* darkening every instant with the falling twilight.

When Peter perceived the village, he burst into a shout of joy. 'Thank God,' said he, 'we are near home; there is my dear native place. It looks just as it did twenty years ago; and there are the same old trees growing round our cottage yonder, and the huge rock that rises above it. My poor father died there, Ma'amselle. Pray heaven my sister be alive; it is a long while since I saw her.' Adeline listened with a melancholy pleasure to these artless expressions of Peter, who, in retracing the scenes of his former days, seemed to live them over again. As they approached the village, he continued to point out various objects of his remembrance. 'And there too is the good pastor's chateau;* look, Ma'amselle, that white house, with the smoke curling, that stands on the edge of the lake yonder. I wonder whether he is alive yet. He was not old when I left the place, and as much beloved as ever man was; but death spares nobody!'

They had by this time reached the village which was extremely neat, though it did not promise much accommodation. Peter had hardly advanced ten steps before he was accosted by some of his old acquaintance, who shook hands, and seemed not to know how to part with him. He inquired for his sister, and was told she was alive and well. As they passed on, so many of his old friends flocked round him, that Adeline became quite weary of the delay. Many whom he had left in the vigour of life were now tottering under infirmities of age, while their sons and daughters, whom he had known only in the playfulness of infancy, were grown from his remembrance, and in the pride of youth. At length they approached the cottage, and were met by his sister, who, having heard of his arrival, came and welcomed him with unfeigned joy.

On seeing Adeline, she seemed surprised, but assisted her to alight, and conducting her into a small but neat cottage, received her with a warmth of ready kindness which would have graced a better situation. Adeline desired to speak with her alone, for the room was now crowded with Peter's friends, and then acquainting her with such particulars of her circumstances as it was necessary to communicate, desired to know if she could be accommodated with lodging in the cottage. 'Yes, Ma'amselle,' said the good woman, 'such as it is, you are heartily welcome. I am only sorry it is not better. But you seem ill, Ma'amselle; what shall I get you?'

Adeline, who had been long struggling with fatigue and indisposition, now yielded to their pressure. She said she was, indeed, ill; but hoped that rest would restore her, and desired a bed might be immediately prepared. The good woman went out to obey her, and soon returning, shewed her to a little cabin, where she retired to a bed, whose cleanliness was its only recommendation.

But, notwithstanding her fatigue, she could not sleep, and her mind, in spite of all her efforts, returned to the scenes that were passed, or presented gloomy and imperfect visions of the future.

The difference between her own condition and that of other persons, educated as she had been, struck her forcibly, and she wept. 'They,' said she, 'have friends and relations, all striving to save them not only from what may hurt, but what may displease them; watching not only for their present safety, but for their future advantage, and preventing them even from injuring themselves. But during my whole life I have never known a friend;* have been in general surrounded by enemies, and very seldom exempt from some circumstance either of danger or calamity. Yet surely I am not born to be for ever wretched; the time will come when'——She began to think she might one time be happy; but recollecting the desperate situation of Theodore, 'No,' said she, 'I can never hope even for peace!'

Early the following morning the good woman of the house came to inquire how she had rested, and found she had slept little, and was much worse than on the preceeding night. The uneasiness of her mind contributed to heighten the feverish symptoms that attended her, and in the course of the day her disorder began to assume a serious aspect. She observed its progress with composure, resigning herself to the will of God, and feeling little to regret in life. Her kind hostess did every thing in her power to relieve her, and there was neither physician nor apothecary in the village, so that nature was deprived of none of her advantages. Notwithstanding this, the disorder rapidly increased, and on the third day from its first attack she became delirious; after which she sunk into a state of stupefaction.

How long she remained in this deplorable condition she knew not; but, on recovering her senses, she found herself in an apartment very different from any she remembered. It was spacious and almost beautiful, the bed and every thing around being in one stile of elegant simplicity. For some minutes she lay in a trance of surprise, endeavouring to recollect her scattered ideas of the past, and almost fearing to move, lest the pleasing vision should vanish from her eyes.

At length she ventured to raise herself, when she presently heard a soft voice speaking near her, and the bed curtain on one side was gently undrawn by a beautiful girl. As she leaned forward over the bed, and with a smile of mingled tenderness and joy inquired of her patient how she did, Adeline gazed in silent admiration upon the most interesting female countenance she had ever seen, in which the expression of sweetness, united with lively sense and refinement, was chastened by simplicity.

Adeline at length recollected herself sufficiently to thank her kind inquirer, and begged to know to whom she was obliged, and where she was? The lovely girl pressed her hand, ''Tis we who are obliged,' said she. 'Oh! how I rejoice to find that you have recovered your recollection.' She said no more, but flew to the door of the apartment, and disappeared. In a few minutes she returned with an elderly lady, who, approaching the bed with an air of tender interest, asked concerning the state of Adeline; to which the latter replied, as well as the agitation of her spirits would permit, and repeated her desire of knowing to whom she was so greatly obliged. 'You shall know that hereafter,' said the lady; 'at present be assured that you are with those who will think their care much overpaid by your recovery; submit, therefore, to every thing that may conduce to it, and consent to be kept as quiet as possible.'

Adeline gratefully smiled, and bowed her head in silent assent. The lady now quitted the room for a medicine; having given which to Adeline, the curtain was closed, and she was left to repose. But her thoughts were too busy to suffer her to profit by the opportunity. She contemplated the past, and viewed the present, and, when she compared them, the contrast struck her with astonishment. The whole appeared like one of those sudden transitions so frequent in dreams, in which we pass from grief and despair, we know not how, to comfort and delight.

Yet she looked forward to the future with a trembling anxiety, that threatened to retard her recovery, and which, when she remembered the words of her generous benefactress, she endeavoured to suppress. Had she better known the disposition of the persons in whose house she now was, her anxiety, as far as it regarded herself, must in a great measure have been done away; for La Luc, its owner, was one of those rare characters to whom misfortune seldom looks in vain, and whose native goodness, confirmed by principle, is uniform and unassuming in its acts. The following little picture of his domestic life, his family and his manners, will more fully illustrate his character. It was drawn from the life, and its exactness will, it is hoped, compensate for its length.

THE FAMILY OF LA LUC

'But half mankind, like Handel's fool, destroy,
Through rage and ignorance, the strain of joy;
Irregularly wild their passions roll
Through Nature's finest instrument, the soul:

While men of sense, with Handel's happier skill,
Correct the taste and harmonize the will;
Teach their affections, like his notes, to flow
Nor rais'd too high, nor ever sunk too low;
Till ev'ry virtue, measur'd and refin'd,
As fits the concert of the master mind,
Melts in its kindred sounds, and pours along
Th' according music of the moral song.'
                                    CAWTHORNE.*

In the village of Leloncourt, celebrated for its picturesque
situation at the foot of the Savoy Alps,* lived Arnaud La
Luc,* a clergyman, descended from an ancient family of
France, whose decayed fortunes occasioned them to seek a
retreat in Switzerland,* in an age when the violence of civil
commotion seldom spared the conquered. He was minister of
the village, and equally loved for the piety and benevolence of
the Christian as respected for the dignity and elevation of the
philosopher. His was the philosophy of nature, directed by
common sense.* He despised the jargon of the modern schools
and the brilliant absurdities of systems, which have dazzled
without enlightening, and guided without convincing, their
disciples.*

His mind was penetrating; his views extensive; and his
systems, like his religion, were simple, rational, and sublime.*
The people of his parish looked up to him as to a father; for
while his precepts directed their minds, his example touched
their hearts.*

In early youth La Luc lost a wife,* whom he tenderly
loved. This event threw a tincture of soft and interesting
melancholy over his character, which remained when time
had mellowed the remembrance that occasioned it.
Philosophy had strengthened, not hardened, his heart; it
enabled him to resist the pressure of affliction, rather than to
overcome it.

Calamity taught him to feel with peculiar sympathy the
distresses of others. His income from the parish was small,
and what remained from the divided and reduced estates of his
ancestors did not much increase it; but though he could not
always relieve the necessities of the indigent, his tender pity

and holy conversation seldom failed in administering consolation to the mental sufferer.* On these occasions the sweet and exquisite emotions of his heart have often induced him to say, that could the voluptuary be once sensible of these feelings, he would never after forego 'the luxury of doing good.'*—'Ignorance of true pleasure,' he would say, 'more frequently than temptation to that which is false, leads to vice.'

La Luc had one son and a daughter, who were too young, when their mother died, to lament their loss. He loved them with peculiar tenderness, as the children of her whom he never ceased to deplore; and it was for some time his sole amusement to observe the gradual unfolding of their infant minds, and to bend them to virtue.* His was the deep and silent sorrow of the heart; his complaints he never obtruded upon others, and very seldom did he even mention his wife. His grief was too sacred for the eye of the vulgar. Often he retired to the deep solitude of the mountains, and amid their solemn and tremendous scenery would brood over the remembrance of times past, and resign himself to the luxury of grief. On his return from these little excursions he was always more placid and contented. A sweet tranquillity, which arose almost to happiness, was diffused over his mind, and his manners were more than usually benevolent. As he gazed on his children, and fondly kissed them, a tear would sometimes steal into his eye, but it was a tear of tender regret, unmingled with the darker qualities of sorrow, and was most precious to his heart.

On the death of his wife he received into his house a maiden sister, a sensible, worthy woman, who was deeply interested in the happiness of her brother. Her affectionate attention and judicious conduct anticipated the effect of time in softening the poignancy of his distress, and her unremitted care of his children, while it proved the goodness of her own heart, attracted her more closely to his.

It was with inexpressible pleasure that he traced in the infant features of Clara the resemblance of her mother. The same gentleness of manner and the same sweetness of disposition soon displayed themselves, and as she grew up her actions frequently reminded him so strongly of his lost wife as to fix him in reveries, which absorbed all his soul.

Engaged in the duties of his parish, the education of his children, and in philosophic research, his years passed in tranquillity. The tender melancholy with which affliction had tinctured his mind was, by long indulgence, become dear to him, and he would not have relinquished it for the brightest dream of airy happiness. When any passing incident disturbed him, he retired for consolation to the idea of her he so faithfully loved, and yielding to a gentle, and what the world would call a romantic, sadness, gradually reassumed his composure. This was the secret luxury to which he withdrew from temporary disappointment—the solitary enjoyment which dissipated the cloud of care, and blunted the sting of vexation—which elevated his mind above this world, and opened to his view the sublimity of another.

The spot he now inhabited, the surrounding scenery, the romantic beauties of the neighbouring walks, were dear to La Luc, for they had once been loved by Clara; they had been the scenes of her tenderness, and of his happiness.*

His chateau stood on the borders of a small lake that was almost environed by mountains of stupendous height, which, shooting into a variety of grotesque forms, composed a scenery singularly solemn and sublime.* Dark woods, intermingled with bold projections of rock, sometimes barren, and sometimes covered with the purple bloom of wild flowers, impended over the lake, and were seen in the clear mirror of its waters. The wild and alpine heights which rose above were either crowned with perpetual snows, or exhibited tremendous crags and masses of solid rock, whose appearance was continually changing as the rays of light were variously reflected on their surface, and whose summits were often wrapt in impenetrable mists. Some cottages and hamlets, scattered on the margin of the lake, or seated in picturesque points of view on the rocks above, were the only objects that reminded the beholder of humanity.*

On the side of the lake, nearly opposite to the chateau, the mountains receded, and a long chain of alps were seen stretching in perspective. Their innumerable tints and shades, some veiled in blue mists, some tinged with rich purple, and others glittering in partial light, gave luxurious and magical colouring to the scene.

The chateau was not large, but it was convenient, and was characterisied by an air of elegant simplicity and good order. The entrance was a small hall, which opening by a glass door into the garden, afforded a view of the lake, with the magnificent scenery exhibited on its borders. On the left of the hall was La Luc's study, where he usually passed his mornings; and adjoining was a small room fitted up with chymical apparatus, astronomical instruments, and other implements of science. On the right was the family parlour, and behind it a room which belonged exclusively to Madame La Luc. Here were deposited various medicines and botanical distillations, together with the apparatus for preparing them. From this room the whole village was liberally supplied with physical comfort; for it was the pride of Madame to believe herself skilful in relieving the disorders of her neighbours.*

Behind the chateau rose a tuft of pines, and in front a gentle declivity, covered with verdure and flowers, extended to the lake, whose waters flowed even with the grass, and gave freshness to the acacias that waved over its surface. Flowering shrubs, intermingled with mountain ash, cypress, and evergreen oak, marked the boundary of the garden.

At the return of spring it was Clara's care to direct the young shoots of the plants, to nurse the budding flowers, and to shelter them with the luxuriant branches of the shrubs from the cold blasts that descended from the mountains. In summer she usually rose with the sun, and visited her favourite flowers while the dew yet hung glittering on their leaves. The freshness of early day, with the glowing colouring which then touched the scenery, gave a pure and exquisite delight to her innocent heart. Born amid scenes of grandeur and sublimity, she had quickly imbibed a taste for their charms, which taste was heightened by the influence of a warm imagination. To view the sun rising above the alps, tinging their snowy heads with light, and suddenly darting his rays over the whole face of nature—to see the fiery splendour of the clouds reflected in the lake below, and the roseate tints first steal upon the rocks above—were among the earliest pleasures of which Clara was susceptible. From being delighted with the observance of nature, she grew pleased with seeing her finely imitated, and soon displayed a taste for poetry and painting. When she was about sixteen she often selected from her father's library those of the Italian poets most celebrated for picturesque beauty, and would spend the first hours of morning in reading them under the shade of the acacias that bordered the lake. Here too she would often attempt rude sketches of the surrounding scenery, and at length by repeated efforts, assisted by some instruction from her brother, she succeeded so well as to produce twelve drawings in crayon, which were judged worthy of decorating the parlour of the chateau.*

Young La Luc played the flute, and she listened to him with exquisite delight, particularly when he stood on the margin of the lake, under her beloved acacias. Her voice was sweet and flexible, though not strong, and she soon learned to modulate it to the instrument. She knew nothing of the intricacies of execution; her airs were simple, and her style equally so, but she soon gave them a touching expression, inspired by the sensibility of her heart, which seldom left those of her hearers unaffected.

It was the happiness of La Luc to see his children happy, and in one of his excursions to Geneva, whither he went to visit some relations of his late wife, he bought Clara a lute. She received it with more gratitude than she could express; and having learned one air, she hastened to her favourite acacias, and played it again and again till she forgot every thing besides. Her little domestic duties, her books, her drawing, even the hour which her father dedicated to her improvement, when she met her brother in the library, and with him partook of knowledge, even this hour passed unheeded by. La Luc suffered it to pass. Madame was displeased that her niece neglected her domestic duties, and wished to reprove her, but La Luc begged she would be silent. 'Let experience teach her her error,' said he; 'precept seldom brings conviction to young minds.'*

Madame objected that experience was a slow teacher. 'It is a sure one,' replied La Luc, 'and is not unfrequently the quickest of all teachers: when it cannot lead us into serious evil, it is well to trust to it.'

The second day passed with Clara as the first, and the third as the second. She could now play several tunes; she came to her father and repeated what she had learnt.

At supper the cream was not dressed, and there was no fruit on the table. La Luc inquired the reason; Clara recollected it, and blushed. She observed that her brother was absent, but nothing was said. Toward the conclusion of the repast he appeared; his countenance expressed unusual satisfaction, but he seated himself in silence. Clara inquired what had detained him from supper, and learnt that he had been to a sick family in the neighbourhood with the weekly allowance which her father gave them. La Luc had entrusted the care of this family to his daughter, and it was her duty to have carried them their little allowance on the preceding day, but she had forget every thing but music.

'How did you find the woman?' said La Luc to his son. 'Worse, Sir,' he replied, 'for her medicines had not been regularly given, and the children had had little or no food today.'

Clara was shocked. 'No food to-day!' said she to herself, 'and I have been playing all day on my lute, under the acacias by the lake!' Her father did not seem to observe her emotion, but turned to his son. 'I left her better,' said the latter; 'the medicines I carried eased her pain, and I had the pleasure to see her children make a joyful supper.'

Clara, perhaps for the first time in her life, envied him his pleasure; her heart was full, and she sat silent. 'No food to-day!' thought she.

She retired pensively to her chamber. The sweet serenity with which she usually went to rest was vanished, for she could no longer reflect on the past day with satisfaction.

'What a pity,' said she, 'that what is so pleasing should be the cause of so much pain! This lute is my delight, and my torment!' This reflection occasioned her much internal debate; but before she could come to any resolution upon the point in question, she fell asleep.

She awoke very early the next morning, and impatiently

watched the progress of the dawn. The sun at length appearing, she arose, and, determined to make all the atonement in her power for her former neglect, hastened to the cottage.

Here she remained a considerable time, and when she returned to the chateau her countenance had recovered all its usual serenity. She resolved, however, not to touch her lute that day.

Till the hour of breakfast she busied herself in binding up the flowers, and pruning the shoots that were too luxuriant, and she at length found herself, she scarcely knew how, beneath her beloved acacias by the side of the lake. 'Ah!' said she, with a sigh, 'how sweetly would the song I learned yesterday, sound now over the waters!' But she remembered her determination, and checked the step she was involuntarily taking towards the chateau.

She attended her father in the library at the usual hour, and learned, from his discourse with her brother on what had been read the two preceding days, that she had lost much entertaining knowledge. She requested her father would inform her to what this conversation alluded; but he calmly replied, that she had preferred another amusement at the time when the subject was discussed, and must therefore content herself with ignorance. 'You would reap the rewards of study from the amusements of idleness,' said he; 'learn to be reasonable—do not expect to unite inconsistencies.'

Clara felt the justness of this rebuke, and remembered her lute. 'What mischief has it occasioned!' sighed she. 'Yes, I am determined not to touch it at all this day. I will prove that I am able to control my inclinations when I see it is necessary so to do.' Thus resolving, she applied herself to study with more than usual assiduity.

She adhered to her resolution, and towards the close of day went into the garden to amuse herself. The evening was still and uncommonly beautiful. Nothing was heard but the faint shivering of the leaves, which returned but at intervals, making silence more solemn,* and the distant murmurs of the torrents that rolled among the cliffs. As she stood by the lake, and watched the sun slowly sinking below the alps, whose summits were tinged with gold and purple; as she saw the last rays of light gleam upon the waters whose surface was not curled by the lightest air, she sighed, 'Oh! how enchanting would be the sound of my lute at this moment, on this spot, and when every thing is so still around me!'

The temptation was too powerful for the resolution of Clara: she ran to the chateau, returned with the instrument to her dear acacias, and beneath their shade continued to play till the surrounding objects faded in darkness from her sight. But the moon arose, and shedding, a trembling lustre on the lake, made the scene more captivating than ever.

It was impossible to quit so delightful a spot; Clara repeated her favourite airs again and again. The beauty of the hour awakened all her genius; she never played with such expression before, and she listened with increasing rapture to the tones as they languished over the waters and died away on the distant air. She was perfectly enchanted 'No! nothing was ever so delightful as to play on the lute beneath her acacias, on the margin of the lake, by moon-light!'

When she returned to the chateau, supper was over. La Luc had observed Clara, and would not suffer her to be interrupted.

When the enthusiasm of the hour was passed she recollected that she had broken her resolution, and the reflection gave her pain. 'I prided myself on controling my inclinations,' said she, 'and I have weakly yielded to their direction. But what evil have I incurred by indulging them this evening? I have neglected no duty, for I had none to perform. Of what then have I to accuse myself? It would have been absurd to have kept my resolution, and denied myself a pleasure when there appeared no reason for this self-denial.'

She paused, not quite satisfied with this reasoning. Suddenly resuming her enquiry, 'But how,' said she, 'am I certain that I should have resisted my inclinations if there *had* been a reason for opposing them? If the poor family whom I neglected yesterday had been unsupplied to-day, I fear I should again have forgotten them while I played on my lute on the banks of the lake.'

She then recollected all that her father had at different times said on the subject of self-command, and she felt some pain.

'No,' said she, 'if I do not consider that to preserve a resolution, which I have once solemnly formed, is a sufficient reason to control my inclinations, I fear no other motive would long restrain me. I seriously determined not to touch my lute this whole day, and I have broken my resolution. To-morrow perhaps I may be tempted to neglect some duty, for I have discovered that I cannot rely on my own prudence. Since I cannot conquer temptation, I will fly from it.'

On the following morning she brought her lute to La Luc, and begged he would receive it again, and at least keep it till she had taught her inclinations to submit to control.

The heart of La Luc swelled as she spoke. 'No, Clara,' said he, 'it is unnecessary that I should receive your lute; the sacrifice you would make proves you worthy of my confidence. Take back the instrument; since you have sufficient resolution to resign it when it leads you from duty, I doubt not that you will be able to control its influence now that it is restored to you.'

Clara felt a degree of pleasure and pride at these words, such as she had never before experienced; but she thought, that to deserve the commendation they bestowed, it was necessary to complete the sacrifice she had begun. In the virtuous enthusiasm of the moment the delights of music were forgotten in those of aspiring to well-earned praise, and when she refused the lute thus offered, she was conscious only of exquisite sensations. 'Dear Sir,' said she, tears of pleasure swelling in her eyes, 'allow me to deserve the praises you bestow, and then I shall indeed be happy.'

La Luc thought she had never resembled her mother so much as at this instant, and, tenderly kissing her, he for some moments, wept in silence. When he was able to speak, 'You do already deserve my praises,' said he, 'and I restore your lute as a reward for the conduct which excites them.' This scene called back recollections too tender for the heart of La Luc, and giving Clara the instrument, he abruptly quitted the room.

La Luc's son, a youth of much promise, was designed by his father for the church, and had received from him an excellent education, which, however, it was thought necessary he should finish at an university. That of Geneva was fixed upon by La Lúc. His scheme had been to make his son not a scholar only; he was ambitious that he should also be enviable as a man. From early infancy he had accustomed him to hardihood and endurance, and, as he advanced in youth, he encouraged him in manly exercises, and acquainted him with the useful arts as well as with abstract science.·

He was high spirited and ardent in his temper, but his heart was generous and affectionate. He looked forward to Geneva, and to the new world it would disclose, with the sanguine expectations of youth; and in the delight of these expectations was absorbed the regret he would otherwise have felt at a separation from his family.

A brother of the late Madame La Luc, who was by birth an Englishwoman, resided at Geneva with his family. To have been related to his wife was a sufficient claim upon the heart of La Luc, and he had, therefore, always kept up an intercourse with Mr Audley, though the difference in their characters and manner of thinking would never permit this association to advance into friendship. La Luc now wrote to him, signifying an intention of sending his son to Geneva, and recommending him to his care; to this letter Mr Audley returned a friendly answer, and a short time after an acquaintance of La Luc's being called to Geneva, he determined that his son should accompany him. The separation was painful to La Luc, and almost insupportable to Clara. Madame was grieved, and took care that he should have a sufficient quantity of medicines put up in his travelling trunk; she was also at some pains to point out their virtues, and the different complaints for which they were requisite; but she was careful to deliver her lecture during the absence of her brother.

La Luc, with his daughter, accompanied his son on horseback to the next town, which was about eight miles from Leloncourt, and there again enforcing all the advice he had formerly given him respecting his conduct and pursuits, and again yielding to the tender weakness of the father, he bade him farewell. Clara wept, and felt more sorrow at this parting than the occasion could justify; but this was almost the first time she had known grief, and she artlessly yielded to its influence.

La Luc and Clara travelled pensively back, and the day was closing when they came within view of the lake, and soon after of the chateau. Never had it appeared gloomy till now; but now Clara wandered forlornly through every deserted apartment where she had been accustomed to see her brother, and recollected a thousand little cirumstances which, had he been present, she would have thought immaterial, but on which imagination now stamped a value. The garden, the scenes around, all wore a melancholy aspect, and it was long ere they resumed their natural character and Clara recovered her vivacity.

Near four years had elapsed since this separation, when one evening, as Madame La Luc and her niece were sitting at work together in the parlour, a good woman in the neighbourhood desired to be admitted. She came to ask for some medicines, and the advice of Madame La Luc. 'Here is a sad accident happened at our house, Madame,' said she; 'I am sure my heart aches for the poor young creature.'— Madame La Luc desired she would explain herself, and the woman proceeded to say, that her brother Peter, whom she had not seen for so many years, was arrived, and had brought a young lady to her cottage, who she verily believed was dying. She described her disorder, and acquainted Madame with what particulars of her mournful story Peter had related, failing not to exaggerate such as her compassion for the unhappy stranger and her love of the marvellous prompted.

The account appeared a very extraordinary one to Madame; but pity for the forlorn condition of the young sufferer induced her to inquire farther into the affair. 'Do let me go to her, Madam,' said Clara, who had been listening with ready compassion to the poor woman's narrative: 'do suffer me to go—she must want comforts, and I wish much to see how she is.' Madame asked some farther questions concerning her disorder, and then, taking off her spectacles, she rose from her chair and said she would go herself. Clara desired to accompany her. They put on their hats and followed the good woman to the cottage, where, in a very small, close room, on a miserable bed, lay Adeline, pale, emaciated, and unconscious of all around her. Madame turned to the woman, and asked how long she had been in this way, while Clara went up to the bed, and taking the almost lifeless hand that lay on the quilt, looked anxiously in her face. 'She observes nothing,' said she, 'poor creature! I wish she was at the chateau, she would be better accommodated, and I could nurse her there.' The woman told Madame La Luc, that the young lady had lain in that state for several hours. Madame examined her pulse, and shook her head. 'This room is very close,' said she.—'Very close indeed,' cried Clara, eagerly; 'surely she would be better at the chateau, if she could be moved.'

'We will see about that,' said her aunt. 'In the mean time let me speak to Peter; it is some years since I saw him.' She went to the outer room, and the woman ran out of the cottage to look for him. When she was gone, 'This is a miserable habitation for the poor stranger,' said Clara; 'she will never be well here: do, Madam, let her be carried to our house; I am sure my father would wish it. Besides, there is something in her features, even inanimate as they now are, that prejudices me in her favour.'

'Shall I never persuade you to give up that romantic notion of judging people by their faces,'* said her aunt. 'What sort of a face she has is of very little consequence—her condition is lamentable, and I am desirous of altering it; but I wish first to ask Peter a few questions concerning her.'

'Thank you, my dear aunt,' said Clara; 'she will be removed then.' Madame La Luc was going to reply; but Peter now entered, and, expressing great joy at seeing her again, inquired how Monsieur La Luc and Clara did. Clara immediately welcomed honest Peter to his native place, and he returned her salutation with many expressions of surprise at finding her *so much grown*. 'Though I have so often dandled you in my arms, Ma'amselle, I should never have known you again. Young twigs shoot fast, as they say.'

Madame La Luc now inquired into the particulars of Adeline's story, and heard as much as Peter knew of it, being only that his late master found her in a very distressed situation, and that he had himself brought her from the Abbey to save her from a French Marquis. The simplicity of Peter's manner would not suffer her to question his veracity, though some of the circumstances he related excited all her surprise, and awakened all her pity. Tears frequently stood in Clara's eyes during the course of his narrative, and when he concluded, she said, 'Dear Madam, I am sure when my father learns the history of this unhappy young woman he will not refuse to be a parent to her, and I will be her sister.'

'She deserves it all,' said Peter, 'for she is very good indeed.' He then proceeded in a strain of praise, which was very unusual with him.—'I will go home and consult with my brother about her,' said Madame La Luc, rising: 'she certainly ought to be removed to a more airy room. The chateau is so near, that I think she may be carried thither without much risk.'

'Heaven bless you! Madam,' cried Peter, rubbing his hands, 'for your goodness to my poor young lady.'

La Luc had just returned from his evening walk when they reached the chateau. Madame told him where she had been, and related the history of Adeline and her present condition. 'By all means have her removed hither,' said La Luc, whose eyes bore testimony to the tenderness of his heart. 'She can be better attended to here than in Susan's cottage.'

'I knew you would say so, my dear father,' said Clara: 'I will go and order the green bed to be prepared for her.'

'Be patient, niece,' said Madame La Luc: 'there is no occasion for such haste: some things are to be considered first; but you are young and romantic.'—La Luc smiled.—'The evening is now closed,' resumed Madame; 'it will, therefore, be dangerous to remove her before morning. Early to-morrow a room shall be got ready, and she shall be brought here; in the mean time I will go and make up a medicine, which I hope may be of service to her.'—Clara reluctantly assented to this delay, and Madame La Luc retired to her closet.

On the following morning Adeline, wrapped in blankets, and sheltered as much as possible from the air, was brought to the chateau, where the good La Luc desired she might have every attention paid her, and where Clara watched over her with unceasing anxiety and tenderness. She remained in a state of torpor during the greater part of the day, but towards evening she breathed more freely; and Clara, who still watched by her bed, had at length the pleasure of perceiving that her senses were restored. It was at this moment that she found herself in the situation from which we have digressed to give this account of the venerable La Luc and his family. The reader will find that his virtues and his friendship to Adeline deserved this notice.

CHAPTER XVII

'Still Fancy, to herself unkind,
Awakes to grief the soften'd mind,
And points the bleeding friend.'
                    COLLINS*

ADELINE, assisted by a fine constitution, and the kind attentions of her new friends, was in a little more than a week so much recovered as to leave her chamber. She was introduced to La Luc, whom she met with tears of gratitude, and thanked for his goodness in a manner so warm, yet so artless, as interested him still more in her favour. During the progress of her recovery, the sweetness of her behaviour had entirely won the heart of Clara, and greatly interested that of her aunt, whose reports of Adeline, together with the praises bestowed by Clara, had excited both esteem and curiosity in the breast of La Luc; and he now met her with an expression of benignity which spoke peace and comfort to her heart. She had acquainted Madame La Luc with such particulars of her story as Peter, either through ignorance or inattention, had not communicated, suppressing only, through a false delicacy, perhaps, an acknowledgement of her attachment to Theodore. These circumstances were repeated to La Luc, who, ever sensible to the sufferings of others, was particularly interested by the singular misfortunes of Adeline.

Near a fortnight had elapsed since her removal to the

chateau, when one morning La Luc desired to speak with her alone. She followed him into his study, and then in a manner the most delicate he told her, that, as he found she was so unfortunate in her father, he desired she would henceforth consider him as her parent, and his house as her home. 'You and Clara shall be equally my daughters,' continued he; 'I am rich in having such children.' The strong emotions of surprise and gratitude for some time kept Adeline silent. 'Do not thank me,' said La Luc; 'I know all you would say, and I know also that I am but doing my duty. I thank God that my duty and my pleasures are generally in unison.' Adeline wiped away the tears which his goodness had excited, and was going to speak; but La Luc pressed her hand, and, turning away to conceal his emotion, walked out of the room.

Adeline was now considered as a part of the family, and in the parental kindness of La Luc, the sisterly affection of Clara, and the steady and uniform regard of Madame, she would have been happy as she was thankful, had not unceasing anxiety for the fate of Theodore, of whom in this solitude she was less likely than ever to hear, corroded her heart, and embittered every moment of reflection. Even when sleep obliterated for a while the memory of the past, his image frequently arose to her fancy, accompanied by all the exaggerations of terror. She saw him in chains, and struggling in the grasp of ruffians, or saw him led, amidst the dreadful preparations for execution, into the field: she saw the agony of his look and heard him repeat her name in frantic accents, till the horrors of the scene overcame her, and she awoke.

A similarity of taste and character attached her to Clara, yet the misery that preyed upon her heart was of a nature too delicate to be spoken of, and she never mentioned Theodore even to her friend. Her illness had yet left her weak and languid, and the perpetual anxiety of her mind contributed to prolong this state. She endeavoured, by strong and almost continual efforts, to abstract her thoughts from their mournful subject, and was often successful. La Luc had an excellent library, and the instruction it offered at once gratified her love of knowledge, and withdrew her mind from painful recollections. His conversation too afforded her another refuge from misery.

But her chief amusement was to wander among the sublime scenery of the adjacent country, sometimes with Clara, though often with no other companion than a book. There were indeed times when the conversation of her friend imposed a painful restraint, and, when given up to reflection, she would ramble alone through scenes, whose solitary grandeur assisted and soothed the melancholy of her heart.* Here she would retrace all the conduct of her beloved Theodore, and endeavour to recollect his exact countenance, his air, and manner. Now she would weep at the remembrance and then, suddenly considering that he had perhaps already suffered an ignominious death for her sake, even in consequence of the very action which had proved his love, a dreadful despair would seize her, and, arresting her tears, would threaten to bear down every barrier that fortitude and reason could oppose.

Fearing longer to trust her own thoughts, she would hurry home, and by a desperate effort would try to lose, in the conversation of La Luc, the remembrance of the past. Her melancholy, when he observed it, La Luc attributed to a sense of the cruel treatment she had received from her father; a circumstance which, by exciting his compassion, endeared her more strongly to his heart; while that love of rational conversation, which in her calmer hours so frequently appeared, opened to him a new source of amusement in the cultivation of a mind eager for knowledge, and, susceptible of all the energies of genius. She found a melancholy pleasure in listening to the soft tones of Clara's lute, and would often soothe her mind by attempting to repeat the airs she heard.

The gentleness of her manners, partaking so much of that pensive character which marked La Luc's, was soothing to his heart, and tinctured his behaviour with a degree of tenderness that imparted comfort to her, and gradually won her entire confidence and affection. She saw with extreme concern the declining state of his health, and united her efforts with those of the family to amuse and revive him.

The pleasing society of which she partook, and the

quietness of the country, at length restored her mind to a state of tolerable composure. She was now acquainted with all the wild walks of the neighbouring mountains, and, never tired of viewing their astonishing scenery, she often indulged herself in traversing alone their unfrequented paths, where now and then a peasant from a neighbouring village was all that interrupted the profound solitude. She generally took with her a book, that if she perceived her thoughts inclined to fix on the one object of her grief, she might force them to a subject less dangerous to her peace. She had become a tolerable proficient in English while at the convent where she received her education, and the instruction of La Luc, who was well acquainted with the language, now served to perfect her. He was partial to the English; he admired their character, and the constitution of their laws, and his library contained a collection of their best authors, particularly of their philosophers and poets. Adeline found that no species of writing had power so effectually to withdraw her mind from the contemplation of its own misery as the higher kinds of poetry, and in these her taste soon taught her to distinguish the superiority of the English from that of the French. The genius of the language, more perhaps than the genius of the people, if indeed the distinction may be allowed, occasioned this.

She frequently took a volume of Shakespear or Milton,* and, having gained some wild eminence, would seat herself beneath the pines, whose low murmurs soothed her heart, and conspired with the visions of the poet to lull her to forgetfulness of grief.

One evening, when Clara was engaged at home, Adeline wandered alone to a favourite spot among the rocks that bordered the lake. It was an eminence which commanded an entire view of the lake, and of the stupendous mountains that environed it. A few ragged thorns grew from the precipice beneath, which descended perpendicularly to the water's edge; and above rose a thick wood of larch, pine, and fir, intermingled with some chesnut and mountain ash. The evening was fine, and the air so still, that it scarcely waved the light leaves of the trees around, or rimpled* the broad expanse of the waters below. Adeline gazed on the scene with a kind of still rapture, and watched the sun sinking amid a crimson glow, which tinted the bosom of the lake and the snowy heads of the distant alps.* The delight which the scenery inspired,

> 'Soothing each gust of passion into peace,
> All but the swellings of the soften'd heart,
> That waken, not disturb, the tranquil mind!'*

was now heightened by the tones of a French horn, and, looking on the lake, she perceived at some distance a pleasure boat. As it was a spectacle rather uncommon in this solitude, she concluded the boat contained a party of foreigners come to view the wonderful scenery of the country, or perhaps of Genevois, who chose to amuse themselves on a lake as grand, though much less extensive, than their own;* and the latter conjecture was probably just.

As she listened to the mellow and enchanting tones of the horn, which gradually sunk away in distance, the scene appeared more lovely than before, and finding it impossible to forbear attempting to paint in language what was so beautiful in reality, she composed the following

STANZAS

> How smooth that lake expands its ample breast!
>   Where smiles in soften'd glow the summer sky:
> How vast the rocks that o'er its surface rest!
>   How wild the scenes its winding shores supply!
>
> Now down the western steep slow sinks the sun,
>   And paints with yellow gleam the tufted woods;
> While here the mountain-shadows, broad and dun,
>   Sweep o'er the chrystal mirror of the floods.
>
> Mark how his splendour tips with partial light
>   Those shatter'd battlements! that on the brow
> Of yon bold promontory burst to sight
>   From o'er the woods that darkly spread below.
>
> In the soft blush of light's reflected power,
>   The ridgy rock, the woods that crown its steep,
> Th' illumin'd battlement, and darker tower,
>   On the smooth wave in trembling beauty sleep.
>
> But lo! the sun recalls his fervid ray,
>   And cold and dim the wat'ry visions fail;

While o'er yon cliff, whose pointed craggs decay,
  Mild Evening draws her thin empurpled veil!

How sweet that strain of melancholy horn!
  That floats along the slowly-ebbing wave,
And up the far-receding mountains borne,
  Returns a dying close from Echo's cave!

Hail! shadowy forms of still, expressive Eve!
  Your pensive graces stealing on my heart,
Bid all the fine-attun'd emotions live,
  And Fancy all her loveliest dreams impart.

La Luc observing how much Adeline was charmed with the features of the country, and desirous of amusing her melancholy, which, notwithstanding her efforts, was often too apparent, wished to shew her other scenes than those to which her walks were circumscribed. He proposed a party on horseback to take a nearer view of the Glaciers; to attempt their ascent was a difficulty and fatigue to which neither La Luc, in his present state of health, nor Adeline, were equal. She had not been accustomed to ride single, and the mountainous road they were to pass made the experiment rather dangerous; but she concealed her fears, and they were not sufficient to make her wish to forego an enjoyment such as was now offered her.

The following day was fixed for this excursion. La Luc and his party arose at an early hour, and having taken a slight breakfast, they set out towards the Glacier of Montanvert,* which lay at a few leagues distance. Peter carried a small basket of provisions; and it was their plan to dine on some pleasant spot in the open air.

It is unnecessary to describe the high enthusiasm of Adeline, the more complacent pleasure of La Luc, and the transports of Clara, as the scenes of this romantic country shifted to their eyes. Now frowning in dark and gloomy grandeur, it exhibited only tremendous rocks, and cataracts rolling from the heights into some deep and narrow valley, along which their united waters roared and foamed, and burst away to regions inaccessible to mortal foot: and now the scene arose less fiercely wild;*

'The pomp of groves and garniture of fields'*

were intermingled with the ruder features of nature, and while
the snow froze on the summit of the mountain, the vine
blushed at its foot.

Engaged in interesting conversation, and by the admiration
which the country excited, they travelled on till noon, when
they looked round for a pleasant spot where they might rest
and take refreshment. At some little distance they perceived
the ruins of a fabric which had once been a castle; it stood
almost on a point of rock that overhung a deep valley; and its
broken turrets rising from among the woods that embosomed
it, heightened the picturesque beauty of the object.*

The edifice invited curiosity, and the shades repose—La
Luc and his party advanced.

'Deep struck with awe, they mark'd the dome o'erthrown,
Where once the beauty bloom'd, the warrior shone:
They saw the *castle*'s mould'ring towers decay'd,
The loose stone tott'ring o'er the trembling shade.'*

They seated themselves on the grass under the shade of
some high trees near the ruins. An opening in the woods
afforded a view of the distant alps—the deep silence of solitude
reigned. For some time they were lost in meditation. Adeline
felt a sweet complacency, such as she had long been a stranger
to.* Looking at La Luc, she perceived a tear stealing down his
cheek, while the elevation of his mind was strongly expressed
on his countenance. He turned on Clara his eyes, which were
now filled with tenderness, and made an effort to recover
himself.

'The stillness and total seclusion of this scene,' said Adeline,
'those stupendous mountains, the gloomy grandeur of these
woods, together with that monument of faded glory on which
the hand of time is so emphatically impressed, diffuse a sacred
enthusiasm over the mind, and awaken sensations truly
sublime.'*

La Luc was going to speak; but Peter coming forward,
desired to know whether he had not better open the wallet, as
he fancied his honour and the young ladies must be main
hungry,* jogging on so far up hill and down before

dinner. They acknowledged the truth of honest Peter's suspicion, and accepted his hint.

Refreshments were spread on the grass, and having seated themselves under the canopy of waving woods, surrounded by the sweets of wild flowers, they inhaled the pure breeze of the alps, which might be called spirit of air, and partook of a repast which these circumstances rendered delicious.*

When they arose to depart, 'I am unwilling,' said Clara, 'to quit this charming spot. How delightful would it be to pass one's life beneath these shades with the friends who are dear to one!'—La Luc smiled at the romantic simplicity of the idea; but Adeline sighed deeply to the image of felicity, and of Theodore, which it recalled, and turned away to conceal her tears.

They now mounted their horses, and soon after arrived at the foot of Montanvert. The emotions of Adeline, as she contemplated in various points of view the astonishing objects around her, surpassed all expression; and the feelings of the whole party were too strong to admit of conversation.* The profound stillness which reigned in these regions of solitude inspired awe, and heightened the sublimity of the scenery to an exquisite degree.

'It seems,' said Adeline, 'as if we were walking over the ruins of the world, and were the only persons who had survived the wreck.* I can scarcely persuade myself that we are not left alone on the globe.'

'The view of these objects,' said La Luc, 'lift the soul to their Great Author, and we contemplate with a feeling almost too vast for humanity—the sublimity of his nature in the grandeur of his works.*—La Luc raised his eyes, filled with tears, to heaven, and was for some moments lost in silent adoration.

They quitted these scenes with extreme reluctance; but the hour of the day, and the appearance of the clouds, which seemed gathering for a storm, made them hasten their departure. Could she have been sheltered from its fury, Adeline almost wished to have witnessed the tremendous effect of a thunder storm in these regions.

They returned to Leloncourt by a different route, and the

shade of the overhanging precipices was deepened by the gloom of the atmosphere. It was evening when they came within view of the lake, which the travellers rejoiced to see, for the storm so long threatened was now fast approaching; the thunder murmured among the alps; and the dark vapours that rolled heavily along their sides heightened their dreadful sublimity. La Luc would have quickened his pace, but the road winding down the steep side of a mountain made caution necessary. The darkening air and the lightnings that now flashed along the horizon terrified Clara, but she withheld the expression of her fear in consideration of her father. A peal of thunder, which seemed to shake the earth to its foundations, and was reverberated in tremendous echoes from the cliffs, burst over their heads.* Clara's horse took fright at the sound, and, setting off, hurried her with amazing velocity down the mountain towards the lake, which washed its foot.* The agony of La Luc, who viewed her progress in the horrible expectation of seeing her dashed down the precipice that bordered the road, is not to be described.

Clara kept her seat, but terror had almost deprived her of sense. Her efforts to preserve herself were mechanical, for she scarcely knew what she did. The horse, however, carried her safely almost to the foot of the mountain, but was making towards the lake, when a gentleman who travelled along the road caught the bridle as the animal endeavoured to pass. The sudden stopping of the horse threw Clara to the ground, and, impatient of restraint, the animal burst from the hand of the stranger, and plunged into the lake. The violence of the fall deprived her of recollection; but while the stranger endeavoured to support her, his servant ran to fetch water.

She soon recovered, and unclosing her eyes, found herself in the arms of a chevalier, who appeared to support her with difficulty. The compassion expressed in his countenance, while he inquired how she did, revived her spirits, and she was endeavouring to thank him for his kindness when La Luc and Adeline came up. The terror impressed on her father's features was perceived by Clara; languid as she was, she tried to raise herself, and said, with a faint smile, which betrayed, instead of disguising, her sufferings, 'Dear Sir, I am not hurt.'

Her pale countenance and the blood that trickled down her cheek contradicted her words. But La Luc, to whom terror had suggested the utmost possible evil, now rejoiced to hear her speak; he recalled some presence of mind, and while Adeline applied her salts, he chafed her temples.

When she revived she told him how much she was obliged to the stranger. La Luc endeavoured to express his gratitude; but the former interrupting him, begged he might be spared the pain of receiving thanks for having followed only an impulse of common humanity.

They were now not far from Leloncourt; but the evening was almost shut in, and the thunder murmured deeply among the hills. La Luc was distressed how to convey Clara home.

In endeavouring to raise her from the ground, the stranger betrayed such evident symptoms of pain, that La Luc inquired concerning it. The sudden jerk which the horse had given the arm of the chevalier, in escaping from his hold, had violently sprained his shoulder, and rendered his arm almost useless. The pain was exquisite, and La Luc, whose fears for his daughter were now subsiding, was shocked at the circumstance, and pressed the stranger to accompany him to the village, where relief might be obtained. He accepted the invitation, and Clara, being at length placed on a horse led by her father, was conducted to the chateau.

When Madame, who had been looking out for La Luc some time, perceived the cavalcade approaching, she was alarmed, and her apprehensions were confirmed when she saw the situation of her niece. Clara was carried into the house, and La Luc would have sent for a surgeon, but there was none within several leagues of the village, neither were there any of the physical profession within the same distance. Clara was assisted to her chamber by Adeline, and Madame La Luc undertook to examine the wounds. The result restored peace to the family; for though she was much bruised, she had escaped material injury; a slight contusion on the forehead had occasioned the bloodshed which at first alarmed La Luc. Madame undertook to restore her niece in a few days with the assistance of a balsam composed by herself, on the virtues of which she descanted with great eloquence, till La Luc interrupted her by reminding her of the condition of her patient.

Madame having bathed Clara's bruises, and given her a cordial of incomparable efficacy, left her, and Adeline watched in the chamber of her friend till she retired to her own for the night.

La Luc, whose spirits had suffered much perturbation, was now tranquillized by the report his sister made of Clara. He introduced the stranger, and having mentioned the accident he had met with, desired that he might have immediate assistance. Madame hastened to her closet, and it is perhaps difficult to determine whether she felt most concern for the sufferings of her guest or pleasure at the opportunity thus offered of displaying her physical skill. However this might be, she quitted the room with great alacrity, and very quickly returned with a phial containing her inestimable balsam, and having given the necessary directions for the application of it, she left the stranger to the care of his servant.

La Luc insisted that the chevalier, M. Verneuil, should not leave the chateau that night, and he very readily submitted to be detained. His manners during the evening were as frank and engaging as the hospitality and gratitude of La Luc were sincere, and they soon entered into interesting conversation. M. Verneuil conversed like a man who had seen much, and thought more, and if he discovered any prejudice in his opinions, it was evidently the prejudice of a mind which, seeing objects through the medium of its own goodness, tinges them with the hue of its predominant quality. La Luc was much pleased, for in his retired situation he had not often an opportunity of receiving the pleasure which results from a communion of intelligent minds. He found that M. Verneuil had travelled. La Luc having asked some questions relative to England, they fell into discourse concerning the national characters of the French and English.

'If it is the privilege of wisdom,' said M. Verneuil, 'to look beyond happiness, I own I had rather be without it. When we observe the English, their laws, writings, and conversation, and at the same time mark their countenances, manners, and the frequency of suicide among them, we are apt to believe that wisdom and happiness are incompatible. If, on the other hand, we turn to their neighbours, the French, and see[1] their wretched policy, their sparkling, but sophistical discourse, frivolous occupations, and, withal, their gay animated air, we shall be compelled to acknowledge that happiness and folly too often dwell together.'*

'It is the end of wisdom,' said La Luc, 'to attain happiness, and I can hardly dignify that conduct or course of thinking which tends to misery with the name of wisdom. By this rule, perhaps, the folly, as we term it, of the French deserves, since its effect is happiness, to be called wisdom. That airy thoughtlessness, which seems alike to contemn reflection and anticipation, produces all the effect of it without reducing its subjects to the mortification of philosophy. But in truth wisdom is an exertion of mind to subdue folly; and as the happiness of the French is less the consequence of mind than of constitution, it deserves not the honours of wisdom.'

Discoursing on the variety of opinions that are daily formed on the same conduct, La Luc observed how much that which is commonly called opinion is the result of passion and temper.

'True,' said M. Verneuil, 'there is a tone of thought, as there is a key note in music, that leads all its weaker affections. Thus where the powers of judging may be equal, the disposition to judge is different, and the actions of men are at least but too often arraigned by whim and caprice, by partial vanity and the humour of the moment.'

Here La Luc took occasion to reprobate the conduct of those writers, who, by shewing the dark side only of human nature, and by dwelling on the evils only which are incident to humanity, have sought to degrade man in his own eyes, and to make him discontented with life. 'What should we say of a painter,' continued La Luc, 'who collected in his piece objects of a black hue only, who presented you with a black man, a black horse, a black dog, &c. &c., and tells you that his is a picture of nature, and that nature is black?'—"Tis true,' you would reply, 'the objects you exhibit do exist in nature, but they form a very small part of her works. You say that

[1] It must be remembered that this was said in the seventeenth century.*

nature is black, and, to prove it, you have collected on your canvass all the animals of this hue that exist. But you have forgot to paint the green earth, the blue sky, the white man, and objects of all those various hues with which creation abounds, and of which black is a very inconsiderable part.'

The countenance of M. Verneuil lightened with peculiar animation during the discourse of La Luc.—'To think well of his nature,' said he, 'is necessary to the dignity and the happiness of man. There is a decent pride which becomes every mind, and is congenial to virtue. That consciousness of innate dignity, which shews him the glory of his nature, will be his best protection from the meanness of vice. Where this consciousness is wanting,' continued M. Verneuil, 'there can be no sense of moral honour, and consequently none of the higher principles of action. What can be expected of him who says it is his nature to be mean and selfish? Or who can doubt that he who thinks thus, thinks from the experience of his own heart, from the tendency of his own inclinations? Let it always be remembered, that he who would persuade men to be good, ought to shew them that they are great.'*

'You speak,' La Luc, 'with the honest enthusiasm of a virtuous mind; and in obeying the impulse of your heart, you utter the truths of philosophy: and, trust me, a bad heart and a *truly* philosophic head has never yet been united in the same individual. Vicious inclinations not only corrupt the heart, but the understanding, and thus lead to false reasoning. Virtue only is on the side of truth.'

La Luc and his guest, mutually pleased with each other, entered upon the discussion of subjects so interesting to them both, that it was late before they parted for the night.

CHAPTER XVIII

''Twas such a scene as gave a kind relief
To memory, in sweetly pensive grief.'
                    VIRGIL'S TOMB*

'Mine be the breezy hill, that skirts the down,
Where a green grassy turf is all I crave,
With here and there a violet bestrown,
And many an evening sun shine sweetly on my grave.'
                    THE MINSTREL*

REPOSE had so much restored Clara, that when Adeline, anxious to know how she did, went early in the morning to her chamber, she found her already risen, and ready to attend the family at breakfast. Monsieur Verneuil appeared also, but his looks betrayed a want of rest, and indeed he had suffered during the night a degree of anguish from his arm, which it was an effort of some resolution to endure in silence. It was now swelled and somewhat inflamed, and this might in some degree be attributed to the effect of Madame La Luc's balsam, whose restorative qualities had for once failed. The whole family sympathised with his sufferings, and Madame, at the request of M. Verneuil, abandoned her balsam, and substituted an emollient fomentation.

From an application of this he, in a short time, found an abatement of the pain, and returned to the breakfast table with greater composure. The happiness which La Luc felt at seeing his daughter in safety was very apparent, but the warmth of his gratitude towards her preserver he found it difficult to express. Clara spoke the genuine emotions of her heart with artless, but modest, energy, and testified sincere concern for the suffering which she had occasioned M. Verneuil.

The pleasure received from the company of his guest, and the consideration of the essential services he had rendered him, co-operated with the natural hospitality of La Luc, and he pressed M. Verneuil to remain some time at the chateau.— 'I can never repay the services you have done me,' said La Luc;

'yet I seek to increase my obligations to you by requesting you will prolong your visit, and thus allow me an opportunity of cultivating your acquaintance.'

M. Verneuil, who at the time he met La Luc was travelling from Geneva to a distant part of Savoy, merely for the purpose of viewing the country, being now delighted with his host and with every thing around him, willingly accepted the invitation. In this circumstance prudence concurred with inclination, for to have pursued his journey on horseback, in his present situation, would have been dangerous, if not impracticable.

The morning was spent in conversation, in which M. Verneuil displayed a mind enriched with taste, enlightened by science, and enlarged by observation. The situation of the chateau and the features of the surrounding scenery charmed him, and in the evening he found himself able to walk with La Luc and explore the beauties of this romantic region.* As they passed through the village, the salutations of the peasants, in whom love and respect were equally blended, and their eager inquiries after Clara, bore testimony to the character of La Luc, while his countenance expressed a serene satisfaction, arising from the consciousness of deserving and possessing their love.—'I live surrounded by my children,' said he, turning to M. Verneuil, who had noticed their eagerness, 'for such I consider my parishioners. In discharging the duties of my office, I am repaid not only by my own conscience, but by their gratitude. There is a luxury in observing their simple and honest love, which I would not exchange for any thing the world calls blessings.'*

'Yet the world, Sir, would call the pleasures of which you speak romantic,' said M. Verneuil; 'for to be sensible of this pure and exquisite delight requires a heart untainted with the vicious pleasures of society—pleasures that deaden its finest feelings and poison the source of its truest enjoyments.'*—They pursued their way along the borders of the lake, sometimes under the shade of hanging woods, and sometimes over hillocks of turf, where the scene opened in all its wild magnificence. M. Verneuil often stopped in raptures to observe and point out the singular beauties it exhibited, while La Luc, pleased with the delight his friend expressed, surveyed with more than usual satisfaction the objects which had so often charmed him before. But there was a tender melancholy in the tone of his voice and his countenance, which arose from the recollection of having often traced those scenes, and partook of the pleasure they inspired, with her who had long since bade them an eternal farewell.

They presently quitted the lake, and, winding up a steep ascent between the woods, came, after an hour's walk, to a green summit, which appeared, among the savage rocks that environed it, like the blossom on the thorn. It was a spot formed for solitary delight, inspiring that soothing tenderness so dear to the feeling mind, and which calls back to memory the images of passed regret, softened by distance and endeared by frequent recollection. Wild shrubs grew from the crevices of the rocks beneath, and the high trees of pine and cedar that waved above, afforded a melancholy and romantic shade.* The silence of the scene was interrupted only by the breeze as it rolled over the woods, and by the solitary notes of the birds that inhabited the cliffs.

From this point the eye commanded an entire view of those majestic and sublime alps whose aspect fills the soul with emotions of indescribable awe, and seems to lift it to a nobler nature. The village, and the chateau of La Luc appeared in the bosom of the mountains, a peaceful retreat from the storms that gathered on their tops. All the faculties of M. Verneuil were absorbed in admiration, and he was for some time quite silent; at length, bursting into a rhapsody, he turned, and would have addressed La Luc, when he perceived him at a distance leaning against a rustic urn, over which drooped, in beautiful luxuriance, the weeping willow.

As he approached, La Luc quitted his position, and advanced to meet him, while M. Verneuil inquired upon what occasion the urn had been erected. La Luc, unable to answer, pointed to it, and walked silently away, and M. Verneuil, approaching the urn, read the following inscription:

TO

THE MEMORY OF CLARA LA LUC,

THIS URN

IS ERECTED ON THE SPOT WHICH SHE LOVED,

IN TESTIMONY OF THE AFFECTION OF

A HUSBAND.*

M. Verneuil now comprehended the whole, and, feeling for his friend, was hurt that he had noticed this monument of his grief. He rejoined La Luc, who was standing on the point of the eminence contemplating the landscape below with an air more placid, and touched with the sweetness of piety and resignation. He perceived that M. Verneuil was somewhat disconcerted, and he sought to remove his uneasiness. 'You will consider it,' said he, 'as a mark of my esteem that I have brought you to this spot. It is never prophaned by the presence of the unfeeling. They would deride the faithfulness of an attachment which has so long survived its object, and which, in their own breasts, would quickly have been lost amidst the dissipation of general society. I have cherished in my heart the remembrance of a woman whose virtues claimed all my love: I have cherished it as a treasure to which I could withdraw from temporary cares and vexations, in the certainty of finding a soothing, though melancholy, comfort.'

La Luc paused. M. Verneuil expressed the sympathy he felt, but he knew the sacredness of sorrow, and soon relapsed into silence. 'One of the brightest hopes of a future state,' resumed La Luc, 'is, that we shall meet again those whom we have loved upon earth. And perhaps our happiness may be permitted to consist very much in the society of our friends, purified from the frailties of mortality, with the finer affections more sweetly attuned, and with the faculties of mind infinitely more elevated and enlarged. We shall then be enabled to comprehend subjects which are too vast for human conception; to comprehend, perhaps, the sublimity of the Deity who first called us into being. These views of futurity, my friend, elevate us above the evils of this world, and seem to communicate to us a portion of the nature we contemplate.'

'Call them not the illusions of a visionary brain,' proceeded

La Luc: 'I trust in their reality. Of this I am certain, that whether they are illusions or not, a faith in them ought to be cherished for the comfort it brings to the heart, and reverenced for the dignity it imparts to the mind. Such feelings make a happy and an important part of our belief in future existence: they give energy to virtue, and stability to principle.'

'This,' said M. Verneuil, 'is what I have often felt, and what every ingenuous mind must acknowledge.'

La Luc and M. Verneuil continued in conversation till the sun had left the scene. The mountains, darkened by twilight, assumed a sublimer aspect, while the tops of some of the highest alps were yet illumined by the sun's rays, and formed a striking contrast to the shadowy obscurity of the world below. As they descended through the woods, and traversed the margin of the lake, the stillness and solemnity of the hour diffused a pensive sweetness over their minds, and sunk them into silence.

They found supper spread, as was usual, in the hall, of which the windows opened upon a garden, where the flowers might be said to yield their fragrance in gratitude to the refreshing dews. The windows were embowered with eglantine and other sweet shrubs, which hung in wild luxuriance around, and formed a beautiful and simple decoration. Clara and Adeline loved to pass the evenings in this hall, where they had acquired the first rudiments of astronomy, and from which they had a wide view of the heavens. La Luc pointed out to them the planets and the fixed stars, explained their laws, and from thence taking occasion to mingle moral with scientific instruction, would often ascend towards that great first cause, whose nature soars beyond the grasp of human comprehension.

'No study,' he would sometimes say, 'so much enlarges the mind, or impresses it with so sublime an idea of the Deity, as that of astronomy. When the imagination launches into the regions of space, and contemplates the innumerable worlds which are scattered through it, we are lost in astonishment and awe. This globe appears as a mass of atoms in the immensity of the universe, and man a mere insect. Yet how wonderful! that man, whose frame is so diminutive in the scale of being, should have powers which spurn the narrow boundaries of time and place, soar beyond the sphere of his existence, penetrate the secret laws of nature, and calculate their progressive effects.'*

'O! how expressively does this prove the spirituality of our Being! Let the materialist consider it, and blush that he has ever doubted.'*

In this hall the whole family now met at supper, and during the remainder of the evening the conversation turned upon general subjects, in which Clara joined in modest and judicious remark. La Luc had taught her to familiarize her mind to reasoning, and had accustomed her to deliver her sentiments freely: she spoke them with a simplicity extremely engaging, and which convinced her hearers that the love of knowledge, not the vanity of talking, induced her to converse.* M. Verneuil evidently endeavoured to draw forth her sentiments, and Clara, interested by the subjects he introduced, a stranger to affectation, and pleased with the opinions he expressed, answered them with frankness and animation. They retired mutually pleased with each other.

M. Verneuil was about six and thirty; his figure manly, his countenance frank and engaging. A quick penetrating eye, whose fire was softened by benevolence, disclosed the chief traits of his character; he was quick to discern, but generous to excuse, the follies of mankind; and while no one more sensibly felt an injury, none more readily accepted the concession of an enemy.

He was by birth a Frenchman. A fortune lately devolved to him, had enabled him to execute the plan, which his active and inquisitive mind had suggested, of viewing the most remarkable parts of the continent. He was peculiarly susceptible of the beautiful and sublime in nature. To such a taste Switzerland and the adjacent country was, of all others, the most interesting; and he found the scenery it exhibited infinitely surpassing all that his glowing imagination had painted; he saw with the eye of a painter, and felt with the rapture of a poet.

In the habitation of La Luc he met with the hospitality, the frankness, and the simplicity, so characteristic of the country: in his venerable host he saw the strength of philosophy united with the finest tenderness of humanity—a philosophy which taught him to correct his feelings, not to annihilate them; in Clara, the bloom of beauty, with the most perfect simplicity of heart; and in Adeline all the charms of elegance and grace, with a genius deserving of the highest culture. In this family picture the goodness of Madame La Luc was not unperceived or forgotten. The chearfulness and harmony that reigned within the chateau was delightful; but the philanthropy which, flowing from the heart of the pastor, was diffused though the whole village, and united the inhabitants in the sweet and firm bonds of social compact, was divine. The beauty of its situation conspired with these circumstances to make Leloncourt seem almost a Paradise. M. Verneuil sighed that he must so soon quit it. 'I ought to seek no farther,' said he, 'for here wisdom and happiness dwell together.'

The admiration was reciprocal; La Luc and his family found themselves much interested in M. Verneuil, and looked forward to the time of his departure with regret. So warmly they pressed him to prolong his visit, and so powerfully his own inclinations seconded theirs, that he accepted the invitation. La Luc omitted no circumstance which might contribute to the amusement of his guest, who having in a few days recovered the use of his arm, they made several excursions among the mountains. Adeline and Clara, whom the care of Madame had restored to her usual health, were generally of the party.

After spending a week at the chateau, M. Verneuil bade adieu to La Luc and his family; they parted with mutual regret, and the former promised that when he returned to Geneva, he would take Leloncourt in his way. As he said this, Adeline, who had for some time observed, with much alarm, La Luc's declining health, looked mournfully on his languid countenance, and uttered a secret prayer that he might live to receive the visit of M. Verneuil.

Madame was the only person who did not lament his departure, she saw that the efforts of her brother to entertain his guest were more than his present state of health would admit of, and she rejoiced in the quiet that would now return to him.

But this quiet brought La Luc no respite from illness; the fatigue he had suffered in his late excursions seemed to have encreased his disorder, which in a short time assumed the aspect of a consumption. Yielding to the solicitations of his family, he went to Geneva for advice, and was there recommended to try the air of Nice.*

The journey thither, however, was of considerable length, and believing his life to be very precarious, he hesitated whether to go. He was also unwilling to leave the duty of his parish unperformed for so long a period as his health might require; but this was an objection which would not have withheld him from Nice, had his faith in the climate been equal to that of his physicians.

His parishioners felt the life of their pastor to be of the utmost consequence to them. It was a general cause, and they testified at once his worth, and their sense of it, by going in a body to solicit him to leave them. He was much affected by this instance of their attachment. Such a proof of regard, joined with the entreaties of his own family, and a consideration that for their sakes it was a duty to endeavour to prolong his life, was too powerful to be withstood, and he determined to set out for Italy.

It was settled that Clara and Adeline, whose health La Luc thought required change of air and scene, should accompany him, attended by the faithful Peter.

On the morning of his departure, a large body of his parishioners assembled round the door to bid him farewell. It was an affecting scene; they might meet no more. At length, wiping the tears from his eyes, La Luc said, 'Let us trust in God, my friends; he has power to heal all disorders both of body and mind. We shall meet again, if not in this world, I hope in a better. Let our conduct be such as to ensure that better.'

The sobs of his people prevented any reply. There was scarcely a dry eye in the village;* for there was scarcely an inhabitant of it that was not now assembled in the presence of La Luc. He shook hands with them all, 'Farewell, my friends,' said he, 'we shall meet again.' 'God grant we may,' said they, with one voice of fervent petition.

Having mounted his horse, and Clara and Adeline being ready, they took a last leave of Madame La Luc, and quitted the chateau. The people, unwilling to leave La Luc, the greater part of them accompanied him to some distance from the village. As he moved slowly on he cast a last lingering look at his little home, where he had spent so many peaceful years, and which he now gazed on, perhaps for the last time, and tears rose to his eyes; but he checked them. Every scene of the adjacent country called up, as he passed, some tender remembrance. He looked towards the spot consecrated to the memory of his deceased wife; the dewy vapours of the morning veiled it. La Luc felt the disappointment more deeply, perhaps, than reason could justify; but those who know from experience how much the imagination loves to dwell on any object, however remotely connected with that of our tenderness, will feel with him. This was an object round which the affections of La Luc had settled themselves; it was a memorial to the eye, and the view of it awakened more forcibly in the memory every tender idea that could associate with the primary subject of his regard. In such cases fancy gives to the illusions of strong affection, the stamp of reality, and they are cherished by the heart with romantic fondness.*

His people accompanied him for near a mile from the village, and could scarcely then be prevailed on to leave him; at length he once more bade them farewell, and went on his way, followed by their prayers and blessings.

La Luc and his little party travelled slowly on, sunk in pensive silence—a silence too pleasingly sad to be soon relinquished, and which they indulged without fear of interruption. The solitary grandeur of the scenes through which they passed, and the soothing murmur of the pines that waved above, aided this soft luxury of meditation.

They proceeded by easy stages; and after travelling for some days among the romantic mountains and green vallies of Piedmont,* they entered the rich country of Nice. The gay and luxuriant views which now opened upon the travellers as they wound among the hills, appeared like scenes of fairy enchantment, or those produced by the lonely visions of the Poets. While the spiral summits of the mountains exhibited the snowy severity of winter, the pine, the cypress, the olive, and the myrtle shaded their sides with the green tints of spring, and groves of orange, lemon, and citron, spread over their feet the full glow of autumn.* As they advanced, the scenery became still more diversified;* and at length, between the receding heights, Adeline caught a glimpse of the distant waters of the Mediterranean, fading into the blue and cloudless horizon. She had never till now seen the ocean;* and this transient view of it roused her imagination, and made her watch impatiently for a nearer prospect.

It was towards the close of day when the travellers, winding round an abrupt projection of that range of Alps which crowns the amphitheatre that environs Nice, looked down upon the green hills that stretch to the shores, on the city, and its antient castle, and on the wide waters of the Mediterranean; with the mountains of Corsica in the farthest distance.* Such a sweep of sea and land, so varied with the gay, the magnificient, and the awful, would have fixed any eye in admiration:—for Adeline and Clara novelty and enthusiasm added their charms to the prospect.* The soft and salubrious air seemed to welcome La Luc to this smiling region, and the serene atmosphere to promise invariable summer.* They at length descended upon the little plain where stands the city of Nice, and which was the most extensive piece of level ground they had passed since they entered the county. Here, in the bosom of the mountains, sheltered from the north and the east, where the western gales alone seemed to breathe, all the blooms of spring and the riches of autumn were united. Trees of myrtle bordered the road, which wound among groves of orange, lemon, and bergamot, whose delicious fragrance came to the sense mingled with the breath of roses and carnations that blossomed in their shade.* The gently swelling hills that rose from the plain were covered with vines, and crowned with cypresses, olives and date trees; beyond, there appeared the sweep of lofty mountains whence the travellers had descended,* and whence rose the little river Paglion, swoln by the snows that melt on their summits, and which, after meandering through the plain, washes the walls of Nice, where it falls into the Mediterranean.* In this blooming region Adeline observed that the countenances of the peasants, meagre and discontented, formed a melancholy contrast to the face of the country, and she lamented again the effects of an arbitrary government, where the bounties of nature, which were designed for all, are monopolized by a few, and the many are suffered to starve tantalized by surrounding plenty.*

The city lost much of its enchantment on a nearer approach: its narrow streets and shabby houses* but ill answered the expectation which a distant view of its ramparts and its harbour, gay with vessels, seemed to authorise. The appearance of the inn at which La Luc now alighted did not contribute to soften his disappointment; but if he was surprised to find such indifferent accommodation at the inn of a town celebrated as the resort of valetudinarians, he was still more so when he learned the difficulty of procuring furnished lodgings.*

After much search he procured apartments in a small but pleasant house, situated a little way out of the town: it had a garden, and a terrace which overlooked the sea, and was distinguished by an air of neatness very unusual in the houses of Nice. He agreed to board with the family, whose table likewise accommodated a gentleman and lady, their lodgers, and thus he became a temporary inhabitant of this charming climate.

On the following morning Adeline rose at an early hour, eager to indulge the new and sublime emotion with which a view of the ocean inspired her, and walked with Clara toward the hills that afforded a more extensive prospect. They pursued their way for some time between high embowering banks, till they arrived at an eminence, whence

'Heaven, earth, ocean, smil'd!'*

They sat down on a point of rock, overshadowed by lofty palm-trees, to contemplate at leisure the magnificent scene. The sun was just emerged from the sea, over which his rays shed a flood of light, and darted a thousand brilliant tints on the vapours that ascended the horizon, and floated there in light clouds, leaving the bosom of the waters below clear as chrystal, except where the white surges were seen to beat upon the rocks; and discovering the distant sails of the fishing boats, and the far distant highlands of Corsica, tinted with ætherial blue. Clara, after some time, drew forth her pencil, but threw it aside in despair. Adeline, as they returned home through a romantic glen, when her senses were no longer absorbed in the contemplation of this grand scenery, and when its images floated on her memory, only, in softened colours, repeated the following lines:

SUNRISE: A SONNET*

Oft let me wander, at the break of day,
  Thro' the cool vale o'erhung with waving woods,
Drink the rich fragrance of the budding May,
  And catch the murmur of the distant floods;
Or rest on the fresh bank of limpid rill,
  Where sleeps the vi'let in the dewy shade,
Where op'ning lilies balmy sweets distill,
  And the wild musk-rose weeps along the glade:
Or climb the eastern cliff, whose airy head
  Hangs rudely o'er the blue and misty main;
Watch the fine hues of morn through æther spread,
  And paint with roseate glow the chrystal plain.
Oh! who can speak the rapture of the soul
  When o'er the waves the sun first steals to sight,
And all the world of waters, as they roll,
  And Heaven's vast vault unveils in living light!
So life's young hour to man enchanting smiles,
  With sparkling health, and joy, and fancy's fairy wiles!

La Luc in his walks met with some sensible and agreeable companions, who like himself came to Nice in search of health.* Of these he soon formed a small but pleasant society, among whom was a Frenchman, whose mild manners, marked with a deep and interesting melancholy, had particularly attracted La Luc. He very seldom mentioned himself, or any circumstance that might lead to a knowledge of his family, but on other subjects conversed with frankness and much intelligence. La Luc had frequently invited him to his lodgings, but he had always declined the invitation, and this in a manner so gentle as to disarm displeasure, and convince La Luc that his refusal was the consequence of a certain dejection of mind which made him reluctant to meet other strangers.

The description which La Luc had given of this foreigner had excited the curiosity of Clara; and the sympathy which the unfortunate feel for each other called forth the commiseration of Adeline; for that he was unfortunate she could not doubt. On their return from an evening walk La Luc pointed out the chevalier, and quickened his pace to overtake him. Adeline was for a moment impelled to follow, but delicacy checked her steps, she knew how painful the presence of a stranger often is to a wounded mind, and forbore to intrude herself on his notice for the sake of only satisfying an idle curiosity. She turned therefore, into another path; but the delicacy which now prevented the meeting, accident in a few days defeated, and La Luc introduced the stranger. Adeline received him with a soft smile, but endeavoured to restrain the expression of pity which her features had involuntarily assumed; she wished him not to know that she observed he was unhappy.

After this interview he no longer rejected the invitations of La Luc, but made him frequent visits, and often accompanied Adeline and Clara in their rambles. The mild and sensible conversation of the former seemed to sooth his mind, and in her presence he frequently conversed with a degree of animation which La Luc till then had not observed in him. Adeline too derived from the similarity of their taste, and his intelligent conversation, a degree of satisfaction which contributed, with the compassion his dejection inspired, to win her confidence, and she conversed with an easy frankness rather unusual to her.

His visits soon became more frequent. He walked with La Luc and his family; he attended them on their little excursions to view those magnificent remains of Roman antiquity which enrich the neighbourhood of Nice.* When the ladies sat at home and worked, he enlivened the hours by reading to them, and they had the pleasure to observe his spirits somewhat relieved from the heavy melancholy that had oppressed him.

M. Amand was passionately fond of music. Clara had not forgot to bring her beloved lute: he would sometimes strike the chords in the most sweet and mournful symphonies, but never could be prevailed on to play. When Adeline or Clara played, he would sit in deep reverie, and lost to every object around him, except when he fixed his eyes in mournful gaze on Adeline, and a sigh would sometimes escape him.

One evening Adeline having excused herself from accompanying La Luc and Clara in a visit to a neighbouring family, she retired to the terrace of the garden, which overlooked the sea, and as she viewed the tranquil splendour of the setting sun, and his glories reflected on the polished surface of the waves, she touched the strings of the lute in softest harmony, her voice accompanying it with words which she had one day written after having read that rich effusion of Shakespeare's genius, 'A Midsummer Night's Dream.'

TITANIA TO HER LOVE

O! fly with me through distant air
　　To isles that gem the western deep!
For laughing Summer revels there,
　　And hangs her wreath on ev'ry steep.

As through the green transparent sea
　　Light floating on its waves we go,
The nymphs shall gaily welcome me
　　Far in their coral caves below.

For oft upon their margin sands,
　　When Twilight leads the fresh'ning Hours,
I come with all my jocund bands
　　To charm them from their sea-green bow'rs.

And well they love our sports to view,
　　And on the Ocean's breast to lave;
And oft, as we the dance renew,
　　They call up music from the wave.

Swift hie we to that splendid clime,
　　Where gay Jamaica spreads her scene,
Lifts the blue mountain—wild—sublime!
　　And smooths her vales of vivid green.

Where throned high, in pomp of shade,
    The *Power of Vegetation* reigns,
Expanding wide, o'er hill and glade,
    Shrubs of all growth—fruit of all stains:

She steals the sun-beams' fervid glow
    To paint her flow'rs of mingling hue;
And o'er the grape the purple throw,
    Breaking from verdant leaves to view.

There, myrtle bow'rs, and citron grove,
    O'ercanopy our airy dance;
And there the sea-breeze loves to rove
    When trembles Day's departing glance.

And when the false moon steals away,
    Or e'er the chacing morn doth rise,
Oft, fearless, we our gambols play
    By the fire-worm's radiant eyes.

And suck the honey'd reeds that swell
    In tufted plumes of silver white;
Or pierce the cocoa's milky cell,
    To sip the nectar of delight!

And when the shaking thunders roll,
    And lightnings strike athwart the gloom,
We shelter in the cedar's bole,
    And revel 'mid the rich perfume!

But chief we love beneath the palm,
    Or verdant plantain's spreading leaf,
To hear, upon the midnight calm,
    Sweet Philomela pour her grief.

To mortal sprite such dulcet sound,
    Such blissful hours, were never known!
O! fly with me my airy round,
    And I will make them all thine own!

Adeline ceased to sing—when she immediately heard
repeated in a low voice,

> 'To mortal sprite such dulcet sound,
>   Such blissful hours, were never known!'

and turning her eyes whence it came, she saw M. Amand. She

blushed and laid down the lute, which he instantly took up, and with a tremulous hand drew forth tones

'That might create a soul under the ribs of Death.'*

In a melodious voice, that trembled with sensibility, he sang the following

SONNET*

How sweet is Love's first gentle sway,
   When crown'd with flow'rs he softly smiles!
   His blue eyes fraught with tearful wiles,
Where beams of tender transport play:
Hope leads him on his airy way,
   And Faith and Fancy still beguiles—
   Faith quickly tangled in her toils—
Fancy, whose magic forms so gay
   The fair Deceiver's self deceive—
'How sweet is Love's first gentle sway!'
   Ne'er would that heart he bids to grieve
From Sorrow's soft enchantments stray—
   Ne'er—till the God, exulting in his art,
   Relentless frowns, and wings th' envenom'd dart!

Monsieur Amand paused: he seemed much oppressed, and at length, bursting into tears, laid down the instrument and walked abruptly away to the farther end of the terrace. Adeline, without seeming to observe his agitation, rose and leaned upon the wall, below which a group of fishermen were busily employed in drawing a net. In a few moments he returned, with a composed and softened countenance. 'Forgive this abrupt conduct,' said he; 'I know not how to apologize for it but by owning its cause. When I tell you, Madam, that my tears flow to the memory of a lady who strongly resembled you, and who is lost to me for ever, you will know how to pity me.'—His voice faultered, and he paused. Adeline was silent. 'The lute,' he resumed, 'was her favourite instrument, and when you touched it with such melancholy expression, I saw her very image before me. But alas! why do I distress you with a knowledge of my sorrows! she is gone, and never to return! And you, Adeline—you'——He checked his speech; and Adeline, turning on him a look of mournful regard, observed a wildness in his eyes which alarmed her. 'These recollections are too painful,' said she, in a gentle voice; 'let us return to the house; M. La Luc is probably come home.'—'O no!' replied M. Amand; 'No—this breeze refreshes me. How often at this hour have I talked with *her*, as I now talk with you!—Such were the soft tones of her voice—such the ineffable expression of her countenance.'—Adeline interrupted him. 'Let me beg of you to consider your health—this dewy air cannot be good for invalids.' He stood with his hands clasped, and seemed not to hear her. She took up the lute to go, and passed her fingers lightly over the chords. The sounds recalled his scattered senses: he raised his eyes, and fixed them in long unsettled gaze upon hers. 'Must I leave you here?' said she, smiling, and standing in an attitude to depart—'I entreat you to play again the air I heard just now,' said M. Amand, in a hurried voice.—'Certainly;' and she immediately began to play. He leaned against a palm tree in an attitude of deep attention, and as the sounds languished on the air, his features gradually lost their wild expression, and he melted into tears. He continued to weep silently till the song concluded, and it was some time before he recovered voice enough to say, 'Adeline, I cannot thank you for this goodness. My mind has recovered its bias, you have soothed a broken heart. Increase the kindness you have shewn me by promising never to mention what you have witnessed this evening, and I will endeavour never again to wound your sensibility by a similiar offence.'—Adeline gave the required promise; and M. Amand, pressing her hand, with a melancholy smile, hurried from the garden, and she saw him no more that night.

La Luc had been near a fortnight at Nice, and his health, instead of amending, seemed rather to decline, yet he wished to make a longer experiment of the climate. The air, which failed to restore her venerable friend, revived Adeline, and the variety and novelty of the surrounding scenes amused her mind,* though, since they could not obliterate the memory of past, or suppress the pang of present affection, they were ineffectual to dissipate the sick languor of melancholy.

Company, by compelling her to withdraw her attention from the subject of her sorrow, afforded her a transient relief, but the violence of the exertion generally left her more depressed. It was in the stillness of solitude, in the tranquil observance of beautiful nature, that her mind recovered its tone, and indulging the pensive inclination now became habitual to it, was soothed and fortified. Of all the grand objects which nature had exhibited, the ocean inspired her with the most sublime admiration.* She loved to wander alone on its shores, and, when she could escape so long from the duties or the forms of society, she would sit for hours on the beach watching the rolling waves, and listening to their dying murmur, till her softened fancy recalled long lost scenes, and restored the image of Theodore, when tears of despondency too often followed those of pity and regret. But these visions of memory, painful as they were, no longer excited that phrenzy of grief they formerly awakened in Savoy; the sharpness of misery was passed, though its heavy influence was not perhaps less powerful. To these solitary indulgences generally succeeded calmness, and what Adeline endeavoured to believe was resignation.

She usually rose early, and walked down to the shore to enjoy, in the cool and silent hours of the morning, the cheering beauty of nature, and inhale the pure sea-breeze. Every object then smiled in fresh and lively colours. The blue sea, the brilliant sky, the distant fishing boats, with their white sails, and the voices of the fishermen borne at intervals on the air, were circumstances which re-animated her spirits, and in one of her rambles, yielding to that taste for poetry which had seldom forsaken her, she repeated the following lines:

MORNING, ON THE SEA SHORE

What print of fairy feet is here
On Neptune's smooth and yellow sands?
What midnight revel's airy dance,
Beneath the moon-beams' trembling glance,
Has blest these shores?—What sprightly bands
Have chac'd the waves uncheck'd by fear?
Whoe'er they were they fled from morn,

For now all silent and forlorn
These tide-forsaken sands appear—
  Return, sweet sprites! the scene to cheer!

In vain the call!—Till moonlight's hour
Again diffuse its softer pow'r,
Titania, nor her fairy loves,
Emerge from India's spicy groves.
  Then, when the shad'wy hour returns,
When silence reigns o'er air and earth,
  And ev'ry star in æther burns,
They come to celebrate their mirth;
  In frolic ringlet trip the ground,
Bid Music's voice on Silence win,
  Till magic echoes answer round—
Thus do their festive rites begin.

O fairy forms! so coy to mortal ken,
  Your mystic steps to poets only shewn,
O! lead me to the brook, or hallow'd glen,
  Retiring far, with winding woods o'ergrown!
    Where'er ye best delight to rule;
  If in some forest's lone retreat,
  Thither conduct my willing feet
    To the light brink of fountain cool,
  Where, sleeping in the midnight dew,
  Lie Spring's young buds of ev'ry hue,
    Yielding their sweet breath to the air;
  To fold their silken leaves from harm,
  And their chill heads in moonshine warm,
    To bright Titania's tender care.

There, to the night-bird's plaintive chaunt
  Your carols sweet ye love to raise,
  With oaten reed and past'ral lays;
And guard with forceful spell her haunt,
  Who, when your antic sports are done,
Oft lulls ye in the lily's cell,
Sweet flow'r! that suits your slumbers well,
  And shields ye from the rising sun.
When not to India's steeps ye fly
  After twilight and the moon,
In honey'd buds ye love to lie,
  While reigns supreme Light's fervid noon;

Nor quit the cell where peace pervades
Till night leads on the dews and shades.

E'en now your scenes enchanted meet my sight!
   I see the earth unclose, the palace rise,
The high dome swell, and long arcades of light
   Glitter among the deep embow'ring woods,
     And glance reflected from the trembling floods!
While to soft lutes the portals wide unfold,
     And fairy forms, of fine aetherial dyes,
     Advance with frolic step and laughing eyes,
Their hair with pearl, their garments deck'd with gold;
Pearls that in Neptune's briny waves they sought,
And gold from India's deepest caverns brought.
Thus your light visions to my eyes unveil,
Ye sportive pleasures, sweet illusions, hail!
   But ah! at morn's first blush again ye fade!
So from youth's ardent gaze life's landscape gay,
   And forms in Fancy's summer hues array'd,
Dissolve at once in air at Truth's resplendent day!*

During several days succeeding that on which M. Amand
had disclosed the cause of his melancholy, he did not visit La
Luc. At length Adeline met him in one of her solitary rambles
on the shore. He was pale and dejected, and seemed much
agitated when he observed her; she therefore endeavoured to
avoid him, but he advanced with quickened steps and accosted
her. He said it was his intention to leave Nice in a few days.
'I have found no benefit from the climate,' added M. Amand;
'Alas! what climate can relieve the sickness of the heart! I go
to lose in the varieties of new scenes the remembrance of past
happiness; yet the effort is vain; I am every where equally
restless and unhappy.' Adeline tried to encourage him to hope
much from time and change of place. 'Time *will* blunt the
sharpest edge of sorrow,' said she; 'I know it from experience.'
Yet while she spoke, the tears in her eyes contradicted the
assertion of her lips. 'You have been unhappy, Adeline!—
Yes—I knew it from the first. The smile of pity which you
gave me, assured me that you knew what it was to suffer.'
The desponding air with which he spoke renewed her
apprehension of a scene similar to the one she had lately
witnessed, and she changed the subject, but he soon returned

to it. 'You bid me hope much from time!—My dear wife!'——
his tongue faultered—'It is now many months since I lost
her—yet the moment of her death seems but as yesterday.'
Adeline faintly smiled. 'You can scarcely judge of the effect
of time yet, you have much to hope for.' He shook his head.
'But I am again intruding my misfortunes on your notice;
forgive this perpetual egotism. There is a comfort in the pity
of the good such as nothing else can impart; this must plead
my excuse; may you, Adeline, never want it. Ah! those
tears——' Adeline hastily dried them. M. Amand forbore to
press the subject, and immediately began to converse on
indifferent topics. They returned towards the chateau, but La
Luc being from home, M. Amand took leave at the door.
Adeline retired to her chamber, oppressed by her own sorrows
and those of her amiable friend.

Near three weeks had now elapsed at Nice, during which
the disorder of La Luc seemed rather to encrease than to
abate, when his physician very honestly confessed the little
hope he entertained from the climate, and advised him to try
the effect of a sea voyage, adding, that if the experiment
failed, even the air of Montpellier appeared to him more likely
to afford relief than that of Nice.* La Luc received this
disinterested advice with a mixture of gratitude and disappointment. The circumstances which had made him reluctant
to quit Savoy, rendered him yet more so to protract his
absence, and encrease his expences; but the ties of affection
that bound him to his family, and the love of life, which so
seldom leaves us, again prevailed over inferior considerations,
and he determined to coast the Mediterranean as far as
Languedoc, where, if the voyage did not answer his
expectations, he would land and proceed to Montpellier.

When M. Amand learned that La Luc designed to quit Nice
in a few days, he determined not to leave it before him.
During this interval he had not sufficient resolution to deny
himself the frequent conversation of Adeline, though her
presence, by reminding him of his lost wife, gave him more
pain than comfort. He was the second son of a French
gentleman of family, and had been married about a year to a
lady to whom he had long been attached when she died in her

lying-in. The infant soon followed its mother, and left the disconsolate father abandoned to grief, which had preyed so heavily on his health, that his physician thought it necessary to send him to Nice. From the air of Nice, however, he had derived no benefit, and he now determined to travel farther into Italy,* though he no longer felt any interest in those charming scenes which in happier days, and with her whom he never ceased to lament, would have afforded him the highest degree of mental luxury—now he sought only to escape from himself, or rather from the image of her who had once constituted his truest happiness.

La Luc having laid his plan, hired a small vessel, and in a few days embarked, with a sick hope bidding adieu to the shores of Italy* and the towering alps, and seeking on a new element the health which hitherto mocked his pursuit.

M. Amand took a melancholy leave of his new friends, whom he attended to the sea side. When he assisted Adeline on board, his heart was too full to suffer him to say farewell; but he stood long on the beach pursuing with his eyes her course over the waters, and waving his hand, till tears dimmed his sight. The breeze wafted the vessel gently from the coast, and Adeline saw herself surrounded by the undulating waves of the ocean. The shore appeared to recede, its mountains to lessen, the gay colours of its landscape to melt into each other, and in a short time the figure of M. Amand was seen no more: the town of Nice, with its castle and harbour, next faded away in distance, and the purple tint of the mountains was at length all that remained on the verge of the horizon. She sighed as she gazed, and her eyes filled with tears. 'So vanished my prospect of happiness,' said she; 'and my future view is like the waste of waters that surround me.' Her heart was full, and she retired from observation to a remote part of the deck, where she indulged her tears as she watched the vessel cut its way through the liquid glass. The water was so transparent that she saw the sun-beams playing at a considerable depth, and fish of various colours glance athwart the current. Innumerable marine plants spread their vigorous leaves on the rocks below, and the richness of their verdure formed a beautiful contrast to the glowing scarlet of the coral that branched beside them.

The distant coast, at length, entirely disappeared. Adeline gazed with an emotion the most sublime, on the boundless expanse of waters that spread on all sides: she seemed as if launched into a new world; the grandeur and immensity of the view astonished and overpowered her: for a moment she doubted the truth of the compass, and believed it to be almost impossible for the vessel to find its way over the pathless waters to any shore. And when she considered that a plank alone separated her from death, a sensation of unmixed terror superceded that of sublimity, and she hastily turned her eyes from the prospect, and her thoughts from the subject.*

CHAPTER XIX

'Is there a heart that music cannot melt?
  Alas! how is that rugged heart forlorn!
Is there who ne'er the mystic transports felt
  Of solitude and melancholy born?
He need not woo the Muse—he is her scorn.'
                                    BEATTIE*

TOWARDS evening the captain, to avoid the danger of encountering a Barbary corsair, steered for the French coast, and Adeline distinguished in the gleam of the setting sun the shores of Provence, feathered with wood and green with pasturage. La Luc, languid and ill, had retired to the cabin, whither Clara attended him. The pilot at the helm, guiding the tall vessel through the sounding waters, and one solitary sailor, leaning with crossed arms against the mast, and now and then singing parts of a mournful ditty, were all of the crew, except Adeline, that remained upon deck—and Adeline silently watched the declining sun, which threw a saffron glow upon the waves, and on the sails, gently swelling in the breeze that was now dying away. The sun, at length, sunk below the ocean, and twilight stole over the scene, leaving the shadowy shores yet visible, and touching with a solemn tint the waters that stretched wide around. She sketched the picture, but it was with a faint pencil.

NIGHT

O'er the dim breast of Ocean's wave
   Night spreads afar her gloomy wings,
   And pensive thought, and silence brings,
Save when the distant waters lave;
   Or when the mariner's lone voice
Swells faintly in the passing gale,
   Or when the screaming sea-gulls poise
O'er the tall mast and swelling sail,
      Bounding the gray gleam of the deep,
   Where fancy'd forms arouse the mind,
      Dark sweep the shores, on whose rude steep
   Sighs the sad spirit of the wind.
Sweet is its voice upon the air
   At Ev'ning's melancholy close,
   When the smooth wave in silence flows!
Sweet, sweet the peace its stealing accents bear!
Blest be thy shades, O Night! and blest the song
Thy low winds breathe the distant shores along!

As the shadows thickened the scene sunk into deeper repose.
Even the sailor's song had ceased; no sound was heard but that
of the waters dashing beneath the vessel, and their fainter
murmur on the pebbly coast. Adeline's mind was in unison
with the tranquillity of the hour: lulled by the waves, she
resigned herself to a still melancholy, and sat lost in reverie.
The present moment brought to her recollection her voyage
up the Rhone, when seeking refuge from the terrors of the
Marquis de Montalt, she so anxiously endeavoured to
anticipate her future destiny. She then, as now, had watched
the fall of evening and the fading prospect, and she
remembered what a desolate feeling had accompanied the
impression which those objects made. She had then no
friends—no asylum—no certainty of escaping the pursuit of
her enemy. Now she had found affectionate friends—a secure
retreat—and was delivered from the terrors she then
suffered—but still she was unhappy. The remembrance of
Theodore—of Theodore who had loved her so truly, who had
encountered and suffered so much for her sake, and of whose
fate she was now as ignorant as when she traversed the Rhone,
was an incessant pang to her heart. She seemed to be more

remote than ever from the possibility of hearing of him. Sometimes a faint hope crossed her that he had escaped the malice of his persecutor; but when she considered the inveteracy and power of the latter, and the heinous light in which the law regards an assault upon a superior officer, even this poor hope vanished, and left her to tears and anguish, such as this reverie, which began with a sensation of only gentle melancholy, now led to. She continued to muse till the moon arose from the bosom of the ocean, and shed her trembling lustre upon the waves, diffusing peace, and making silence more solemn; beaming a soft light on the white sails, and throwing upon the waters the tall shadow of the vessel, which now seemed to glide along unopposed by any current. Her tears had somewhat relieved the anguish of her mind, and she again reposed in placid melancholy, when a strain of such tender and entrancing sweetness stole on the silence of the hour, that it seemed more like celestial than mortal music—so soft, so soothing, it sunk upon her ear, that it recalled her from misery to hope and love. She wept again—but these were tears which she would not have exchanged for mirth and joy. She looked round, but perceived neither ship or boat; and as the undulating sounds swelled on the distant air, she thought they came from the shore. Sometimes the breeze wafted them away, and again returned them in tones of the most languishing softness. The links of the air thus broken, it was music rather than melody that she caught, till, the pilot gradually steering nearer the coast, she distinguished the notes of a song familiar to her ear. She endeavoured to recollect where she had heard it, but in vain; yet her heart beat almost unconsciously with a something resembling hope. Still she listened, till the breeze again stole the sounds. With regret she now perceived that the vessel was moving from them, and at length they trembled faintly on the waves, sunk away at distance, and were heard no more. She remained upon the deck a considerable time, unwilling to relinquish the expectation of hearing them again, and their sweetness still vibrating on her fancy, and at length retired to the cabin oppressed by a degree of disappointment which the occasion did not appear to justify.

La Luc grew better during the voyage, his spirits revived, and when the vessel entered that part of the Mediterranean called the Gulf of Lyons, he was sufficiently animated to enjoy from the deck the noble prospect which the sweeping shores of Provence, terminating in the far distant ones of Languedoc, exhibited. Adeline and Clara, who anxiously watched his looks, rejoiced in their amendment; and the fond wishes of the latter already anticipated his perfect recovery. The expectations of Adeline had been too often checked by disappointment to permit her now to indulge an equal degree of hope with that of her friend, yet she confided much in the effect of this voyage.

La Luc amused himself at intervals with discoursing, and pointing out the situations of considerable ports on the çoast, and the mouths of the rivers that, after wandering through Provence, disembogue themselves* into the Mediterranean. The Rhone, however, was the only one of much consequence which he passed. On this object, though it was so distant that fancy, perhaps, rather than the sense, beheld it, Clara gazed with peculiar pleasure, for it came from the banks of Savoy; and the wave which she thought she perceived, had washed the feet of her dear native mountains. The time passed with mingled pleasure and improvement as La Luc described to his attentive pupils the manners and commerce of the different inhabitants of the coast, and the natural history of the country; or as he traced in imagination the remote wanderings of rivers to their source, and delineated the characteristic beauties of their scenery.

After a pleasant voyage of a few days, the shores of Provence receded, and that of Languedoc, which had long bounded the distance, became the grand object of the scene, and the sailors drew near their port. They landed in the afternoon at a small town situated at the foot of a woody eminence, on the right overlooking the sea, and on the left the rich plains of Languedoc, gay with the purple vine. La Luc determined to defer his journey till the following day, and was directed to a small inn at the extremity of the town, where the accommodation, such as it was, he endeavoured to be contented with.

In the evening the beauty of the hour, and the desire of exploring new scenes, invited Adeline to walk. La Luc was fatigued, and did not go out, and Clara remained with him. Adeline took her way to the woods that rose from the margin of the sea, and climbed the wild eminence on which they hung. Often as she went she turned her eyes to catch between the dark foliage the blue waters of the bay, the white sail that flitted by, and the trembling gleam of the setting sun. When she reached the summit, and looked down over the dark tops of the woods on the wide and various prospect, she was seized with a kind of still rapture impossible to be expressed, and stood unconscious of the flight of time, till the sun had left the scene, and twilight threw its solemn shade upon the mountains. The sea alone reflected the fading splendor of the West; its tranquil surface was partially disturbed by the low wind that crept in tremulous lines along the waters, whence rising to the woods, it shivered their light leaves, and died away. Adeline, resigning herself to the luxury of sweet and tender emotions, repeated the following lines:

SUNSET

Soft o'er the mountain's purple brow
　　Meek Twilight draws her shadows gray;
From tufted woods, and vallies low,
　　Light's magic colours steal away.
Yet still, amid the spreading gloom,
　　Resplendent glow the western waves
　　That roll o'er Neptune's coral caves,
A zone of light on Ev'ning's dome.
　　On this lone summit let me rest,
And view the forms to Fancy dear,
　　Till on the Ocean's darken'd breast
The stars of Ev'ning tremble clear;
Or the moon's pale orb appear,
　　Throwing her line of radiance wide, ⎫
　　Far o'er the lightly-curling tide, ⎬
　　That seems the yellow sands to chide. ⎭
No sounds o'er silence now prevail,
　　Save of the dying wave below,
Or sailor's song borne on the gale,

> Or oar at distance striking slow.
> So sweet! so tranquil! may my ev'ning ray
> Set to this world—and rise in future day!

Adeline quitted the heights, and followed a narrow path that wound to the beach below: her mind was now particularly sensible to fine impressions, and the sweet notes of the nightingale amid the stillness of the woods again awakened her enthusiasm.

TO THE NIGHTINGALE

> Child of the melancholy song!
> O yet that tender strain prolong!
>
> Her lengthen'd shade, when Ev'ning flings,
>   From mountain-cliffs and forest's green,
> And sailing slow on silent wings
>   Along the glimm'ring West is seen;
> I love o'er pathless hills to stray,
>   Or trace the winding vale remote,
> And pause, sweet Bird! to hear thy lay
>   While moon-beams on the thin clouds float,
> Till o'er the mountain's dewy head
> Pale Midnight steals to wake the dead.
>
> Far through the Heav'ns' ætherial blue,
>   Wafted on Spring's light airs you come,
> With blooms, and flow'rs, and genial dew,
>   From climes where Summer joys to roam,
>   O! welcome to your long-lost home!
> 'Child of the melancholy song!'
> Who lov'st the lonely woodland-glade
> To mourn, unseen, the boughs among,
>   When Twilight spreads her pensive shade,
> Again thy dulcet voice I hail!
>   O! pour again the liquid note
> That dies upon the ev'ning gale!
>   For Fancy loves the kindred tone;
>   Her griefs the plaintive accents own.
>   She loves to hear thy music float
> At solemn Midnight's stillest hour,
>   And think on friends for ever lost,

On joys by disappointment crost,
And weep anew Love's charmful pow'r!

Then Memory wakes the magic smile,
   Th' impassion'd voice, the melting eye,
That won't the trusting heart beguile,
   And *wakes again* the hopeless sigh!
Her skill the glowing tints revive
   Of scenes that Time had bade decay;
She bids the soften'd Passions live—
   The Passions urge again their sway.
Yet o'er the long-regretted scene
   Thy song the grace of sorrow throws;
A melancholy charm serene,
   More rare than all that mirth bestows.
Then hail, sweet Bird! and hail thy pensive tear!
To Taste, to Fancy, and to Virtue, dear!

The spreading dusk at length reminded Adeline of her
distance from the inn, and that she had her way to find
through a wild and lonely wood: she bade adieu to the syren
that had so long detained her, and pursued the path with
quick steps. Having followed it for some time, she became
bewildered among the thickets, and the increasing darkness
did not allow her to judge of the direction she was in. Her
apprehensions heightened her difficulties: she thought she
distinguished the voices of men at some little distance, and she
increased her speed till she found herself on the sea sands over
which the woods impended. Her breath was now exhausted—
she paused a moment to recover herself, and fearfully listened;
but, instead of the voices of men, she heard faintly swelling
in the breeze the notes of mournful music.—Her heart, ever
sensible to the impression of melody, melted with the tones,
and her fears were for a moment lulled in sweet enchantment.
Surprise was soon mingled with delight when, as the sounds
advanced, she distinguished the tone of that instrument, and
the melody of that well-known air, she had heard a few
preceding evenings from the shores of Provence. But she had
no time for conjecture—footsteps approached, and she
renewed her speed. She was now emerged from the darkness
of the woods, and the moon, which shone bright, exhibited

along the level sands the town and port in the distance. The steps that had followed now came up with her, and she perceived two men, but they passed in conversation without noticing her, and as they passed she was certain she recollected the voice of him who was then speaking. Its tones were so familiar to her ear, that she was surprised at the imperfect memory which did not suffer her to be assured by whom they were uttered. Another step now followed, and a rude voice called to her to stop. As she hastily turned her eyes she saw imperfectly by the moonlight a man in a sailor's habit pursuing, while he renewed the call. Impelled by terror, she fled along the sands, but her steps were short and trembling— those of her pursuer's strong and quick.

She had just strength sufficient to reach the men who had before passed her, and to implore their protection, when her pursuer came up with them, but suddenly turned into the woods on the left, and disappeared.*

She had no breath to answer the inquiries of the strangers who supported her, till a sudden exclamation, and the sound of her own name, drew her eyes attentively upon the person who uttered them, and in the rays which shone strong upon his features, she distinguished M. Verneuil!—Mutual satisfaction and explanation ensued, and when he learned that La Luc and his daughter were at the inn, he felt an increased pleasure in conducting her thither. He said that he had accidentally met with an old friend in Savoy, whom he now introduced by the name of Mauron, and who had prevailed on him to change his route and accompany him to the shores of the Mediterranean. They had embarked from the coast of Provence only a few preceding days, and had that evening landed in Languedoc on the estate of M. Mauron. Adeline had now no doubt that it was the flute of M. Verneuil, and which had so often delighted her at Leloncourt, that she had heard on the sea.

When they reached the inn they found La Luc under great anxiety for Adeline, in search of whom he had sent several people. Anxiety yielded to surprize and pleasure, when he perceived her with M. Verneuil, whose eyes beamed with unusual animation on seeing Clara. After mutual congratulations, M. Verneuil observed, and lamented, the very indifferent accommodation which the inn afforded his friends, and M. Mauron immediately invited them to his chateau with a warmth of hospitality that overcame every scruple which delicacy or pride could oppose. The woods that Adeline had traversed formed a part of his domain, which extended almost to the inn; but he insisted that his carriage should take his guests to the chateau, and departed to give orders for their reception. The presence of M. Verneuil, and the kindness of his friend, gave to La Luc an unusual flow of spirits; he conversed with a degree of vigour and liveliness to which he had long been unaccustomed, and the smile of satisfaction that Clara gave to Adeline expressed how much she thought he was already benefited by the voyage. Adeline answered her look with a smile of less confidence, for she attributed his present animation to a more temporary cause.

About half an hour after the departure of M. Mauron, a boy who served as waiter brought a message from a chevalier then at the inn, requesting permission to speak with Adeline. The man who had pursued her along the sands instantly occurred to her, and she scarcely doubted that the stranger was some person belonging to the Marquis de Montalt, perhaps the Marquis himself, though that he should have discovered her accidentally, in so obscure a place, and so immediately upon her arrival, seemed very improbable. With trembling lips, and a countenance pale as death, she inquired the name of the chevalier. The boy was not acquainted with it. La Luc asked what sort of a person he was; but the boy, who understood little of the art of describing, gave such a confused account of him, that Adeline could only learn he was not large, but of the middle stature. This circumstance, however, convincing her it was not the Marquis de Montalt who desired to see her, she asked whether it would be agreeable to La Luc to have the stranger admitted. La Luc said, 'By all means;' and the waiter withdrew. Adeline sat in trembling expectation till the door opened, and Louis de la Motte entered the room. He advanced with an embarrassed and melancholy air, though his countenance had been enlightened with a momentary pleasure when he first beheld Adeline—Adeline, who was still the idol of his heart. After the first salutations were over, all apprehensions of the Marquis being now dissipated, she inquired when Louis had seen Monsieur and Madame La Motte.

'I ought rather to ask you that question,' said Louis, in some confusion, 'for I believe you have seen them since I have; and the pleasure of meeting you thus is equalled by my surprise. I have not heard from my father for some time, owing probably to my regiment being removed to new quarters.'

He looked as if he wished to be informed with whom Adeline now was; but as this was a subject upon which it was impossible she could speak in the presence of La Luc, she led the conversation to general topics, after having said that Monsieur and Madame La Motte were well when she left them. Louis spoke little, and often looked anxiously at Adeline, while his mind seemed labouring under strong oppression. She observed this, and recollecting the declaration he had made her on the morning of his departure from the Abbey, she attributed his present embarrassment to the effect of a passion yet unsubdued, and did not appear to notice it. After he had sat near a quarter of an hour, under a struggle of feelings which he could neither conquer or conceal, he rose to leave the room, and as he passed Adeline, said, in a low voice, 'Do permit me to speak with you alone for five minutes.' She hesitated in some confusion, and then saying there were none but friends present, begged he would be seated.—'Excuse me,' said he, in the same low accent; 'What I would say nearly concerns you, and you only. Do favour me with a few moments attention.' He said this with a look that surprized her; and having ordered candles in another room, she went thither.

Louis sat for some moments silent, and seemingly in great perturbation of mind. At length he said, 'I know not whether to rejoice or to lament at this unexpected meeting, though, if you are in safe hands, I ought certainly to rejoice, however hard the task that now falls to my lot. I am not ignorant of the dangers and persecutions you have suffered, and cannot forbear expressing my anxiety to know how you are now circumstanced. Are you indeed with friends?'—'I am,' said

Adeline; 'M. la Motte has informed you'——'No,' replied Louis, with a deep sigh, 'not my father.'—He paused.—'But I do indeed rejoice! that you are in safety. Could you know, lovely Adeline, what I have suffered!'——He checked himself.—'I understood you had something of importance to say, Sir,' said Adeline; 'you must excuse me if I remind you that I have not many moments to spare.'

'It is indeed of importance,' replied Louis; 'yet I know not how to mention it—how to soften——This task is too severe. Alas! my poor friend!'

'Who is it you speak of, Sir!' said Adeline, with quickness. Louis rose from his chair, and walked about the room. 'I would prepare you for what I have to say,' he resumed, 'but upon my soul I am not equal to it.'

'I entreat you to keep me no longer in suspence,' said Adeline, who had a wild idea that it was Theodore he would speak of. Louis still hesitated. 'Is it—O is it?—I conjure you tell me the worst at once,' said she, in a voice of agony. 'I can bear it—indeed I can.'

'My unhappy friend!' exclaimed Louis, 'O Theodore!'—'Theodore!' faintly articulated Adeline, 'he lives then!'——'He does,' said Louis, 'but'—He stopped.—'But what?' cried Adeline, trembling violently; 'If he is living you cannot tell me worse than my fears suggest; I entreat you, therefore, not to hesitate.'—Louis resumed his seat, and, endeavouring to assume a collected air, said, 'He is living, Madam, but he is a prisoner, and—for why should I deceive you? I fear he has little hope in this world.'

'I have long feared so, Sir,' said Adeline, in a voice of forced composure; 'you have something more terrible than this to relate, and I again intreat you will explain yourself.'

'He has every thing to apprehend from the Marquis de Montalt,' said Louis. 'Alas! why do I say to apprehend? His judgment is already fixed—he is condemned to die.'

At this confirmation of her fears a death-like paleness diffused itself over the countenance of Adeline; she sat motionless, and attempted to sigh, but seemed almost suffocated. Terrified at her situation, and expecting to see her faint, Louis would have supported her, but with her hand she waved him from her, and was unable to speak. He now called for assistance, and La Luc and Clara, with M. Verneuil, informed of Adeline's indisposition, were quickly by her side.

At the sound of their voices she looked up, and seemed to recollect herself, when uttering a heavy sigh she burst into tears. La Luc rejoiced to see her weep, encouraged her tears, which, after some time, relieved her, and when she was able to speak, she desired to go back to La Luc's parlour. Louis attended her thither; when she was better he would have withdrawn, but La Luc begged he would stay.

'You are perhaps a relation of this young lady, Sir,' said he, 'and may have brought news of her father.'—'Not so, Sir,' replied Louis, hesitating.—'This gentleman,' said Adeline, who had now recollected her dissipated thoughts, 'is the son of the M. La Motte, whom you may have heard me mention.'—Louis seemed shocked to be declared the son of a man that had once acted so unworthily towards Adeline, who, instantly perceiving the pain her words occasioned, endeavoured to soften their effect by saying that La Motte had saved her from imminent danger, and had afforded her an asylum for many months. Adeline sat in a state of dreadful solicitude to know the particulars of Theodore's situation, yet could not acquire courage to renew the subject in the presence of La Luc; she ventured, however, to ask Louis if his own regiment was quartered in the town.

He replied that his regiment lay at Vaceau, a French town on the frontiers of Spain; that he had just crossed a part of the Gulph of Lyons, and was on his way to Savoy, whither he should set out early in the morning.

'We are lately come from thence,' said Adeline; 'may I ask to what part of Savoy you are going?'—'To Leloncourt,' he replied.—'To Leloncourt!' said Adeline, in some surprize.—'I am a stranger to the country,' resumed Louis; 'but I go to serve my friend. You seem to know Leloncourt.'—'I do indeed,' said Adeline.—'You probably know then that M. La Luc lives there, and will guess the motive of my journey.'

'O heavens! is it possible?' exclaimed Adeline—'is it possible that Theodore Peyrou is a relation of M. La Luc!'

'Theodore! what of my son?' asked La Luc, in surprize and

apprehension.—'Your son!' said Adeline, in a trembling voice, 'your son!'—The astonishment and anguish depictured on her countenance increased the apprehensions of this unfortunate father, and he renewed his question. But Adeline was totally unable to answer him; and the distress of Louis, on thus unexpectedly discovering the father of his unhappy friend, and knowing that it was his task to disclose the fate of his son, deprived him for some time of all power of utterance, and La Luc and Clara, whose fears were every instant heightened by this dreadful silence, continued to repeat their questions.

At length a sense of the approaching sufferings of the good La Luc overcoming every other feeling, Adeline recovered strength of mind sufficient to try to soften the intelligence Louis had to communicate, and to conduct Clara to another room. Here she collected resolution to tell her, and with much tender consideration, the circumstances of her brother's situation, concealing only her knowledge of his sentence being already pronounced. This relation necessarily included the mention of their attachment, and in the friend of her heart Clara discovered the innocent cause of her brother's destruction. Adeline also learned the occasion of that circumstance which had contributed to keep her ignorant of Theodore's relationship to La Luc; she was told the former had taken the name of Peyrou, with an estate which had been left him about a year before by a relation of his mother's upon that condition. Theodore had been designed for the church, but his disposition inclined him to a more active life than the clerical habit would admit of, and on accession to this estate he had entered into the service of the French king.

In the few and interrupted interviews which had been allowed them at Caux, Theodore had mentioned his family to Adeline only in general terms, and thus, when they were so suddenly separated, had, without designing it, left her in ignorance of his father's name and place of residence.

The sacredness and delicacy of Adeline's grief, which had never permitted her to mention the subject of it even to Clara, had since contributed to deceive her.

The distress of Clara, on learning the situation of her brother, could endure no restraint; Adeline, who had commanded her feelings so as to impart this intelligence with tolerable composure, only by a strong effort of mind, was now almost overwhelmed by her own and Clara's accumulated suffering. While they wept forth the anguish of their hearts, a scene, if possible, more affecting passed between La Luc and Louis, who perceived it was necessary to inform him, though cautiously and by degrees, of the full extent of his calamity. He therefore told La Luc, that though Theodore had been first tried for the offence of having quitted his post, he was now condemned on a charge of assault made upon his general officer, the Marquis de Montalt, who had brought witnesses to prove that his life had been endangered by the circumstance; and who having pursued the prosecution with the most bitter rancour, had at length obtained the sentence which the law could not withhold, but which every other officer in the regiment deplored.

Louis added, that the sentence was to be executed in less than a fortnight, and that Theodore being very unhappy at receiving no answers to the letters he had sent his father, wishing to see him once more, and knowing that there was now no time to be lost, had requested him to go to Leloncourt and acquaint his father with his situation.

La Luc received the account of his son's condition with a distress that admitted neither of tears or complaint. He asked where Theodore was, and desiring to be conducted to him, he thanked Louis for all his kindness, and ordered post horses immediately.

A carriage was soon ready, and this unhappy father, after taking a mournful leave of M. Verneuil, and sending a compliment to M. Mauron, attended by his family, set out for the prison of his son. The journey was a silent one; each individual of the party endeavoured, in consideration of each other, to suppress the expression of grief, but was unable to do more. La Luc appeared calm and complacent; he seemed frequently to be engaged in prayer; but a struggle for resignation and composure was sometimes visible upon his countenance, notwithstanding the efforts of his mind.

CHAPTER XX

'And venom'd with disgrace the dart of Death.'
SEWARD*

WE now return to the Marquis de Montalt, who having seen
La Motte safely lodged in the prison of D——y, and learning
the trial would not come on immediately, had returned to his
villa on the borders of the forest, where he expected to hear
news of Adeline. It had been his intention to follow his
servants to Lyons; but he now determined to wait a few days
for letters, and he had little doubt that Adeline, since her
flight had been so quickly pursued, would be overtaken, and
probably before she could reach that city. In this expectation
he had been miserably disappointed; for his servants informed
him, that though they traced her thither, they had neither
been able to follow her route beyond, not to discover her at
Lyons. This escape she probably owed to having embarked on
the Rhone, for it does not appear that the Marquis's people
thought of seeking her on the course of that river.

His presence was soon after required at Vaceau, where the
court martial was then sitting; thither, therefore, he went,
with passions still more exasperated by his late disappointment, and procured the condemnation of Theodore. The
sentence was universally lamented, for Theodore was much
beloved in his regiment; and the occasion of the Marquis's
personal resentment towards him being known, every heart
was interested in his cause.

Louis de la Motte happening at this time to be stationed in
the same town, heard an imperfect account of his story, and
being convinced that the prisoner was the young chevalier
whom he had formerly seen with the Marquis at the Abbey,
he was induced partly from compassion, and partly with a
hope of hearing of his parents, to visit him. The compassionate
sympathy which Louis expressed, and the zeal with which he
tendered his services, affected Theodore, and excited in him a
warm return of friendship. Louis made him frequent visits,

did every thing that kindness could suggest to alleviate his sufferings, and a mutual esteem and confidence ensued.

Theodore at length communicated the chief subject of his concern to Louis, who discovered, with inexpressible grief, that it was Adeline whom the Marquis had thus cruelly persecuted, and Adeline for whose sake the generous Theodore was about to suffer. He soon perceived also that Theodore was his favoured rival; but he generously suppressed the jealous pang this discovery occasioned, and determined that no prejudice of passion should withdraw him from the duties of humanity and friendship. He eagerly inquired where Adeline then resided. 'She is yet, I fear, in the power of the Marquis,' said Theodore, sighing deeply. 'O God!—these chains!'—and he threw an agonizing glance upon them. Louis sat silent and thoughtful; at length starting from his reverie, he said he would go to the Marquis, and immediately quitted the prison. The Marquis was, however, already set off for Paris, where he had been summoned to appear at the approaching trial of La Motte; and Louis, yet ignorant of the late transactions at the Abbey, returned to the prison, where he endeavoured to forget that Theodore was the favoured rival of his love, and to remember him only as the defender of Adeline. So earnestly he pressed his offers of service, that Theodore, whom the silence of his father equally surprized and afflicted, and who was very anxious to see him once again, accepted his proposal of going himself to Savoy. 'My letters I strongly suspect to have been intercepted by the Marquis,' said Theodore; 'if so, my poor father will have the whole weight of this calamity to sustain at once, unless I avail myself of your kindness, and I shall neither see him nor hear from him before I die. Louis! there are moments when my fortitude shrinks from the conflict, and my senses threaten to desert me.'

No time was to be lost; the warrant for his execution had already received the king's signature, and Louis immediately set forward for Savoy. The letters of Theodore had indeed been intercepted by order of the Marquis, who, in the hope of discovering the asylum of Adeline, had opened and afterwards destroyed them.

But to return to La Luc, who now drew near Vaceau, and

who his family observed to be greatly changed in his looks since he had heard the late calamitous intelligence; he uttered no complaint; but it was too obvious that his disorder had made a rapid progress. Louis, who, during the journey, proved the goodness of his disposition by the delicate attentions he paid this unhappy party, concealed his observation of the decline of La Luc, and, to support Adeline's spirits, endeavoured to convince her that her apprehensions on this subject were groundless. Her spirits did indeed require support, for she was now within a few miles of the town that contained Theodore; and while her increasing perturbation almost overcame her, she yet tried to appear composed. When the carriage entered the town, she cast a timid and anxious glance from the window in search of the prison; but having passed through several streets without perceiving any building which corresponded with her idea of that she looked for, the coach stopped at the inn. The frequent changes in La Luc's countenance betrayed the violent agitation of his mind, and when he attempted to alight, feeble and exhausted, he was compelled to accept the support of Louis, to whom he faintly said, as he passed to the parlour, 'I am indeed sick at heart, but I trust the pain will not be long.' Louis pressed his hand without speaking, and hastened back for Adeline and Clara, who were already in the passage. La Luc wiped the tears from his eyes, (they were the first he had shed) as they entered the room. 'I would go immediately to my poor boy,' said he to Louis; 'yours, Sir, is a mournful office—be so good as to conduct me to him.' He rose to go, but, feeble and overcome with grief, again sat down. Adeline and Clara united in entreating that he would compose himself, and take some refreshment, and Louis urging the necessity of preparing Theodore for the interview, prevailed with him to delay it till his son should be informed of his arrival, and immediately quitted the inn for the prison of his friend. When he was gone, La Luc, as a duty he owed those he loved, tried to take some support, but the convulsions of his throat would not suffer him to swallow the wine he held to his parched lips, and he was now so much disordered, that he desired to retire to his chamber, where alone, and in prayer, he passed the dreadful interval of Louis's absence.

Clara on the bosom of Adeline, who sat in calm but deep distress, yielded to the violence of her grief. 'I shall lose my dear father too,' said she; 'I see it; I shall lose my father and my brother together.' Adeline wept with her friend for some time in silence; and then attempted to persuade her that La Luc was not so ill as she apprehended.

'Do not mislead me with hope,' she replied, 'he will not survive the shock of this calamity—I saw it from the first.' Adeline knowing that La Luc's distress would be heightened by the observance of his daughter's, and that indulgence would only encrease its poignancy, endeavoured to rouse her to an exertion of fortitude by urging the necessity of commanding her emotion in the presence of her father. 'This is possible,' added she, 'however painful may be the effort. You must know, my dear, that my grief is not inferior to your own, yet I have hitherto been enabled to support my sufferings in silence, for M. La Luc I do, indeed, love and reverence as a parent.'

Louis meanwhile reached the prison of Theodore, who received him with an air of mingled surprize and impatience. 'What brings you back so soon,' said he, 'have you heard news of my father?' Louis now gradually unfolded the circumstances of their meeting, and La Luc's arrival at Vaceau. A various emotion agitated the countenance of Theodore on receiving this intelligence. 'My poor father!' said he, 'he has then followed his son to this ignominious place! Little did I think when last we parted he would meet me in a prison, under condemnation!' This reflection roused an impetuosity of grief which deprived him for some time of speech. 'But where is he?' said Theodore, recovering himself; 'now he is come, I shrink from the interview I have so much wished for. The sight of his distress will be dreadful to me. Louis! when I am gone—comfort my poor father.' His voice was again interrupted by sobs; and Louis, who had been fearful of acquainting him at the same time of the arrival of La Luc, and the discovery of Adeline, now judged it proper to administer the cordial of this latter intelligence.

The glooms of a prison, and of calamity, vanished for a transient moment; those who had seen Theodore would have believed this to be the instant which gave him life and liberty. When his first emotions subsided, 'I will not repine,' said he; 'since I know that Adeline is preserved, and that I shall once more see my father, I will endeavour to die with resignation.' He enquired if La Luc was there in the prison; and was told he was at the inn with Clara and Adeline. 'Adeline! Is Adeline there too!—This is beyond my hopes. Yet why do I rejoice? I must never see her more: this is no place for Adeline.' Again he relapsed into an agony of distress—and again repeated a thousand questions concerning Adeline, till he was reminded by Louis that his father was impatient to see him—when, shocked that he had so long detained his friend, he entreated him to conduct La Luc to the prison, and endeavoured to recollect fortitude for the approaching interview.

When Louis returned to the inn La Luc was still in his chamber, and Clara quitting the room to call him, Adeline seized with trembling impatience the opportunity to enquire more particularly concerning Theodore, than she chose to do in the presence of his unhappy sister. Louis represented him to be much more tranquil than he really was: Adeline was somewhat soothed by the account; and her tears, hitherto restrained, flowed silently and fast, till La Luc appeared. His countenance had recovered its serenity, but was impressed with a deep and steady sorrow, which excited in the beholder a mingled emotion of pity and reverence. 'How is my son? sir,' said he as he entered the room. 'We will go to him immediately.'

Clara renewed the entreaties that had been already rejected, to accompany her father, who persisted in a refusal. 'To-morrow you shall see him,' added he; 'but our first meeting must be alone. Stay with your friend, my dear; she has need of consolation.' When La Luc was gone, Adeline, unable longer to struggle against the force of grief, retired to her chamber and her bed.

La Luc walked silently towards the prison, resting on the arm of Louis. It was now night: a dim lamp that hung above shewed them the gates, and Louis rung a bell; La Luc, almost overcome with agitation, leaned against the postern till the porter appeared. He enquired for Theodore, and followed the man; but when he reached the second court yard he seemed ready to faint, and again stopped. Louis desired the porter would fetch some water; but La Luc, recovering his voice, said he should soon be better, and would not suffer him to go. In a few minutes he was able to follow Louis, who led him through several dark passages, and up a flight of steps to a door, which being unbarred, disclosed to him the prison of his son. He was seated at a small table, on which stood a lamp that threw a feeble light across the place sufficient only to shew its desolation and wretchedness. When he perceived La Luc he sprung from his chair, and in the next moment was in his arms. 'My father!' said he in a tremulous voice. 'My son!' exclaimed La Luc; and they were for some time silent, and locked in each other's embrace. At length Theodore led him to the only chair the room afforded, and seating himself with Louis at the foot of the bed, had leisure to observe the ravages which illness and calamity had made on the features of his parent. La Luc made several efforts to speak, but unable to articulate, laid his hand upon his breast and sighed deeply. Fearful of the consequence of so affecting a scene on his shattered frame, Louis endeavoured to call off his attentions from the immediate object of his distress, and interrupted the silence; but La Luc shuddering, and complaining he was very cold, sunk back in his chair. His condition roused Theodore from the stupor of despair; and while he flew to support his father, Louis ran out for other assistance.—'I shall soon be better, Theodore,' said La Luc, unclosing his eye, 'the faintness is already going off. I have not been well of late; and this sad meeting!' Unable any longer to command himself, Theodore wrung his hand, and the distress which had long struggled for utterance burst in convulsive sobs from his breast. La Luc gradually revived, and exerted himself to calm the transports of his son; but the fortitude of the latter had now entirely forsaken him, and he could only utter exclamation and complaint. 'Ah! little did I think we should ever meet under circumstances so dreadful as the present! But I have not deserved them, my father! the motives of my conduct have still been just.'

'That is my supreme consolation,' said La Luc, 'and ought

to support you in this hour of trial. The Almighty God, who is the judge of hearts, will reward you hereafter. Trust in him, my son; I look to him with no feeble hope, but with a firm reliance on his justice!' La Luc's voice faultered; he raised his eyes to heaven with an expression of meek devotion, while the tears of humanity fell slowly on his cheek.

Still more affected by his last words, Theodore turned from him, and paced the room with quick steps: the entrance of Louis was a very seasonable relief to La Luc, who, taking a cordial he had brought, was soon sufficiently restored to discourse on the subject most interesting to him. Theodore tried to attain a command of his feelings, and succeeded. He conversed with tolerable composure for above an hour, during which La Luc endeavoured to elevate, by religious hope, the mind of his son, and to enable him to meet with fortitude the aweful hour that approached. But the appearance of resignation which Theodore attained always vanished when he reflected that he was going to leave his father a prey to grief, and his beloved Adeline for ever. When La Luc was about to depart he again mentioned her. 'Afflicting as an interview must be in our present circumstances,' said he, 'I cannot bear the thought of quitting the world without seeing her once again, yet I know not how to ask her to encounter, for my sake, the misery of a parting scene. Tell her that my thoughts never, for a moment, leave her; that'——La Luc interrupted, and assured him, that since he so much wished it, he should see her, though a meeting could serve only to heighten the mutual anguish of a final separation.

'I know it—I know it too well,' said Theodore; 'yet I cannot resolve to see her no more, and thus spare her the pain this interview must inflict. O my father! when I think of those whom I must soon leave for ever, my heart breaks. But I will indeed try to profit by your precept and example, and shew that your paternal care has not been in vain. My good Louis, go with my father—he has need of support. How much I owe this generous friend,' added Theodore, 'you well know, Sir.'—'I do, in truth,' replied La Luc, 'and can never repay his kindness to you. He has contributed to support us all; but you require comfort more than myself—he shall remain with you—I will go alone.'

This Theodore would not suffer; and La Luc no longer opposing him, they affectionately embraced, and separated for the night.

When they reached the inn La Luc consulted with Louis on the possibility of addressing a petition to the sovereign time enough to save Theodore. His distance from Paris, and the short interval before the period fixed for the execution of the sentence, made this design difficult; but believing it was practicable, La Luc, incapable as he appeared of performing so long a journey, determined to attempt it. Louis, thinking that the undertaking would prove fatal to the father, without benefiting the son, endeavoured, though faintly, to dissuade him from it—but his resolution was fixed.—'If I sacrifice the small remains of my life in the service of my child,' said he, 'I shall lose little: if I save him, I shall gain every thing. There is no time to be lost—I will set off immediately.'

He would have ordered post horses, but Louis, and Clara, who was now come from the bed-side of her friend, urged the necessity of his taking a few hours repose: he was at length compelled to acknowledge himself unequal to the immediate exertion which parental anxiety prompted, and consented to seek rest.

When he had retired to his chamber, Clara lamented the condition of her father.—'He will not bear the journey,' said she; 'he is greatly changed within these few days'—Louis was so entirely of her opinion, that he could not disguise it, even to flatter her with a hope. She added, what did not contribute to raise his spirits, that Adeline was so much indisposed by her grief for the situation of Theodore, and the sufferings of La Luc, that she dreaded the consequence.

It has been seen that the passion of young La Motte had suffered no abatement from time or absence; on the contrary, the persecution and the dangers which had pursued Adeline awakened all his tenderness, and drew her nearer to his heart. When he had discovered that Theodore loved her, and was beloved again, he experienced all the anguish of jealousy and disappointment; for though she had forbade him to hope, he found it too painful an effort to obey her, and had secretly cherished the flame which he ought to have stifled. His heart

was, however, too noble to suffer his zeal for Theodore to
abate because he was his favoured rival, and his mind too
strong not to conceal the anguish this certainty occasioned.
The attachment which Theodore had testified towards
Adeline even endeared him to Louis, when he had recovered
from the first shock of disappointment, and that conquest over
jealousy which originated in principle, and was pursued with
difficulty, became afterwards his pride and his glory. When,
however, he again saw Adeline—saw her in the mild dignity
of sorrow more interesting than ever—saw her, though sinking
beneath its pressure, yet tender and solicitous to soften the
afflictions of those around her—it was with the utmost
difficulty he preserved his resolution, and forbore to express
the sentiments she inspired. When he farther considered that
her acute sufferings arose from the strength of her affection,
he more than ever wished himself the object of a heart capable
of so tender a regard, and Theodore in prison and in chains
was a momentary object of envy.

In the morning, when La Luc arose from short and
disturbed slumbers, he found Louis, Clara, and Adeline,
whom indisposition could not prevent from paying him this
testimony of respect and affection, assembled in the parlour
of the inn to see him depart. After a slight breakfast, during
which his feelings permitted him to say little, he bade his
friends a sad farewell, and stepped into the carriage, followed
by their tears and prayers.—Adeline immediately retired to
her chamber, which she was too ill to quit that day. In the
evening Clara left her friend, and, conducted by Louis, went
to visit her brother, whose emotions, on hearing of his father's
departure, were various and strong.

CHAPTER XXI

'Tis only when with inbred horror smote
At some base act, or done, or to be done,
That the recoiling soul, with conscious dread,
Shrinks back into itself.'

MASON*

WE return now to Pierre De la Motte, who, after remaining some weeks in the prison of D——y, was removed to take his trial in the courts of Paris, whither the Marquis de Montalt followed to prosecute the charge. Madame De la Motte accompanied her husband to the prison of the Chatelet.* His mind sunk under the weight of his misfortunes; nor could all the efforts of his wife rouse him from the torpidity of despair which a consideration of his circumstances occasioned. Should he be even acquitted of the charge brought against him by the Marquis, (which was very unlikely) he was now in the scene of his former crimes, and the moment that should liberate him from the walls of his prison would probably deliver him again into the hands of offended justice.

The prosecution of the Marquis was too well founded, and its object of a nature too serious, not to justify the terror of La Motte. Soon after the latter had settled at the Abbey of St. Clair, the small stock of money which the emergency of his circumstances had left him being nearly exhausted, his mind became corroded with the most cruel anxiety concerning the means of his future subsistence. As he was one evening riding alone in a remote part of the forest, musing on his distressed circumstances, and meditating plans to relieve the exigencies which he saw approaching, he perceived among the trees at some distance a chevalier on horseback, who was riding deliberately along, and seemed wholly unattended. A thought darted across the mind of La Motte that he might be spared the evils which threatened him by robbing this stranger. His former practices had passed the boundary of honesty—fraud was in some degree familiar to him—and the thought was not dismissed. He hesitated——every moment of hesitation increased the power of temptation—the opportunity was such as might never occur again. He looked round, and as far as the trees opened saw no person but the chevalier, who seemed by his air to be a man of distinction. Summoning all his courage, La Motte rode forward and attacked him. The Marquis de Montalt, for it was him, was unarmed, but knowing that his attendants were not far off, he refused to yield. While they were struggling for victory, La Motte saw several horsemen enter the extremity of the avenue, and, rendered desperate by opposition and delay, he drew from his pocket a pistol, (which an apprehension of banditti made him usually carry when he rode to a distance from the Abbey) and fired at the Marquis, who staggered and fell senseless to the ground. La Motte had time to tear from his coat a brilliant star, some diamond rings from his fingers, and to rifle his pockets, before his attendants came up. Instead of pursuing the robber, they all, in their first confusion, flew to assist their lord, and La Motte escaped.

He stopped before he reached the Abbey at a little ruin, the tomb formerly mentioned, to examine his booty. It consisted of a purse containing seventy louis d'ors; of a diamond star, three rings of great value, and a miniature set with brilliants of the Marquis himself, which he had intended as a present for his favourite mistress. To La Motte, who but a few hours before had seen himself nearly destitute, the view of this treasure excited an almost ungovernable transport; but it was soon checked when he remembered the means he had employed to obtain it, and that he had paid for the wealth he contemplated the price of blood. Naturally violent in his passions, this reflection sunk him from the summmit of exultation to the abyss of despondency. He considered himself a murderer, and startled as one awakened from a dream, would have given half the world, had it been his, to have been as poor, and, comparatively, as guiltless as a few preceding hours had seen him. On examining the portrait he discovered the resemblance, and believing that his hand had deprived the original of life, he gazed upon the picture with unutterable anguish. To the horrors of remorse succeded the perplexities of fear. Apprehensive of he knew not what, he lingered at the tomb, where he at length deposited his treasure, believing that if his offence should awaken justice, the Abbey might be searched, and these jewels betray him. From Madame La Motte it was easy to conceal his increase of wealth; for as he had never made her acquainted with the exact state of his finances, she had not suspected the extreme poverty which menaced him, and as they continued to live as usual, she believed that their expences were drawn from the usual supply. But it was not so easy to disguise the workings of remorse and horror: his manner became gloomy and reserved, and his frequent visits to the tomb, where he went partly to examine his treasure, but chiefly to indulge in the dreadful pleasure of contemplating the picture of the Marquis, excited curiosity. In the solitude of the forest, where no variety of objects occurred to renovate his ideas, the horrible one of having committed murder was ever present to him.—When the Marquis arrived at the Abbey, the astonishment and terror of La Motte, for at first he scarce knew whether be beheld the shadow or the substance of a human form, were quickly succeeded by apprehension of the punishment due to the crime he had really committed. When his distress had prevailed on the Marquis to retire, he informed him that he was by birth a chevalier: he then touched upon such parts of his misfortunes as he thought would excite pity, expressed such abhorrence of his guilt, and voluntarily uttered such a solemn promise of returning the jewels he had yet in his possession, for he had ventured to dispose only of a small part, that the Marquis at length listened to him with some degree of compassion. This favourable sentiment, seconded by a selfish motive, induced the Marquis to compromise with La Motte. Of quick and inflammable passions, he had observed the beauty of Adeline with an eye of no common regard, and he resolved to spare the life of La Motte upon no other condition than the sacrifice of this unfortunate girl. La Motte had neither resolution or virtue sufficient to reject the terms—the jewels were restored, and he consented to betray the innocent Adeline. But as he was too well acquainted with her heart to believe that she would easily be won to the practice of vice, and as he still felt a degree of pity and tenderness for her, he endeavoured to prevail on the Marquis to forbear precipitate measures, and to attempt gradually to undermine her principles by seducing her affections. He approved and adopted this plan: the failure of his first scheme induced him to employ the stratagems he afterwards pursued, and thus to multiply the misfortunes of Adeline.

Such were the circumstances which had brought La Motte to his present deplorable situation. The day of trial was now come, and he was led from prison into the court, where the

Marquis appeared as his accuser. When the charge was delivered, La Motte, as is usual, pleaded not guilty, and the Advocate Nemours, who had undertaken to plead for him, afterwards endeavoured to make it appear that the accusation, on the part of the Marquis de Montalt, was false and malicious. To this purpose he mentioned the circumstance of the latter having attempted to persuade his client to the murder of Adeline: he farther urged that the Marquis had lived in habits of intimacy with La Motte for several months immediately preceding his arrest, and that it was not till he had disappointed the designs of his accuser, by conveying beyond his reach the unhappy object of his vengeance, that the Marquis had thought proper to charge La Motte with the crime for which he stood indicted: Nemours urged the improbability of one man's keeping up a friendly intercourse with another from whom he had suffered the double injury of assault and robbery; yet it was certain that the Marquis had observed a frequent intercourse with La Motte for some months following the time specified for the commission of the crime. If the Marquis intended to prosecute, why was it not immediately after his discovery of La Motte? and if not then, what had influenced him to prosecute at so distant a period?

To this nothing was replied on the part of the Marquis; for as his conduct on this point had been subservient to his designs on Adeline, he could not justify it but by exposing schemes which would betray the darkness of his character, and invalidate his cause. He, therefore, contented himself with producing several of his servants as witnesses of the assault and robbery, who swore without scruple to the person of La Motte, though not one of them had seen him otherwise than through the gloom of evening and riding off at full speed. On a cross examination most of them contradicted each other; their evidence was of course rejected; but as the marquis had yet two other witnessess to produce, whose arrival at Paris had been hourly expected, the event of the trial was postponed, and the court adjourned.

La Motte was re-conducted to his prison under the same pressure of despondency with which he had quitted it. As he walked through one of the avenues he passed a man who stood by to let him proceed, and who regarded him with a fixed and earnest eye. La Motte thought he had seen him before; but the imperfect view he caught of his features through the duskiness of the place made him uncertain as to this, and his mind was in too perturbed a state to suffer him to feel an interest on the subject. When he was gone the stranger inquired of the keeper of the prison who La Motte was; on being told, and receiving answers to some farther questions he put, he desired he might be admitted to speak with him. The request, as the man was only a debtor, was granted; but as the doors were now shut for the night, the interview was deferred till the morrow.

La Motte found Madame in his room, where she had been waiting for some hours to hear the event of the trial. They now wished more earnestly then ever to see their son; but they were, as he had suspected, ignorant of his change of quarters, owing to the letters which he had, as usual, addressed to them under an assumed name, remaining at the post-house of Auboin. This circumstance occasioned Madame La Motte to address her letters to the place of her son's late residence, and he had thus continued ignorant of his father's misfortunes and removal. Madame La Motte, surprized at receiving no answers to her letters, sent off another, containing an account of the trial as far as it had proceeded, and a request that her son would obtain leave of absence, and set out for Paris instantly. As she was still ignorant of the failure of her letters, and had it been otherwise, would not have known whither to have sent them, she directed this as usual.

Mean while his approaching fate was never absent for a moment from the mind of La Motte, which, feeble by nature, and still more enervated by habits of indulgence, refused to support him at this dreadful period.

While these scenes were passing at Paris, La Luc arrived there without any accident after performing a journey, during which he had been supported almost entirely by the spirit of his resolution. He hastened to throw himself at the feet of the sovereign, and such was the excess of his feeling on presenting the petition which was to decide the fate of his son, that he could only look silently up, and then fainted. The king received the paper, and giving orders for the unhappy father to be taken care of, passed on. He was carried back to his hotel, where he awaited the event of this his final effort.

Adeline, mean while, continued at Vaceau in a state of anxiety too powerful for her long-agitated frame, and the illness in consequence of this, confined her almost wholly to her chamber. Sometimes she ventured to flatter herself with a hope that the journey of La Luc would be successful: but these short and illusive intervals of comfort served only to heighten, by contrast, the despondency that succeeded, and in the alternate extremes of feeling she experienced a state more torturing than that produced either by the sharp sting of unexpected calamity, or the sullen pain of settled despair.

When she was well enough she came down to the parlour to converse with Louis, who brought her frequent accounts of Theodore, and who passed every moment he could snatch from the duty of his profession in endeavours to support and console his afflicted friends. Adeline and Theodore both looked to him for the little comfort allotted them, for he brought them intelligence of each other, and whenever he appeared a transient melancholy kind of pleasure played round their hearts. He could not conceal from Theodore Adeline's indisposition, since it was necessary to account for her not indulging the earnest wish he repeatedly expressed to see her again. To Adeline he spoke chiefly of the fortitude and resignation of his friend, not however forgetting to mention the tender affection he constantly expressed for her. Accustomed to derive her sole consolation from the presence of Louis, and to observe his unwearied friendship towards him whom she so truly loved, she found her esteem for him ripen into gratitude, and her regard daily increase.

The fortitude with which he had said Theodore supported his calamities was somewhat exaggerated. He could not sufficiently forget those ties which bound him to life to meet his fate with firmness; but though the paroxysms of grief were acute and frequent, he sought, and often attained in the presence of his friends, a manly composure. From the event of his father's journey he hoped little, yet that little was sufficient to keep his mind in the torture of suspence till the issue should appear.

On the day preceding that fixed for the execution of the sentence La Luc reached Vaceau. Adeline was at her chamber window when the carriage drew up to the inn; she saw him alight, and with feeble steps, supported by Peter, enter the house. From the languor of his air she drew no favourable omen, and, almost sinking under the violence of her emotion, she went to meet him. Clara was already with her father when Adeline entered the room. She approaching him, but, dreading to receive from his lips a confirmation of the misfortune his countenance seemed to indicate, she looked expressively at him and sat down, unable to speak the question she would have asked. He held out his hand to her in silence, sunk back in his chair, and seemed to be fainting under oppression of heart. His manner confirmed all her fears; at this dreadful conviction her senses failed her, and she sat motionless and stupified.

La Luc and Clara were too much occupied by their own distress to observe her situation; after some time she breathed a heavy sigh, and burst into tears. Relieved by weeping, her spirits gradually returned, and she at length said to La Luc, 'It is unnecessary, Sir, to ask the success of your journey; yet, when you can bear to mention the subject, I wish'—

La Luc waved his hand—'Alas!' said he, 'I have nothing to tell but what you already guess too well. My poor Theodore!—His voice was convulsed with sorrow, and some moments of unutterable anguish followed.

Adeline was the first who recovered sufficient recollection to notice the extreme languor of La Luc, and attend his support. She ordered him refreshments, and entreated he would retire to his bed and suffer her to send for a physician; adding, that the fatigue he had suffered made repose absolutely necessary. 'Would that I could find it, my dear child,' said he; 'it is not in this world that I must look for it, but in a better, and that better, I trust, I shall soon attain. But where is our good friend, Louis La Motte? He must lead me to my son.'—Grief again interrupted his utterance, and the entrance of Louis was a very seasonable relief to them all. Their tears explained the question he would have asked; La Luc immediately inquired for his son, and thanking Louis for all his kindness to him, desired to be conducted to the prison. Louis endeavoured to persuade him to defer his visit till the morning, and Adeline and Clara joined their entreaties with his, but La Luc determined to go that night.—'His time is short,' said he; 'a few hours and I shall see him no more, at least in this world; let me not neglect these precious moments. Adeline! I had promised my poor boy that he should see you once more; you are not now equal to the meeting. I will try to reconcile him to the disappointment; but if I fail, and you are better in the morning, I know you will exert yourself to sustain the interview.'—Adeline looked impatient, and attempted to speak. La Luc rose to depart, but could only reach the door of the room, where, faint and feeble, he sat down in a chair. 'I must submit to necessity,' said he; 'I find I am not able to go farther to-night. Go to him, La Motte, and tell him I am somewhat disordered by my journey, but that I will be with him early in the morning. Do not flatter him with a hope; prepare him for the worst.'——There was a pause of silence; La Luc at length recovering himself, desired Clara would order his bed to be got ready, and she willingly obeyed. When he withdrew, Adeline told Louis, what was indeed unnecessary, the event of La Luc's journey, 'I own,' continued she, 'that I had sometimes suffered myself to hope, and I now feel this calamity with double force. I fear too that M. La Luc will sink under its pressure; he is much altered for the worse since he set out for Paris. Tell me your opinion sincerely.'

The change was so obvious, that Louis could not deny it, but he endeavoured to sooth her apprehension by ascribing this alteration, in a great measure, to the temporary fatigue of travelling. Adeline declared her resolution of accompanying La Luc to take leave of Theodore in the morning. 'I know not how I shall support the interview,' said she; 'but to see him once more is a duty I owe both to him and myself. The remembrance of having neglected to give him this last proof of affection would pursue me with incessant remorse'

After some farther conversation on this subject Louis withdrew to the prison, ruminating on the best means of imparting to his friend the fatal intelligence he had to communicate. Theodore received it with more composure than he had expected; but he asked, with impatience, why he did not see his father and Adeline, and on being informed that indisposition withheld them, his imagination seized on the worst possibility, and suggested that his father was dead. It was a considerable time before Louis could convince him of the contrary, and that Adeline was not dangerously ill; when, however, he was assured that he should see them in the morning, he became more tranquil. He desired his friend would not leave him that night. 'These are the last hours we can pass together,' added he; 'I cannot sleep! Stay with me and lighten their heavy moments. I have need of comfort, Louis. Young as I am, and held by such strong attachments, I cannot quit the world with resignation. I know not how to credit those stories we hear of philosophic fortitude; wisdom cannot teach us cheerfully to resign a good, and life in my circumstances is surely such.'

The night was passed in embarrassed conversation; sometimes interrupted by long fits of silence, and sometimes by the paroxysms of despair; and the morning of that day which was to lead Theodore to death at length dawned through the grates of his prison.

La Luc mean while passed a sleepless and dreadful night. He prayed for fortitude and resignation both for himself and Theodore; but the pangs of nature were powerful in his heart, and not to be subdued. The idea of his lamented wife, and of what she would have suffered had she lived to witness the ignominious death which awaited her son, frequently occurred to him.

It seemed as if a destiny had hung over the life of Theodore, for it is probable that the king might have granted the petition of the unhappy father, had it not happened that the Marquis de Montalt was present at court when the paper was presented. The appearance and singular distress of the petitioner had interested the monarch, and, instead of putting by the paper, he opened it. As he threw his eyes over it, observing that the criminal was of the Marquis de Montalt's regiment: he turned to him and inquired the nature of the offence for which the culprit was about to suffer. The answer was such as might have been expected from the Marquis, and the king was convinced that Theodore was not a proper object of mercy.

But to return to La Luc, who was called, according to his order, at a very early hour. Having passed some time in prayer, he went down to the parlour, where Louis, punctual to the moment, already waited to conduct him to the prison. He appeared calm and collected, but his countenance was impressed with a fixed despair that sensibly affected his young friend. While they waited for Adeline he spoke little, and seemed struggling to attain the fortitude necessary to support him through the approaching scene. Adeline not appearing, he at length sent to hasten her, and was told she had been ill, but was recovering. She had indeed passed a night of such agitation, that her frame had sunk under it, and she was now endeavouring to recover strength and composure sufficient to sustain her in this dreadful hour. Every moment that brought her nearer to it had increased her emotion, and the apprehension of being prevented seeing Theodore had alone enabled her to struggle against the united pressure of illness and grief.

She now, with Clara, joined La Luc, who advanced as they entered the room, and took a hand of each in silence. After some moments he proposed to go, and they stepped into a carriage which conveyed them to the gates of the prison. The crowd had already began to assemble there, and a confused murmur arose as the carriage moved forward; it was a grievous sight to the friends of Theodore. Louis supported Adeline when she alighted, she was scarcely able to walk, and with trembling steps she followed La Luc, whom the keeper led towards that part of the prison where his son was confined. It was now eight o'clock, the sentence was not to be executed till twelve, but a guard of soldiers was already placed in the court, and as this unhappy party passed along the narrow avenues they were met by several officers who had been to take a last farewell of Theodore. As they ascended the stairs that led to his apartment, La Luc's ear caught the clink of chains, and heard him walking above with a quick irregular step. The unhappy father, overcome by the moment which now pressed upon him, stopped, and was obliged to support himself by the bannister. Louis fearing the consequence of his grief might be fatal, shattered as his frame already was, would have gone for assistance, but he made a sign to him to stay. 'I am better;' said La Luc, 'O God! support me through this hour!' and in a few minutes he was able to proceed.

As the warder unlocked the door, the harsh grating of the key shocked Adeline, but in the next moment she was in the presence of Theodore, who sprung to meet her, and caught her in his arms before she sunk to the ground. As her head reclined on his shoulder, he again viewed that countenance so dear to him, which had so often lighted rapture in his heart, and which though pale and inanimate as it now was, awakened him to momentary delight. When at length she unclosed her eyes, she fixed them in long and mournful gaze upon Theodore, who pressing her to his heart could answer her only with a smile of mingled tenderness and despair; the tears he endeavoured to restrain trembled in his eyes, and he forgot for a time every thing but Adeline. La Luc, who had seated himself at the foot of the bed, seemed unconscious of what passed around him, and entirely absorbed in his own grief; but Clara, as she clasped the hand of her brother, and hung weeping on his arm, expressed aloud all the anguish of her heart, and at length recalled the attention of Adeline, who in a voice scarcely audible entreated she would spare her father. Her words roused Theodore, and supporting Adeline to a chair, he turned to La Luc. 'My dear child!' said La Luc, grasping his hand and bursting into tears, 'My dear child!' They wept together. After a long interval of silence, he said, 'I thought I could have supported this hour, but I am old and feeble. God knows my efforts for resignation, my faith in his goodness!'

Theodore by a strong and sudden exertion assumed a composed and firm countenance, and endeavoured by every gentle argument to sooth and comfort his weeping friends. La Luc at length seemed to conquer his sufferings; drying his eyes, he said, 'My son, I ought to have set you a better example, and practised the precepts of fortitude I have so often given you. But it is over; I know, and will perform, my duty.' Adeline breathed a heavy sigh, and continued to weep. 'Be comforted, my love, we part but for a time,' said Theodore as he kissed the tears from her cheek; and uniting her hand with that of his father's, he earnestly recommended her to his protection. 'Receive her,' added he, 'as the most precious legacy I can bequeath; consider her as your child. She will console you when I am gone, she will more than supply the loss of your son.'

La Luc assured him that he did now, and should continue to, regard Adeline as his daughter. During those afflicting hours he endeavoured to dissipate the terrors of approaching death by inspiring his son with religious confidence. His conversation was pious, rational and consolatory: he spoke not from the cold dictates of the head, but from the feelings of a heart which had long loved and practised the pure precepts of christianity, and which now drew from them a comfort such as nothing earthly could bestow.

'You are young, my son,' said he, 'and are yet innocent of any great crime; you may therefore look on death without terror, for to the guilty only is his approach dreadful. I feel that I shall not long survive you, and I trust in a merciful God that we shall meet in a state where sorrow never comes; *where the Son of Righteousness shall come with healing in his wing!* As he spoke he looked up; the tears still trembled in his eyes, which beamed with meek yet fervent devotion, and his countenance glowed with the dignity of a superior being.

'Let us not neglect the awful moments,' said La Luc, rising, 'let our united prayers ascend to Him who alone can comfort and support us!' They all knelt down, and he prayed with that simple and sublime eloquence which true piety inspires. When he rose he embraced his children separately, and when he came to Theodore he paused, gazed upon him with an earnest, mournful expression, and was for some time unable to speak. Theodore could not bear this; he drew his hand before his eyes, and vainly endeavoured to stifle the deep sobs which convulsed his frame. At length recovering his voice, he entreated his father would leave him. 'This misery is too much for us all,' said he, 'let us not prolong it. The time is now drawing on—leave me to compose myself. The sharpness of death consists in parting with those who are dear to us; when that is passed, death is disarmed.'

'I will not leave you, my son,' replied La Luc, 'My poor

girls shall go, but for me, I will be you in your last moments.'
Theodore felt that this would be too much for them both,
and urged every argument which reason could suggest to
prevail with his father to relinquish his design. But he
remained firm in his determination. 'I will not suffer a selfish
consideration of the pain I may endure,' said La Luc, 'to
tempt me to desert my child when he will most require my
support. It is my duty to attend you, and nothing shall
withhold me.'

Theodore seized on the words of La Luc—'As you would
that I should be supported in my last hour,' said he, 'I entreat
that you will not be witness of it. Your presence, my dear
father, would subdue all my fortitude—would destroy what
little composure I may otherwise be able to attain. Add not to
my sufferings the view of your distress, but leave me to forget,
if possible, the dear parent I must quit for ever.' His tears
flowed anew. La Luc continued to gaze on him in silent
agony; at length he said, 'Well, be it so. If indeed my presence
would distress you, I will not go.' His voice was broken and
interrupted. After a pause of some moments he again
embraced Theodore—'We must part,' said he, 'we *must* part,
but it is only for a time—we shall soon be re-united in a higher
world!—O God! thou seest my heart—thou seest all its feelings
in this bitter hour!'—Grief again overcame him. He pressed
Theodore in his arms; and at length, seeming to summon all
his fortitude, he again said, 'We *must* part—Oh! my son,
farewell for ever in this world!—The mercy of Almighty God
support and bless you!'

He turned away to leave the prison, but, quite worn out
with grief, sunk into a chair near the door he would have
opened. Theodore gazed, with a distracted countenance,
alternately on his father, on Clara, and on Adeline, whom he
pressed to his throbbing heart, and their tears flowed together.
'And do I then,' cried he, 'for the last time look upon that
countenance!—Shall I never—never more behold it?—O!
exquisite misery! Yet once again—once more,' continued he,
pressing her cheek, but it was insensible and cold as marble.

Louis, who had left the room soon after La Luc arrived, that
his presence might not interrupt their farewell grief, now

returned. Adeline raised her head, and perceiving who entered, it again sunk on the bosom of Theodore.

Louis appeared much agitated. La Luc arose. 'We must go,' said he: 'Adeline, my love, exert yourself—Clara—my children, let us depart.—Yet one last—last embrace, and then!'——Louis advanced and took his hand; 'My dear Sir, I have something to say; yet I fear to tell it.'—'What do you mean?' said La Luc, with quickness: 'No new misfortune can have power to afflict me at this moment. Do not fear to speak.'—'I rejoice that I cannot put you to the proof,' replied Louis; 'I have seen you sustain the most trying affliction with fortitude. Can you support the transports of hope?' -La Luc gazed eagerly on Louis—'Speak!' said he, in a faint voice. Adeline raised her head, and, trembling between hope and fear, looked at Louis as if she would have searched his soul. He smiled cheerfully upon her. 'Is it—O! is it possible!' she exclaimed, suddenly re-animated—'He lives! He lives!'—She said no more, but ran to La Luc, who sunk fainting in his chair, while Theodore and Clara with one voice called on Louis to relieve them from the tortures of suspence.

He proceeded to inform them that he had obtained from the commanding officer a respite for Theodore till the king's farther pleasure could be known, and this in consequence of a letter received that morning from his mother, Madame De la Motte, in which she mentioned some very extraordinary circumstances that had appeared in the course of a trial lately conducted at Paris, and which so materially affected the character of the Marquis de Montalt as to render it possible a pardon might be obtained for Theodore.

These words darted with the rapidity of lightning upon the hearts of his hearers. La Luc revived, and that prison so lately the scene of despair now echoed only to the voices of gratitude and gladness. Le Luc, raising his clasped hands to Heaven, said, 'Great God! support me in this moment as thou hast already supported me!—If my son lives, I die in peace.'

He embraced Theodore, and remembering the anguish of his last embrace, tears of thankfulness and joy flowed to the contrast. So powerful indeed was the effect of this temporary reprieve, and of the hope it introduced, that if an absolute pardon had been obtained, it could scarcely for the moment have diffused a more lively joy. But when the first emotions were subsided, the uncertainty of Theodore's fate once more appeared. Adeline forebore to express this, but Clara without scruple lamented the possibility that her brother might yet be taken from them, and all their joy be turned to sorrow. A look from Adeline checked her. Joy was, however, so much the predominant feeling of the present moment, that the shade which reflection threw upon their hopes passed away like the cloud that is dispelled by the strength of the sun-beam; and Louis alone was pensive and abstracted.

When they were sufficiently composed, he informed them that the contents of Madame De la Motte's letter obliged him to set out for Paris immediately; and that the intelligence he had to communicate intimately concerned Adeline, who would undoubtedly judge it necessary to go thither also as soon as her health would permit. He then read to his impatient auditors such passages in the letter as were necessary to explain his meaning; but as Madame De la Motte had omitted to mention some circumstances of importance to be understood, the following is a relation of the occurrences that had lately happened at Paris.

It may be remembered, that on the first day of his trial, La Motte, in passing from the courts to his prison, saw a person whose features, though imperfectly seen through the dusk, he thought he recollected; and that this same person, after inquiring the name of La Motte, desired to be admitted to him. On the following day the warder complied with his request, and the surprise of La Motte may be imagined when, in the stronger light of his apartment, he distinguished the countenance of the man from whose hands he had formerly received Adeline.

On observing Madame De la Motte in the room, he said, he had something of consequence to impart, and desired to be left alone with the prisoner. When she was gone, he told De la Motte that he understood he was confined at the suit of the Marquis de Montalt. La Motte assented.—'I know him for a villain,' said the stranger boldly.—'Your case is desperate. Do you wish for life?'

'Need the question be asked!'

'Your trial, I understand, proceeds to-morrow. I am now under confinement in this place for debt; but if you obtain leave for me to go with you into the courts, and a condition from the judge that what I reveal shall not criminate myself, I will make discoveries that shall confound that same Marquis; I will prove him a villain; and it shall then be judged how far his word ought to be taken against you.'

La Motte, whose interest was now strongly excited, desired he would explain himself; and the man proceeded to relate a long history of the misfortunes and consequent poverty which had tempted him to become subservient to the schemes of the Marquis, till he suddenly checked himself, and said, 'When I obtain from the court the promise I require, I will explain myself fully; till then I cannot say more on the subject.'

La Motte could not forbear expressing a doubt of his sincerity, and a curiosity concerning the motive that had induced him to become the Marquis's accuser.—'As to my motive, it is a very natural one,' replied the man: 'it is no easy matter to receive ill usage without resenting it, particularly from a villain whom you have served.'—La Motte, for his own sake, endeavoured to check the vehemence with which this was uttered. 'I care not who hears me,' continued the stranger, but at the same time he lowered his voice; 'I repeat it—the Marquis has used me ill—I have kept his secret long enough. He does not think it worth while to secure my silence, or he would relieve my necessities. I am in prison for debt, and have applied to him for relief: since he does not chuse to give it, let him take the consequence. I warrant he shall soon repent that he has provoked me, and 'tis fit he should.'

The doubts of La Motte were now dissipated; the prospect of life again opened upon him, and he assured Du Bosse, (which was the stranger's name) with much warmth, that he would commission his Advocate to do all in his power to obtain leave for his appearance on the trial, and to procure the necessary condition. After some farther conversation they parted.

CHAPTER XXII

'Drag forth the legal monster into light,
Wrench from his hand Oppression's iron rod,
And bid the cruel feel the pains they give.'*

LEAVE was at length granted for the appearance of Du Bosse, with a promise that his words should not criminate him, and he accompanied La Motte into court.

The confusion of the Marquis de Montalt on perceiving this man was observed by many persons present, and particularly by La Motte, who drew from this circumstance a favourable presage for himself.

When Du Bosse was called upon, he informed the court, that on the night of the twenty-first of April, in the preceding year, one Jean d'Aunoy, a man he had known many years, came to his lodging. After they had discoursed for some time on their circumstances, d'Aunoy said he knew a way by which du Bosse might change all his poverty to riches, but that he would not say more till he was certain he would be willing to follow it. The distressed state in which du Bosse then was made him anxious to learn the means which would bring him relief; he eagerly inquired what his friend meant, and after some time d'Aunoy explained himself. He said he was employed by a nobleman, (whom he afterwards told du Bosse was the Marquis de Montalt) to carry off a young girl from a convent, and that she was to be taken to a house at a few leagues distant from Paris. 'I knew the house he described well,' said du Bosse, 'for I had been there many times with d'Aunoy, who lived there to avoid his creditors, though he often passed his nights at Paris.' He would not tell me more of the scheme, but said he should want assistants, and if I and my brother, who is since dead, would join him, his employer would grudge no money, and we should be well rewarded. I desired him again to tell me more of the plan, but he was obstinate, and after I had told him I would consider of what he said, and speak to my brother, he went away.

'When he called the next night for his answer, my brother and I agreed to engage, and accordingly we went home with him. He then told us that the young lady he was to bring thither was a natural daughter of the Marquis de Montalt, and of a nun belonging to a convent of Ursalines; that his wife had received the child immediately on its birth, and had been allowed a handsome annuity to bring it up as her own, which she had done till her death. The child was then placed in a convent and designed for the veil; but when she was of an age to receive the vows, she had steadily persisted in refusing them. This circumstance had so much exasperated the Marquis, that in his rage he ordered, that if she persisted in her obstinacy she should be removed from the convent, and got rid of any way, since if she lived in the world her birth might be discovered, and in consequence of this, her mother, for whom he had yet a regard, would be condemned to expiate her crime by a terrible death.'

Du Bosse was interrupted in his narrative by the council of the Marquis, who contended that the circumstances alledged tending to criminate his client, the proceeding was both irrelevant and illegal. He was answered that it was not irrelevant, and therefore not illegal, for that the circumstances which threw light upon the character of the Marquis, affected his evidence against La Motte. Du Bosse was suffered to proceed.

'D'Aunoy then said that the Marquis had ordered him to dispatch her, but that as he had been used to see her from her infancy, he could not find in his heart to do it, and wrote to tell him so. The Marquis then commanded him to find those who would, and this was the business for which he wanted us. My brother and I were not so wicked as this came to, and so we told d'Aunoy, and I could not help asking why the Marquis resolved to murder his own child rather than expose her mother to the risque of suffering death. He said the Marquis had never seen his child, and that therefore it could not be supposed he felt much kindness towards it, and still less that he could love it better than he loved its mother.'

Du Bosse proceded to relate how much he and his brother had endeavoured to soften the heart of d'Aunoy towards the

Marquis's daughter, and that they prevailed with him to write again and plead for her. D'Aunoy went to Paris to await the answer, leaving them and the young girl at the house on the heath, where the former had consented to remain, seemingly for the purpose of executing the orders they might receive, but really with a design to save the unhappy victim from the sacrifice.

It is probable that Du Bosse, in this instance, gave a false account of his motive, since if he was really guilty of an intention so atrocious as that of murder, he would naturally endeavour to conceal it. However this might be, he affirmed that on the night of the twenty-sixth of April, he received an order from d'Aunoy for the destruction of the girl whom he had afterwards delivered into the hands of La Motte.

La Motte listened to this relation in astonishment; when he knew that Adeline was the daughter of the Marquis, and remembered the crime to which he had once devoted her, his frame thrilled with horror. He now took up the story, and added an account of what had passed at the Abbey between the Marquis and himself concerning a design of the former upon the life of Adeline; and urged, as a proof of the present prosecution originating in malice, that it had commenced immediately after he had effected her escape from the Marquis. He concluded, however, with saying, that as the Marquis had immediately sent his people in pursuit of her, it was possible she might yet have fallen a victim to his vengeance.

Here the Marquis's council again interfered, and their objections were again overruled by the court. The uncommon degree of emotion which his countenance betrayed during the narrations of Du Bosse, and De la Motte, was generally observed. The court suspended the sentence of the latter, ordered that the Marquis should be put under immediate arrest, and that Adeline (the name given by her foster mother), and Jean d'Aunoy should be sought for.

The Marquis was accordingly seized at the suit of the crown, and put under confinement till Adeline should appear, or proof could be obtained that she died by his order, and till d'Aunoy should confirm or destroy the evidence of De la Motte.

Madame, who at length obtained intelligence of her son's residence from the town where he was formerly stationed, had acquainted him with his father's situation, and the proceedings of the trial; and as she believed that Adeline, if she had been so fortunate as to escape the Marquis's pursuit, was still in Savoy, she desired Louis would obtain leave of absence, and bring her to Paris, where her immediate presence was requisite to substantiate the evidence, and probably to save the life of La Motte.

On the receipt of her letter, which happened on the morning appointed for the execution of Theodore, Louis went immediately to the commanding officer to petition for a respite till the king's further pleasure should be known. He founded his plea on the arrest of the Marquis, and shewed the letter he had just received. The commanding officer readily granted a reprieve, and Louis, who, on the arrival of this letter, had forborne to communicate its contents to Theodore, lest it should torture him with false hope, now hastened to him with this comfortable news.

CHAPTER XXIII

'Low on his fun'ral couch he lies!
No pitying heart, no eye, afford
A tear to grace his obsequies.'
                              GRAY*

ON learning the purpose of Madame de la Motte's letter, Adeline saw the necessity of her immediate departure for Paris. The life of La Motte, who had more than saved her's, the life, perhaps, of her beloved Theodore, depended on the testimony she should give. And she who had so lately been sinking under the influence of illness and despair, who could scarcely raise her languid head, or speak but in the faintest accents, now reanimated with hope, and invigorated by a sense of the importance of the business before her, prepared to perform a rapid journey of some hundred miles.

Theodore tenderly intreated that she would so far consider her health as to delay this journey for a few days; but with a smile of enchanting tenderness she assured him, that she was now too happy to be ill, and that the same cause which would confirm her happiness would confirm her health. So strong was the effect of hope upon her mind now, that it succeeded to the misery of despair, that it overcame the shock she suffered on believing herself a daughter of the Marquis, and every other painful reflection. She did not even foresee the obstacle that circumstance might produce to her union with Theodore, should he at last be permitted to live.

It was settled that she should set off for Paris in a few hours with Louis, and attended by Peter. These hours were passed by La Luc and his family in the prison.

When the time of her departure arrived the spirits of Adeline again forsook her, and the illusions of joy disappeared. She no longer beheld Theodore as one respited from death, but took leave of him with a mournful pre-sentiment that she should see him no more. So strongly was this presage impressed upon her mind, that it was long before she could summons resolution to bid him farewel; and when she had done so, and even left the apartment, she returned to take of him a last look. As she was once more quitting the room, her melancholy imagination represented Theodore at the place of execution, pale and convulsed in death; she again turned her lingering eyes upon him; but fancy affected her sense, for she thought as she now gazed that his countenance changed, and assumed a ghastly hue. All her resolution vanished, and such was the anguish of her heart, that she resolved to defer her journey till the morrow, though she must by this means lose the protection of Louis, whose impatience to meet his father would not suffer the delay. The triumph of passion, however, was transient; soothed by the indulgence she promised herself, her grief subsided, reason resumed its influence; she again saw the necessity of her immediate departure, and recollected sufficient resolution to submit. La Luc would have accompanied her for the purpose of again soliciting the King in behalf of his son, had not the extreme weakness and lassitude to which he was reduced made travelling impracticable.

At length, Adeline, with a heavy heart, quitted Theodore, notwithstanding his entreaties, that she would not undertake the journey in her present weak state, and was accompanied by Clara and La Luc to the inn. The former parted from her friend with many tears, and much anxiety for her welfare, but under a hope of soon meeting again. Should a pardon be granted to Theodore La Luc designed to fetch Adeline from Paris; but should this be refused, she was to return with Peter. He bade her adieu with a father's kindness, which she repaid with a filial affection, and in her last words conjured him to attend to the recovery of his health: the languid smile he assumed seemed to express that her solicitude was vain, and that he thought his health past recovery.

Thus Adeline quitted the friends so justly dear to her, and so lately found, for Paris, where she was a stranger, almost without protection, and compelled to meet a father, who had pursued her with the utmost cruelty, in a public court of justice. The carriage in leaving Vaceau passed by the prison; she threw an eager look towards it as she passed; its heavy black walls, and narrow-grated windows, seemed to frown upon her hopes—but Theodore was there, and leaning from the window, she continued to gaze upon it till an abrupt turning in the street concealed it from her view. She then sunk back in the carriage, and yielding to the melancholy of her heart, wept in silence. Louis was not disposed to interrupt it; his thoughts were anxiously employed on his father's situation, and the travellers proceeded many miles without exchanging a word.

At Paris, whither we shall now return, the search after Jean d'Aunoy was prosecuted without success. The house on the heath, described by du Bosse, was found uninhabited, and to the places of his usual resort in the city, where the officers of the police awaited him, he no longer came. It even appeared doubtful whether he was living, for he had absented himself from the houses of his customary rendezvous some time before the trial of La Motte; it was therefore certain that his absence was not occasioned by any thing which had passed in the courts.

In the solitude of his confinement the Marquis de Montalt

had leisure to reflect on the past, and to repent of his crimes; but reflection and repentance formed as yet no part of his disposition. He turned with impatience from recollections which produced only pain, and looked forward to the future with an endeavour to avert the disgrace and punishment which he saw impending. The elegance of his manners had so effectually veiled the depravity of his heart, that he was a favourite with his Sovereign; and on this circumstance he rested his hope of security. He, however, severely repented that he had indulged the hasty spirit of revenge which had urged him to the prosecution of La Motte, and had thus unexpectedly involved him in a situation dangerous—if not fatal—since if Adeline could not be found he would be concluded guilty of her death. But the appearance of d'Aunoy was the circumstance he most dreaded; and to oppose the possibility of this, he employed secret emissaries to discover his retreat, and to bribe him to his interest. These were, however, as unsuccessful in their research as the officers of police, and the Marquis at length began to hope the man was really dead.

La Motte mean while awaited with trembling impatience the arrival of his son, when he should be relieved, in some degree, from his uncertainty concerning Adeline. On his appearance he rested his only hope of life, since the evidence against him would lose much of its validity from the confirmation she would give of the bad character of his prosecutor; and if the Parliament even condemned La Motte, the clemency of the King might yet operate in his favour.

Adeline arrived at Paris after a journey of several days, during which she was chiefly supported by the delicate attentions of Louis, whom she pitied and esteemed, though she could not love. She was immediately visited at the hotel by Madame La Motte: the meeting was affecting on both sides. A sense of her past conduct excited in the latter an embarrassment which the delicacy and goodness of Adeline would willingly have spared her; but the pardon solicited was given with so much sincerity, that Madame gradually became composed and re-assured. This forgiveness, however, could not have been thus easily granted, had Adeline believed her former conduct was voluntary; a conviction of the restraint and terror under which Madame had acted, alone induced her to excuse the past. In this first meeting they forbore dwelling on particular subjects; Madame La Motte proposed that Adeline should remove from the hotel to her lodgings near the Chatelet, and Adeline, for whom a residence at a public hotel was very improper, gladly accepted the offer.

Madame there gave her a circumstantial account of La Motte's situation, and concluded with saying, that as the sentence of her husband had been suspended till some certainty could be obtained concerning the late criminal designs of the Marquis, and as Adeline could confirm the chief part of La Motte's testimony, it was probable that now she was arrived the Court would proceed immediately. She now learnt the full extent of her obligation to La Motte; for she was till now ignorant that when he sent her from the forest he saved her from death. Her horror of the Marquis, whom she could not bear to consider as her father, and her gratitude to her deliverer, redoubled, and she became impatient to give the testimony so necessary to the hopes of her preserver. Madame then said, she believed it was not too late to gain admittance that night to the Chatelet; and as she knew how anxiously her husband wished to see Adeline, she entreated her consent to go thither. Adeline, though much harassed and fatigued, complied. When Louis returned from M. Nemour's, his father's advocate, whom he had hastened to inform of her arrival, they all set out for the Chatelet. The view of the prison into which they were now admitted so forcibly recalled to Adeline's mind the situation of Theodore, that she with difficulty supported herself to the apartment of La Motte. When he saw her a gleam of joy passed over his countenance; but again relapsing into despondency, he looked mournfully at her, and then at Louis, and groaned deeply. Adeline, in whom all remembrance of his former cruelty was lost in his subsequent kindness, expressed her thankfulness for the life he had preserved, and her anxiety to serve him, in warm and repeated terms. But her gratitude evidently distressed him; instead of reconciling him to himself, it seemed to awaken a remembrance of the guilty designs he had once assisted, and to strike the pangs of conscience deeper in his heart. Endeavouring to conceal his emotions, he entered on the subject of his present danger, and informed Adeline what testimony would be required of her on the trial. After above an hour's conversation with La Motte, she returned to the lodgings of Madame, where, languid and ill, she withdrew to her chamber, and tried to obliviate her anxieties in sleep.

The Parliament which conducted the trial re-assembled in a few days after the arrival of Adeline, and the two remaining witnesses of the Marquis, on whom he now rested his cause against La Motte, appeared. She was led trembling into the Court, where almost the first object that met her eyes was the Marquis de Montalt, whom she now beheld with an emotion entirely new to her, and which was strongly tinctured with horror. When du Bosse saw her he immediately swore to her identity; his testimony was confirmed by her manner; for on perceiving him she grew pale, and a universal tremor seized her. Jean d'Aunoy could no where be found, and La Motte was thus deprived of an evidence which essentially affected his interest. Adeline, when called upon, gave her little narrative with clearness and precision; and Peter, who had conveyed her from the Abbey, supported the testimony she offered. The evidence produced was sufficient to criminate the Marquis of the intention of murder, in the minds of most people present; but it was not sufficient to affect the testimony of his two last witnesses, who positively swore to the commission of the robbery, and to the person of La Motte, on whom sentence of death was accordingly pronounced. On receiving this sentence the unhappy criminal fainted, and the compassion of the assembly, whose feelings had been unusually interested in the decision, was expressed in a general groan.

Their attention was quickly called to a new object—it was Jean d'Aunoy who now entered the Court. But his evidence, if it could ever, indeed, have been the means of saving La Motte, came too late. He was re-conducted to prison; but Adeline, who, extremely shocked by his sentence, was much indisposed, received orders to remain in the Court during the examination of d'Aunoy. This man had been at length found in the prison of a provincial town, where some of his creditors had thrown him, and from which even the money which the Marquis had remitted to him for the purpose of satisfying the craving importunities of du Bosse, had been insufficient to release him. Meanwhile the revenge of the latter had been roused against the Marquis by an imaginary neglect, and the money which was designed to relieve his necessities was spent by d'Aunoy in riotous luxury.

He was confronted with Adeline and with du Bosse, and ordered to confess all he knew concerning this mysterious affair, or to undergo the torture. D'Aunoy, who was ignorant how far the suspicions concerning the Marquis extended; and who was conscious that his own words might condemn him, remained for some time obstinately silent; but when the *question* was administered his resolution gave way, and he confessed a crime of which he had not even been suspected.

It appeared, that in the year 1642 d'Aunoy, together with one Jacques Martigny, and Francis Balliere, had waylaid, and seized, Henry Marquis de Montalt, half brother to Phillipe; and after having robbed him, and bound his servant to a tree, according to the orders they had received, they conveyed him to the Abbey of St. Clair, in the distant forest of Fontangville. Here he was confined for some time till farther directions were received from Phillipe de Montalt, the present Marquis, who was then on his estates in a northern province of France. These orders were for death, and the unfortunate Henry was assassinated in his chamber in the third week of his confinement at the Abbey.

On hearing this Adeline grew faint; she remembered the MS. she had found, together with the extraordinary circumstances that had attended the discovery; every nerve thrilled with horror, and raising her eyes she saw the countenance of the Marquis overspread with the livid paleness of guilt. She endeavoured, however, to arrest her fleeting spirits while the man proceeded in his confession.

When the murder was perpetrated d'Aunoy had returned to his employer, who gave him the reward agreed upon, and in a few months after delivered into his hands the infant daughter of the late Marquis, whom he conveyed to a distant part of the kingdom, where, assuming the name of St. Pierre, he brought her up as his own child, receiving from the present Marquis a considerable annuity for his secrecy.

Adeline, no longer able to struggle with the tumult of emotions that now rushed upon her heart, uttered a deep sigh and fainted away. She was carried from the Court, and, when the confusion occasioned by this circumstance subsided, Jean d'Aunoy went on. He related, that on the death of his wife, Adeline was placed in a convent, from whence she was afterwards removed to another, where the Marquis had destined her to receive the vows. That her determined rejection of them had occasioned him to resolve upon her death, and that she had accordingly been removed to the house on the heath. D'Aunoy added, that by the Marquis's order he had misled du Bosse with a false story of her birth. Having after some time discovered that his comrades had deceived him concerning her death, d'Aunoy separated from them in enmity; but they unanimously determined to conceal her escape from the Marquis that they might enjoy the recompence of their supposed crime. Some months subsequent to this period, however, d'Aunoy received a letter from the Marquis, charging him with the truth, and promising him a large reward if he would confess where he had placed Adeline. In consequence of this letter he acknowledged that she had been given into the hands of a stranger; but who he was, or where he lived, was not known.

Upon these depositions Phillipe de Montalt was committed to take his trial for the murder of Henry, his brother; d'Aunoy was thrown into a dungeon of the Chatelet, and du Bosse was bound to appear as evidence.

The feelings of the Marquis, who, in a prosecution stimulated by revenge, had thus unexpectedly exposed his crimes to the public eye, and betrayed himself to justice, can only be imagined. The passions which had tempted him to the commission of a crime so horrid as that of murder—and what, if possible, heightened its atrocity, the murder of one connected with him by the ties of blood, and by habits of even infantine association—the passions which had stimulated him to so monstrous a deed were ambition, and the love of pleasure. The first was more immediately gratified by the title of his brother; the latter by the riches which would enable him to indulge his voluptuous inclinations.

The late Marquis de Montalt, the father of Adeline, received from his ancestors a patrimony very inadequate to support the splendour of his rank; but he had married the heiress of an illustrious family, whose fortune amply supplied the deficiency of his own. He had the misfortune to lose her, for she was amiable and beautiful, soon after the birth of a daughter, and it was then that the present Marquis formed the diabolical design of destroying his brother. The contrast of their characters prevented that cordial regard between them which their near relationship seemed to demand. Henry was benevolent, mild, and contemplative. In his heart reigned the love of virtue; in his manners the strictness of justness was tempered, not weakened, by mercy; his mind was enlarged by science, and adorned by elegant literature. The character of Phillipe has been already delineated in his actions; its nicer shades were blended with some shining tints; but these served only to render more striking by contrast the general darkness of the portrait.

He had married a lady, who, by the death of her brother, inherited considerable estates, of which the Abbey of St. Clair, and the villa on the borders of the forest of Fontangville, were the chief. His passion for magnificence and dissipation, however, soon involved him in difficulties, and pointed out to him the conveniency of possessing his brother's wealth. His brother and his infant daughter only stood between him and his wishes; how he removed the father has been already related; why he did not employ the same means to secure the child, seems somewhat surprizing, unless we admit that a destiny hung over him on this occasion, and that she was suffered to live as an instrument to punish the murderer of her parent. When a retrospect is taken of the vicissitudes and dangers to which she had been exposed from her earliest infancy, it appears as if her preservation was the effect of something more than human policy, and affords a striking instance that Justice, however long delayed, will overtake the guilty.

While the late unhappy Marquis was suffering at the

Abbey, his brother, who, to avoid suspicion, remained in the north of France, delayed the execution of his horrid purpose from a timidity natural to a mind not yet inured to enormous guilt. Before he dared to deliver his final orders he waited to know whether the story he contrived to propagate of his brother's death would veil his crime from suspicion. It succeeded but too well; for the servant, whose life had been spared that he might relate the tale, naturally enough concluded that his Lord had been murdered by banditti; and the peasant, who a few hours after found the servant wounded, bleeding, and bound to a tree, and knew also that the spot was infested by robbers, as naturally believed him, and spread the report accordingly.

From this period the Marquis, to whom the Abbey of St. Clair belonged in right of his wife, visited it only twice, and that at distant times, till after an interval of several years he accidentally found La Motte its inhabitant. He resided at Paris, and on his estate in the north, except that once a year he usually passed a month at his delightful villa on the borders of the forest. In the busy scenes of the Court, and in the dissipations of pleasure, he tried to lose the remembrance of his guilt; but there were times when the voice of conscience would be heard, though it was soon again lost in the tumult of the world.

It is probable, that on the night of his abrupt departure from the Abbey, the solitary silence and gloom of the hour, in a place which had been the scene of his former crime, called up the remembrance of his brother with a force too powerful for fancy, and awakened horrors which compelled him to quit the polluted spot. If it was so, it is however certain that the spectres of conscience vanished with the darkness; for on the following day he returned to the Abbey, though it may be observed, he never attempted to pass another night there. But though terror was roused for a transient moment, neither pity or repentance succeeded, since when the discovery of Adeline's birth excited apprehension for his own life, he did not hesitate to repeat the crime, and would again have stained his soul with human blood. This discovery was effected by means of a seal, bearing the arms of her mother's family, which was impressed on the note his servant had found, and had delivered to him at Caux. It may be remembered, that having read this note, he was throwing it from him in the fury of jealousy; but that after examining it again, it was carefully deposited in his pocket-book. The violent agitation which a suspicion of this terrible truth occasioned deprived him for a while of all power to act. When he was well enough to write he dispatched a letter to d'Aunoy. The purport of which has been already mentioned. From d'Aunoy he received that confirmation of his fears. Knowing that his life must pay the forfeiture of his crime, should Adeline ever obtain a knowledge of her birth, and not daring again to confide in the secrecy of a man who had once deceived him, he resolved, after some deliberation, on her death. He immediately set out for the Abbey, and gave those directions concerning her which terror for his own safety, still more than a desire of retaining her estates, suggested.

As the history of the seal which revealed the birth of Adeline is rather remarkable, it may not be amiss to mention, that it was stolen from the Marquis, together with a gold watch, by Jean d'Aunoy: the watch was soon disposed of, but the seal had been kept as a pretty trinket by his wife, and at her death went with Adeline among her clothes to the convent. Adeline had carefully preserved it, because it had once belonged to the woman whom she believed to have been her mother.

CHAPTER XXIV

'While anxious doubt distracts the tortur'd heart'*

WE now return to the course of the narrative, and to Adeline, who was carried from the court to the lodging of Madame De la Motte. Madame was, however, at the Chatelet with her husband, suffering all the distress which the sentence pronounced against him might be supposed to inflict. The feeble frame of Adeline, so long harassed by grief and fatigue, almost sunk under the agitation which the discovery of her birth excited. Her feelings on this occasion were too complex to be analysed. From an orphan, subsisting on the bounty of others, without family, with few friends, and pursued by a cruel and powerful enemy, she saw herself suddenly transformed to the daughter of an illustrious house, and the heiress of immense wealth. But she learned also that her father had been murdered—murdered in the prime of his days—murdered by means of his brother, against whom she must now appear, and in punishing the destroyer of her parent doom her uncle to death.

When she remembered the manuscript so singularly found, and considered that when she wept to the sufferings it described, her tears had flowed for those of her father, her emotion cannot easily be imagined. The circumstances attending the discovery of these papers no longer appeared to be a work of chance, but of a Power whose designs are great and just. 'O my father!' she would exclaim, 'your last wish is fulfilled—the pitying heart you wished might trace your sufferings shall avenge them.'

On the return of Madame La Motte Adeline endeavoured, as usual, to suppress her own emotions, that she might sooth the affliction of her friend. She related what had passed in the courts after the departure of La Motte, and thus excited, even in the sorrowful heart of Madame, a momentary gleam of satisfaction. Adeline determined to recover, if possible, the manuscript. On inquiry she learned that La Motte, in the confusion of his departure, had left it among other things at the Abbey. This circumstance much distressed her, the more so because she believed its appearance might be of importance on the approaching trial: she determined, however, if she should recover her rights, to have the manuscript sought for.

In the evening Louis joined this mournful party: he came immediately from his father, whom he left more tranquil than he had been since the fatal sentence was pronounced. After a silent and melancholy supper they separated for the night, and Adeline, in the solitude of her chamber, had leisure to meditate on the discoveries of this eventful day. The sufferings of her dead father, such as she had read them recorded by his *own hand*, pressed most forcibly to her thoughts. The narrative had formerly so much affected her heart, and interested her imagination, that her memory now faithfully reflected each particular circumstance there disclosed. But when she considered that she had been in the very chamber where her parent had suffered, where even his life had been sacrificed, and that she had probably seen the very dagger, seen it stained with rust, the rust of blood! by which he had fallen, the anguish and horror of her mind defied all control.

On the following day Adeline received orders to prepare for the prosecution of the Marquis de Montalt, which was to commence as soon as the requisite witnesses could be collected. Among these were the Abbess of the Convent, who had received her from the hands of d'Aunoy; Madame La Motte, who was present when Du Bosse compelled her husband to receive Adeline; and Peter, who had not only been witness to this circumstance, but who had conveyed her from the Abbey that she might escape the designs of the Marquis. La Motte, and Theodore La Luc, were incapacitated by the sentence of the law from appearing on the trial.

When La Motte was informed of the discovery of Adeline's birth, and that her father had been murdered at the Abbey of St. Clair, he instantly remembered, and mentioned to his wife, the skeleton he found in the stone room leading to the subterranean cells. Neither of them doubted, from the situation in which it lay, hid in a chest in an obscure room strongly guarded, that La Motte had seen the remains of the late Marquis. Madame, however, determined not to shock Adeline with the mention of this circumstance till it should be necessary to declare it on the trial.

As the time of this trial drew near the distress and agitation of Adeline increased. Though justice demanded the life of the murderer, and though the tenderness and pity which the idea of her father called forth urged her to avenge his death, she could not, without horror, consider herself as the instrument of dispensing that justice which would deprive a fellow being of existence; and there were times when she wished the secret of her birth had never been revealed. If this sensibility was, in her peculiar circumstances, a weakness, it was at least an amiable one, and as such deserves to be reverenced.

The accounts she received from Vaceau of the health of M. La Luc did not contribute to tranquillize her mind. The symptoms described by Clara seemed to say that he was in the last stage of a consumption, and the grief of Theodore and herself on this occasion was expressed in her letters with the lively eloquence so natural to her. Adeline loved and revered La Luc for his own worth, and for the parental tenderness he had shewed her, but he was still dearer to her as the father of Theodore, and her concern for his declining state was not inferior to that of his children. It was increased by the reflection that she had probably been the means of shortening his life, for she too well knew that the distress occasioned him by the situation in which it had been her misfortune to involve Theodore, had shattered his frame to its present infirmity. The same cause also with-held him from seeking in the climate of Montpellier the relief he had formerly been taught to expect there. When she looked round on the condition of her friends, her heart was almost overwhelmed with the prospect; it seemed as if she was destined to involve all those most dear to her in calamity. With respect to La Motte, whatever were his vices, and whatever the designs in which he had formerly engaged against her, she forgot them all in the service he had finally rendered her, and considered it to be as much her duty, as she felt it to be her inclination, to intercede in his behalf. This, however, in her present situation, she could not do with any hope of success; but if the suit, upon which depended the establishment of her rank, her fortune, and consequently her influence, should be decided in her favour, she determined to throw herself at the king's feet, and, when she pleaded the cause of Theodore, ask the life of La Motte.

A few days preceding that of the trial Adeline was informed a stranger desired to speak with her, and on going to the room where he was she found M. Vernueil. Her countenance expressed both surprize and satisfaction at this unexpected meeting, and she inquired, though with little expectation of an affirmative, if he had heard of M. La Luc. 'I have seen him,' said M. Vernueil; 'I am just come from Vaceau. But I am sorry I cannot give you a better account of his health. He is greatly altered since I saw him before.'

Adeline could scarcely refrain from tears at the recollection these words revived of the calamities which had occasioned this lamented change. M. Verneuil delivered her a packet from Clara; as he presented it he said, 'Beside this introduction to your notice, I have a claim of a different kind, which I am proud to assert, and which will perhaps justify the permission I ask of speaking upon your affairs.'—Adeline bowed, and M. Verneuil, with a countenance expressive of the most tender solicitude, added that he had heard of the late proceeding of the parliament of Paris, and of the discoveries that so intimately concerned her. 'I know not,' continued he, 'whether I ought to congratulate or condole with you on this trying occasion. That I sincerely sympathize in all that concerns you I hope you will believe, and I cannot deny myself the pleasure of telling you that I am related, though distantly, to the late Marchioness, your mother, for that she *was your mother* I cannot doubt.'

Adeline rose hastily and advanced towards M. Verneuil; surprize and satisfaction re-animated her features. 'Do I indeed see a relation?' said she in a sweet and tremulous voice, 'and one whom I can welcome as a friend?' Tears trembled in her eyes; and she received M. Verneuil's embrace in silence. It was some time before her emotion would permit her to speak.

To Adeline, who from her earliest infancy had been abandoned to strangers, a forlorn and helpless orphan; who had never till lately known a relation, and who then found one in the person of an inveterate enemy, to her this discovery was as delightful as unexpected. But after struggling for some time with the various emotions that pressed upon her heart, she begged M. Verneuil permission to withdraw till she could recover composure. He would have taken leave, but she entreated him not to go.

The interest which M. Verneuil took in the concern of La Luc, which was strengthened by his increasing regard for Clara, had drawn him to Vaceau, where he was informed of the family and peculiar circumstances of Adeline. On receiving this intelligence he immediately set out for Paris to offer his protection and assistance to his newly-discovered relation, and to aid, if possible, the cause of Theodore.

Adeline in a short time returned, and could then bear to converse on the subject of her family. M. Verneuil offered her his support and assistance, if they should be found necessary. 'But I trust,' added he, 'to the justness of your cause, and hope it will not require any adventitious aid. To those who remember the late Marchioness, your features bring sufficient evidence of your birth. As a proof that my judgement in this instance is not biassed by prejudice, the resemblance struck me when I was in Savoy, though I knew the Marchioness only by her portrait; and I believe I mentioned to M. La Luc that you often reminded me of a deceased relation. You may form some judgement of this yourself,' added M. Verneuil, taking a miniature from his pocket. 'This was your amiable mother.'

Adeline's countenance changed; she received the picture eagerly, gazed on it for a long time in silence, and her eyes filled with tears. It was not the resemblance she studied, but the countenance—the mild and beautiful countenance of her parent, whose blue eyes, full of tender sweetness, seemed bent upon her's; while a soft smile played on her lips; Adeline pressed the picture to her's, and again gazed in silent reverie. At length, with a deep sigh, she said, 'This surely *was* my mother. Had she *but* lived, O my poor father! you had been spared.' This reflection quite overcame her, and she burst into tears. M. Verneuil did not interrupt her grief but took her hand and sat by her without speaking till she became more composed. Again kissing the picture, she held it out to him with a hesitating look. 'No,' said he, 'it is already with its true owner.' She thanked him with a smile of ineffable sweetness, and after some conversation on the subject of the approaching trial, on which occasion she requested M. Verneuil would support her by his presence, he withdrew, having begged leave to repeat his visit on the following day.

Adeline now opened her packet, and saw once more the well-known characters of Theodore; for a moment she felt as if in his presence, and the conscious blush overspread her cheek; with a trembling hand she broke the seal, and read the tenderest assurances and solicitudes of his love; she often paused that she might prolong the sweet emotions which these assurances awakened, but while tears of tenderness stood trembling on her eyelids, the bitter recollection of his situation would return, and they fell in anguish on her bosom.

He congratulated her, and with peculiar delicacy, on the prospects of life which were opening to her; said every thing that might tend to animate and support her, but avoid dwelling on his own circumstances, except by expressing his sense of the zeal and kindness of his commanding officer, and adding, that he did not despair of finally obtaining a pardon.

This hope, though but faintly expressed, and written evidently for the purpose of consoling Adeline, did not entirely fail of the desired effect. She yielded to its enchanting influence, and forgot for a while the many subjects of care and anxiety which surrounded her. Theodore said little of his father's health; what he did say was by no means so discouraging as the accounts of Clara, who, less anxious to conceal a truth that must give pain to Adeline, expressed, without reserve, all her apprehension and concern.

CHAPTER XXV

— 'Heaven is just!
And, when the measure of his crimes is full,
Will bare its red right arm, and launch its lightnings'
MASON*

THE day of the trial so anxiously awaited, and on which the fate of so many persons depended, at length arrived. Adeline, accompanied by M. Verneuil and Madame la Motte, appeared as the prosecutor of the Marquis de Montalt; and d'Aunoy, du Bosse, Louis de la Motte, and several other persons, as witness in her cause. The judges were some of the most distinguished in France; and the advocates on both sides men of eminent abilities. On a trial of such importance the court, as may be imagined, was crowded with persons of distinction, and the spectacle it presented was strikingly solemn, yet magnificent.

When she appeared before the tribunal, Adeline's emotion surpassed all the arts of disguise, but adding to the natural dignity of her air an expression of soft timidity, and to her downcast eyes a sweet confusion, it rendered her an object still more interesting; and she attracted the universal pity and admiration of the assembly. When she ventured to raise her eyes, she perceived that the Marquis was not yet in the court, and while she awaited his appearance in trembling expectation, a confused murmuring rose in a distant part of the hall. Her spirits now almost forsook her; the certainty of seeing immediately, and consciously, the murderer of her father chilled her with horror, and she was with difficulty preserved from fainting. A low sound now ran through the court, and an air of confusion appeared, which was soon communicated to the tribunal itself. Several of the members arose, some left the hall, the whole place exhibited a scene of disorder, and a report at length reached Adeline that the Marquis de Montalt was dying. A considerable time elapsed in uncertainty; but the confusion continued; the Marquis did not appear; and at Adeline's request M. Verneuil went in quest of more positive information.

He followed a crowd which was hurrying towards the Chatelet, and with some difficulty gained admittance into the prison; but the porter at the gate, whom he had bribed for a passport, could give him no certain information on the subject of his enquiry, and not being at liberty to quit his post, furnished M. Verneuil with only a vague direction to the Marquis's apartment. The courts were silent and deserted, but as he advanced a distant hum of voices led him on, till perceiving several persons running towards a staircase which appeared beyond the archway of a long passage, he followed thither, and learned that the Marquis was certainly dying. The staircase was filled with people; he endeavoured to press through the crowd, and after much struggle and difficulty he reached the door of an anti-room which communicated with the apartment where the Marquis lay, and whence several persons now issued. Here he learned that the object of his enquiry was already dead. M. Verneuil, however, pressed through the anti-room to the chamber where lay the Marquis on a bed surrounded by officers of the law, and two notaries, who appeared to have been taking down depositions. His countenance was suffused with a black, and deadly hue, and impressed with the horrors of death; M. Verneuil turned away, shocked by the spectacle, and on enquiry heard that the Marquis had died by poison.

It appeared that convinced he had nothing to hope from his trial, he had taken this method of avoiding an ignominious death. In the last hours of life, while tortured with the remembrance of his crime, he resolved to make all the atonement that remained for him, and having swallowed the potion, he immediately sent for a confessor to take a full confession of his guilt, and two notaries, and thus established Adeline beyond dispute in the rights of her birth; and also bequeathed her a considerable legacy.

In consequence of these depositions she was soon after formally acknowledged as the daughter and heiress of Henry Marquis de Montalt, and the rich estates of her father were restored to her. She immediately threw herself at the feet of the king in behalf of Theodore and of La Motte. The character of the former, the cause in which he had risked his life, and the occasion of the late Marquis's enmity towards him, were circumstances so notorious, and so forcible, that it is more than probable the monarch would have granted his pardon to a pleader less irresistible than was Adeline de Montalt. Theodore La Luc not only received an ample pardon, but in consideration of his gallant conduct towards Adeline, he was soon after raised to a post of considerable rank in the army.

For La Motte, who had been condemned for the robbery on full evidence, and who had been also charged with the crime which had formerly compelled him to quit Paris, a pardon could not be obtained; but at the earnest supplication of Adeline, and in consideration of the service he had finally rendered her, his sentence was softened from death to banishment. This indulgence, however, would have availed him little, had not the noble generosity of Adeline silenced other prosecutions that were preparing against him, and bestowed on him a sum more than sufficient to support his family in a foreign country. This kindness operated so powerfully upon his heart, which had been betrayed through weakness rather than natural depravity, and awakened so keen a remorse for the injuries he had once meditated against a benefactress so noble, that his former habits became odious to him, and his character gradually recovered the hue which it would probably always have worn had he never been exposed to the tempting dissipations of Paris.

The passion which Louis had so long owned for Adeline was raised almost to adoration by her late conduct; but he now relinquished even the faint hope which he had hitherto almost unconsciously cherished, and, since the life which was granted to Theodore rendered this sacrifice necessary, he could not repine. He resolved, however, to seek in absence the tranquillity he had lost, and to place his future happiness on that of two persons so deservedly dear to him.

On the eve of his departure La Motte and his family took a very affecting leave of Adeline; he left Paris for England, where it was his design to settle; and Louis, who was eager to fly from her enchantments, set out on the same day for his regiment.

Adeline remained some time at Paris to settle her affairs, where she was introduced by M. V— to the few and distant relations that remained of her family. Among these were the Count and Countess D—, and the Mon. Amand, who had so much engaged her pity and esteem at Nice. The lady, whose death he lamented, was of the family of de Montalt; and the resemblance which he had traced between her features and those of Adeline, her cousin, was something more than the effect of fancy. The death of his elder brother had abruptly recalled him from Italy; but Adeline had the satisfaction to observe, that the heavy melancholy which formerly oppressed him, had yielded to a sort of placid resignation, and that his countenance was often enlivened by a transient gleam of cheerfulness.

The Count and Countess D—, who were much interested by her goodness and beauty, invited her to make their hotel her residence while she remained at Paris.

Her first care was to have the remains of her parent removed from the Abbey of St. Clair, and deposited in the vault of his ancestors. D'Aunoy was tried, condemned, and hanged, for the murder. At the place of execution he had described the spot where the remains of the Marquis were concealed, which was in the stone room already mentioned, belonging to the Abbey. M. V—— accompanied the officers appointed for the search, and attended the ashes of the Marquis to St. Maur, an estate in one of the northern provinces. There they were deposited with the solemn funeral pomp becoming his rank: Adeline attended as chief mourner; and this last duty paid to the memory of her parent, she became more tranquil and resigned. The MS. that recorded his sufferings had been found at the Abbey, and delivered to her by M. V——, and she preserved it with the pious enthusiasm so sacred a relique deserved.

On her return to Paris, Theodore La Luc, who was come from Montpelier, awaited her arrival. The happiness of this meeting was clouded by the account he brought of his father, whose extreme danger had alone withheld him from hastening the moment he obtained his liberty to thank Adeline for the life she had preserved. She now received him as the friend to whom she was indebted for her preservation, and as the lover who deserved, and possessed, her tenderest affection. The remembrance of the circumstances under which they had last met, and of their mutual anguish, rendered more exquisite the happiness of the present moments, when no longer oppressed by the horrid prospect of ignominious death and final separation, they looked forward only to the smiling days that awaited them when hand in hand they should tread the flowery scenes of life. The contrast which memory drew of the past with the present, frequently drew tears of tenderness and gratitude to their eyes, and the sweet smile which seemed struggling to dispel from the countenance of Adeline those gems of sorrow, penetrated the heart of Theodore, and brought to his recollection a little song which in other circumstances he had formerly sung to her. He took up a lute that lay on the table, and touching the dulcet chords, accompanied it with the following words:

SONG

The rose that weeps with morning dew,
And glitters in the sunny ray,

> In tears and smiles resembles you,
>   When Love breaks Sorrow's cloud away,
>
> The dews that bend the blushing flow'r,
>   Enrich the scent—renew the glow;
> So Love's sweet tears exalt his pow'r,
>   So bliss more brightly shines by woe!

Her affection for Theodore had induced Adeline to reject several suitors which her goodness, beauty, and wealth, had already attracted, and whom, though infinitely his superiors in point of fortune, were many of them inferior to him in family, and all of them in merit.

The various and tumultuous emotions which the late events had called forth in the bosom of Adeline were now subsided; but the memory of her father still tinctured her mind with a melancholy that time only could subdue; and she refused to listen to the supplications of Theodore till the period she had prescribed for her mourning should be expired. The necessity of re-joining his regiment obliged him to leave Paris within the fortnight after his arrival; but he carried with him assurance of receiving her hand soon after she should lay aside her sable habit, and departed therefore with tolerable composure.

M. La Luc's very precarious state was a source of incessant disquietude to Adeline, and she determined to accompany M. V——, who was now the declared lover of Clara, to Montpelier, whither La Luc had immediately gone on the liberation of his son. For this journey she was preparing when she received from her friend a flattering account of his amendment; and as some farther settlement of her affairs required her presence at Paris, she deferred her design, and M. V—— departed alone.

When Theodore's affairs assumed a more favourable aspect, M. Verneuil had written to La Luc, and communicated to him the secret of his heart respecting Clara. La Luc, who admired and esteemed M. V——, and who was not ignorant of his family connections, was pleased with the proposed alliance; Clara thought she had never seen any person whom she was so much inclined to love; and M. V—— received an answer favourable to his wishes, and which encouraged him to undertake the present journey to Montpelier.

The restoration of his happiness and the climate of Montpelier did all for the health of La Luc that his most anxious friends could wish, and he was at length so far recovered as to visit Adeline at her estate of St. Maur. Clara and M. V—— accompanied him, and a cessation of hostilities between France and Spain* soon after permitted Theodore to join this happy party. When La Luc, thus restored to those most dear to him, looked back on the miseries he had escaped, and forward to the blessings that awaited him, his heart dilated with emotions of exquisite joy and gratitude; and his venerable countenance, softened by an expression of complacent delight, exhibited a perfect picture of happy age.

CHAPTER XXVI

'Last came Joy's ecstatic trial:
They would have thought who heard the strain,
They saw in Tempe's vale her native maids
Amidst the festal sounding shades,
To some unweary'd minstrel dancing,
While as his flying fingers kiss'd the strings,
Love fram'd with Mirth a gay fantastic round.'
ODE TO THE PASSIONS*

ADELINE, in the society of friends so beloved, lost the impression of that melancholy which the fate of her parent had occasioned; she recovered all her natural vivacity; and when she threw off the mourning habit which filial piety had required her to assume, she gave her hand to Theodore. The nuptials, which were celebrated at St. Maur, were graced by the presence of the Count and Countess D——, and La Luc had the supreme felicity of confirming on the same day the flattering destinies of both his children. When the ceremony was over he blessed and embraced them all with tears of fatherly affection. 'I thank thee, O God! that I have been permitted to see this hour;' said he, 'whenever it shall please thee to call me hence, I shall depart in peace.'

'Long, very long, may you be spared to bless your children,' replied Adeline. Clara kissed her father's hand and wept: 'Long, very long,' she repeated in a voice scarcely audible. La Luc smiled cheerfully, and turned the conversation to a subject less affecting.

But the time now drew nigh when La Luc thought it necessary to return to the duties of his parish, from which he had so long been absent. Madame La Luc too, who had attended him during the period of his danger at Montpelier, and hence returned to Savoy, complained much of the solitude of her life; and this was with her brother an additional motive for his speedy departure. Theodore and Adeline, who could not support the thought of a separation, endeavoured to persuade him to give up his chateau, and to reside with them in France; but he was held by many ties to Leloncourt. For many years he had constituted the comfort and happiness of his parishioners; they revered and loved him as a father—he regarded them with an affection little short of parental. The attachment they discovered towards him on his departure was not forgotten either; it had made a deep impression on his mind, and he could not bear the thought of forsaking them now that Heaven had showered on him its abundance. 'It is sweet to live for them,' said he, 'and I will also die amongst them.' A sentiment also of a more tender nature,—(and let not the stoic prophane it with the name of weakness, or the man of the world scorn it as unnatural)—a sentiment still more tender attracted him to Leloncourt,—the remains of his wife reposed there.

Since La Luc would not reside in France, Theodore and Adeline, to whom the splendid gaieties that courted them at Paris were very inferior temptations to the sweet domestic pleasures and refined society which Leloncourt would afford, determined to accompany La Luc and Mon. and Madame Verneuil abroad. Adeline arranged her affairs so as to render her residence in France unnecessary; and having bade an affectionate adieu to the Count and Countess D——, and to M. Amand, who had recovered a tolerable degree of cheerfulness, she departed with her friends for Savoy.

They travelled leisurely, and frequently turned out of their way to view whatever was worthy of observation. After a long and pleasant journey they came once more within view of the Swiss mountains, the sight of which revived a thousand interesting recollections in the mind of Adeline. She remembered the circumstances and the sensations under which she had first seen them—when an orphan, flying from persecution to seek shelter among strangers, and lost to the only person on earth whom she loved—she remembered this, and the contrast of the present moment struck with all its force upon her heart.

The countenance of Clara brightened into smiles of the most animated delight as she drew near the beloved scenes of her infant pleasures; and Theodore, often looking from the windows, caught with patriotic enthusiasm the magnificent and changing scenery which the receding mountains successively disclosed.

It was evening when they approached within a few miles of Leloncourt, and the road winding round the foot of a stupendous cragg, presented them a full view of the lake, and of the peaceful dwelling of La Luc. An exclamation of joy from the whole party announced the discovery, and the glance of pleasure was reflected from every eye. The sun's last light gleamed upon the waters that reposed in 'chrystal purity'* below, mellowed every feature of the landscape, and touched with purple splendour the clouds that rolled along the mountain tops.

La Luc welcomed his family to his happy home, and sent up a silent thanksgiving that he was permitted thus to return to it. Adeline continued to gaze upon each well-known object, and again reflecting on the vicissitudes of grief and joy, and the surprising change of fortune which she had experienced since last she saw them, her heart dilated with gratitude and complacent delight. She looked at Theodore, whom in these very scenes she had lamented as lost to her for ever; who, when found again, was about to be torn from her by an ignominious death, but who was sat by her side her secure and happy husband, the pride of his family and herself; and while the sensibility of her heart flowed in tears from her eyes, a smile of ineffable tenderness told him all she felt. He gently pressed her hand, and answered her with a look of love.

Peter, who now rode up to the carriage with a face full of joy and of importance, interrupted a course of sentiment which was become almost too interesting. 'Ah! my dear master!' cried he, 'welcome home again. Here is the village, God bless! It is worth a million such places as Paris. Thank St. Jacques, we are all come safe back again!'

This effusion of honest Peter's joy was received and answered with the kindness it deserved. As they drew near the lake music sounded over the water, and they presently saw a large party of the villagers assembled on a green spot that sloped to the very margin of the waves, and dancing in all their holiday finery. It was the evening of a festival. The elder peasants sat under the shade of the trees that crowned this little eminence, eating milk and fruits, and watching their sons and daughters frisk it away to the sprightly notes of the tabor* and pipe, which was joined by the softer tones of a mandolin.

The scene was highly interesting, and what added to its picturesque beauty was a group of cattle that stood, some on the brink, some half in the water, and others reposing on the green bank, while several peasant girls, dressed in the neat simplicity of their country, were dispensing the milky feast. Peter now rode on first, and a crowd soon collected round him, who learning that their beloved master was at hand, went forth to meet and welcome him. Their warm and honest expressions of joy diffused an exquisite satisfaction over the heart of the good La Luc, who met them with the kindness of a father, and who could scarcely forbear shedding tears to this testimony of their attachment. When the younger part of the peasants heard the news of his arrival, the general joy was such, that, led by the tabor and pipe, they danced before his carriage to the chateau, where they again welcomed him and his family with the enlivening strains of music. At the gate of the chateau they were received by Madame La Luc, and a happier party never met.

As the evening was uncommonly mild and beautiful, supper was spread in the garden. When the repast was over, Clara, whose heart was all glee, proposed a dance by moonlight. 'It will be delicious,' said she; 'the moon-beams are already dancing on the waters. See what a stream of radiance they throw across the lake, and how they sparkle round that little promontory on the left. The freshness of the hour too invites to dancing.'

They all agreed to the proposal.—'And let the good people who have so heartily welcomed us home be called in too,' said La Luc: 'they shall *all* partake our happiness. There is devotion in making others happy, and gratitude ought to make us devout. Peter, bring more wine, and set some tables under the trees.' Peter flew, and, while chairs and tables were placing, Clara ran for her favourite lute, the lute which had formerly afforded her such delight, and which Adeline had often touched with a melancholy expression. Clara's light hand now ran over the chords, and drew forth tones of tender sweetness, her voice accompanying the following

AIR

Now at Moonlight's fairy hour,
   When faintly gleams each dewy steep,
And vale and mountain, lake and bow'r,
   In solitary grandeur sleep;

When slowly sinks the evening breeze,
   That lulls the mind in pensive care,
And Fancy loftier visions sees,
   Bid Music wake the silent air.

Bid the merry, merry tabor sound,
   And with the Fays of lawn or glade,
In tripping circlet beat the ground
   Under the high trees' trembling shade.

'Now at Moonlight's fairy hour'
   Shall Music breathe her dulcet voice,
And o'er the waves, with magic pow'r,
   Call on Echo to rejoice!

Peter, who could not move in a sober step, had already spread refreshments under the trees, and in a short time the lawn was encircled with peasantry. The rural pipe and tabor were placed, at Clara's request, under the shade of her beloved acacias on the margin of the lake; the merry notes of music sounded, Adeline led off the dance, and the mountains answered only to the strains of mirth and melody.

The venerable La Luc, as he sat among the elder peasants, surveyed the scene—his children and people thus assembled round him in one grand compact of harmony and joy—the frequent tear bedewed his cheek, and he seemed to taste the fulness of an exalted delight.

So much was every heart roused to gladness, that the morning dawn began to peep upon the scene of their festivity, when every cottager returned to his home blessing the benevolence of La Luc.

After passing some weeks with La Luc, M. Verneuil bought a chateau in the village of Leloncourt, and as it was the only one not already occupied, Theodore looked out for a residence in the neighbourhood. At the distance of a few leagues, on the beautiful banks of the lake of Geneva, where the waters retire into a small bay, he purchased a villa. The chateau was characterized by an air of simplicity and taste, rather than of magnificence, which however was the chief trait in the surrounding scene. The chateau was almost encircled with woods, which forming a grand amphitheatre swept down to the water's edge, and abounded with wild and romantic walks. Here nature was suffered to sport in all her beautiful luxuriance, except where here, and there, the hand of art formed the foliage to admit a view of the blue waters of the lake, with the white sail that glided by, or of the distant mountains. In front of the chateau the woods opened to a lawn, and the eye was suffered to wander over the lake, whose bosom presented an ever moving picture, while its varied margin sprinkled with villas, woods, and towns, and crowned beyond with the snowy and sublime alps, rising point behind point in aweful confusion, exhibited a scenery of almost unequalled magnificence.

Here, contemning the splendour of false happiness, and possessing the pure and rational delights of a love refined into the most tender friendship, surrounded by the friends so dear to them, and visited by a select and enlightened society—here, in the very bosom of felicity, lived Theodore and Adeline La Luc.

The passion of Louis De la Motte yielded at length to the powers of absence and necessity. He still loved Adeline, but it was with the placid tenderness of friendship, and when, at the earnest invitation of Theodore, he visited the villa, he beheld their happiness with a satisfaction unalloyed by any emotions of envy. He afterwards married a lady of some fortune at Geneva, and resigning his commission in the French service, settled on the borders of the lake, and increased the social delights of Theodore and Adeline.

Their former lives afforded an example of trials well endured—and their present, of virtues greatly rewarded; and this reward they continued to deserve—for not to themselves was their happiness contracted, but diffused to all who came within the sphere of their influence. The indigent and unhappy rejoiced in their benevolence, the virtuous and enlightened in their friendship, and their children in parents whose example impressed upon their hearts the precepts offered to their understandings.

FINIS

EXPLANATORY NOTES

A few preliminary points should be made about the scope and organization of the explanatory notes:

1. The references which *The Romance of the Forest* makes to other writings and areas of writing are indicated in the notes as briefly as possible; the roles which such references assume within this work of Gothic fiction—and within the Gothic genre in general—are explored more fully, however, in the Introduction.

2. Where a feature selected for commentary here recurs many times throughout the novel—or throughout certain sections of the novel—an explanatory note is appended to the first instance of this feature only (unless the feature then undergoes changes which require some further explanation). For features which recur with rather less frequency, cross-references are provided.

3. Where passages from the works of Rousseau are quoted, the quotation is taken, in every case, from a contemporary English translation. (A reference to a French edition is always included as well.)

4. The identification of a play by title only, without any information about its authorship, indicates that it is one of the works of Shakespeare.

ABBREVIATIONS

Initials

OED   *Oxford English Dictionary*

Titles

(a) Works by Ann Radcliffe

The Mysteries of Udolpho   edited by Bonamy Dobrée, World's Classics (Oxford, 1980)

The Italian   *The Italian; or, The Confessional of the Black Penitents. A Romance*, edited by Frederick Garber, World's Classics (Oxford, 1981)

(b) Works by Jean Jacques Rousseau

La Nouvelle Héloïse	*Julie; ou, La Nouvelle Héloïse*, edited by Michel Launay (Paris, 1967)
Eloisa	*Eloisa: or, A Series of Original Letters Collected and Published by J. J. Rousseau*, [translated by William Kenrick,] 4 vols (Dublin, 1761)
Emile	*Emile; ou, De l'Education*, edited by Michel Launay (Paris, 1966)
Emilius and Sophia	*Emilius and Sophia; or, A New System of Education*, [translated by William Kenrick,] 4 vols (London, 1762)
Rêveries	*Les Rêveries du promeneur solitaire*, edited by Henri Roddier (Paris, 1960)
Reveries	*The Reveries of the Solitary Walker*, in *The Confessions of J. J. Rousseau*, [translated by William Combe?,] 2 vols (London, 1783), II, 143–296.

(c) Others

Clermont	Regina Maria Roche, *Clermont: A Tale*, 4 vols (London, 1798)
The Man of Feeling	Henry Mackenzie, edited by Brian Vickers (Oxford, 1967)

Names of authors and compilers

Alison	Archibald Alison, *Essays on the Nature and Principles of Taste* (Edinburgh, 1790)
Blair	Hugh Blair, *Lectures on Rhetoric and Belles Lettres*, 2 vols (London, 1783)
Bourrit	Marc Théodore Bourrit, *A Relation of a Journey to the Glaciers, in the Dutchy of Savoy*, translated [from the original, French edition of 1771] by C. and F. Davy (Norwich, 1775)
Burke	Edmund Burke, *A Philosophical Enquiry into the Origin of our Ideas of the Sublime and Beautiful* (London, 1757)
Dodsley	*A Collection of Poems*, compiled by Robert Dodsley, [fifth edition?,] 6 vols (London, 1758)
Gilpin	William Gilpin, *Three Essays: on Picturesque Beauty; on Picturesque Travel; and on Sketching Landscape* (London, 1792)

Gray   [Thomas] Gray, *The Poems of Mr. Gray, to which are prefixed Memoirs of his Life and Writings*, edited by William Mason (York, 1775)

Johnson   Samuel Johnson, *A Dictionary of the English Language*, 2 vols (London, 1755)

Kames   [Henry Home,] Lord Kames, *Elements of Criticism*, 3 vols (Edinburgh, 1762)

Partridge   Eric Partridge, *A Dictionary of Slang and Unconventional English*, revised by Paul Beale (London, 1984)

Piozzi   Hester Lynch Piozzi, *Observations and Reflections Made in the Course of a Journey through France, Italy, and Germany*, edited by Herbert Barrows (Ann Arbor, 1967)

Smollett   Tobias Smollett, *Travels through France and Italy*, edited by Frank Felsenstein, World's Classics (Oxford, 1981)

Author and title

Swinburne, *Travels*   Henry Swinburne, *Travels in the Two Sicilies . . . in the Years 1777, 1778, 1779, and 1780*, 2 vols (London, 1783–5)

Swinburne, 'Journey'   Henry Swinburne, 'A Journey from Bayonne to Marseilles', in *Travels through Spain, in the Years 1775 and 1776*, second edition, 2 vols (London, 1787), II, 279–469

xxx *Advertisement . . .*: the *Gazetteer and New Daily Advertiser* was a newspaper which published poems by a fairly wide range of writers, including Anna Seward (from whose works Radcliffe quotes in *The Romance of the Forest*, p. 307) and Robert Burns. One of the poems by Radcliffe to be printed in this newspaper was 'Song of a Spirit' (see *The Romance of the Forest*, pp. 161–2), which appeared on Friday, 28 January 1791, under the pseudonym 'Adeline'.

1 *epigraph*: adapted from Macbeth, III. i. 110–13. Lines from this same play (II. ii. 40–4) are quoted on the title pages of each of the three volumes of the first and second editions.

Nemours: a name made famous by the part played in French politics by various Dukes of Nemours from the Middle Ages to the seventeenth century.

Pierre de la Motte: the name which La Motte (as he is subsequently called) is given is one which had become notorious in the seventeen-eighties as a result of the trial, in France, resulting from the 'affair of the queen's necklace' (a scandal which did some harm to the standing of the French monarchy), in which one of the accused was Jeanne de Luz, de Saint-Rémy, or de Valois, comtesse de la Motte. This name might also have been suggested, however, by that of the 'Monsieur De La Motte' (the French poet and critic Antoine Houdart de la Motte, 1672–1731) whose fables are cited as the source of several poems in Dodsley (an anthology which contains a number of the works quoted in *The Romance in the Forest*). See Dodsley, III, 202, 205 and V, 223. See, too, the reference to 'the isle of La Motte' in *Rêveries*, p. 61 (*Reveries*, II, 211).

Guyot de Pitaval . . . the seventeenth century: François Gayot de Pitaval's *Causes célèbres et intéressantes, avec les jugements des cours souveraines qui les ont décidées* (published in 1734, and for some years after), was used as the basis of a smaller collection of tales compiled by Charlotte Smith, entitled *The Romance of Real Life* (3 vols, London, 1787). Radcliffe follows this latter publication, I, vi, in referring to the original author as 'Guyot de Pitaval'. The narrative that follows does not, in fact, form part of either collection of stories, although C. F. McIntyre points out in *Ann Radcliffe in Relation to her Time* (New Haven, 1920), 57–8, that the story of 'Mademoiselle de Choiseul' in *The Romance of Real Life* bears a certain resemblance to *The Romance of the Forest* in its plot.

2 *He was a man . . . conscience*: Smith's *The Romance of Real Life* (see p. 1, note 4) declares that the compiler has been advised by 'a literary friend' to select from Gayot de Pitaval's *Causes célèbres* such stories as 'might lead us to form awful ideas of the force and danger of the human passions' (I, vi). The suggestion that 'it is our passions that render us feeble' is found in Rousseau's *Emile*, p. 212 (*Emilius and Sophia*, II, 2), a work to which the final section of *The Romance of the Forest* refers very frequently indeed.

See also Introduction, pp. x–xi.

3 *the extreme darkness*: the account of the darkness which prevails

throughout this episode, like many of the other descriptions of darkness in this novel, appeals to a principle put forward in Burke, p. 43: 'To make any thing very terrible, obscurity seems in general to be necessary. When we know the full extent of any danger, when we accustom our eyes to it, a great deal of the apprehension vanishes.'

4 *no sound . . . the waste*: Burke, p. 50, names silence as well as darkness (see note to p. 3)—and in addition, too, to certain types of sound—as a source of sublimity and terror: 'All *general* privations are great, because they are all terrible; *Vacuity, Darkness, Solitude* and *Silence*.' Alison, p. 143, suggests that the sound of rising gusts of wind may itself produce an effect of sublimity: 'as the forerunner of the storm, and the sign of all the imagery we connect with it, it is sublime in a very great degree'.

The 'pitiless pelting' of the storm: a quotation which refers to *King Lear*, III. iv. 29: 'the pelting of this pitiless storm'.

5 *Her features . . . the utmost distress*: the heroine's first appearance in the novel strongly emphasizes her role as a victim (see Introduction, p. xvii). Like many other accounts of women in Gothic novels, the description of Adeline, as she is presented to La Motte, incorporates the assumption—stated directly in Burke, p. 91—that 'beauty in distress is much the most affecting beauty'.

7 *'An eye . . . purest white'*: James Thomson, *The Tragedy of Sophonisba*, II. i. 76–8.

A habit of grey camlet, with short slashed sleeves: the term *habit* is used here in the sense of 'a gown or robe' (*OED*). *Camlet* is defined in the *OED* as 'a name originally applied to some beautiful and costly eastern fabric, afterwards to imitations and substitutes the nature of which has changed many times over'. Johnson asserts that this fabric 'is now made with wool and silk'. 'Slashed' sleeves consist of sleeves with vertical slits, through which a contrasting lining is visible (*OED*).

. . . shewed, but did not adorn, her figure: see the description of excessive adornment as 'unbecoming', and the assertion that those garments 'which most distinguish the wearer, are often such as are least remarkable in themselves', in *Emile*, p. 485 (*Emilius and Sophia*, IV, 36).

9 *The fresh breeze . . . beauties of nature*: the first of many passages in which Adeline is soothed or revived by the aesthetic delights

of the landscape. A receptiveness to such delights is always, in Gothic fiction, a mark of virtue: *The Italian*, p. 255, for example, establishes a sharp contrast between the power of the heroine to yield her cares 'to the influence of majestic nature' and the indifference to natural scenery displayed by the villainous Schedoni.

the varied landscape: variety is named as a source of pleasure in most eighteenth-century works of aesthetic theory: Kames, I, 298, for example, mentions 'the extreme delight we have in viewing the face of nature, when sufficiently enriched and diversified by objects'. The Gothic novel, in its accounts of variety, as in its descriptions of many of the other aesthetic categories discussed in eighteenth-century theoretical writings, refers not only to these writings themselves but also to contemporary travel literature. The principle that the impressions made by natural scenery 'become more agreeable, as the objects which excite them are more varied' is put forward, for example, in Bourrit, p. 1. The 'varied' nature of the landscape to be viewed on a journey between Paris and Lyons is affirmed in Piozzi, p. 15 ('Here is no tedious uniformity to fatigue the eye').

the charms . . . those of novelty: 'the charm of novelty' is noted in Burke, p. 1, and in many other eighteenth-century works of aesthetic theory (see, for example, Kames, i, 319 and Blair, I, 91), with direct or indirect reference back to Addison's discussion of novelty as one of the three major sources of aesthetic pleasure (the other two being 'beauty' and 'greatness'). (See Joseph Addison, *Critical Essays from the Spectator*, edited by Donald F. Bond (Oxford, 1970), 178–9.)

the grandeur . . . a wide horizon: the term *grandeur* is regularly employed in eighteenth-century writings on aesthetic theory to name a quality—or effect—which is presented as one related very closely indeed to that of sublimity, if not actually identical with it (see, for example, Burke, p. 60 and Clair, p. 55), and which is therefore, like sublimity, a source of admiration and delight (see p. 15, note 5). 'Vastness of extent' is described in Burke, p. 51, as a quality which, like 'greatness of dimension', operates as 'a powerful cause of the sublime'. (See also Blair, I, 47.) The term *magnificence*, as employed in Burke, p. 60, indicates the 'great profusion' of 'things which are splended or valuable in themselves' which a prospect such as 'a wide horizon' might comprehend.

the picturesque beauties of more confined scenery: the term *picturesque* was often employed in later eighteenth-century accounts of landscape, even before the publication of Gilpin (1792) and of Uvedale Price's *Essay on the Picturesque* (1794–8). Until these two works appeared, however, this term was not subjected to any very rigorous process of definition, but was applied, fairly loosely, to any qualities which might be considered suitable for representation in painting. (In descriptions of the landscape, picturesque qualities were not, in fact, as this passage might be taken to imply, usually located within 'more confined scenery' alone.) An account of a journey alongside two Sicilian rivers in Swinburne, *Travels*, II, 347, for example, asserts that 'the country on each side of these streams is exceedingly handsome, and the view of Augusta at the bottom of a valley, through which the water meanders, remarkably picturesque'.

13 *romantic glades*: Johnson defines *romantick*, in the context of the landscape, as 'full of wild scenery'. The term is employed very frequently in this sense in eighteenth-century landscape description: Gray, p. 59, for example, characterizes a view of mountainous scenery in Savoy as 'one of the most solemn, the most romantic, and the most astonishing scenes I ever beheld'.

The Romance of the Forest also employs the term *romantic* in ways which correspond to at least two of Johnson's other definitions': 'improbable; false' (see, for example, p. 99: 'a romantic tale') and 'fanciful' (see, for example, p. 256: 'that romantic notion').

14 *'melancholy boughs'*: *As You Like It*, II. vii. 111 ('Under the shade of melancholy boughs').

through which . . . the travellers: like other Gothic novels, *The Romance of the Forest* contains a great many descriptions of evening, which establish implicit allusions to eighteenth-century allegorical poetry in their emphasis on such emotions as melancholy, pensiveness, and solemnity (see Introduction, pp. xxii–xxiii), and which often, as in this instance, refer also to Burke's principle that obscurity is a source of terror (see note to p. 3).

15 *epigraph*: adapted from Horace Walpole, *The Mysterious Mother*, I. i. 1–7. (The line-scheme has been completely changed.)

The Mysterious Mother (1768) was noted above all for the story which it tells of incest between a mother and her son, and narrowly avoided incest between that son and his daughter— who, as she is his mother's daughter too, is also his sister! (For an account of the delays in general distribution of this work occasioned by the preoccupations of its plot, see the *Monthly Review*, 23 (1797), 248–54.) This quotation, therefore, like quotations from the same play in *The Italian* (p. 5, p. 48, p. 98) serves, indirectly, to emphasize the role which the threat of incest is liable to assume within the Gothic scenario of horror and terror. (In *The Romance of the Forest*, this threat is, in fact, only mentioned explicitly towards the end of the narrative.)

a romantic gloom: Burke's discussion of obscurity in general (see note to p. 3) includes an observation on obscurity in buildings, in particular: 'I think then, that all edifices calculated to produce an idea of the sublime, ought rather to be dark and gloomy' (p. 63).

the lofty battlements: the vastness of the abbey is mentioned several times in the description which follows, with implicit reference to Burke, p. 58: 'To the sublime in building, greatness of dimension seems requisite' (see also p. 9, note 4).

'The thistle . . . the wind': quoted (with one slight adjustment) from 'Carthon: a Poem', in [James Macpherson,] *The Works of Ossian, the Son of Fingal*, 2 vols (London, 1775), I, 186.

a sensation . . . astonishment and awe: Burke, p. 13, explains the close link between sublimity and terror as follows: 'Whatever is fitted in any sort to excite the ideas of pain, and danger, that is to say, whatever is in any sort terrible, or is conversant about terrible objects, or operates in a manner analogous to terror, is a source of the *sublime*; that is, it is productive of the strongest emotion which the mind is capable of feeling.' The effect of sublimity, however, as described in Burke's *Philosophical Enquiry*, necessarily includes an element of 'delight' (defined on p. 129 as 'not pleasure, but a sort of delightful horror, a sort of tranquillity tinged with terror'), whereas the effect of terror may or may not be combined with an aesthetic 'delight' of this kind: 'When danger or pain press too nearly, they are incapable of giving any delight, and are simply terrible; but at certain distances, and with certain modifications, they may be, and they are delightful, as we every day experience' (13–14).

The other two forms of emotional response mentioned in this passage also have precise meanings attached to them in eighteenth-century aesthetic theory. Burke, p. 130, explains the relation between them in the following comment on the sublime: 'Its highest degree I call *astonishment*; the subordinate degrees are awe, reverence, and respect.' Astonishment is further defined (p. 4) as 'that state of the soul, in which all its motions are suspended, with some degree of horror'.

16 *as he contemplated . . . to past ages*: the power of a ruin to 'revive the memory of former times', a common theme in late eighteenth-century literature, is noted, for example, in [Thomas Whately,] *Observations on Modern Gardening* (London, 1770), p. 155 (quoted in Alison, p. 43).

The comparison . . . 'into the dust': many similar reflections are found in other eighteenth-century literary contexts. See, for example, the account of Gaius Marius's meditations on the ruins of Carthage in William Shenstone's 'Elegy XVII', lines 65–8:

> Genius of Carthage! paint thy ruin'd pride;
> Tow'rs, arches, fanes, in wild confusion strown;
> Let banish'd Marius, low'ring by thy side,
> Compare thy fickle fortunes with his own.

18 *As they proceeded . . . scenes of horror*: this passage appeals not only to Burke's argument that obscurity is a powerful source of sublimity, and of horror and terror (see note to p. 3), but also to the principle that an effect of horror is produced by dramatic contrasts between light and shade. An association of this kind between horror and striking effects of *chiaroscuro* is incorporated in many eighteenth-century accounts of works of art (see, for example, the account of how Salvator Rosa would have painted 'a saint calling down lightning from heaven to destroy blasphemers' in Smollett, p. 278).

A kind of pleasing dread . . . filled all her soul: an appeal to Burke's account of horror, terror, and sublimity as qualities comparable with 'delight' (see p. 15, note 5). The distinction between the response of Adeline, who is able to feel not only 'fear' but also 'admiration', and Madame La Motte's unreflective 'terrors', unmixed with any such element of aesthetic delight, is used to define the novel itself as the product of an informed sensibility, capable of recognizing and expounding the complex and paradoxical forms of aesthetic pleasure offered by the sublime.

19 *they had 'nothing to fear'*: this episode provides one example of the narrative device by which fears of some imminent danger are raised, and are then revealed to be groundless—a device used very frequently in the Gothic novel to postpone impending moments of terror (see Introduction, pp. vii–viii).

20 *she observed . . . not strictly Gothic*: the assertion of a knowledge of

architectural history, in this remark, is used here as a means of reinforcing the self-definition of *The Romance of the Forest* as the product of informed taste and sensibility (see p. 18, note 2).

22 *The scene before her . . . 'future evil'*: the suggestion that the presence of God may be felt in the works of nature is in close accordance with the references, later in *The Romance of the Forest*, to the 'Profession de foi du vicaire savoyard', in *Emile* (although this suggestion is one which is also found in many other eighteenth-century literary contexts: see, for example, Thomson, *Seasons*, 'Spring', lines 847–902). The 'vicaire savoyard', in advocating a form of religion which is based not on revelation but on reason, attaches great importance to the contemplation of nature, declaring, for example, that the book of nature 'lies open to every eye', and that 'it is from this sublime and wonderful volume that I learn to serve and adore its Divine Author' (*Emile*, p. 401 (*Emilius and Sophia*, III, 135)).

23 *various*: see p. 9, note 2.

26 *'Discovered! . . .' 'Discoloured! I suppose you mean'*: in representing Peter as a comically naïve figure, given to prolixity, digression, and confusion when clear information is urgently required of him, *The Romance of the Forest* follows a convention which is established as a feature of the Gothic genre in Horace Walpole's *The Castle of Otranto: A Gothic Story* (1764). The Preface to the second edition of this novel claims that in introducing comic 'domestics' into the action, 'that great master of nature, Shakespeare, was the model I copied' (edited by W. S. Lewis, World's Classics (Oxford, 1982), p. 8).

drubbing: 'a beating, a thrashing' (*OED*).

27 *a douse o' the chops*: 'a dull heavy blow' on the parts of the face about the mouth (*OED*).

29 *when she smiled . . . Hebe*: Hebe, in Greek mythology, was the handmaiden of the gods, for whom she poured out nectar, and was also associated with perpetual youth. This reference to her implicitly invokes Milton's 'L'Allegro', lines 28–30.

> Nods and Becks and wreathèd Smiles,
> Such as hang on Hebe's cheek.

'That might . . . scann'd': unidentified.

33 *epigraph*: *As You Like It*, II. i. 3–7.

35 *To the Visions of Fancy . . .*: the central theme of this sonnet is a common one in eighteenth-century poetry from the seventeen-

forties onwards. The title closely follows that of John Langhorne's poem 'The Visions of Fancy. In Four Elegies', whilst the range of passions prompted or heightened by Fancy is similar to that named in Joseph Warton's ode 'To Fancy', lines 107–10. Like all the other poems by Radcliffe which are included in the novel, 'To the Visions of Fancy' establishes multiple allusions to the general themes of eighteenth-century allegorical poetry and to words and phrases which are in common use in such poetry (see Introduction, pp. xxii–xxiii).

The theme of the 'illusive powers' of the imagination is one which plays a large part in the accounts of superstitious fear in *The Romance of the Forest* (see, for example, p. 141). By its range of references to allegorical poetry, this poem implicitly links the novel's concern with superstitious imaginative distortion to a preoccupation with 'wild illusions' of a more abstractedly literary nature.

38 *I looked around me . . . the Giver of all good!*: this contrast between the terror and misery of the convent, in which the Abbess 'never forgave an offence against ceremony' (p. 36), and the adoration of the Divinity prompted by the sight of natural scenery, invokes the principle formulated by the 'vicaire savoyard' in *Emile*, p. 385 (*Emilius and Sophia*, III, 103): 'Let us not confound the ceremonials of religion with religion itself. The worship of God demands that of the heart'. For the *vicaire's* account of the role which the spectacle of nature is to assume in prompting this religion 'of the heart', see note to p. 22.

44 *epigraph*: *Macbeth*, V. iii. 22–3 (a variant on the more usual wording of this passage, which begins 'My *way* of life . . .' (my italics)).

epigraph: Thomas Warton, 'The Suicide', lines 25–9.

46 *The operation of strong passion . . . direction*: see note to p. 2.

54 *That thrilling curiosity . . . spectacle*: La Motte's reaction serves to emphasize the form of response which the Gothic novel itself invites from the reader, as he or she pursues the mysteries which the narrative promises to reveal (see Introduction, pp. vii–viii).

55 *He had by this time . . . so much terror*: the strategy of postponing the full effect of horror or terror which the reader expects by revealing, after a period of suspense, that fears of some imminent danger are in fact unfounded (see note to p. 19) often, as in this case, takes the form of a narrative of pursuit, or

apparent pursuit, in which the pursuer is eventually discovered to be innocent of harmful intent.

57 *the Bicêtre, or the Bastille*: the Bicêtre was founded as a Parisian military hospital in 1632, but from 1672 onwards it was used as a house of correction and a prison. The fortress and prison of the Bastille had, by the end of the eighteenth century, assumed immense notoriety as an emblem of oppression; at the time when *The Romance of the Forest* was published, the storming and capture of this fortress by the people of Paris (14 July 1789), in revolt against the system of government which it represented, was still a relatively recent event.

66 *He was turning . . . each other's arms*: see note to p. 55.

73 *'Here,' said he, 'are probably deposited . . . upon earth'*: see p. 16, note 1.

75 *that soft and pleasing melancholy, so dear to the feeling mind*: see *Emile*, p. 298 (*Emilius and Sophia*, II, 183): 'Solitude and silence are friends to true pleasure. Tender emotions and tears are the companions of enjoyment.'

76 *Sonnet . . .*: the description of this poem as a 'sonnet' is not in fact (as the current usage of the term would suggest) at variance with eighteenth-century literary terminology; Johnson defines the word *sonnet* as one which may be applied not only to 'a short poem, consisting of fourteen lines, of which the rhymes are adjusted by a particular rule', but also to 'a small poem'.

The second and third stanzas of this 'Sonnet', like many of the poems in this novel (see Introduction, pp. xxii–xxiii), establish a number of allusions to Collins's 'Ode to Evening'; the term 'dying gales' (line 6), for example, is found in line 4 of that poem (and also in line 159 of Pope's *Eloisa to Abelard*).

79 *'Trifles . . . Holy Writ'*: *Othello*, III. iii. 322–4.

'to twist the true cause the wrong way.': misquoted from *2 Henry IV*, II. i. 110–11: 'I am well acquainted with your manner of wrenching the true cause the false way.'

82 *Self-love . . . virtue*: this passage takes as the starting-point of its argument the assertion, in *Emile*, p. 275 and *Emilius and Sophia*, II, 137, that 'the source of our passions, the origin and chief of every other . . . is SELF-LOVE'. In *Emile*, however, this passion of 'self-love' ('l'amour de soi') is not presented as one to be censured, but, on the contrary, is described as an emotion which 'regards our own personal good only', and 'is contented when

our real wants are supplied', in contrast to 'self-interest' ('l'amour-propre'), 'which stands in competition with the good of others': 'Thus we see how the soft and affectionate passions arise from self-love, and the hateful and irascible ones from self-interest' (*Emile*, p. 276, p. 277 (*Emilius and Sophia*, II, 140, 141)).

83 *La Motte had several . . . enthusiastic delight*: the Gothic novel's attempt to establish affiliations with a tradition of English poetry (see Introduction, pp. xxii–xxiii) sometimes takes the form of an assertion or implication that characters in a particular work of Gothic fiction are actually acquainted with that tradition themselves. In *The Mysteries of Udolpho*, p. 6, for example, it is explained that the French heroine has been taught Latin and English 'chiefly that she might understand the sublimity of their best poets', and a Frenchman in *Clermont* prefaces a quotation with the words: 'In the language of a poet of a sister country I might have said—' (IV, 85).

85 *epigraph*: *Macbeth*, III. iv. 105–6.

86 *The storm was now loud . . . any other sound*: see Burke, p. 65: 'Excessive loudness alone is sufficient to overpower the soul, to suspend its action, and to fill it with terror. The noise of vast cataracts, raging storms, thunder, or artillery, awakes a great and aweful sensation in the mind.'

88 *The noble deportment . . . the apartment*: so far, this episode has followed the narrative sequence outlined in the note to p. 19; the next paragraph, however, marks a variation on this sequence.

91 *His impassioned gestures . . . the obscurity of the subject*: Burke, pp. 43–4, applies the term *obscurity* not only to darkness (see note to p. 3), but also to uncertainty. (The two concepts are, in fact, very closely linked, since uncertainty is presented as the form of response which usually accompanies a state of darkness, and which contributes very strongly towards the effect of terror and sublimity that darkness produces.) The account of Madame La Motte's response to the 'obscurity' of the topic on which her husband and the Marquis are conversing appeals to Burke's observations that 'it is our nature, that, when we do not know what may happen to us, to fear the worst that can happen to us' (p. 67) and that 'it is our ignorance of things that . . . chiefly excites our passions' (pp. 47–8).

97 *epigraph*: *Macbeth*, I. iii. 137–8 (a misquotation of 'Present fears . . .').

99 *His conversation was lively, amusing, sometimes even witty*: see Introduction, pp. xiv–xvi.

109 *She now thought herself . . . as if for a funeral*: this part of Adeline's third dream closely resembles that of Edmund in *The Old English Baron: A Gothic Story* (1777; edited by James Trainer (Oxford, 1977), pp. 44–5); the circumstances in which Adeline's three dreams take place, moreover, are very similar to those which form the setting for Edmund's dream.

111 *epigraph*: *Julius Caesar*, I. iii. 28–31.

112 *Theodore Peyrou*: Theodore's surname might have been suggested by the description of 'the square walk, called le Peyrou', in Montpellier, in Swinburne, 'Journey', p. 380, or by an account of this same feature in some other travel book. (Smollett, p. 103, also mentions 'the peirou'.)

113 *She was awakened . . . unpleasant to be alone*: see p. 18, note 1 and note to p. 86.

127 *epigraph*: Thomas Warton, 'The Suicide', lines 19–24.

128 *the immortal Henry*: presumably Henri IV, King of France from 1594 to 1610.

131 *horrors more terrible than any, perhaps, which certainty could give*: for an account of Burke's discussion of the terrors of uncertainty, see note to p. 91.

137 *epigraph*: *King Lear*, I, i. 151–2 (slightly misquoted).

we are all blown up: 'our secrets would be discovered, with disastrous consequences'. (See Partridge, *blow-up* (noun) and *OED, blow up* (verb).)

144 *This account of the voice she had heard relieved Adeline's spirits*: the device of providing a rational explanation for an apparently supernatural effect has often been considered as one of the main distinguishing features of the form of Gothic novel written by Radcliffe and her followers (as opposed to the form of Gothic novel represented by *The Monk*, in which supernatural effects are allowed to remain unexplained). The *Critical Review*, likening *The Mysteries of Udolpho* to *The Romance of the Forest*, notes that 'the same mysterious terrors are continually exciting in the mind the idea of a supernatural appearance, keeping us, as it were, upon the very edge and confines of the world of spirits, and yet are ingeniously explained by familiar causes' (11 (1794), 361–72 (p. 361)); see, for example, *The Mysteries of Udolpho*, p. 460.

Rational explanations of the supernatural, by demonstrating that fears of supernatural forces are in fact groundless, provide one of the strategies by which the Gothic novel defers impending moments of horror and terror (see note to p. 19, and Introduction pp. vii–viii).

145 *fudge*: ' a lie, nonsense', a deception (Partridge).

151 *bumpers of wine*: a *bumper* is defined in Johnson as 'a cup filled till the liquour swells over the brims'.

his libations to Bacchus: Bacchus was the Roman god of wine. The term *libations* refers to wine or some other liquid poured out in honour of a god, and was commonly used, in the eighteenth century, in this 'somewhat jocular' manner (*OED*), to refer to glasses of wine poured out to be drunk.

152 *Chapter XI*: this chapter is the eleventh in the novel, but is nevertheless headed 'Chapter X' in both the first and second editions. The numbering both of this chapter and of those which follow has been changed in the present edition.

epigraph: William Collins, 'Ode to Fear', lines 1–8. Lines from this same poem are also quoted in the epigraph to Chapter XV (p. 224), and in epigraphs in *The Mysteries of Udolpho* (p. 222) and *The Italian* (p. 192).

it set . . . indifference: as noted in the Introduction, p. xviii, landscape description is used here to keep the reader in a state of suspense.

156 *saloon*: 'a large and lofty apartment serving as one of the principal reception rooms in a palace or other great house' (*OED*).

scenes from Ovid: as the author of the *Ars amatoria* and (according to rumour) the lover of Julia, the daughter of the Emperor Augustus, the Latin poet Ovid (Publius Ovidius Naso, 43 BC–AD 18) had a reputation for profligacy which would have made the representation of scenes from his poetry seem particularly suited to the château of the libidinous Marquis de Montalt. Ovid is characterized in *As You Like It* (III. iii. 9), for example, as 'that most capricious [i.e. lascivious] poet'. Several decades after the publication of *The Romance of the Forest*, this reputation is reaffirmed in Byron's *Don Juan* (1819–24; canto I, stanza XLII, line 1): 'Ovid's a rake, as half his verses show him'.

a scene from the Armida of Tasso: Armida is in fact the name not of a work by the Italian poet Torquato Tasso, but of a character in that poet's epic *La Gierusalemme liberata* (1580). An opera based on the story of this character and entitled *Armida*, however, was given at least two separate productions on the London stage in the decades preceding the publication of *The Romance of the Forest*; it was presumably either on this opera or on another adaptation of *La Gierusalemme liberata*, such as John Dennis's play *Rinaldo and Armida* (1699), that Radcliffe's knowledge of Tasso's epic was based.

The appropriateness of the story of Armida to the Marquis's château lies in Armida's role as a seductress and enchantress; the theme of 'enchantment' and delusive, treacherous delight is emphasized very strongly in the description of the château and its diversions that follows. *La Gierusalemme liberata* presents Armida, during the siege of Jerusalem by the Christians, luring away many of the principal Christian knights from their camp by her beauty. She then uses her magic powers to inveigle these knights into an enchanted garden, where they are overcome by indolence.

a silver lamp of Etruscan form: (see also the reference to *Etruscan vases*, below) the 'Etruscan' style of interior decoration, fashionable in the late eighteenth century, and especially in the seventeen-seventies, entailed the adoption of forms and colour-schemes based on those of Greek black-figure and red-figure vase-painting, which was erroneously termed 'Etruscan'.

pier glasses: a pier glass consists of 'a large tall mirror, originally one fitted to fill up the pier or space between two windows, or over a chimney-piece' (*OED*).

Horace, Ovid, Anacreon, Tibullus, and Petronius Arbiter: Anacreon (sixth century BC) was a Greek lyric poet; the other writers mentioned were all Romans. The listing of their names serves to emphasize both the Marquis's ability to appropriate for his own use the delights of literature and the importance, within his château, of the vices or—more often—the forms of light-hearted hedonism with which each of these writers was, on occasion, associated. An 'Ode to the Genius of Italy, occasioned by the Earl of Corke's going abroad', by J. Duncombe (in Dodsley, VI, 263–4), for example, characterizes the first of these poets (Quintus Horatius Flaccus, 65–8 BC) by describing the 'Sabine . . . plain' as a spot 'Where playful Horace tun'd his amorous strain' (lines 14–15). Ovid's reputation is described in note 2 above. Byron's characterization of Ovid in *Don Juan* is followed by the assertion that 'Anacreon's morals are a still worse sample' (canto I, stanza XLII, line 2); an earlier, less ironically inflated account of Anacreon's reputation, however, is found in James Scott's 'Ode to the Muse', lines 19–20: 'I hear Anacreon's honey'd tongue | To love and wine repeat the song' (in *A Collection of Poems . . . by Several Hands*, edited by G. Pearch, 2 vols (London, 1768), II, 207–11). The major role assumed by playful dalliance in the work of Albius Tibullus (*c.* 60–19 BC) is indicated in 'Part of an Elegy of Tibullus, translated', by George, Lord Lyttleton (Dodsley, II, 52–4), lines 65–6: 'We'll live, my Delia, and from life remove | All care, all bus'ness, but delightful Love'. Gaius Petronius Arbiter (died AD 65) was described by Tacitus as a man who led a life of luxury and dissipation.

a collation . . . liquors: the term *collation* indicates 'a light meal or repast: one consisting of light viands or delicacies' (*OED*).

157 *varied*: see p. 9, note 2.

'*Is this a charm to lure me to destruction?*': the most immediately evident literary reference here is to Milton's *Comus* (quoted on p. 286 of *The Romance of the Forest*, and a number of times, too, in Radcliffe's other novels), in which the eponymous evil spirit attempts to exert a delusive charm of this kind. Adeline's question might also be seen, however, as a reference to the story of Armida, mentioned on p. 156 (see note 3).

'*music such as charmeth sleep*': *A Midsummer Night's Dream*, IV. i. 83.

a hautboy: an oboe.

160 *his sophistry*: see Introduction, pp. xiv–xvi.

161 *the banquet*: i.e. the 'collation' named on p. 156 (see note 7). The term *banquet*, in the eighteenth century, referred not only to 'a feast' but also to various forms of 'slight repast', including 'a course of sweetmeats, fruit and wine, served . . . as a separate entertainment' (*OED*). The term refers, in this case, to the food itself, but is used below ('In the midst of the banquet') to describe the social occasion at which the food is consumed.

164 *Parian marble*: the white marble, 'highly valued among the ancients for statuary' (*OED*), which came from the island of Paros, one of the Cyclades.

the toilet: i.e. 'a dressing table' (Johnson).

parterres: the ornamental arrangements of flower-beds, areas of lawn and paths, on level ground, which were characteristic of the French, formal style of gardening, as opposed to the taste for 'picturesque' irregularity and ordered wildness which had superseded more formal conceptions of garden design in eighteenth-century England.

167 *She looked earnestly . . . who spoke*: see note to 55.

172 *epigraph*: William Collins, 'The Passions, An Ode for Music', lines 38–40.

   trembled through the clouds: an echo of the quotation on p. 7 (see note).

   'Oh! . . . with passion weak': 'Cynthia, an Elegiac Poem', from which these two stanzas are quoted (lines 49–56), appears in Dodsley, VI, 234–9, where it is attributed to 'T. P***cy'.

183 *another physician was consulted*: although the surgeon talks of this physician as a colleague whose professional status is much the same as his own (see also, for example, the reference, on p. 184, to 'my brother physician'), it is assumed here that the reader is aware of the sharp social division which in fact existed between physicians and surgeons in eighteenth-century England (and which had assumed a similar form in seventeenth-century France). Physicians were gentlemen of university education (though it was not from this education that their knowledge of medicine was derived). Surgeons, on the other hand, were craftsmen who engaged in practical work: Johnson defines a surgeon as 'one who cures by manual operations; one whose duty it is to act in external maladies by the direction of the physician'. The distinction between the two professions is indicated more clearly on p. 189, when Adeline succeeds in finding a physician to treat Theodore, and the physician at once recommends a new surgeon to work with him.

194 *roquelaure*: 'a cloak reaching to the knee worn by men during the eighteenth century and the early part of the nineteenth' (*OED*).

199 *epigraph*: unidentified.

205 *epigraph*: *King John*, IV. i. 41–2.

   epigraph: *King John*, III. ii. 47–53 and 62–3. (The words 'the midnight bell' are used as the title of a later Gothic novel, by Francis Lathom, published in 1798).

208 *Lethean*: i.e. inducing forgetfulness of the past. Lethe, in the works of Latin poets, was a river in Hades, the water of which, when drunk by souls about to be reincarnated, caused them to forget their previous existence.

222 *While the refined Europeans . . . wisdom*: as indicated in the Introduction (p. xvi), the libertines in the novels of Sade often make similar appeals to the customs of other societies— especially to those of primitive societies—in order to justify their own conduct, and to question the moral values or rules of decorum in operation in their own society. In *Justine; ou, Les Malheurs de la Vertu* (1791), for example, the Comte de Gernande, defending his cruel treatment of his wife, refers to the contempt in which women are or have been held in a wide range of different societies and declares: 'je traiterai ma femme comme j'en trouve le droit dans tous les codes de l'univers, dans mon coeur et dans la Nature' (edited by Béatrice Didier (Paris, 1973), p. 285; 'I shall treat my wife as I find the right to treat her in all the codes of the Universe, in my heart and in Nature').

the Turk . . . does not call it murder: many seventeenth-century and eighteenth-century travel writings define the Turkish character as a potentially violent one, and describe the Turks as brutally tyrannical in their exercise of power. See, for example, [Pierre Augustin] Guys, *A Sentimental Journey through Greece*, 3 vols (London, 1772), I, 19 (translated from *Voyage littéraire de la Grèce*, 2 vols (Paris, 1771), I, 16): 'Turks in power and under the sanction of the government, are very dangerous to have concerns with; they are unacquainted with any law, but that of their own despotic will.'

Even the polished Italian . . . his purpose: see Introduction, pp. xiii–xiv. Almost all seventeenth-century and eighteenth-century accounts of the Grand Tour make some reference to the prevalence, amongst the Italians, of 'the horrid practice of drawing the knife and stabbing each other' (John Moore, *A View of Society and Manners in Italy* (London, 1781), I, 461–2; see also, for example, Samuel Sharp, *Letters from Italy* (London, 1766), p. 129).

224 *epigraph*: William Collins, 'Ode to Fear', lines 10–13, 16–17, 22–4.

230 *When he approached . . . he stopped*: this episode refers back, in a very general sense, to *Macbeth*, II. ii. 20–3.

232 *he advised her . . . Savoy*: Savoy was an independent state from the early Middle Ages onwards. Piedmont was incorporated in the Duchy of Savoy as a dependency, and the government of Savoy, from 1562 onwards, was based in Turin. Its territories also included Nice, to which Adeline travels later in the

narrative. In 1720, Sardinia too was annexed to Savoy, which was usually known, after that date, by the name of the Kingdom of Sardinia. All these territories except Sardinia were lost to the French in the decade following the publication of *The Romance of the Forest*, but were regained in 1814–15. Savoy and Nice were finally ceded to France in 1858.

235 *from the rich plains . . . sublime emotions*: see Gray, p. 55: 'the rich plains of the Lyonnois, with the rivers winding among them, and the Alps, with the mountains of Dauphiné, to bound the view'. See also Bourrit, p. 2: 'of all the pictures she [nature] presents us, those of mountains covered with eternal snows, whose summits reach beyond the clouds, and whose forms are so majestic, are by far the most affecting, as they fill the mind with an idea of her grandeur and sublimity'.

In a few hours . . . circumstances: see the account of Lyons and its surroundings in Gray, p. 55: 'we shall leave the city, and proceed to its environs, which are beautiful beyond expression; it is surrounded with mountains, and those mountains all bedroped and bespeckled with houses, gardens and plantations of the rich Bourgeois, who have from thence a prospect of the city in the vale below'.

that busy city: the 'busy' state of commercial activity in Lyons is indicated, for example, in Smollett, p. 72 and Gray, p. 55.

A new and striking scene . . . busy faces: Gray, p. 55, notes the effect of extreme liveliness produced, in this same city, by 'the number of people, and the face of commerce diffused about it'.

whose steep banks . . . scenery: the 'steep banks' of the Rhône, the mountains which rise from these banks, and the 'romantic beauty' of the landscape are described in Smollett, p. 74, in an account of a journey from Lyons alongside the river as it flows towards the coast (i.e. in the opposite direction from the journey described here). For an account of the aesthetic pleasure located in the 'varied' or 'various' landscape, see p. 9, note 2, and note 7 below.

novelty: see p. 9, note 3.

now frowning with savage grandeur, and now smiling in fertility: eighteenth-century descriptions of landscape very frequently construct contrasts between the wild and the cultivated, the barren and the fertile, the 'savage' and the gentle. A description of 'a surprising mixture of wild, and cultivated nature', for example, is found in *La Nouvelle Héloïse* , p. 44 (*Eloisa*, I, 56), whilst Bourrit, pp. 253–4, notes 'the astonishing contrast between the rugged Mountains of *Savoy* . . . and the beautiful country under the Government of *Berne*'. Wild and barren elements, in the later eighteenth century, are almost invariably identified, implicitly or explicitly, with sublimity and grandeur, whilst cultivated, fertile and 'smiling' scenes of nature are identified with 'the beautiful'—the category which is set in direct opposition to that of the sublime in works of aesthetic theory (see, for example, Burke, p. 155). It is usually the presence of both wild and cultivated, sublime and beautiful elements which is indicated when a landscape is praised for its varied (or 'various') character (see p. 9, note 2, and note 5 above).

235 *gay with towns and villages*: the 'great number of towns and villages' along the banks of the Rhône is noted in Smollett, p. 74.

236 *her sorrow gradually softened into a gentle and not unpleasing melancholy*: see the account of the therapeutic effect of a similarly 'various' landscape in *La Nouvelle Héloïse*, p. 44 (*Eloisa*, I, 56): 'To this pleasing variety of scenes I attributed the serenity of my mind during my first day's journey.'

Sonnet: see note to p. 76.

239 *this great truth, 'That where guilt is, there peace cannot enter.'*: the maxim closest to this one (though still somewhat different in its implications) which is cited in *The Oxford Dictionary of Proverbs* (revised by F. P. Wilson, third edition, Oxford, 1970) is that formulated in Michael Drayton's *The Owle*, line 174: 'A guiltie Conscience feeles continuall feare'.

240 *epigraph*: James Beattie, *The Minstrel*, Book 2, lines 82–3.

When he came . . . ' . . . with ours': the appreciation of the landscape by servants in Gothic novels is always limited to—at most—a form of local patriotism. See, for example, the description of Vesuvius as '*our* mountain' by the Neapolitan servant Paulo [*sic*] in *The Italian*, p. 159. Like accounts of the indifference to landscape exhibited by Gothic villains (see p. 9, note 1), and of the imperfect appreciation displayed by characters such as Madame La Motte (see p. 18, note 2), such allusions to a limited form of aesthetic enjoyment serve to emphasize by contrast the taste and sensibility of the heroine, and to define the novel itself as one which is written from a position of superior discernment, which allows all attitudes to the landscape except that of true taste and sensibility to be judged as inadequate.

its disadvantages . . . the inhabitants: Gray, p. 61, describes Savoy as 'a country naturally, indeed, fine and fertile; but you meet with nothing in it but meager, ragged, bare-footed peasants, with their children, in extreme misery and nastiness'.

the usual effects of an arbitrary government: see the comparison between Savoy and the Swiss canton of Geneva in Gray, p. 61, which sets the poverty of the former region in contrast to the prosperity of the latter, and relates this contrast to the difference between the absolutist government of the Kingdom of Sardinia (see note to p. 232) and the republican government of Switzerland. For a similar contrast between the effects of the two governments, see *La Nouvelle Héloïse*, p. 387 (*Eloisa*, III, 159).

Her spirits . . . terror: for an account of the distinction between 'delightful sublimity' and 'terror', see p. 15, note 5.

241 *It stood . . . the sublime scenery on its borders*: the immensity of the mountains of Savoy is constantly emphasized in the descriptions that follow, as it is in Bourrit (see, for example, pp. 113–14). The portrayal of vast, 'stupendous' mountains as instances of sublimity implicitly refers back to the discussion of vastness in works of aesthetic theory. Burke, pp. 51–2, for example, asserts that the sublimity of an object of vast height, such as a mountain, is greater than that of an object of vast extent, such as a wide stretch of even ground, and notes, too, that 'a perpendicular has more force in forming the sublime, than an inclined plane'. (See also p. 9, note 4.)
  Vermil is a common variant of *vermilion*.

the good pastor's chateau: the term *pastor* does not necessarily indicate a Protestant clergyman, although La Luc is in fact soon revealed to be a Protestant (see p. 245, note 9). The term is used, in *Emilius and Sophia*, (III, 143), to translate the French *curé* (*Emile*, p. 405), in referring to the post which the Roman Catholic 'vicaire savoyard', on whom this 'good pastor', La Luc, is modelled, expresses a desire to hold. (The term *vicaire*, indicating an inferior rank, is translated in *Emilius and Sophia*, III, 16 (*Emile*, p. 345) by the title of *curate*.)

242 *The difference between her own condition . . . a friend*: Adeline's reflections follow a similar course to those of the 'promeneur solitaire' in *Rêveries*, p. 3 (*Reveries*, II, 145): 'Here I am, then,

alone on the earth, having neither brother, neighbour, friend, or society but myself.'

245 '*But half mankind . . .*' . . . *Cawthorne*: James Cawthorn, 'Life Unhappy, because We Use It Improperly: A Moral Essay', lines 165–76 (slightly misquoted).

at the foot of the Savoy Alps: a location which echoes the description of the two lovers in *La Nouvelle Héloïse* as 'habitants d'une petite ville au pied des Alpes' (or, in *Eloisa*, I, v, 'inhabitants of a small village at the foot of the Alps') in the subtitle of that novel.

Arnaud La Luc: this name may be based on that of the 'Monsieur de Luc'—Jean André de Luc, a geologist—whose explorations in Savoy are described in Bourrit, pp. 148–229. The selection of this name may also have been determined by its association with the anti-materialist views of Jacques François de Luc, the geologist's father.

whose decayed fortunes occasioned them to seek a retreat in Switzerland: the account of La Luc's parish on p. 240 clearly indicates, however, that this clergyman himself lives not in Switzerland but in Savoy.

His was the philosophy of nature, directed by common sense: a reference to the 'natural religion' expounded by the 'vicaire savoyard' in *Emile*. The *vicaire*, emphasizing the superiority of 'rational' belief over a religion based on revelation, and the superiority of the 'simple' and 'sublime' tenets of the gospels over the elaborate, ritualistic religion of the (Roman Catholic) Church (see, for example, *Emile*, p. 405 (*Emilius and Sophia*, III, 144)), sums up the principles of this 'natural religion' as follows: 'The most sublime ideas of the Deity are inculcated by reason alone. Take a view of the works of nature, listen to the voice within, and then tell me what God hath omitted to say to your sight, your conscience, your understanding? Where are the men who can tell us more of him than he tells us of himself?' (*Emile*, p. 385 (*Emilius and Sophia*, III, 101)).

He despised . . . their disciples: see *Emile*, p. 356 (*Emilius and Sophia*, III, 40): 'General and abstract ideas form the source of our greatest errors. The jargon of metaphysics never discovered one truth; but it has filled philosophy with absurdities of which we are ashamed, as soon as they are stript of their pompous expressions.'

his systems, like his religion, were simple, rational, and sublime: see note 5 above.

The people . . . their hearts: see the account by the 'vicaire savoyard', in *Emile*, p. 405 (*Emilius and Sophia*, III, 144), of how he would perform the duties of a *curé* towards his parishioners: 'Before I should teach them their duty, I should always endeavour to practise it myself, in order to let them see that I really thought as I spoke.'

a wife: La Luc, it becomes clear at this point, is not a Roman Catholic priest, as might be expected in Catholic Savoy, but a Protestant minister. (See p. 241, note 2)

246 *His income . . . the mental sufferer*: see *Emile*, p. 405 (*Emilius and Sophia*, III, 143): 'I cannot but think that I should make my parishioners happy! I should never, indeed, make them rich, but I should partake their poverty; I would raise them above meanness and contempt, more insupportable than indigence itself.'

On these occasions . . . '. . . of doing good': see *Emile*, p. 379 (*Emilius and Sophia*, III, 89–90): 'But can you believe there exists on earth a creature so depraved as never to have given up his heart to the inclination of doing good? The temptation is so natural and seductive, that it is impossible always to resist it, and the remembrance of the pleasure it hath once given us, is sufficient to represent it to us ever afterwards.'

it was for some time . . . to virtue: the discussion of how this last task may be accomplished occupies a major role in *Emile*: see, for example, p. 289 (*Emilius and Sophia*, II, 165).

247 *The spot . . . of his happiness*: see Alison, p. 15: 'There is no man, who has not some interesting associations with particular scenes, or airs, or books, and who does not feel their beauty or sublimity enhanced to him, by such connections.' This exposition of Alison's doctrine of associationism then goes on to emphasize the powerful imaginative effect of scenes which 'recal . . . images of past happiness, and past affections'.

which, shooting . . . sublime: this passage appeals not only to the principle that vastness is a source of the sublime (see p. 9, note 4, and p. 241, note 1), but also to the principle that irregularity, too, contributes towards an effect of sublimity. See the declaration, in Burke, p. 115, that 'the great' (i.e. the sublime) should be 'rugged and negligent'.

Some cottages . . . humanity: Alison, p. 29, cites 'a cottage on a precipice' as an example of the category of 'Picturesque Objects'. 'The effect which such objects have on every one's mind', according to Alison's definition, 'is to suggest an additional train of conceptions, beside what the scene or description itself would have suggested.'

248 *it was the pride . . . her neighbours*: the association of an interest in 'medicines and botanical distillations' with Madame La Luc, a character who is presented in the course of the narrative as a woman of limited imagination (though of great benevolence), is in line with the portrayal of such an interest as a rather prosaic preoccupation in *Rêveries*, pp. 92–3 (*Reveries*, II, 245).

249 *Here too . . . the chateau*: in describing Clara's efforts at landscape drawing, as in the later reference to her acquisition of the ability to reason (p. 276), *The Romance of the Forest* departs from the very restricted view of women's education put forward in *Emile* (see p. 480 (*Emilius and Sophia*, IV, 27)).

'Let experience . . . young minds': see *Emile*, p. 328 (*Emilius and Sophia*, II, 240): 'I cannot repeat it too often: let your lessons to youth consist in action rather than words; they must learn nothing from books which may be taught by experience.'

251 *Nothing was heard . . . more solemn*: Burke, as well as naming both silence and loud noises as sources of sublimity (see p. 4 note 1, and note to p. 86), asserts that 'a low, tremulous, intermitting sound . . . is productive of the sublime' (p. 67).

256 *'Shall I never . . . by their faces'*: the judgement of character by the face was a particular focus of interest at the end of the eighteenth century; at least two different English translations of Johann Caspar Lavater's *Physiognomische Fragmente* (1775–8) were published in the course of the seventeen-eighties. Appealing to arguments which are found both in Burke, p. 104 and *Emile*, p. 298 (*Emilius and Sophia*, II, 184), *The Romance of the Forest* suggests at several points that both character and inner emotional experience are manifested in the human countenance. (See, for example, the description of Adeline on p. 9, and the account of the Marquis's anger on p. 238.) The scepticism of Clara's aunt towards the tracing of character in the countenance echoes that of Harley's aunt in *The Man of Feeling*, p. 44.

258 *epigraph*: William Collins, 'Ode, to a Lady on the Death of Colonel Ross in the Action of Fontenoy', lines 10–13.

260 *There were indeed . . . of her heart*: Adeline's predilection for solitary, reflective rambles suggests a general allusion to *Rêveries*, in which the quest for solitude, and the delights of 'seating myself sometimes in the most pleasing and solitary retreats, to meditate at my ease' (on an island in a Swiss, Alpine lake) are repeatedly emphasized (*Rêveries*, p. 68; see also pp. 88–91 (*Reveries*, II, 218; see also II, 240–4)).

261 *She frequently took a volume of Shakespear or Milton*: see note to p. 83.

rimpled: the verb *to rimple* is defined in Johnson as 'to pucker; to contract into corrugations'. A similar effect of gentle movement on the surface of 'a small lake' in Savoy is described in Bourrit, p. 46.

262 *a crimson glow . . . alps*: the 'beautiful roseate colour' of the Alpine glaciers, both during and after sunset, is decribed in a footnote to *La Nouvelle Héloïse*, p. 389 (*Eloisa*, III, 163).

'*Soothing . . . mind*': James Thomson, *The Seasons*, 'Spring', lines 464–6 (slightly altered).

or perhaps of Genevois . . . than their own: a detail which suggests an oblique reference to the well-known description of an eventful party of pleasure on Lake Geneva in *La Nouvelle Héloïse*, pp. 386–8 (*Eloisa*, III, 157–61).

263 *the Glacier of Montanvert*: a visit to this glacier is described in Bourrit, pp. 75–83. The narrative of the excursion to view the glaciers, however, bears a close resemblance not to the account of this visit, but to the description of another expedition, to 'the Mountain called *Breven*', in this same travel book (pp. 63–74).

Now frowning . . . less fiercely wild: see p. 235, note 7.

264 '*The pomp of groves and garniture of fields*': James Beattie, *The Minstrel*, Book I, line 76.

its broken turrets . . . heightened the picturesque beauty of the object: the castle is presented as a 'Picturesque Object' of the kind described in Alison, p. 29 (see p. 247, note 3). The mention of the 'broken turrets' also suggests that this description is invoking the principle that roughness and irregularity constitute sources of the picturesque—a principle which was to be formulated explicitly in Gilpin (p. 26). The description refers, too, to Milton's 'L'Allegro', 77–8.

'*Deep struck . . . trembling shade*': unidentified.

Adeline . . . a stranger to: see Saint-Preux's letter from the mountains of the Valais in *La Nouvelle Héloïse*, p. 45 (*Eloisa*, I, 57): 'Here it was that I plainly discovered, in the purity of the air, the true cause of that returning tranquillity of soul, to which I had been so long a stranger.'

'The stillness . . . truly sublime': see the declaration by Saint-Preux, in *La Nouvelle Héloïse*, p. 45 (*Eloisa*, I, 57), that, in the mountains, 'our meditations acquire a degree of sublimity from the grandeur of the objects around us'.

main hungry: i.e. (in a variety of English dialects) 'very hungry'. (See *The English Dialect Dictionary*, edited by Joseph Wright, Oxford, 1970.)

265 *they inhaled . . . delicious*: see Bourrit, p. 71: 'we . . . took our repast, which the fatigue we had gone thro' and the purity of the air we breathed, rendered delicious'.

The emotions of Adeline . . . of conversation: see Bourrit, p. 72: 'we gave one parting glance at those magnificent objects; which we never could be tired with surveying. We looked at one another, without uttering a word; our eyes alone could speak what we had seen, and told what passed in our hearts; they were affected and softened.' (This same description also notes the regret of the travellers at quitting such a scene—a detail which is reproduced below.)

'It seems . . . the wreck': Adeline's speech implicitly refers to the suggestion, put forward in Thomas Burnet's *Telluris Theoria Sacra* (Amsterdam, 1694), pp. 46–53, that mountains were not created directly by God, but were formed as a product of the Flood, and constitute 'ruins' of previous natural formations. (An allusion to this same theory is made in *The Mysteries of Udolpho*, p. 602.)

'The view . . . his works': see note to p. 22.

266 *They returned to Leloncourt . . . over their heads*: this description resembles in some of its details a similarly dramatic account of a thunderstorm in Bourrit, pp. 69–70. See also note to p. 86.

Clara's horse . . . its foot: the account of a return from the mountains after a storm in Bourrit, pp. 73–4, suggests the possibility of an incident of this kind occurring, in its description of the local villagers 'looking out with anxious expectation . . . apprehensive that we might have met with some unfortunate accident'.

269 *If, on the other hand . . . dwell together*: see Introduction, p. xv.

It must . . . the seventeenth century: this footnote serves to disclaim the implication that the reference to the 'wretched policy' of the French might have some relevance to contemporary politics—in which case it might be seen as a gesture of support for the Revolution of 1789. See Introduction, p. xxiv.

270 *'Let it always . . . great'*: both La Luc and M. Verneuil, in the preceding discussion, echo the accounts of the superior qualities displayed by the human species which are found in the 'Profession de foi du vicaire savoyard'. See, for example, *Emile*, p. 361 (*Emilius and Sophia*, III, 51): 'am I capable of loving what is good, and doing it, and shall I compare myself to the brutes? Abject soul, it is your gloomy philosophy alone that renders you at all like them.'

271 *epigraph*: Joseph Trapp the Younger, 'Virgil's Tomb', lines 27–8.

epigraph: James Beattie, *The Minstrel*, Book II, lines 5–7 and line 9.

272 *the beauties of this romantic region*: see Bourrit, pp. 5–6: 'The farther we penetrate, the more the sight is animated with the beauties of this romantic region.'

'I live surrounded . . . blessings.': La Luc's account of the joys of his 'office' as a pastor refers to the desire for a post of this kind expressed by the 'vicaire savoyard' in *Emile*, p. 405 (*Emilius and Sophia*, III, 143): 'O, that I enjoyed but some little benefice among the poor people in our mountains! how happy should I then be!'

'to be sensible . . . enjoyments.': although this theme is obviously too common to be traceable to any individual source, compare the contrast between the pleasures of society and true happiness in *Emile*, pp. 295–8 (*Emilius and Sophia*, II, 177–84).

273 *It was a spot . . . romantic shade*: see *La Nouvelle Héloïse*, p. 389, *Eloisa*, III, 162: 'This solitary spot formed a wild and desert nook, but full of those sorts of beauties, which are only agreeable to susceptible minds', and *La Nouvelle Héloïse*, p. 389 (*Eloisa*, III, 163): 'Forest of gloomy fir-trees afforded us a melancholy shade.'

274 *La Luc, unable to answer . . . a husband*: see p. 247, note 1.

276 *'This globe . . . effects'*: see *Emile*, p. 361 (*Emilius and Sophia*, III, 50–1): 'It is then true that man is lord of the creation, that

he is, at least, sovereign over the habitable earth; for it is certain that he not only subdues all other animals, and even disposes of the elements at his pleasure by his industry; but he alone of all other terrestrial beings knows how to subject the earth to his convenience, and even to appropriate to his use, by contemplation, the very stars and planets he cannot approach.'

'O! how expressively . . . doubted.': in Emile, accounts of the superior powers which the human species enjoys (see note 1 above) are used as a means of reinforcing the argument that man cannot be seen as a purely material being (an argument put forward in opposition to the various forms of materialism propounded by—among other figures of the French Enlightenment—La Mettrie and Diderot). In affirming that 'man is . . . a free agent, and as such animated by an immaterial substance', the 'vicaire savoyard' asserts, for example: 'No material being can be self-active, and I perceive that I am so . . . I have a body, on which other bodies act; and which acts reciprocally on them. This reciprocal action is indubitable; but my will is independent of my senses' (Emile, p. 365, p. 364 (Emilius and Sophia, III, 60, 57-8)).

La Luc had taught her . . . to converse: see p. 249, note 1. (Compare, in particular, Emile, p. 507 (Emilius and Sophia, IV, 74).)

278 and was there recommended to try the air of Nice: the reputation of the climate of Nice as one beneficial to health is mentioned, for example, in Smollett, p. 8 and p. 193. In the same travel book, pp. 301-2, certain reservations about this reputation are expressed, but the benefits of the air of Nice are not entirely denied. (The scepticism of Smollett is echoed in the doubts of La Luc, described below.)

There was scarcely a dry eye in the village: the final section of The Romance of the Forest is characterized by a number of displays of lachrymosity; see, for example, the references to the tears of Adeline, on p. 259, and of La Luc, above and on p. 313 and p. 362. The use of description of tears as a means of emphasizing the intensity of emotion generated by particular situations is derived from the sentimental novel. One instance of this genre, for example, The Man of Feeling, recounts the story of a repentant prostitute, who, confronted with her long-lost father, who has just 'burst into tears' (p. 67), 'fell to the ground, and bathed his feet with her tears!', at which the hero, pleading with

EXPLANATORY NOTES 393

her father to forgive her, 'fell on her neck, and mingled his tears with hers' (p. 68).

279 *This was an object . . . romantic fondness*: see p. 247, note 1.

the romantic mountains and green vallies of Piedmont: see Smollett, p. 309: 'I need not tell you that Piedmont is one of the most fertile and agreeable countries in Europe.'

280 *While the spiral summits . . . autumn*: see p. 235, note 7. The strategy of describing the 'diversified' landscape of alternating fertility and barrenness as one in which different seasons appear to coexist is often employed in eighteenth-century topographical description, in order to present juxtapositions between contrasting elements as more sharply paradoxical—and, therefore, to identify these juxtapositions with the element of drama which the traveller expects the foreign or unfamiliar landscape to provide. See, for example, Smollett, pp. 109–10 and *La Nouvelle Héloïse*, p. 44 (*Eloisa*, I, 56).

As they advanced the scenery became still more diversified: see p. 9, note 2.

the ocean: the term is employed here, as it is in Burke, p. 43, to refer to any vast expanse of salt water—as a form of natural scenery associated with a particular aesthetic effect.

It was towards the close of day . . . in the farthest distance: this description draws heavily on the account of Nice in Smollett, pp. 115–19, which notes, for example, the 'sweep or amphitheatre' of mountains around the city (p. 115), the greanness of the hills (p. 119), the fact that these hills rise 'from the sea-shore' (p. 115), and 'the ruins of an old castle' (p. 116). Smollett's description of Nice also informs the reader that 'in a clear morning, one can perceive the high lands of Corsica' (p. 119).

for Adeline and Clara . . . to the prospect: see p. 9, note 3.

The soft and salubrious air . . . invariable summer: see Smollett, p. 334: 'The air of Nice is pure and penetrating, yet mild, generally dry, and elastic; and the sky is remarkably clear and serene.'

Trees of myrtle . . . in their shade: many of these same plants are mentioned in Smollett, p. 118, in a passage which suggests a similar admiration for the abundant vegetation of the countryside around Nice.

The gently swelling hills . . . had descended: see Smollett, p. 115 ('hills of a gentle ascent') and pp. 118–19: 'The hills are shaded to the tops with olive-trees, which are always green, and those hills are over-topped by more distant mountains, covered with snow.'

281 *whence rose the little river Paglion . . . into the Mediterranean*: see the reference to 'the little river Paglion' in Smollett, p. 115, and the description of this river, in the same travel book, as one which is 'fed by melted snow and rain in the mountains', and sometimes 'swelled by sudden rains' (p. 115), and which, when it reaches the city, 'washes the walls upon the west, and falls into the Mediterranean' (p. 333; see also p. 115). (This river is now known as the *Paillon*, and is mainly covered over.)

In this blooming region . . . surrounding plenty: 'the great poverty of the people' in Nice is described in Smollett, p. 169. Accounts of a waste of natural fertility, and of peasants starving amidst great abundance, are common in eighteenth-century descriptions of southern Europe (see, for example, Patrick Brydone, *A Tour through Sicily and Malta*, second edition (London, 1774), II, 62–3). These observations on the condition of the peasants in Nice bear a particularly close resemblance to a passage in Swinburne's *Travels*, I, 299, which describes the small town of Corigliano, in southern Italy, as one which contains 'about eight thousand inhabitants, who have an appearance of extreme poverty, and, like Tantalus, starve in the midst of plenty'. This description itself refers back to Pope's 'Epistle to Burlington', line 163: 'In plenty starving, tantaliz'd in state'.

This description of the peasantry also reproduces the equation between poverty and 'an arbitrary government' which is found in Gray's account of Savoy (see p. 240, note 4), and this same passage (Gray, p. 61) in using the 'discontented face' as an index of the conditions in which the peasantry live.

its narrow streets and shabby houses: see the description of the city of Nice in Smollett, pp. 116–17: 'The streets are narrow . . . and the windows in general are fitted with paper instead of glass.'

The appearance of the inn . . . furnished lodgings: Smollett, p. 113, asserts that 'Unless you . . . hire a whole house for a length of time, you will find no ready-furnished lodgings at Nice', and describes a week-long stay in 'a paltry inn' before finding apartments. (The combined features of these apartments and of some lodgings which Smollett moves into whilst furnishing them are reproduced in the apartments which La Luc eventually finds, as described below.) The same travel book also mentions, in the course of its descriptions of Nice, the 'valetudinarians, who come hither for the benefit of this climate' (p. 193).

'*Heaven, earth, ocean, smil'd!*': James Beattie, *The Minstrel*, Book 1, line 180.

282 *A Sonnet*: see note to p. 76.

who like himself came to Nice in search of health: see p. 278, note 1.

283 *he attended them . . . the neighbourhood of Nice*: see Smollett, p. 119: 'Though Nice itself retains few marks of antient splendor, there are considerable monuments of antiquity in its neighbourhood.'

286 '*That might create a soul under the ribs of Death*': Milton, *Comus*, lines 561–2.

Sonnet: see note to p. 76. (The poem, though of fourteen lines, does not accord with the more stringent definition of the term *sonnet*, which requires that all the lines should be decasyllabic.)

287 *the variety and novelty of the surrounding scenes amused her mind*: see p. 9, notes 2 and 3.

288 *Of all the grand objects . . . the most sublime admiration*: Burke, p. 43, argues that 'the ocean' (see p. 280, note 3) produces an even stronger effect of sublimity than other forms of vast expanse. This particularly powerful effect, Burke claims, is largely due to the fact that 'the ocean is an object of no small terror'.

290 *Morning, on the Sea Shore . . .*: this poem incorporates allusions not only to *A Midsummer Night's Dream*, in the references to Titania, but also to *The Tempest*: the words 'yellow sands' and 'sweet sprites', for example, appear in 'Ariel's Song' in this latter play, I. ii. 337 and 382.

291 *even the air of Montpellier . . . Nice*: Swinburne, in his 'Journey', comments on Montpellier: 'Its climate has long been celebrated for wholesomeness, and incredible numbers of invalids have visited it in hopes of relief from their complaints, or at least of finding an atmosphere more congenial to their delicate frames; but I suspect its merits have been over-rated.' Smollett, p. 88 and p. 101, is even more disparaging about the effects of this city's climate.

292 *he now determined to travel farther into Italy*: Nice, as a

territory included within the Duchy of Savoy—or, after 1720, the Kingdom of Sardinia—and administered from Turin (see note to p. 232), was often considered, in the eighteenth century, as part of Italy. Smollett, p. 174, notes the propensity of the 'Nissards' to claim either Italian or Provencal identity, as occasion demands. See also, below, the account of La Luc, as he sails away from Nice, 'bidding adieu to the shores of Italy'.

293 *Adeline gazed with an emotion the most sublime . . . from the subject*: see p. 15, note 5 and note to p. 288.

epigraph: James Beattie, *The Minstrel*, Book I, lines 496–500.

296 *disembogue themselves*: Johnson defines *disembogue* as 'to pour out at the mouth of a river; to vent'.

300 *her pursuer . . . disappeared*: see note to p. 55.

307 *epigraph*: Anna Seward, 'Monody on Major André', line 402.

315 *epigraph*: William Mason, *Caractacus* (London, 1759), p. 46.

316 *the prison of the Chatelet*: the Châtelet, in the seventeenth and eighteenth centuries, housed the central criminal courts and prison of Paris.

332 *epigraph*: James Thomson, *The Seasons*, 'Winter', lines 379–81 (with slight alterations).

335 *epigraph*: Thomas Gray, 'The Bard: A Pindaric Ode', lines 64–6.

345 *epigraph*: unidentified.

351 *epigraph*: William Mason, *Elfrida* (London, 1752), p. 72.

357 *a cessation of hostilities between France and Spain*: long-standing hostilities between these two countries were in fact brought to an end with the Peace of the Pyrenees in 1659.

epigraph: William Collins, 'The Passions, An Ode for Music', lines 80 and 85–90.

359 *'chrystal purity'*: the metaphor of crystal is employed very frequently in eighteenth-century poetry to describe the clarity, or 'purity', of streams and fountains, with reference to Horace's ode 'Ad Fontem Bandusiam', line 1 ('O Fons Bandusiae, splendidior vitro'). Joseph Warton's 'To a Fountain', for example, an imitation of this ode, mentions both 'Ye waves, that gushing fall with purest stream' (line 1) and 'thy crystal clear' (line 12). See also James Thomson, *The Seasons*, 'Summer', lines 308–9: 'Nor is the stream | Of purest crystal' and Edward

Jerningham, 'Sensibility', line 3: 'the pure crystal of thy fountain'.

360 *the tabor*: 'A small drum beaten with one stick to accompany a pipe' (Johnson).

The Oxford World's Classics Website

www.worldsclassics.co.uk

- Information about new titles
- Explore the full range of Oxford World's Classics
- Links to other literary sites and the main OUP webpage
- Imaginative competitions, with bookish prizes
- Peruse the Oxford World's Classics Magazine
- Articles by editors
- Extracts from Introductions
- A forum for discussion and feedback on the series
- Special information for teachers and lecturers

www.worldsclassics.co.uk

American Literature

British and Irish Literature

Children's Literature

Classics and Ancient Literature

Colonial Literature

Eastern Literature

European Literature

History

Medieval Literature

Oxford English Drama

Poetry

Philosophy

Politics

Religion

The Oxford Shakespeare

A complete list of Oxford Paperbacks, including Oxford World's Classics, Oxford Shakespeare, Oxford Drama, and Oxford Paperback Reference, is available in the UK from the Academic Division Publicity Department, Oxford University Press, Great Clarendon Street, Oxford OX2 6DP.

In the USA, complete lists are available from the Paperbacks Marketing Manager, Oxford University Press, 198 Madison Avenue, New York, NY 10016.

Oxford Paperbacks are available from all good bookshops. In case of difficulty, customers in the UK can order direct from Oxford University Press Bookshop, Freepost, 116 High Street, Oxford OX1 4BR, enclosing full payment. Please add 10 per cent of published price for postage and packing.